Tim Gautreaux

Born and raised in Louisiana, Tim Gautreaux lives there still and is writer in residence at Southeastern Louisiana University. His work has appeared in *Harper's*, the *Atlantic Monthly*, *GQ*, *Zoetrope*, *Prize Stories: The O. Henry Awards*, and *Best American Short Stories*, and he is the author of two short story collections, now published in one volume as *Waiting for the Evening News*. His first novel, *The Next Step in the Dance*, was published in 1999 and won the SEBA Book Award. It was followed by the widely acclaimed *The Clearing* in 2003 and *The Missing* in 2009.

'Gautreaux writes with sustained grace and creates memorable characters . . . What really sets *The Missing* apart, though, is his remarkable ability to realise the period . . . a rare and rather uncanny achievement: a novel about the South in the early Twenties that reads as though it was actually written there and then' John Dugdale, *Literary Review*

'A novelist aims for the payoff between forward narrative and the inbuilt magic of the text . . . Gautreaux always achieves this. From the soup of a gripping, almost cinematic plot are lifted the dripping bones of a poetic literary experience . . . . The anticipation clutching your throat makes you race towards the novel's climax.' Alan Warner, *Guardian*

'Full of vivid evocations of the sights, sounds and smells of the South. As Simoneaux pursues his morally driven detective mission the scent of the steaming mud of the cypress swamps and the sound of 1920s New Orleans jazz rise off the page' Claire Prentice, *Scotsman*

'A joy to read' Barclay McBain, *Herald*

'Gautreaux has placed each character and scene – every comma – with the care and skill of a master . . . *The Missing* is a culmination of his excellent body of work. It is a riveting, neat-but-never-tidy joy of a story that readers should savour but will more likely devour.'
Jennifer Levasseur, *The Australian*

'A prodigious book by a talent who deserves wider recognition and unstinting praise' Mark Thomas, *Canberra Times*

'Gautreaux's paragraphs linger like a Southern afternoon, warm and languorous . . . this book is that rare thing: a needful lesson that nourishes and delights' Laurel Maury, *San Francisco Chronicle*

'Gautreaux has a mythic sense of plot, a keen ear for dialect and vivid powers of description . . . Make no mistake, vengeance begets vengeance. But love is an equally powerful force in this novel, which comes to a moving and resonant conclusion as Sam's life and the missing girl's converge in an unexpected way.' Malena Watrous, *New York Times*

Tim Gautreaux

The Missing

SCEPTRE

First published in Great Britain in 2009 by Sceptre
An imprint of Hodder & Stoughton
An Hachette UK company

First published in the US by Alfred A Knopf
A division of Random House, Inc

First published in paperback in 2010

5

A CIP catalogue record for this title is available from the British Library.

ISBN 978 0 340 97795 8

Typeset in Sabon MT by Palimpsest Book Production Limited,
Grangemouth, Stirlingshire

Printed and bound by Clays Ltd, St Ives plc

Hodder & Stoughton Ltd
338 Euston Road
London NW1 3BH

www.hodder.co.uk

For my father,
Minos Lee Gautreaux,
who taught me to love children and steamboats

Acknowledgements

I'd like to thank Southeastern Louisiana University for their continued support of my writing; my agent, Peter Matson of Sterling-Lord Literistic, for his encouragement and expert management; my family, especially my wife, Winborne, for all her help and her careful reading of the manuscript; Tom Piazza, for his helpful writing on the world of jazz; *The S&D Reflector*, published by the sons and daughters of pioneer rivermen, a bottomless vault of information on inland waterways during the age of steam; the stories and research of Captain Fred Way; the wonderful Internet resource Red Hot Jazz Archive; and I am grateful for two books in particular, *Moonlite at Eight Thirty* by Alan Bates and Clarke Hawley and *Jazz* on the River by William Kenney. Finally, I give thanks for my editor, Gary Fisketjon, whose care and carefulness show amazing love for his work.

I

Sam Simoneaux leaned against the ship's rail, holding on in the snarling wind as his lieutenant struggled toward him through the spray, grabbing latches, guy wires, valve handles.

'Pretty bad belowdecks,' the lieutenant cried out against the blow.

'That's a fact. Stinks too bad to eat.'

'I noticed you have a bit of an accent. Where are you from?'

Sam felt sorry for him. The lieutenant was trying to be popular with his men, but none of them could imagine such a white-blond beanpole from a farm in Indiana leading anyone into battle. 'I don't think I have an accent. But you do.'

The lieutenant gave him a startled look. 'Me?'

'Yeah. Where I was raised in south Louisiana, nobody talks like you.'

The lieutenant smiled. 'Everybody's got an accent, then.'

Sam looked at the spray running over the man's pale freckles, thinking that in a heavy frost he'd be nearly invisible. 'You come up on a farm?'

'Yeah, sure. My family moved down from Canada about twenty years ago.'

'I was raised on a farm but figured I could do better,' Sam yelled. 'The lady down the road from us had a piano and she taught it to me. Moved to New Orleans when I was sixteen to be close to the music.'

The lieutenant bent into the next blast of wind. 'I'm with you there. I can't throw bales far enough to farm.'

'How many days till we get to France?'

'The colonel says three more, the captain, two, the pilot, four.'

Sam nodded. 'Nobody knows what's goin' on, like usual.'

'Well, it's a big war,' the lieutenant said. They watched a huge swell climb the side of the rusty ship and engulf a machine-gun crew hunkered down below them in a makeshift nest of sandbags, the deluge flushing men out on deck, where they slid on their bellies in the foam.

The next few days were a lurching penance of bad ocean, flint-topped rollers breaking against the bows and spray blowing by the portholes like broken glass. Inside the ship, Sam slept among the thousands of complaining, groaning, and heaving men, but spent his waking hours at the rails, sometimes with his friend Melvin Robicheaux, a tough little fellow from outside of Baton Rouge. On November 11, 1918, their steamer escaped the mountainous Atlantic and landed at Saint-Nazaire, where the wharves were jammed with people cheering, some dancing together, others running in wild rings.

Robicheaux pointed down over the rusty side of the ship. 'How come everybody's dancin'? They all got a bottle of wine. You think they glad to see us?'

Tugboats and dock locomotives were blowing their whistles through a hanging gauze of coal smoke. As he watched the celebration, Sam felt happy that he'd shown up with his rifle. The French looked like desperate people ecstatic about an approaching rescue. However, as the tugboats whistled and pushed the ship against the dock, he sensed the festival wasn't for this boatload of soldiers but for some more important event. Hardly anybody was waving at the ship.

Four thousand troops unloaded onto the dock, and when all the men were lined up under the freight sheds and out of the wind, a colonel climbed onto a pile of ammunition crates and announced through a megaphone that an armistice had just been signed and the war was over.

Many cheered, but a portion of the young recruits seemed disappointed that they wouldn't get to shoot at anybody. The weapons hanging on them, the ammunition stacked around in wooden crates, the cannons still being unloaded by the puffing dock cranes were suddenly redundant. Sam wondered what he would tell his friends back home of his war experience. The most valuable trophies of war were the stories, and this one was good only for a derisive laugh.

Robicheaux poked him in the back with the tip of his bayonet scabbard. 'This like that time you tried workin' at Stein's?'

'What?'

'Stein, the shoe man.'

'Oh. I guess so.' He had tried for two weeks to get a job at Stein's Shoe Emporium on Canal Street, but the morning after the old man had finally decided to take him on, Sam showed up for work only to find a wreath on the door and a typed note announcing the death of Solomon Stein and the permanent closure of his shop.

He stood in his ranks for an hour feeling awkward and unnecessary while the officers tried to figure what to do with all these soldiers and their tons of gear. Sam's long suit was patience, or at least an ability to wait for something good to happen, so he stood there, watching the civilians cheer as the men around him grumbled that they might have to file onto the ship for a lurching voyage back to New Orleans. It was cold, and he was hungry. After a long while, boys pushing carts of food came up and fed each man a miniature loaf of hard bread with a slice of cheese hanging out like a pale tongue. Then they were marched five miles to the edge of the city, where they pitched camp in a bald field that, judging by the stumps and posturing bronze statues, must once have been a landscaped park. An icy breeze flowed down a boulevard feeding into the camp, and Sam fastened the top button on his tunic and closed his coat. He had never felt a wind that cold in his life.

That night he was sure he would freeze to death. Robicheaux, his tent mate, lay on his cot talking nonstop.

'Hey, Simoneaux, I'm thinkin' of a warm fire, me. Hot potatoes in each pocket. How about you?'

'I'm thinkin' about those recruiting posters. They made joining up look like a good idea,' he said glumly.

'I liked the one with the Hun molesting them Belgian women.'

Sam raised his head from his cot and looked at him. 'You liked it?'

'I mean it made me mad. Made me want to come over and help 'em out.'

'You wanted to make them Belgian women grateful, huh?'

'You bet.'

Sam covered his head. 'Sometimes I think about the music. I was sales clerk at Gruenwald's when I joined up, and we got in all this sheet music full of sunshine, like "Over There," "Somewhere in France Is Daddy," "Keep Your Head Down, Fritzie Boy"'

Robicheaux sniffed. 'You didn't think you'd need to keep your head down between your legs to keep your ears from freezin' off.'

'So far,' Sam said dreamily, 'it's not a happy song.' At home, the war had seemed a colorful musical production, a gay fox-trot in the key of C, but the voyage on the *Alex Denkman* changed all that. The *Denkman* was a round-bottom, coal-burning nausea machine, its hull so fouled with giant streamers of rust that the government decided painting a camouflage pattern on it was unnecessary. A boy who'd grown up in Sam's hometown had died en route of a burst appendix and was buried at sea after a perfunctory prayer. Sam and several other Louisiana men had stood in snow flurries on the fantail and watched the shrouded figure bob in the ship's rolling wake, refusing to sink, as though the corpse itself didn't feel right about the lead-cold sea and was trying to drift back toward the warm soil of a Louisiana graveyard. He was a Duplechen boy, his father a wiry little farmer who was good with mules. Sam knew the man and could imagine his sorrow, the vacant place at his table, the forever-broken link. This cold camp seemed a minor inconvenience next to that, and he turned over and went to sleep.

One morning, after a week of camping among the statues, he watched a group of officers drive up in an open motorcar and choose squads of ten to travel to Paris and work in hospitals. Sam drew this duty and was put in charge of guarding a narcotics dispensary. Sometimes he was sent through the pungent wards to deliver a dose of morphine to a nurse, and the things he saw on these errands aged him. The amputations, the groaning, the smell of infection and illness were proof of how little he knew about the meanness of warfare. At the end of each day, he felt humbled and simple.

Sometimes he and his contingent would walk to a café where there was a very bad piano, and Sam would practice for an hour straight. The men didn't talk about the things they had seen in the wards, because all of it was beyond words. Sam was afraid that talking about it would make pictures stick in his head forever. They all worked in the ward for those too sick to move, and it was so huge that the ten of them combined had never seen half of it, much less the satellite buildings and compounds. There were French hospitals. English hospitals. American hospitals. Nothing in the patriotic posters or sheet music hinted at the blown-away jawbones, the baked eyeballs, or the trembling black rubber tubes dripping pus.

Eventually, because he could speak Cajun French, which to the Parisians sounded like a very bad seventeenth-century patois from the south of France, he was asked to perform some rudimentary interpreting. But every Frenchman he talked to raised his eyebrows in alarm, studied his pleasant face, and asked which colony he came from.

In January he was pulled off hospital duty and teamed up with eight fellow Louisianans under the Indiana lieutenant, for battlefield cleanup in the Argonne. They were told they were going to a forest, and Robicheaux picked up his rifle and said, 'Hot damn, maybe we can shoot us a deer and get some good meat.' But days later, when they jumped off the muddy, open truck, they saw a dead and ice-glazed countryside convulsed with shell craters and stippled with exploded trees, a vast, botched junkscape of shot-apart wagons, upended tanks, and frost-etched ordnance of every description. They were given a map and told to police two square miles of it.

Sam stepped off the frozen track and his boot broke through a crust of ice, sinking deep into a foul-smelling brook. He pulled free and looked back at his lieutenant, tall, pale-eyed, barely there, his boyish midwestern face full of obedience and confusion.

'Sir, what exactly do they want us to do?'

The lieutenant put a foot up on an abandoned water-cooled machine gun. 'I think it's pretty simple. We should look for the most dangerous ordnance and detonate it.' His voice was thin, and Sam remembered hearing that he was highly educated and had never seen combat. They all looked over the immense battlefield, unable to comprehend any of it. Even in the cold, a stink rose out of the earth, and bristling everywhere were rusted hummocks of barbed wire.

They set up a camp of sorts, erecting a small tent for their supplies, and two hours after they'd arrived, a plodding noise came from the west, and they turned to see the head of an infantryman rise up from a steep swale and then the rest of him, his right hand towing the reins of five saddled horses over the remnant of a road. He plodded on deliberately – like a horse himself, and stopped next to the truck. 'I have orders to let you have these here animals,' he drawled.

'What on earth for?' the lieutenant asked.

The soldier shrugged. 'Each demolition group gets a team.'

Sam pointed over the chaos of no-man's-land. 'They don't expect us to ride these out there, do they?'

'Good idea!' the lieutenant exclaimed, his face brightening. He dismissed the soldier and took the reins, tying them to the truck's side rails. 'From horseback you'll be able to find the shells much better. That's the first thing to go after. The big projectiles. We can stack them and blow them up.' He gestured toward the truck bed. 'We've been sent out with a detonator, electrical wire, and cases of dynamite.'

Sam had been issued a pair of field glasses and was studying a hill to the north, his stomach heavy with foreboding. 'What about the grenades? They're out there like gravel.' He put down the glasses and looked over at the lieutenant.

'I know enough not to handle them. Some might go off with just a nudge. I think we should try shooting them with our Springfields.'

Melvin Robicheaux took off his helmet. 'Will that set them things off?'

The lieutenant raised his shoulders and turned up his hands. 'Pick one and shoot at it. Sort of an experiment.'

Sam again peered through his field glasses. 'I wouldn't do it.'

The lieutenant rose up on the balls of his feet. 'We'll give it a try.'

Robicheaux got his rifle from the rear of the truck and worked the bolt. He glanced over his shoulder. 'Them horses, they been in the fightin' or they like us?'

The lieutenant turned toward the animals. 'I'd guess the gimpy pair and that one with the scarred rump are veterans. The others, I don't know. Maybe they just came up from a transport.' He turned, put his hands behind his back, and looked up the hill. 'Go ahead and shoot one.'

Robicheaux adjusted the sights of the rifle, aimed at a grenade on the lip of a shell crater seventy yards away, and fired. He missed, but at the crack of the rifle one of the horses whinnied and reared, pulling loose from the truck and taking off in a zigzag gallop across the galled field and up the hill. Sam grabbed the bridles of two of the shying horses, and the other pair stood steaming in the light snow as if nothing at all had happened. The men watched the spooked horse run up the far rise for half a mile, dodging stumps and jumping craters and then stepping on God knows what, disappearing at once in a monstrous pink fireball. The ear-flattening concussion roared back across the field like a clap of thunder and they all ran behind the truck, scanning the sky for falling debris.

Once the sound of the explosion had echoed away, the lieutenant turned around and pointed to Dupuis, the only veteran among them. 'What did that animal step on?'

Dupuis, a dour older man from Arnaudville, said, 'I don't know, Cap. I been here a whole year and don't understand none of it.'

A twenty-pound piece of shrapnel came straight down out of the clouds and banged through the hood of the truck. Crouched next to a tire, Sam stared at where the horse had been vaporized and then up at the sky, unable to imagine this cause-and-effect, the power involved, or what they were doing here. Up on the hill, a crater smoked like an entrance to a burning mine.

They fanned out over the blasted countryside shooting at grenades, about half of which exploded. Sam adjusted his sights and began setting off German stick grenades that went up with ear-cutting thuds, both dull and sharp at the same time. After an hour he felt something like a hammer blow on his helmet. Examining a long coppery crease, he guessed it was caused by a stray shot from another man's rifle, for other teams were working adjacent quadrants. After that, he worked in the low places, sighting in from the edge of trenches. Walking along a poisoned trickle of a stream, the water blue and stinking, he looked up the bank and saw a thighbone protruding from the earth. Downstream five German helmets sat as inert as dead turtles. Farther on he saw a mortar hitched to a team of killed horses frozen hard in their harness, and his thoughts began to balk against the math of the place; there were enough unexploded grenades of all nationalities to keep him busy for a hundred years. The smell was a walking presence and a mockery of what he had imagined of war, now blasted out of his mind forever. He understood how brutally the illusion of warfare had ended for the hundreds of thousands who'd struggled here. 'What a damned lie,' he said aloud. Climbing out of the stream, he worked the bolt and fired at a French pear grenade, which tumbled away but didn't detonate.

Suddenly an infantryman raised his head over the next hillock.

'Son of a bitch, didn't they give you a compass? You're not supposed to fire to the northwest.'

They walked toward each other until only a naked ravine graveled with spent machine-gun casings separated them.

'You with a disposal unit?' Sam called.

The man was coated with mud and his helmet was missing. 'What's left of one. Two of us were killed outright this morning when they kicked over grenades. Another caught a bullet in the ass, and we don't even know who did it.'

'I been sure of my backdrop when I took a shot.'

The man held his arms up against the sky and let them drop. He looked behind him into his own sector and then back at Sam. 'Nobody's ever done anything like this before.' Bareheaded, sickly small, he seemed lost and befuddled.

Sam spat into the ravine. 'It's a bitch, all right.'

'A trainload of bitches,' the infantryman said, turning back down the hill.

It took them all afternoon to build a stack of German three-inch shells to the size of a cord of wood, set the dynamite charges, and pay out wire to the detonating machine. They had no idea how far to back off. The lieutenant found a long trench a hundred yards away, and the ten of them piled into it. After Dupuis wired the machine, the lieutenant pushed the plunger. The explosion was astounding, and at the end of the row a man from Lafayette cried out when a chunk of shell came down and fractured his collarbone. Sam crawled through a rain of falling dirt and found that the man's heavy coat had saved his shoulder from being cut off, but that some terrible wound was bleeding under the cloth.

He laid him flat in the trench and as gently as he could, pulled his arm straight down by his side. The soldier roared at the hot star of pain in his shoulder, and Sam, who had never seen such hurt, felt foolish and near tears himself. He turned to the lieutenant. 'What can we do for him?'

The lieutenant's voice rose half an octave. 'Well, I don't know.'

He looked up over the lip of the trench. 'We're not supposed to get hurt.'

Sam opened his canteen and tilted it toward the injured man's white, clenched lips. 'Maybe you could send somebody to that other bunch in the northwest. Maybe their truck works and they can come get him.'

The lieutenant remained silent. Dupuis volunteered to climb over the ridge to find another unit, and the man from Lafayette began screaming about his bones grinding together.

'What can I do, bud?' Sam asked.

The soldier's eyes opened wide and looked past Sam out of a narrow, stubbled face wrinkled even in youth. 'Hit me in the head with somethin',' he rasped.

The rest of the men gathered close, as though the heat of their bodies would collect and offer comfort. The wounded soldier began to fill the trench with his moans, and Sam sensed how minuscule this pain was compared to the vast agonies of the death field they were in. He looked out and saw half a million soldiers going at each other in a freezing rain, their bodies shredded by artillery, their faces torn off, their knees disintegrated into snowy red pulp, their lungs boiled out by poison gas, and all of this for four years, spread out as far and wide as the continent itself.

That night, after the wounded man had been picked up by an ambulance wagon, the rest of them bedded down around their ruined truck. Robicheaux had hobbled the horses but they shuffled among the men all night and one of them stepped on Sam's hand as he slept. In the morning his wrist was swollen and stiff, and he had trouble unbuttoning his trousers. The men washed their rations down with water and started out again, shooting not only at hand grenades, but also a certain type of four-and-a-half-inch shell that would explode if hit near the nose. For these, the lieutenant ordered them to lie flat at least seventy-five yards away before firing so the shrapnel would fly over their backs. They shot until a man named LeBoeuf was hit in the elbow by a fragment and had to be hauled hollering out to the road to wait for the ambulance. The remaining seven continued, gamely picking up grenades now and arranging them like ducks in a shooting gallery. They shot ineffectively at mortar rounds, and even large artillery duds. The sky faired off late, and they went on firing until sundown, their faces smudged gray with gunpowder. Between explosions they could hear teams in other sectors shooting as well, blowing up large caches, all of it a silly echo of the war itself. When the light gave out, Sam's ears were ringing like struck anvils. Taking one last look at the darkening land, he felt fortunate and, at the same time, deeply saddened.

Robicheaux had found a crock jug of brandy in the cellar of a destroyed house, and after everybody finished eating, he brought it from under the truck and passed it around, the men taking swallows with trembling hands and savoring the fine liquid heat. One by one, five of them fell asleep in their blankets. A half-moon came up, glazing the high points of the frost-struck battlefield, the stumps and armaments taking on the muted glow of tombstones. Sam and his friend sat back against the front tire, watching the field gradually luminesce.

Robicheaux took off his helmet, hung it on the bumper, and adjusted his wool cap. 'I'm glad we missed the big dance.' He was a robust man, all muscle, a high-school footballer who'd also worked the New Orleans docks unloading sacks of coffee.

'Ain't you cold?' Sam asked.

'It's all right. The house I grew up in had so many cracks in the wallboards you could read a newspaper by the sunlight leakin' in.'

'You married?'

Robicheaux started to answer in French, but Sam waved him off. 'Talk American.'

'Pourquoi?'

'I moved to the city so I could learn to talk better, pronounce my words, dress nicer, you know. I don't talk like some college boy, but at least people don't think I'm a fool. If you talk French in town people look at you like you're stupid. You notice that?'

Robicheaux nodded. 'You want a indoor job.'

'You got that right.'

'Your old man, he's tanned like a brick from workin' a cane farm, right?'

'I was raised by my uncle Claude and he farmed sweet potatoes.'

'Patates douces,' Robicheaux said dreamily.

'Sweet potatoes.'

'I am.'

'What?'

'Married. I got two little boys up in Baton Rouge. You?'

'Yes.'

'Kids?'

Sam took a pull of the brandy and set the jug down between them. 'I had a son. Oscar. He got a bad fever about two years old and didn't make it.'

Robicheaux turned his head away. 'That's rough.'

'Plenty rough. My uncle came to town for the funeral. He told me he'd lost a boy and a girl before the rest of us came along. He was trying to give me some comfort, I guess. Came to New Orleans and sat in my little rent house and talked, talked, talked. Damned if in the middle of all that comforting he didn't start crying himself about the babies he'd lost, my cousins. Then he starts telling me about his brothers and sisters he'd never seen, about my own brother, sister, mother, and father, people I never knew.'

Robicheaux stretched his legs out over the ground. 'They say mosquitoes cause most of that fever. You got to screen in your cistern. Pour oil in the ditches.'

'I do now. And we got city water.'

'You'll just have to make some more, you and your wife.'

Sam looked up at the craters in the moon and buttoned his tunic and then his overcoat. 'They're not like loaves of bread you give to a neighbor. You remember them.'

Robicheaux put the cork in the jug. 'I know. One minute they're here and the next they ain't, but they don't go away. They're in your head. '

Sam briefly raised an arm. 'I'm looking out at this chopped-up place they sent us. I'm glad I don't know anybody that got killed here, because I'd feel like I was walking on his grave.' He stood up and gathered his blanket from the truck, then knocked the dried mud off his boots and climbed onto the front seat. He wondered briefly how much of the mud was composed of atomized blood and shell-fractured bone, how much was relic of a cause made sacred for no reason other than the sacrifice itself. He thought of how the dead men's families were maimed by the loss that for some would surely grow larger over time, the absence more palpable than the presence. He remembered his dead child and cast a long look over the dim killing fields.

He began to think of his uncle Claude back on the sweet-potato-and-sugar-cane farm, promising himself he'd go way out in the country to see him when he returned. It was a long trip over swampy roads, but he would make it to sit in the kerosene-smelling kitchen and tell him how it was over here, how it wasn't like they'd expected, that the dead men were heroes but also pieces cut forever out of the lives of their families. He thought of his uncle's simple kitchen table, purchased along with six chairs, how he'd moved one chair out to the back porch when Sam had left the farm so they could remember him by its absence.

He settled across the seat, closed his eyes, and began to piece together the many missing parts of his childhood – father, mother, brother, and sister. The details of stories he'd heard whispered around him since infancy formed a whole mural in his mind, a speaking picture – words above everyone's head. His people were from southwest Louisiana and had run cattle there since the 1700s, after the Attakapas cannibals had been civilized. These Acadian *vachers* knew animals well and valued trained beasts as minor souls among them. Sam's father raised and trained oxen and leased the teams to lumber companies in Texas that were beginning to clear out the big stands of longleaf pines in the low country where only an animal could go. One day, this father he never met was waiting outside a saloon in the village of Troumal on the Texas border with his cousins the Ongerons, waiting with two teams he would turn over to lumbermen. They were smoking, sitting on a mud sled, their willow ox whips wedged upright in the box, chatting in French and waiting for drovers to show up, when a drunk little timber-lease buyer came out through the swinging doors and stood staring at them. A week of black stubble ran up to his eye sockets, and his teeth were little yellow stones. An ox shifted his head toward his greasy trousers, took a sniff, and turned away, blowing the stink out of his snout. The man leaned against a porch post and scratched his rear with his gun hand. After a moment he spat on the nearest ox and snapped, 'Why don't you mushmouths talk American? You sound like a bunch of pigeons in a tub.'

The Ongerons had seen him once before and were too smart to fight him. Sam's father had no interest in the bluster of an Arkansas drunk, yet he was the one to answer. 'What you want to know, you?'

'I want some sharp spurs with big rowels. Where do they sell such as that in this shithole town?'

The father's eyes went to the flanks of the drunk's horse, which were scuffed raw and hairless. Around Troumal no one made spurs or anything else. The general store sold what a man could put in his stomach or under a plowshare, but little else. Ten miles away was a poor excuse for a railroad that could take him somewhere, but none of them had ever seen it, though they'd heard the whistle when the wind was out of the south. 'Maybe in Beaumont.'

'That's a forty-mile ride, you idjet.'

The Ongerons were looking at the drunk's horse, which was well formed and bright eyed, though muddy and cut in several places as if forced to jump barbed wire. One of them said, 'Sharp spurs won't work on a smart horse, no.'

The Arkansas man stepped down into the ankle-deep slop surrounding the porch and untied his animal. Sam's father saw the rusty, long-spined Mexican rowels, and he watched the horse's eyes roll in expectation. The man got up and doubled the reins in a gloved fist. The oxmen regarded his movements closely, waiting for him to lean rearward in the saddle and back the animal away from the porch. What he did instead was to give a neck-twisting haul on the reins, bringing the horse's head all the way up, and the backwards stumbling and rearing was hard for them to tolerate. The drunk cursed and rattled the bit in the horse's mouth, jerking the reins high again and again, and the animal began to whinny and lower its hindquarters like a whipped dog. At this point Sam's father reached out with his ox twitch and stung the Arkansas man on the back of his crosshatched neck for being the dumb brute he was. The drunk dropped the reins in surprise, lost his balance as the horse gave a leap, and tumbled backwards out of the saddle, doubling his neck on the edge of the porch.

The saloonkeeper had seen what happened and pushed through the door. Sam's father and the Ongerons, five brothers, joined in a circle and bent down to where the man was quivering toward death. One of them pinched the mud out of the drunk's nose, and two others jiggled his shoulders with their open palms, as if he were hot to the touch. Finally the saloonkeeper jerked down the drunk's collar for a look, and they all straightened up.

'*Eh bien,*' one of the Ongerons said.

'*Quel est son nom?*' Sam's father asked.

'I don't know,' said the saloonkeeper, who understood but didn't speak the local dialect. 'I think he was buying timber rights for some people in Arkansas. But his business ain't around here. I guess he was just passing through.'

The Ongeron brothers were indistinguishable except by age. Their mother made their clothes on a house loom, and they wove their own hats out of palmetto leaves. The youngest asked if someone should go for the sheriff. They all agreed it would be a good idea, but the sheriff was a day's ride and the messenger would have to swim his animal across three bayous. Another Ongeron pointed out that the sheriff wouldn't give a damn since the drunk wasn't from the parish.

Just then five men rode out of the woods on mules, not arriving on the road but struggling out of the tallow trees and stickers on the west side of the saloon. These were the Texans coming for the eight oxen.

One wore store-bought clothes and was obviously in charge. He glanced at the dead man, then up at the saloon. 'Is these ox ready to be bought?'

Sam's father walked over and cast his gray eyes up to him. 'I'm Simoneaux.'

'Here.' The man tossed down a tobacco sack. 'Count your money. Just lookin', I can see these animals is made right. They look like they could pull down a courthouse. Can I have your twitch?'

Sam's father looked at the slender rod in his hand for a moment and then handed it up. The man tapped the left ear of the near ox yoked in a pair, and the animal stepped left. 'All right.'

The Texans got down, mounted the porch, and sat on the bench. They were all the color of schoolhouse brick. The head man looked over the hitch rail. 'Why's he sleepin' in the road?'

'He fell off his horse and died,' the saloonkeeper told him. 'You know him?'

The man turned his head sideways and studied the body's face. 'Naw. And I'm glad of it. You got beer?'

'It's warm.'

'It's still beer, ain't it?'

After the men went inside, the Ongerons and Sam's father stood talking above the dead man and decided they should ride to the priest's house and ask him what to do. They all got in the *traneau*, and the two dark mules lunged into their collars to free the runners and began pulling down the mud path to the south.

The priest was a dour, half-senile man with no teeth or manners, an Estonian exiled to the Louisiana prairie. He stood in the high grass outside his little box of a rectory and yelled out, because he was mostly deaf, 'Is the body Catholic?'

'*Je crois que non,*' the oldest Ongeron answered.

The priest cupped a hand behind an ear. 'How did he die?'

Simoneaux stepped out of the mud sled and explained in French what had happened.

'Ah, violence. Simoneaux, will you confess this?'

'Mais oui. Quand tu veux.'

The priest shook his head slowly. 'Well, he can't be put inside the fence because he's not Catholic and met a bad end, unconfessed. But you can put him outside the fence in the back.'

'All right.'

The priest held out a hand. 'The plot costs a dollar.'

Sam's father looked into his bag and fished out a silver coin. *'Combien s'il est catholique?'*

'Fifty cents.'

He looked sorrowfully at the coin and examined it front and back. *'Tu peux pas lui baptiser?'*

The priest gently took the dollar. 'Simoneaux, you can't buy a ticket after the boat has sailed.'

And Sam's father knew this was right, that something had been done that could not be undone. He and the Ongerons silently went back to the saloon, loaded the body into the sled, and buried it behind the churchyard. The priest watched from the window but did not come out, only opened the door when one of the men returned his shovel. They removed the saddle and bloody bit from the horse and put him in the shed next to the priest's mare, and then they all went home for supper.

That night, Sam's father was the last one to bed, and for the first time he waited at the dark front window to listen for something other than the coarse respirations of his animals. It was like this every night from then on, watchfulness and worry after dark. Whether the song of a night bird or the breaking of a stick, he listened to every sound as if for the beat of a sick heart.

And two months later, when the three children were playing in the house and his wife was washing supper dishes in a pan at the kitchen window, the moonless night stirred with the sound of hooves. He expected to be called out, and maybe he thought for half a moment about seizing his three-dollar shotgun rusting behind the door, but as family stories let it be known in the years to come, there was only enough time for the thing to happen and none for preparation. The house was made of weatherboard nailed on studs, and the insect noise of gun hammers being set in the yard on shotguns loaded with double-ought buckshot, on long-barreled Colt .45 revolvers, on Winchesters and Marlins preceded the coming apart of the building in a splintering volley that swept the rooms with a swarm of deforming lead, the boy and girl killed outright, the mother running toward them knocked back into the next world, and he himself catching a slug under the rib cage that didn't kill him at once, giving him a moment to reach the six-month-old baby lying on the floor, grab him by the foot, sling him through the open door of the cold potbellied stove, and bat it shut as the slugs sailed through the smokestack without even shaking it, rang against a skillet, exploded the mantel clock, pounded through Sam's father's skull, and beat that stove like an anvil until everyone in the dark yard had emptied magazines, breeches, and cylinders of their revenge. The door came off the hinges under the kick of a soggy boot, though the lock hadn't been set in years. The overhead lantern had its globe shot out, but the flame still burned enough for them to check their work in its infernal glow, the assassins hearing in their ringing ears only the muffled mewing of the family cat. They prowled through the house like feral hogs, then mounted up to flee back to Arkansas or Mississippi or North Louisiana, from wherever these wronged blood kin had been drawn. No one afterward knew exactly who they were.

The next morning at daybreak, a lean, sandy-haired man rode up on his mule to help his brother put in seed cane. Claude found them all and sat down on the one standing chair and bawled, looking at the forms on the floor and holding out a hand to each, crying out again and then hearing a miniature echo of his grief begin to rise out of the stove. He opened the door and saw the baby furry with ash, its face black but for the lightning strikes of its tears.

Sam looked up out of the stove, stopped crying, and smiled at his uncle's face caught in the square of light that was the world.

2

The battlefield the next morning was silver plated with frost, and Sam woke shaking with cold. He and the other men stood next to the truck, chewing chalky bread and hiding from the wind before they set to work. By lunchtime he took a long look at the gutted land and understood that they were not making any headway at all and never would against four years' worth of unexploded projectiles and weaponry. Each layer of dirt down to twenty feet was a meat loaf of munitions and the lieutenant told them that deeper still were big, fort-killing shells that no one would find for a hundred years. Sam shook his head and walked over to Robicheaux and told him a joke about a pelican and a duck, and that warmed them, reminding that they were not of this place. In the cold open country their laughter sounded like ice breaking.

At the north end of their quadrant they found a depot of large German artillery projectiles, thirty tons at least. They spent the morning working four men to a shell, stacking as many as they could, and when they finished, the pile was half the size of a railroad boxcar. The lieutenant looked behind him. 'How much wire do we have left?'

Dupuis rolled his eyes up to calculate. 'Maybe two t'ousand feet, yeah. But if we string it that long and I hook up the right amount of caps, the burden might be too much for the machine. Might not light all them caps.'

'Do we have enough fuse?'

'You gonna light this thing and then run half a mile over all this mess?'

The lieutenant folded his arms and slouched backwards. 'You're right. That wouldn't work anyway. A long fuse would give someone a chance to wander up behind it.' He looked west, biting his lip. 'There. We'll post a lookout with a flag on that hill. Give him our good binoculars. When he raises the flag to let us know nobody's nearby, we'll push the plunger.'

Dupuis sucked an eyetooth. 'It'll take me all day to rig the charge and get us far enough away. I got to put boosters in the line and sometimes they don't work worth a damn.' He sucked the other eyetooth. 'Anybody know how to work a cannon?'

The lieutenant pulled out a tab of flesh under his tight chin. 'Cannon?'

'They's a upside-down French 155 over there.' He pointed south. 'In all that junk at the base of that burnt hill. Maybe eight, nine hundred yards.'

Sam followed their line of sight down the gray land through a dusting of snowflakes. 'You want to shoot the pile with a field gun?' Exhausted and cold, he turned and looked at the artillery shells a long time, a shiver of doubt crawling along his spine. He thought it a bad idea, but if they disposed of so much at once, they could go back to the truck, share the brandy, maybe get up a poker game under the canvas in the back. 'Well, most of those rounds are fused. It might could work.'

The squad moved down a hill toward the gun, each man watching where he stepped. It was a large piece, three-quarters turned over, but its breechblock was closed and a proper plug wedged in the muzzle. A metal limber spilled out shells, and the intact one next to it held dry bags of cordite. Two men walked to the truck for ropes, then saddled the horses and led them back along the ridges of shell craters. In a few minutes the animals managed to pull the cannon upright onto its wheels with a crash, clods tumbling from between the spokes. Comeaux, who had washed out of artillery school, selected a shell and two bags of powder as the lieutenant rotated the elevation wheel until the barrel seemed to point directly into the pile of shells on top of the knoll. He struggled with the sighting mechanism, which was caked with rusty mud.

Comeaux looked down the side of the endless barrel. 'Now, I can't guarantee where this t'ing is gonna hit. I figure we should try to put one in the slope below them shells, and maybe that'll tell us how to adjust.'

Sam was twenty-three, an age when a man would just as soon do one thing as another without thinking about it much, but he was uneasy when he looked downrange. If they could figure an impact point with this test shot, he couldn't imagine a miss with a second. Summoning within himself a dumb optimism for the perfect hit, he decided not to ask the lieutenant to reconsider. He even envisioned a commendation for developing a new technique for battlefield disposal. Suddenly, something big detonated two miles off, a cloud of black smoke rising like an Indian's signal, and his confidence shrank. They glanced nervously at one another.

'Be sure to aim low,' Sam told Comeaux, who turned the elevation wheel to lower the barrel and then pulled the plug out of the muzzle.

'All right, all right!' Robicheaux hollered. 'Let's plow us a hole.'

Comeaux held the lanyard tentatively in his hand as the lieutenant shooed the horses away, waving his billed cap and crying out like a schoolboy. Everybody except Comeaux crouched down behind a line of sandbags.

Comeaux turned his back and squinted. 'Fire?'

'Check the lookout first,' the lieutenant told him.

Comeaux raised his field glasses and saw the makeshift flag a thousand yards to the west, waving on the hill.

'He says it's clear.'

'Then fire,' the lieutenant said, squatting low behind the sandbags.

Comeaux opened his mouth wide, bent his knees, then gave the lanyard a jerk.

The gun bucked back with a head-flattening concussion. Sam

thought that his soft palate had fallen down his throat, and his ears strummed as though struck by lightning. They all hugged the ground, Comeaux dove under the gun's axle as it rocked back and forth, everyone preparing, as the shell screamed downrange, for the second explosion to fall on them like a mountain.

They heard nothing. Sam looked up and saw the pile was intact. Stunned, Comeaux unlocked the gun's breach and looked into the smoky hole, as if convinced the shell hadn't been launched. He turned slowly and raised his shoulders. Then, far off, they heard it: a dull and profound *whomp,* maybe five miles away.

'We missed,' Sam announced, and his voice sounded tinny in his singing ears. He knew then he should have stopped the whole thing and that for the rest of his life, whenever he performed some stupid action to save time or inconvenience, he would feel the way he did now, like a lazy, rash fool.

'Oh, my,' the lieutenant said.

They all looked at one another, frozen, knowing.

Sam began running toward one of the horses.

'Where are you going?' the lieutenant shouted.

'I've got to see where that damn thing came down.'

The officer ran after him for a few yards, gesturing wildly, but Sam had jumped on the scarred bay and booted him off. 'Stop, private! That horse might step on a shell.'

The animal, confused at first, gradually fell into a rough gallop around the stumps, craters, and islands of wire to the ruined road that ran up a slope in the direction the shell had flown. When Sam looked back, the men stood watching him, motionless, the thin lieutenant now waving as if to a relative on a departing train. Then he went round a bend and they were gone. He charged on over dry ruts and through the wrecked lorries and tanks and a burned-up aeroplane, reining the horse in when the road veered off in the wrong direction. Praying for luck, he soon found an old stone pasture wall and trotted along that, the horse kicking up rifles in its wake. Hundreds of German Mausers lay abandoned along the fence, and he imagined the fight, the assassination of troops approaching the wall, the bayonet-driven countercharge, the panicked retreat up the hill, the screaming slaughter. In a defile between two long hills he turned the bay through a blasted gap in the stone, but the animal stopped dead. Sam kicked away at its flanks, but the big horse took it and stood like a pillar. He looked around, wondering if the animal remembered what had happened here, and dismounting, he looked into the liquid eyes, which seemed deliberately unfocused. He put a hand on its neck and the muscles were taut as fence wire, and he saw that its legs were trembling. He led it back through the wall by its bridle, remounted, and then put the animal forward along the stones, moving away from the place where twenty shattered limbers and many swollen horses lay about as if rained down from a murdering sky.

He studied the land ahead of him, and within a mile he rode into a squad stacking bags of cordite for demolition and reined up. A lanky private told him that he'd heard a shell rocket overhead. 'They ain't startin' up again, is they?'

'No.'

'I'm glad of it. After I seen all this mess I'm glad I missed the big ruckus. We just turnt over a steam tractor and found two skeletons from Alabama.'

Sam started the horse through a shell crater the size of a city fountain, rode into a dry canal and out again over a dike. Rising in the distance was a plume of white smoke. He whipped the bay with the reins and got up as much speed as he could, riding through a hedge and out into a mud lane, expecting to be blown up at any second. Suddenly he was in a village, coursing among sheds and small houses of bullet-pocked stucco and a large barn missing half its roof. A quarter-mile on, at the edge of an open field, sat the remnants of a small stone house, its blocks dispersed over an acre, its thatch roof on fire. In the dirt lane out front lay a girl, her long hair splayed on the ground as by an electrical charge. He jumped off the horse and carried her away from the flames, propping her against a low stone wall. No one else was around.

She appeared to be about eleven, but when she opened her eyes they were watery and old.

He asked her in French if anyone else had been in the house.

'Non, monsieur.' She seemed alarmed by his voice and asked where he was from, but he ignored her.

'Où sont tes parents?'

'Je ne sais pas.' She raised her right hand and it was streaming blood, the little finger cut off cleanly at the base. Then she told him she thought her parents were in heaven, and that everyone in the village had been killed or driven away. Suddenly she winced, grabbed her arm, and began to sob.

'Quel est ton nom?' he said, trying to distract her as he sat her up on the stone wall.

'Amélie,' she cried.

He pulled out his canteen, washed the wound, poured in disinfectant powder from a kit in his belt pack, and applied a rude bandage meant for gunshot wounds. Leaving her clutching her hand in the folds of her heavy skirt, he walked a circuit through the nearby buildings, all of them empty, though in one house there was a meal on the table, the food dried like scabs on the plates, as though everyone had fled months before and never come back. At the open rear door he looked across a steep field covered with frost-bitten weeds, imagining the panicked family running away from an incoming barrage, hoping to reach safety behind the next hill. He knew the girl was alone and would probably starve to death.

He went back and asked her full name.

'Amélie Melançon.' She squinted up at him. *'Et le vôtre?'*

'Sam Simoneaux.'

She repeated his name, her eyes growing round. *'Il y a des français en Amérique?'*

He explained where he lived and that there were indeed French people in the countryside to the west of there. He described New Orleans and asked if she had heard of it.

'Mais oui, monsieur.' She bent over as another spasm traveled up her arm.

He listened to her shuddering intake of breath and stared at the flames until her pain seemed to lessen. Then he told her he would find her a doctor, though he had no idea of where to start looking. He sat down and comforted her as best he could, asking her to talk about the vanished people of her village.

Staring at him intently, she asked, '*Combien de temps avez vous été en France?*'

'*Je suis arrivé le jour la guerre était finie.*'

She sniffed and gave him a fragment of a rueful smile. '*Eh bien, Monsieur Sam, votre nom devrait être Chanceux.*'

'My name should be Lucky? Me? I don't know about that.'

He heard a sputtering engine and stood as a muddy, open car with British markings came up the road, a one-armed captain sitting behind the driver in the wide rear seat. The captain leaned out and observed the girl now rocking back and forth on the wall, then the blown apart building, then Sam, who saluted. The captain made a face and said, as if to no one, 'American.'

'Yes, sir.'

'Was anyone else hurt?'

'Not that I could find, sir.'

'I see. Shooting at pigeons, I suppose?'

'No, sir. We were trying to detonate a pile of artillery rounds.'

The captain studied him for a long time, as if trying to gauge the workings of a mind accustomed to vast, empty American spaces where one could fire a howitzer all day long and hit nothing of consequence.

'Sir, the little girl was in the house alone and I think she's probably an orphan. What can we do for her?'

The captain seemed amazed by this question. 'Private, how long have you been over here?'

Sam shrugged. 'Maybe a couple months.' He looked helplessly around, feeling bereft of some essential common experience. The driver sniffed.

'I see.' The nub of the captain's arm twitched under the pinned sleeve, a phantom motion. 'Do you know how many orphans are wandering the roads? Living in what forests are left? They are roaming about looking for relatives who are already dealing with children from every other branch of the family. Many of them wind up in orphanages. Do you really want her in one of those?'

'I don't know, sir.'

He looked again at the girl. 'How bad is her hand?'

'She's got a finger off.'

'Clean wound?'

'Yes, sir.'

'My advice is to leave her here, then, if that's what she wants. Somebody she knows will drift back, and she can fit in with them. This is my district. Tell her she can walk the five miles to Pilars to see the army medic if her hand doesn't heal.'

'Leave her?'

The captain raised his chin and looked around. 'There, that house has a roof on it. She can stay there.' He tapped the driver on the shoulder, and the big car heaved up out of a rut and left them.

Sam looked down at the girl and asked if she wanted to stay in that house.

'C'est la maison de mon oncle,' she said. *'Il est mort.'*

He asked if it would frighten her to stay in the house of her dead uncle.

She looked up at him with her pained eyes and said that a live person was more frightening than a dead one. It was a live person who blew up her house.

He looked again at the burning thatch roof. *'C'était un accident,'* he said. *'La guerre est finie.'*

'Non,' she said. The girl told him that it was not over for her, and she began weeping again, thrusting her bloody bandage up at him.

He sat down next to her on the stone wall and pulled her head against his chest. She smelled unwashed, and a louse came up between his fingers, but he held her close, repeating 'It's over, it's over,' as she shook her head, and keened, *'Jamais, jamais pour moi.'*

He spent the rest of the day preparing the house, boarding up a blown-out window, remounting the front door, and as he worked he told her about his childhood, and where he lived now. He showed her how to make fires, though she assured him that she was wise to the chore, and he explained how to clean and rebandage her wound. When the daylight began to fade he told her he was sorry for what happened to the other house, and she gave him a worried look and asked if he was going to shoot his cannon again. He said no, that they'd made an experiment that had failed.

'Bon. Si la fusillade a enfin arrêté, peut-être mes voisins seront de retour.'

He set a plate on the rough kitchen table in front of her, and began rummaging for something to put on it, wondering how she would manage until someone showed up to help. She had lost everyone. He asked her if she knew how to read.

'J'étais la première dans ma classe,' she said, throwing her head up.

In a cabinet in another room he had found a small library, and he brought a few books out for her, setting them next to her plate. She brushed her dark hair back and picked one of them up. There was a translation of Dickens and another of Twain, and editions of Flaubert and Stendhal, names he didn't recognize. *'Peut-être ceux-ci peuvent t'aider à passer le temps.'*

She opened the book with her bloody hand. *'Monsieur Chanceux, ma mère m'a dit que le temps passe sans notre aide.'*

That evening he rode the bay back to his unit, arriving well after dark and reporting what he'd discovered, that he'd left a child with candles and eight shriveled potatoes and some rations from the horse's saddlebags. The men were glad the stray shell hadn't done even more damage, but Sam saw nothing to be happy about. His uncle had taught him that what he did in life, good or bad, could seldom be undone.

The lieutenant pulled from his tunic a packet delivered a half hour earlier by motorcycle courier, then bent next to the truck out of the wind and tried to read a message by matchlight. 'We were so busy waiting for you and sharing the excellent brandy with the poor motorcyclist that I forgot to read this.' After a moment, his head snapped up. 'Well, it's over.'

'What we got to blow up now?' Sam asked, holding his cup out to Robicheaux's jug.

'Nothing.' The lieutenant threw the packet into the ruined truck and smiled all around. 'Most teams have been ordered back to Paris. All cleanup has been ordered stopped, and for some reason our little group's being sent to the south of France. Makes me wonder why they exiled us out here in the first place.'

'They had this fancy idea in their heads,' Sam said, feeling the brandy burn in his throat.

'What? An illusion, you mean?'

'Is that what they call it? I meant some general who's never been out here had a fancy idea we could sweep up this place with a whisk broom and a dustpan. When you think about a problem for thirty seconds instead of a week like you should, you come up with one of those illusions you're talking about.'

'Oh, sit down and have a drink,' the lieutenant told him.

Sam held out an open hand toward the battlefield. 'Do you think I can come back and check on the little girl?'

'No, absolutely not. We have our orders.'

'What about later? On my leave?'

'We're going a long ways away, and I'd bet straight home after that.'

'I have to see about her.'

The lieutenant took a swallow from a tin cup. 'You're not exactly a tourist over here. And you can't pop some French kid into your knapsack for the trip home.' The brandy was making the lieutenant talkative and bold. He drained the cup. 'I'm sorry, but she'll have to take her chances like the rest of us.'

Sam leaned back against the truck and ran his hand along the enormous hole in the hood. The piece of shrapnel could just as well have crashed through him. 'The little French girl called me Lucky. Like a name.'

'Why's that?'

'For getting here the day the Armistice was signed. For missing everything.'

'There's worse nicknames,' the lieutenant said, walking over to where the other men were huddled in blankets, passing the huge jug.

Sam stared at the moonstruck wreckage around him that extended from the North Sea to the Mediterranean and beyond, understanding that Amélie's lot was but one particle of the overall catastrophe, that mothers from Nebraska to Mesopotamia were setting tables for diminished families, and countless children were waiting for the sound of a door opening and the claiming voices of their blood. He wanted in the worst way to help the girl, but he was as carried along by the war's events as she was and would be a hundred miles away by the next evening.

Robicheaux called out from his blanket spread along a fallen tree. '*Simoneaux, viens ici, petit boogalee.*'

He walked toward the voice. 'Let me have a pull on that jug if you haven't dirtied it with your spit.'

'This brandy has a lot of fire,' Comeaux said. 'You could disinfect a urinal with it.'

Sam drank until his eyes watered. '*Maudit fils d'putain!*' he exclaimed.

'I thought you give up speakin' French,' Robicheaux said.

'This stuff'll make you speak Chinese.' But he took another swallow, and after a few minutes, another, for a breeze had come up and the wind was ice. Comeaux told a joke, but no one laughed, and the lieutenant tried to explain what life was like in Indiana, but no one listened to him. After a long period of quiet someone said out of the dark, 'I can't believe they expected us to do any good.'

'Yes,' the lieutenant began, raising an arm toward the north, 'think of all the millions of tons of stuff lying out there that didn't explode.'

Sam's gaze followed the gesture, and saddened by the day's events, he said, 'But think of every bit that did.'

3

1921

Sam returned from Europe with the notion that the surface appearance of things was not to be trusted, that the world was a more dangerous place than he'd thought. Like most of his fellow soldiers, he didn't completely understand what he'd been through. Some of his friends came back shell-shocked, depressed, suspicious, and disoriented. Most got jobs and tried to work their way out of the war, and, in time, succeeded – artillerymen selling cars, machine gunners baking bread. Sam was thankful he hadn't killed anybody, because the men he knew who had were having a rough time just walking down Canal Street, where a car might backfire and send them to the pavement.

For the past two years Sam had been the head floorwalker in Krine's department store, four high-ceilinged floors of clothes for all genders and ages and budgets; shoes ranging from hand-sewn wingtips with waxy oxblood complexions to smelly rubber footgear that would come apart if the wearer stood on a heat register; a like spectrum of furniture, notions, and phonograph records; a lunch counter with both steak and thin soup. On an open mezzanine above the first floor was a lady's parlor of no particular commercial purpose where a pipe organ was manned between ten and five by Maurice, the fourth and most musical son of Isaac Krine, the owner. Sam told his fellow employees to call him Lucky and repeated the Armistice story to everybody because it made them happy. He was glad to be in New Orleans and not on the farm, glad to be getting rid of his bayou accent, his sun-roasted skin, his army clothes, the explosions, and the horse droppings.

Krine's was on Canal Street, not far from neighborhoods fallen on hard times, including the French Quarter, home, in Sam's mind, to people of decayed wealth and logic. The store suffered the slings and arrows of shoplifting, a biannual armed robbery, usually at the jewelry counter, arson, and the occasional fistfight between whores in the foundations department.

Sam stepped out of the office, rolled his shoulders in his freshly pressed summer-wool suit, and checked the wide aisles. Each morning he slipped a fresh flower into his buttonhole, checked his nut-brown hair and square jaw in the jewelry-counter mirror, and began a constant route through the cavernous store, examining both the behavior of customers and the physical plant, including the many-bulbed light fixtures hanging twenty feet above the floor from huge plaster medallions. If Mr Krine spotted a dead bulb before Sam did, his pay would be docked a nickel. On this particular Monday in late June he rolled down the aisle through women's dresses wearing his rubber-heeled lace-ups and stepping easily so no one could hear his approach. He was uncomfortable about wearing such deceptively quiet shoes, but his job required them. The previous week he'd come upon a man wadding silk scarves into his pants pocket. Sam drifted up behind him like a cloud, inserting four fingers into his collar before the thief knew what was happening. He struggled and tried to run, but Sam pulled him down in the purse section, with a knee in his lower back, just as he'd learned in the army and in childhood scuffles with his cousins.

It was eleven o'clock and Maurice began playing 'Down Among the Sugar Cane' with only the ocarina stop pulled out, a signal to the restaurant crew to gear up for lunch. The store was flush with customers, a hundred or more on the main floor, browsing and listening, from time to time glancing up at the pastel-painted organ pipes and Maurice's animated backside bouncing on the bench. People were shopping with music in their feet, and the overall motion in the store was that of a dance floor as lips mouthed the song's words, hands reached out for ties, and fingers tapped shirt-fronts in the rhythm of selection. Everyone was convinced by the chandeliers, decorative plaster, and music that they were happy to spend their money.

Sam enjoyed his clean, snappy clothes and light duties. His wife, a seamstress, worked for a fine upholstery shop uptown, where they rented a cypress shotgun house and comfortably waited for another child to come along. He'd bought himself a decent second-hand Packard piano, and his wife purchased a Singer sewing machine that she could run like a small locomotive when rushed to complete a job. Their lives had found a happy, productive pattern. He now looked up at a store fixture and checked all the bulbs, keeping everything in control, all the nickels in his paycheck. Glancing around the morning-cool store at the pretty counter girls, he tapped a shiny shoe to the fluting pipe organ. He could work this job, he felt, for the rest of his life.

And then the young couple approached him, their faces worried, confused. 'Excuse us,' the man said, 'but we can't find our little girl.' Sam looked at their clothes. The woman showed a nice sense of style that she'd put together on a budget. The man's suit was sharp, but shiny with wear.

Sam remembered learning at his internship in Krine's St Louis store that it was common for a child to wander away from one parent engaged in the art of buying things, but when two lost track of a young one, something was wrong. Maybe the child had run off, or had fallen asleep in some under-counter bin, or was exploring the elevator machinery in the basement. Or worse.

He smiled easily at them, but it was a store-bought smile, and he immediately scanned the nearest doors leading to the street. 'Where was she the last time you saw her?'

'It was over in men's suits,' the man said.

Sam noticed that he was wearing a carefully ironed shirt, and the thought came to him that the man's wife loved him.

She now pointed across the store. 'We've looked for her for five minutes all over that side. We've been in the store a half hour, and honest, she was right around us all that time. She's only three years old. A little blonde in a blue pinafore. Her name's Lily.'

'Has she wandered off before? Does she like to play hide-and-seek?'

The mother, a blonde herself, her hair in a medium bob, shook her head.

Sam smiled at her. 'Don't worry. You two cross over to the south side of the store and look there. I'll recheck men's suits.' While the parents began to filter through the maze of counters, he walked over toward Lillian Clarksby in cosmetics and asked her to close her register and check the front of the store, especially the window displays on the street. Sometimes he'd found young children wandering among the mannequins as if comparing their frozen gestures and shallow eyes with those of the adults they knew.

He toured suits, then mounted the stairs to the mezzanine and stood with his back to the women's parlor to scan the aisles, but saw no children.

Mary Lou Landry, the mezzanine attendant, came up behind him. 'Lucky, what you looking for, darling?'

He caught a whiff of an expensive scent and stared at her, then remembered that she spritzed herself at the perfume counter every morning. 'A little blond girl, a toddler.'

'She got herself lost? Well, stop looking and start listening. She'll be bawling for sure if she's still in the store.'

He watched customers wandering over the chicken-wire tile entranced by the illusion Krine's lavished on them. Sam sometimes felt it himself, a shrinelike ambience like that of a courthouse or a church. 'Do me a favor, Mary. Lillian's checking the front doors, so will you please slip around to the Granier Street entrance and stay there for about ten minutes? She was wearing a little blue pinafore, they told me.'

'Oh, she wouldn't wander that far.' Mary wasn't about to take orders from a floorwalker.

He leaned into her. 'Not without help.'

'Oh.' Mary clopped down the mezzanine steps briskly, her hands turned up on her wrists as if she were displaying her nails.

Sam walked down the line of elevators and put his head in each that was open, asking the same question of the operators, then stepped into the last one and told old Melvin Stine to bring him up to two.

'You checkin' the tills, Lucky?'

'I'm looking for a three-year-old girl in a pinafore.'

'She didn't come up in this car.' He gave Sam a look. 'Lucky, how long you been lookin'?'

He glanced at his watch. 'Nine minutes.'

'Don't forget the stairwells. And Mr Krine's rule.'

He got out and walked through children's clothes, then into toys, telling clerks what to look for as he went. After checking the dressing rooms he unlocked a door with his key and walked through the janitor's area and two large, hot storerooms. Outside again, catching Melvin's car going up, he traveled to the third floor, then the fourth, which was the discount floor, a sweltering place with tall, wide-open windows and many ceiling fans whirring overhead – a repository of returned suits, remaindered shoes, garish suspenders, celluloid collars, and what was referred to derisively as the Country Corner, a few shelves of overalls, blue jeans, straw hats, brogans, red neckerchiefs. This was the province of Hulgana Ditchovich, a blocky woman stuffed into a vertically striped dress made of what seemed to be mattress ticking.

'Mrs Ditchovich, have you seen a little blond girl in a pinafore up here? Her parents lost sight of her downstairs.'

'Lucky, Lucky, when will the cool-air vents come to the fourth floor?'

He imagined Hulgana as a stolid child, holding a wooden bucket and feeding cows in the snow outside of St Petersburg. 'Maybe next season. About that child?'

'No children up here this morning except for some farmer boys come in for shoes.' She focused on him for the first time. 'Such a big man like you can't find a child?'

After a quick tour of the steaming storage area on her floor, he came back out and used the store phone under Hulgana's register to call the candy counter.

'Penny Nickens, candy.'

'Penny, this is Sam.'

'Lucky!' she shouted into the receiver. He liked Penny well enough but found her too exuberant, always likely to spout like a shaken bottle of pop.

'You have a good view of the office. Is anything going on?'

After a pause she said, 'There's a worried-looking couple talking to Mr Krine. Oh, the lady looks so sad.'

'Thin woman in a blue dress. Pretty.'

'Yes. Look, I've got some of those new raspberry slices you like.'

'You can't win me with candy.'

'Oh!' she shrieked. 'And you a married man!'

He imagined all the heads turning toward the candy counter, and hung up.

It had been half an hour since the little girl disappeared. Walking to the elevator, he remembered Melvin's comment about the stair-well and changed direction. No one used the stairs, and they gave off a nose-burning essence of dusty concrete. He started down, and on the third flight something on a gray tread caught his eye, a little piece of yellow hard rubber, some junk missed by the janitor. He stepped past it and continued all the way to the bottom of the stairs, trying not to scuff his mirrory shoes. He was annoyed that he would have to deal with the parents again. By now, the girl had probably turned up.

He put his hand on the knob of the stairwell door and stopped, overcome by the feeling that he'd made some kind of mistake. The whole store's design ghosted through his mind as he tried to think of what he might've missed. He looked back up the stairway and pursed his lips, letting go of the knob and rising several flights to pick up the little piece of yellow tucked against the wall in the corner of a step: a child's barrette, a yellow bar and nickel-plated clasp with a small blue butterfly set on the topside. Suddenly, he was frightened.

Down on the first floor he met the couple, the Wellers, and

when he showed them the barrette, the mother clapped her hands over her mouth.

Mr Krine touched him on the shoulder as if he were adjusting a table lamp. 'Mr Simoneaux, if you found this, why can't you find the child? I was sure you'd come in here leading her by the hand.'

'Now that I know the hair clip was hers, maybe I can.' He looked at Mrs Weller. 'She probably just found the stairs. Kids love stairs.'

Mr Krine raised a marble-hard face to Sam, as though to say, 'Look at me and see how serious this is.' 'Search again,' he said. 'And this time find her.'

The mother cried, 'Why would someone try to take Lily?' and the sound of her voice made him understand that today might not be like every other day, that something terrible could be happening. Some long-dormant fear woke up in him, the mysterious taste of ash welling up on the back of his tongue.

He ran through the milling customers to the first open elevator and told the operator to take him straight to the fourth floor. A middle-aged woman in the back of the car said, 'I have to get off at three,' and he considered saying something sharp, but even now he understood that most people didn't have all the facts. 'I'm sorry for the inconvenience, ma'am,' he said. As soon as the doors opened he bounded into the discount section and in a moment was in the Country Corner. Mrs Ditchovich was dozing behind the register, and he rushed past her back to the only dressing room in the store he hadn't checked, one that was seldom used because people buying bulky triple-stitch denim clothes rarely studied how they looked in a mirror. Behind the showroom partition he entered a dim hall filled with a peculiar smell that stopped him cold. Suddenly the hospitals in France came back to him, with the memory of men returned from surgery reeking of chloroform, which was what Sam was smelling now as he stood frozen, trying to imagine what that odor was doing here. When he understood, he lunged for the door to the dressing room.

The first thing he noticed was a golden blur on the floor, and a surprised older woman sitting on the bench holding a large pair of blued scissors over the head of a child, a very young, short-haired boy – his eyes rolled up in his head, his mouth gaping open – dressed in new trousers and a checkered shirt. Sam thought he had accidentally stumbled upon something horrible yet unrelated to his search, but in the next instant he saw a small blue pinafore lying next to a scattering of fine blond hair and knew he had found the girl, though as he reached out to her, for an instant enjoying the touch of rescue before it actually happened, she disappeared into darkness, all light instantly knocked out of his head by a soundless blow from behind.

For a long time he lay stunned, listening to a scuffling, and then, as from a great distance in the dark, a fleshy pale image like a blurred cameo drifted toward him, out of focus, sliding away from resolution, but finally he willed his brain to fix the vision and it was the bright face of a strangely wise-looking baby girl with soft cheeks and long lashes, and he felt himself running through the dark faster and faster, breathing through his mouth and moaning out loud until he woke up coughing on vomit, a doctor rolling him onto his side and his face plunging into boiled hospital sheets, a nurse coming toward him with a porcelain pan while a bright window beyond her absorbed the dissolving jewel of the child's face.

4

Four days after he'd entered the hospital, he woke with a spinning head and saw his wife, Linda, sitting in a white enamel chair stitching a large canvas of needlepoint. He watched her a moment before he spoke to make sure she was real and not one of the dreams that had been haunting him. He blinked. It was stolid Linda, red hair, milk white complexion, her fingers working needlepoint chair bottoms she sold to a furniture store uptown.

When he spoke her name, she lifted her head and said, 'Do you remember what happened?'

It was like her to check to see if something, in this case his memory, might be broken. He wondered if she'd throw him away if he couldn't think anymore. But after a moment, he decided he could, and told her, 'I'm all right. I remember.'

She leaned in close and studied his eyes, kissing his forehead as she would a feverish child. 'I'll call for the doc to look at you in a minute.' She helped him sit up, and his head began to clear. He then told her about that day in the store, carefully working in all the details, placing them for her like delicate items on a shelf.

'Well,' she said, brushing his hair back. 'That's pretty much the way Mr Krine told it to me when he came by to fire you.'

He looked down at his arms, as though he still expected to be wearing his floorwalker's suit. 'What for?'

Her eyebrows arched, and she looked at him as if he'd just asked what the sun was. 'Why, for losing that little girl.'

He thought about this. For Mr Krine there was no substitute for performance. If something went wrong, it was the employee's fault. Always. 'How did they get away with her?'

'They left you out cold in the dressing room, came downstairs with the child dressed as a sleeping boy and walked right through the doors before the staff got the order from Mr Krine himself to lock them.' She leaned around and inspected the back of his head. 'Nobody found you for half an hour. When they saw all the stuff in the dressing room, they figured out what happened. The parents were really upset, Lucky. They said they should've got more help from the store. They've been by here every day with a policeman wanting to ask you questions. Mr Krine's afraid they'll try to sue.'

'What else could I have done?' But even as he said this, he knew the answer. He'd ignored Mr Krine's rule: If a child was missing in-store for more than fifteen minutes, the floorwalker on duty was responsible for making sure all the doors were locked.

His wife walked back to her chair. 'Whatever needed to be done, you didn't do it.'

'I tried my best.' He turned his face to the wall, wondering if this was true.

'That's what the mezzanine attendant and the candy girl said.' She glanced up at him, then returned to her needlework. 'You sure have a lot of lady friends.'

'Linda, three-quarters of the staff's ladies.'

She drew her work close. 'The city cops said you should've called them first off.'

He groaned and slid down in the sheets. 'City cops wouldn't come for a kid lost in a store.'

'I realize that. But because things turned out bad, you know, after the fact, they're all down on you.'

'They want Krine to hire one of their patrolmen on his off-hours.'

She squinted and drew a stitch. 'They do carry guns.'

'I've got a little gun in the store safe,' he said weakly, knowing he would never have used it. After his experience in the war, he wanted nothing further to do with guns.

Linda shrugged.

He watched her push her needle up and through the pattern,

one he recognized from other chair seats, of an eighteenth-century dandy bowing before his reluctant lady. Her work was beautiful and earned decent money, and he was glad of it.

Two days later he went to the store, and Mr Krine gave him a week's pay along with a lecture. Sam was hoping for a little mercy, but it was a faint hope at best; he'd seen several employees walk out of Krine's flashy doors holding their final pay envelopes because of lesser mistakes.

He stood in front of the mahogany desk in the owner's office. 'How can I come back? I like the job.'

Mr Krine was looking up a phone number, already finished with him. 'If you find that little girl you can have your job back.'

Sam glanced at the family photograph on Mr Krine's desk showing his well-dressed offspring, all of them working in the store. 'You have any idea how I might do that?'

Mr Krine kept his eyes on the phone as he drew it toward him. 'You could use all the free time you have.'

Six blocks from the store was the precinct station on Chartres, and he dawdled through the steamy morning, breathing a nimbus of horse droppings and cigarette butts sopping in the gutters and sewer gas crawling out of the storm drains. He kept back from the curb as the Model T's and fruit wagons splashed down toward the market.

Coming into the station house's lobby, a large open space with wedding-cake plaster on its ceiling, he saw Sergeant Muscarella writing in a ledger, the white dome of his bald head bobbing away under a shivering lightbulb. Last year he was on foot patrol in Sam's neighborhood, but then he had donated a month's pay to the new mayor's campaign fund.

'Mr M.'

Muscarella raised his gray face from the ledger. 'Eh, Lucky, you got out the hospital.' The sergeant's eyes, watching him with detachment, were olives left too long in the jar.

'Yeah. I still got the headache real bad.' He touched his forehead. 'You heard anything about that little girl?'

The sergeant laid his pen in the crack of the ledger. 'You know, somebody steals a coat, he'll sell it or wear it. We can kind of guess where to look. But when somebody steals a kid, what do you do?'

'You sent people to the stations?'

'Yeah, sure. But nowadays they coulda used a car.' He shrugged. 'They coulda left on a ship. They could even still be in town, you know.'

'If you hear anything, I'm in the book.'

Muscarella's face twitched unpleasantly. 'Lucky, why you worried about this? You not a cop.'

He looked at the quarter-sawn oak wall panels behind the sergeant's bench, carved sections that rose up around the policeman like a little throne. He decided not to tell him about the pale cameo floating nightly behind his eyelids, the injured girl he left behind in France, his dead son, or his stolen family. He looked down at his shoes, understanding that the policeman didn't need the complicated truth. He needed a reason. 'Sal, I got fired because of this mess. Krine said he might hire me back if I found the kid.'

The sergeant shrugged. 'Lucky, floorwalker's not much of a job for somebody like you.'

'I like it. The pay's not bad and I can move up some, maybe manage a department.'

'Well, if you that hard up, I can get you on as a bank guard.'

He looked up and shook his head.

The sergeant picked up his pen. 'I guess you're not the shootin' kind.'

'Even my wife says I'm responsible for the little girl.'

Muscarella ranged his dark eyes over him. 'What *you* say?'

He put his hands in his pockets. 'I say I wish it'd been my day off.'

The sound of an argument rolled up the steps outside and the double doors burst open with two small cops fighting a two-hundred-pound whore, her red face rising angry as a boil out of a white feather boa.

He spent the day looking for work at the other big stores downtown. At suppertime he stepped off the streetcar and walked under the live oaks and over the root-buckled sidewalks to his shotgun on Camp Street. Looking forward to playing into the evening on his piano, he stopped half a block away and pushed back his straw boater when he saw a man and a woman sitting on the porch with his wife. He put his head down and walked up.

His wife's voice carried a forced lightness. 'Lucky, these are the Wellers, Ted and Elsie.'

'I know. How are you?' He noticed the mother's lips were determined today, pressed tight. Ted, a thick, balding fellow with a short mustache, held out his hand for Sam's and clasped it with surprisingly long fingers. After Sam sat down in a straight-back chair, the couple told him they'd been to every precinct house in town and explained they were musicians working on a Stewart Line excursion steamer come down from Cincinnati.

Sam nodded. 'One of the big dance boats.'

'The *Excelsior,*' Ted said. 'Elsie and me were in town shopping, you know, getting some fresh duds for a new act. That's what we were doing when our girl got taken.' He looked away, his eyes reddening.

Elsie leaned into the conversation. 'The boat's getting laid up for a couple months for new boilers and hull work. The company's going to put us on another boat they just bought from the St Paul Line. It's tied up south of town, but until it leaves we're spending every spare minute looking for her.'

Sam closed his eyes for a second and saw the little girl. 'Her name's Lily, isn't it?'

'Yes.' Elsie put a hand to her mouth.

He looked uncomfortably from one to the other, not knowing what to say or ask in a situation like this. Finally, he said, 'She is your blood child, right? There's no ex-spouses involved, is there?'

Ted frowned. 'She's our natural child. And we've thought about everybody we know and can't come up with a soul who'd want to make off with her.'

Sam leaned back, listening to the chair creak underneath him. 'Well, I'm not surprised.'

'Why do you say that?' Elsie asked, her hand still next to her mouth.

'The woman I saw didn't look like anybody who'd wanted a pretty little girl. She was old and had seen a lot of hard times. I just caught a glimpse, but her hair was oily-looking and I think, let's see now' – he closed his eyes again – 'she was missing a front tooth.'

'Oh,' Elsie said, 'she sounds awful.'

'Did you see the one who hit you?' her husband asked.

'No, but the bastard – excuse me – he sure knew where to pop me. If you think about it, considering the chloroform and all, it's like somebody hired those people to steal her. They were just too good at it. They'd planned it all out.'

For a long moment everyone on the narrow wood porch seemed to be thinking about what he'd said. In the next block, the clipped yells of a neighborhood baseball game swelled up and died off. Sam was imagining the one bottle of beer at the bottom of the cooler, next to the block of ice.

Ted moved uneasily in his chair. 'It doesn't make sense for someone to hire a thief.'

'I don't know. Tell me something about her.'

The Wellers exchanged looks.

'Well,' the husband began, 'about two months ago we brought her into the act. She's only three and a half, but she's smarter than the two of us multiplied together. The child can remember at least a couple verses of a dozen different songs. When she sings, you can see the music in the way she moves.'

Elsie straightened her back. 'She's got this voice that's very accurate for a child. Good volume, too.'

'I taught her how to dance a little while she sings,' Ted bragged. 'We're part of the big orchestra that the Stewart Line hires, but we only use Lily in two ensemble pieces per set, and the audiences go crazy for her.' He looked up and narrowed his eyes. 'A lot of people have watched her perform since we left Cincinnati four weeks ago.'

'Three and a half and she can do all that?' Sam looked at his wife. 'I'd steal her myself.'

The parents both looked glumly at the street.

During the next half hour he told the Wellers how sorry he was several times, but they didn't make a move to get up. Finally, the street began to darken and he pulled out his watch. 'You know, I've got to go in now.'

Ted also pulled a pocket watch from his vest but wound it without checking the time. 'You're the only one who saw the ones that took her. The cops at the Third District said you're real smart. You can figure all the angles here.'

Sam felt sorry for them, but had no idea of how to help. His brief stay in France had instilled in him the understanding that the world presents unsolvable tragedies at every turn. 'I don't know what to do for you.'

Lightning bugs began to come out of the streetside privet, sparking on and off like flickering hopes.

At last, Elsie stood up. 'We're sorry you got fired.'

'Me too.'

'What will you do?'

He smiled up at her in spite of himself. 'I guess I'll think about some of those angles.'

Later, after supper, Linda opened the beer and poured it into two glasses. Sam walked through the little parlor and picked up a small framed photograph of an infant dressed in baptismal clothes. They went back out onto the porch and sat in the night's breath coming up from the river. He held the photograph in one hand and rubbed a thumb back and forth across the glass.

Linda touched his arm. 'Are you thinking of how to help them?'

'I'm thinking, all right.' There were people missing in his life like big holes cut out of the night sky, and Sam felt powerless to do anything about it. He was only one person in a planet full of incomplete seekers, and now the Wellers had joined him.

5

It had been two weeks since they'd seen the Wellers. Right after a thunderstorm had tortured the neighborhood with sizzling bolts, Sam and his wife were looking through the window screen at the water standing in their small bricked yard. He felt like a piece of wreckage left behind by the wind. Between them on the table was a small loaf of French bread showing a flame of desiccated ham. No lettuce or tomato, no mayonnaise. They were out of everything and the rent was due. They owned only an old Dodge automobile and their clothes. Linda had spent her needlepoint money on the telephone bill, electricity, gasoline. Sam imagined she had a jar of quarters somewhere but never asked about it, for fear it didn't exist. The dry sandwich lay between them like a signal.

'Well, I guess I better go see Muscarella and sign up with the bank militia.'

She looked at him. 'My brother can get you on at the railroad.'

'Switchman?'

'Yes.'

'Your brother with three fingers missing? Or your brother with a thumb cut off?'

She sliced the sandwich in half and pushed the larger portion toward him. 'You're more careful.'

'Linda, there's not a man in your family that can play the piano.'

She bit at her part of the sandwich, twisting on it. 'Well, go on downtown, then. And please find *something*.'

That day and the following, he walked the twenty blocks downtown to look for work in the stores. He went on foot to loosen up his legs, he told himself, but in fact he wanted to save the seven cents' streetcar fare. On the second day, halfway to Canal Street, he didn't know why, some little spark of curiosity or sense of purpose overtook him at Lee Circle and he changed direction toward the river, wondering what he was doing as he walked into the smell of burning coal and roasting coffee. From the foot of Canal he could see a big Stewart Line excursion boat riding high in a dry dock across the river, its paddle wheel dismantled, its rusty stacks laid out on the deck. He caught the Algiers ferry, which cost him seven cents, and from the landing walked down a dirt lane to the shipyard. A watchman told him that most of the boat's crew and performers had been put up in the Gardenia Hotel. He counted out five Indian-head pennies and two Lincolns, took the next boat across, and walked through the French Quarter to the hotel, a place he knew was frequented by vaudevillians and traveling salesmen. He arrived tired and thirsty, the bottoms of his feet burning in his shiny floorwalker's shoes, and he paused on the sidewalk across from the Gardenia, examining the pressed-tin roof frieze that pretended to be stone, the copper-sheeted bay windows that hung over the street like ingots, showing a thinly deceptive elegance.

The desk clerk rang the Wellers' room, and the wife said her husband was out but she would come right down, so Sam waited in the illusory lobby with its puddled curtains and genteel walnut settees and side tables. He knew what the rooms were like, small and hot and plain as toast. He heard Elsie on the stairs before he saw her, and her steps were slow. She joined him on a green plush sofa, sitting down quickly, perhaps pretending not to notice a polite scattering of dust rising from the cushions.

'Do you have any news?' she asked. She was composed and did not smile at him.

He shook his head, once. 'I've been going around town trying to find a job that won't maim me or drive me crazy or get me arrested.' He watched her face, but she seemed unconcerned about what he'd said. He knew what she wanted to hear. 'While I was out and about, I did what I could. Checked with the porters at the stations. Visited some hotels and the one criminal I know.'

She still did not smile. Out in the street the vegetable man's wagon passed by, his falsetto rising about the glories of tomatoes and plums, 'Ahh gotta da bannannnn . . . ,' but her gaze didn't stray toward the window. 'We've paid a private policeman to investigate Lily's disappearance, but he's turned up nothing. I don't think he really cares about her, just our money.' She didn't say this in a bitter voice, and he was glad of it. His uncle had taught him that bitterness solved nothing. 'I don't suppose you have children,' she continued. 'I didn't see any sign of them at your house.'

He looked over at the bald desk clerk, who was watching them. 'I had a son. But we lost him to a fever.'

'How old?'

'Nearly two. I know a little of what you're feeling.'

'A little,' she said. 'At least you know where your son is.'

He reddened at her presumption, bordering on meanness, and had opened his mouth to say something, he wasn't sure what, when a big hand came down on his shoulder. He looked up and saw a large, white-haired gentleman dressed in a bluewater uniform, a soft cap pulled down at an angle with the legend 'Captain' in gold braid above the patent-leather bill.

'Pardon me,' he said, 'but I've got to put a quick question to this lady.' He was about sixty-five years old, the type of blustery fellow used to taking over anyone's conversation. 'Elsie, I need you and Ted to come down to the Industrial Canal out by the cracker works. We've just closed on the *Ambassador* and we've got to get her in shape fast.'

'Is there a piano on board?' She seemed confused.

The big man cocked his head. 'Now, Elsie?'

'Oh, I see. You want us to clean and paint,' she said, frowning.

'The *Ambassador*'s a big old boat and she's been laid up a while down here in all this dampness. You know the routine. So you'll come out tomorrow? Bring your work duds?'

Elsie nodded vaguely, and the captain straightened up and put his hands behind his back. 'I've got to get on and find some men who won't milk me dry for salary.'

Suddenly, her face seemed busy with several ideas at once. 'This man here's looking for work.'

The captain leaned back and examined Sam as though he were a deck chair he might or might not buy. The leather in his shoes creaked in the quiet lobby. 'You're a pretty nice-looking fellow. Ever worked a dance boat before, son?'

'No, but I've gone dancing on a few.'

She stood and put a hand on his shoulder. 'Last night Ted said that if you worked on the boat, you'd be able to go ashore and help us look. Maybe you could watch the crowds while we worked.'

'Watch the crowds for what?'

'The woman you saw. We figured that somebody who caught Lily's act paid that woman to take her.'

Sam stood up, looked through the glass-paneled entry door, and took a step toward it. 'That old lady's not going to show up on your boat.'

'She's on the bank somewhere along our route.'

He stopped, then, admitting to himself that this was probably true.

'You a musician?' the captain asked.

'I'm a pretty bad pianist.'

'And were you in the war?'

'The army.'

The captain's white eyebrows collapsed together, and he lowered his voice. 'Can you break up a fight and keep your hand out of a till?'

Elsie began to shake him. 'Sam, this new boat will work the same landings we did on the way down. You might could spot that old woman in one of the towns.'

He watched the desperation rising in her face, then turned to the captain. 'What kind of work do you have?'

'I need a third mate. One of the main duties is to walk around the dance floor and show some authority. You have any experience walking around and looking like you know what you're doing?'

Elsie sat down on the settee, smoothed her dress, then ran a forefinger along one eyebrow. 'He's the floorwalker I told you about.'

The captain's expression darkened. 'You're the one who couldn't stop those people.'

Sam looked back through the door where three smiling couples were strolling along the street. 'That's me, all right.' Suddenly he seemed to have a new identity: the man to blame.

The captain glanced down at Elsie. 'Well, I'll hire you anyway. Long hours, free room and board.'

'I'm Sam Simoneaux. My friends call me Lucky.'

The other man took his hand soberly. 'My name's Adam Stewart, and you can call me Captain.'

His wife was not happy about this job that would keep him away from home, and seemed suspicious of his motives. It took him until late that night to explain to her why he felt obliged to go on the river, but as he fell asleep he realized that he wasn't sure of his motives himself, though the idea of wearing a snappy uniform and being around musicians had its appeal. He could explore each town on the boat's route, asking questions about the stolen girl, but beyond that he wasn't sure what he might accomplish for the Wellers.

The next morning he kissed Linda goodbye and caught a streetcar down to the Canal line and made the first of several transfers, walking the last leg down the east side of the new Industrial Canal. He could see the boat from a distance as it was nearly three hundred feet long, and he could tell by the kinks in the deck railings that it had seen too much river. He judged it to be at least forty years old, a sternwheeler four decks high that must have started life as a packet, hauling passengers and cotton, and then was made over into an excursion boat after the trade played out. The wooden hull was sprung, planks out of line and seams gorged with oakum. The main stage ramp was hung up over the bow in a tangle of rusted pillow blocks limed with bird droppings. A long two-by-twelve led from the wharf to the first deck. Beyond the boat the wide canal shifted, oily and slow, the new sun caught in it like a yolk. He bounced down the plank onto a deck made of broad cupped planks shedding enamel like red snow. He glanced up a broad central staircase and walked beyond it and then aft along the outside rail, past the boiler room, stepping through a door and walking among the main engines and pumps, expecting to find someone going over the machinery. He stopped in the dark and smelled cold oil, a ferrous mist of rust, and from below deck the sour ghost of a dark, side-rolling bilge. The old noncondensing steam engines looked like dead museum pieces that would never move again, asbestos-stuffed mammoths hulking in the gloom.

He walked forward and pulled himself up the main staircase. The vast second deck opened before him all the way to the stern windows, a maplewood dance floor hundreds of feet long that popped like distant musketry as he walked across it. A bandstand stood amidships on his left, and a long raft of small tables ganged next to cloudy windows slid shut against rain and birds, everything dusted blue with mildew. The ceiling was cross-bracketed every eight feet with gingerbread arches layered with gunpowder mold bred by the waterbound air.

The third deck was a two-tier affair, an outer open promenade called a hurricane deck and, in the center, a raised deck some rivermen called the skylight roof, railed and balustered, topped with a thin plank ceiling, the front half open to the breeze and the rear half a café, walled and windowed, sheltering a jumble of cheap wooden tables and deck chairs stacked in a great logjam. He walked through the café and looked into the kitchen at the big rusted coal ranges and many-doored oak iceboxes that hung open with the bitter smell of rotting rubber gaskets. He shook his head, thinking that every square inch of the busy woodwork, stanchions, hogchains, window frames, braces, brackets, filigree, molding, steam pipes, valve bonnets, smokestacks, and gingerbread would have to be scrubbed and painted.

The fourth level housed most of the crew. Sam remembered it was called the Texas deck and this one held a double row of plain cabins whose doors opened to the outside. On top of the Texas was the pilothouse, trimmed above its wide windows with sooty knickknack millwork and a copper-shelled dome. Sam found an unlocked cabin door and looked inside: two stacked bunks, a small lavatory, a locker with thread spools for pulls, the mattresses no better than what he had seen in a jailhouse. He looked back over the rail and realized for the first time that these old boats were made mostly of thin wood, to keep the weight down – regular wood that wanted to rot and warp and crack and leak and twist, and woe to everybody on board if a fire ever got started. The *Ambassador* had seen its share of summer squalls and upriver ice jams, had banged lock walls, scraped boulders, wormed over sand-bars, and every lurch and shock was recorded in her timbers. He looked aft and saw again the buckles in her guardrails, the swale in her roofline. The boat seemed a used-up, dead and musty thing as still as a gravestone, and he wondered who in his right mind would want to ride on it for fun.

About nine o'clock a bus rattled in on solid rubber tires and men dressed in denim began to pour off, most of them black. A little later four men hopped off a horse-drawn surrey, put on plug caps that identified them as the engine-room crew, then boarded and headed aft. In the next half hour a buggy, several Fords, and one horse showed up at the wharf, soon followed by a steaming stake-bed truck driven by the captain and piled high with cans of paint, brushes, turpentine, rags, and scrapers. The Wellers and other crew members were there, dressed in their worst clothes. Another, smaller truck pulled up carrying two zinc drums of bleach, and the captain climbed up in the bed and gave directions for its dilution and use. Sam was told to work with the second mate, a big hound of an ex-policeman named Charlie Duggs.

'Hey, I know you,' Duggs said. 'You're the head floorwalker at Krine's.'

Sam stuffed a brush in his back pocket. 'Not anymore.'

Duggs waited for a clarification, and after several seconds said, 'We all used to be somebody else, I guess.'

Sam motioned to Duggs's mate's cap. 'How'd you wind up in the steamboat business?'

He shrugged. 'When I got back from France with everybody else I was a cop for a year. Muscarella fired me when the new mayor came in. You know Sergeant Muscarella?'

'Who doesn't?'

They walked up carrying ladders and in a few minutes were scraping the gingerbread along the roofline of the Texas deck. Above them several men were making the chips fly on the pilothouse, and below a crew of seven was scratching away at the balusters on the guardrails, the whole boat vibrating as though gnawed by a million carpenter bees. As the day progressed, the dark water around the *Ambassador* was speckled by a soiled snow of paint flakes.

Something was burning, and Sam looked up to gray smoke bailing out of the starboard smokestack. The engine crew had laid a wood fire on the boiler grates, and after a half hour it was hot enough to ignite coal, the smoke turning to a black column of tarry-sweet bituminous breath. As Sam worked, he figured that the boat had been painted at least thirty times, the paint in places nearly a quarter-inch thick. At first he went after the old paint hard, but Charlie told him to ease off. 'Just get the loose stuff. We not painting a banker's house.'

'The captain won't get on us about it?'

'He knows it can't last. The soot eats it off once a year. Don't you know that?'

'No.'

With his scraper, Charlie knocked a dirt-dauber nest spinning into the canal. 'How'd you get on?'

'The Wellers put in a word for me.'

'You hear about their little girl?'

'Ah, yes.'

'That was a pretty child. Smart, smart. You could see it in her eyes. Little strong eyes that told you she was gonna do some big stuff in her time.'

'You heard her sing?'

'When we tie up I stand by to do the electrics for the band. Keep the microphone goin' and lights. She got a voice like a tiny fiddle and can play it, too. When I was that age I couldn't hardly wipe myself.' He was standing atop the rail and holding on to the molding of the deck above. 'Somebody stole that child right out of a department store and couldn't nobody in the store stop it, not even the puke-brain of a floorwalker who was looking for her.'

Sam stopped working. He was notorious already. 'So, you know it was me.'

'Yep.'

'How many people working today are the regular crew?'

'About most of us. They's a dozen or so extra painters to work this week that'll be paid off.'

'So you're all some type of big family, right? Been working together a few seasons?'

Charlie lowered his arms and balanced. 'So what?'

'Everybody talks about everybody's business? So if I tell you something, it's like having a meeting with everyone else at once, right?'

Charlie ran a thumb along his scraper's blade and looked at him. 'This is goin' somewhere?'

'I might as well say it now. I lost that job because of the child, and here I am, number one, to keep my lights on. And number two, the Wellers think I can help find their girl.'

'Is that how it is?'

'Spread the news.'

Charlie took two steps around a corner of the rail and stood over the paddlewheel, scraping and wincing away the peppering flakes. '*Something's* got to be done. Let's hope you're the something.'

* * *

A susurration began in one of the smokestacks as the boilers started to build steam pressure. The two escape pipes sizzled at their feathered tops. After two hours, the engineers fed steam to the ejectors, which opened with a roar, siphoning out the foul bilge. Sam could tell when the boilers reached the hundred-pound mark, because someone opened a valve and the muted chuff of the dynamo wound up in tempo, the running lights on the stacks coming on slow as candle flames. Soon crew members were mopping down every surface with bleach, for the pumps had brought up the water system and men in slickers began hosing the *Ambassador* down from pilothouse to lower deck, washing off smut, bird droppings, dust, paint chips, wasp nests, and mildew. The day had turned hot, and Sam leaned against the roof bell, letting Charlie stand back with a fire hose and soak him like a dirty rug.

By sundown of the second day, the whole boat was skinned down and drying in the hot breeze. After two days everyone was to come back and paint, unless rain threatened. The second night, the engineers stayed on the boat testing the boilers and chasing rust and tarnish, clogged oil channels, or wrens' nests in the engines' valve works. Sam was told to light the lanterns on the engineers' wagon and drive it back to their house, which was only eight blocks from his own. It'd been a long time since he'd driven a team, but once his hands remembered the feel of reins, he backed and turned the horses for town. The animals were heavy and streetwise, and he ran them alongside the clattering, sparking trolleys and under the streetlamps with no trouble at all. The day was finally cooling, and it was a pleasure to jostle the night air with their iron-shod hooves. Running over the Belgian-block streets downtown the wagon's steel rims and gear sounded like an avalanche of silverware. About ten o'clock he tied them off in back of a house on Magazine Street, where a light came on in the yard and an older woman wearing gray cotton trousers came out to unharness them.

'And thank you for not latherin' the boys up,' she said, bending to unhook the chains.

'You can let me do that.'

'No, get on home, son. As dark as it is, I can tell you're sunburned and coated with paint chips.'

'How's this wagon gonna get back?'

'I'll take it out tomorrow afternoon.' She was a big woman and no stranger to horses. In a moment she was leading the animals to a pair of roofed stalls against the back fence. 'I guess we'll get rid of these fellas after this season. We're the last in the neighborhood to keep any.'

'Do you work on the boat?'

She gave him a quick look. 'Yes. Those engineers are my nephews, and the bunch of us have been on the river all our lives. My late husband was a pilot and two of my sons are pilots on the upper Ohio. I'm Nellie Benton.' She reached out like a man and he looked at her hand for just a heartbeat before taking it. She shook like she meant to hurt his fingers. And she did.

The streets on his way home were fogbound, and the live oaks sucked the light out of the streetlamps. He walked through the gloom nearly asleep and found himself standing on a corner half a block past his door before he understood where he was.

In a few minutes he was in the bathtub, the water cold because the gas had been turned off.

Linda padded in to use the commode, and glanced at his eyes. 'You look like an Indian, honeybunch.'

He covered his face with a hand. 'Can I have your straw hat?'

'Sure. I'll take the sash off so it'll look like a man's.' She stood and looked at him again. 'You see the Wellers any?'

'Yeah. They were scrubbing down the dance floor. I believe they're tireder than I am.'

She put a hand in his hair. 'You don't have to do this.'

'It's sixty bucks a month, plus you don't have to feed me.'

'You know what I mean.'

He pulled his palm away from his face. 'I don't know. I just can't understand it.'

She reached into the tub and rubbed his neck as though claiming him. 'I believe I can.'

By the second day the bilge was pumped dry, and he and Charlie were sent belowdecks with carbide lamps to check the hull. There wasn't much down there other than a potable water tank, some steering and capstan works, and a few steam lines. After his eyes adjusted, he crawled along under the bracing, holding his lamp so Charlie could examine warped areas and test for punky boards with an ice pick. They had been out of daylight for an hour when Sam shone the lamp ahead and then back toward the dim shaft of light falling down the hatch they'd entered.

'You looking for frogs?'

'Everything's wood,' Sam said. 'No watertight compartments.'

'That's a fact.' Charlie took a string of oakum from his shoulder, then set it into a seeping joint with the pick.

'How'd this thing stay afloat all these years?'

'Two eyeballs in the wheelhouse. Shine that light here.'

He was in awe of all the soggy wood. 'One bump on a rock and this tub'll go down like a woodstove.'

Charlie sniffed. 'Kind of makes 'em careful where they steer it, don't it? One thing about a steamboat, it's all wood, and not the best wood or heaviest at that. It's just kind of a glorified chicken coop. If you smack a bridge pier with a wood steamboat, folks downstream will have all the toothpicks they want.'

The next day, fifty people showed up to paint. The stacks were washed down with stove black; the outside of cabin doors, the rails, the first-deck planking, and the boat's name – in four-foot letters on the engine-room bulkhead – were dressed with burgundy gloss enamel. The paddlewheel was painted bright red and everything else, from the circus molding branching out from the deck posts to the balusters and fire buckets, a sun-tossing white. Inside, when everything was scrubbed and enameled white, the spaces loomed larger, the huge dance floor now cavernous, the whole interior glowing like a snow cave. After he used turpentine to get the sticky oil paint from his hands and forearms, Sam jumped on shore and walked way back from the boat to look her over: in the early evening light she was a three-hundred-foot wedding cake. The running lights came on at the top of the stacks, and then the thousand roofline bulbs sent up their ivory fire, the whole boat flashing against the dark canal and floating above it like someone's dream of a traveling good time. Inside, a pianist was running the moths out of the bandstand piano with 'Dill Pickles Rag,' the notes completing the paint-bright illusion that made him want to pat his foot.

Charlie followed over to where he stood by a coal pile. 'Sam, my man. What you think?'

He raised a hand, then let it fall. 'I can't understand it. A few days ago it was a stinking washtub. Now I want to buy a ticket for the moonlight cruise.'

6

Acy White owned the only bank in the riverside town of Graysoner, Kentucky. He was a thin, sallow man, a Presbyterian-for-show, the grandson of a plantation owner who had owned many slaves in Mississippi. He held risky mortgages on dozens of little farms and owned personal loans made to hundreds of the county's lesser inhabitants, in this respect continuing his grandfather's slaver persona. Though he loaned money to most businesses in the area, nobody knew him well. He was not a gregarious and sweating banker, the usual tobacco-soaked, seersucker-wearing steak eater one finds in small Southern towns. He was neither a skinflint nor an easy touch, though now and then a wiry meanness flashed in his eyes. Acy believed in his inalienable right to whatever it was he wanted. He was remarkable for only one thing, his devotion to his wife, Willa, a blank slate of a woman he'd created out of his imagination.

Willa Stanton White, forty-year-old daughter of a wealthy lumber family from Gipson County, spent much of her time reading and rereading a leatherbound and gilt collection of Sir Walter Scott novels her husband had bought her and practicing Franz von Suppé transcriptions on the piano. Willa was an only child who had been spoiled beyond all measure and who'd allowed herself to be chosen by a man bent on honoring that tradition. For a small-town woman she owned brave sexual appetites and was an encouraging partner for Acy, though at times he seemed too tired to meet her demands. She had few close friends in town, though she knew many citizens at a hand-waving distance. Favoring expensive clothes designed to seem modest, she was not a stupid woman, but isolated and logic-deprived, raised on illusions and no work whatsoever.

At noon Acy left the bank in his new Oldsmobile, jittering over the redbrick street up the hill to his house, a three-story Greek revival with a windowed cupola on top from which one could just barely see the river two miles away. He went in and washed his hands in the downstairs bathroom under the stairs and sat in the dining room to wait for his lunch. Vessy, a thin serving girl from out of the eastern Kentucky mountains, hipped open the swinging kitchen door and in one motion set down a plate of beef stew and noodles and a glass of iced tea.

'Are they home?' He raised his chin to her.

She brushed her straight, near-colorless hair out of her gray eyes. 'They'll get down directly.'

'I thought they might have gone out in the other car.'

'Naw. The missus stickin' close to the house.' Vessy pulled the silver condiment rack closer to Acy and left the room.

He'd finished half his meal when his wife and the little girl came in. Willa had her hand on the child's back, guiding her to a chair next to Acy.

The child's hair was an odd two-inch length all over, but her face was composed and engaged. 'Hi,' she said.

Acy looked down at her. 'Hi what?'

She shrugged. 'Hi hi?'

'Madeline, you can call me Daddy now.'

'This lady said my daddy's in heaven.'

He gave his wife an uneasy glance. 'Yes, and I've replaced him. I'm your new daddy. And you shouldn't call Willa "this lady". You can call her Mother.'

The girl looked away and bit her top lip.

Willa sat down. 'Can you call me Mother?' She made a face full of mock deference that the child saw through at once, narrowing her eyes and remaining silent. 'Well, it'll come in time.' She flipped a starched napkin across her lap.

The kitchen door flew open and Vessy swung into the room carrying two plates of food. She didn't look at the child, even as her arm passed around the little head.

'Madeline, can you remember this gal's name?' Acy asked.

The child picked up her fork and then looked at Vessy's face, smiling slightly. 'Miss Vessy,' she said.

Acy wiped his mouth and took a swallow of tea. 'Just Vessy is sufficient,' he said.

'What's "sufficient?" The girl picked up a noodle with her fingers and dangled it like a fishing worm.

'It means good enough,' Acy told her. 'You don't put "Miss" in front of a hillbilly girl's name.'

The child watched as Vessy refilled the man's glass of tea and silently left the room, her face artfully turned away from them.

After lunch the girl was left in the upstairs nursery with the maid, and Willa came down to share an after-dinner drink with her husband. From a decanter kept out of sight in a side table, she poured herself three fingers of bourbon in two fingers of water.

Acy lit a cigar and leaned back into a velvet chair. 'What did you tell Vessy?'

'The same.'

'What, exactly? I've got to keep tabs on all this explaining.'

Willa took a long sip and wiped her lips with a lace handkerchief. 'That Madeline came from an orphanage in Cincinnati. Her head was shaved for sanitary reasons by the orphanage, and her parents were killed in a railroad accident of some sort, just recently.'

He puffed steadily, slowly exhausting the smoke. 'Good,' he said. 'Are you still happy?'

Willa's face brightened. 'Yes. She's everything I could have wished for. Smart as a whip and pretty as can be.'

He looked out of the window down the hill. They had tried to have a baby for ten years, but something was wrong, and their physical enjoyment only mocked them. As more time passed, Willa's longing for a child was something she couldn't put out of her mind, and the barren years had nearly driven her crazy. They'd visited orphanages in several states, but even when they would find a bright-cheeked child, clever and healthy, Willa always saw something in the hopeful face that made it impossible to claim.

She poured herself another splash and took it down like a soft drink. 'What are you thinking?'

'I don't know. I'm glad we found Madeline. Glad she's not an orphan.'

'Oh.' She remembered the trips, the smells of want, the expressions on small faces taught by being passed over for the smarter child, the blue-eyed child. These visits drove home that all orphans were unlucky, and she realized she wanted something else – a child fortunate enough to be currently loved. Perhaps she felt herself incapable of raising a child to whom she could give love. She didn't really understand the feeling and was mystified by her husband's powerful devotion.

Across town the sawmill whistle blew the get-ready signal to bring the workers off their lunch break, and Acy stood up, just a little dizzy from his toddy, and went to retrieve his straw hat from the hook. He moved to where his wife was sitting on an embroidered dining-room chair and gave her a kiss on the softest part of her cheek, next to the mouth, where a drop of bourbon burned his lips.

7

The New Orleans papers advertised that the *Ambassador* would operate one dance trip at eight p.m. as a break-in for her new season. Sam boarded the boat that morning and went up to his cabin on the Texas deck, where his third mate's uniform was laid out on the bunk, a blue jacket with a gold stripe on the sleeve and a billed officer's cap, on its front a gold wreath encircling the name of the boat. He put it on and felt silly at first, but stepping out on deck and climbing upstairs to the Texas roof, he looked the glossy boat over fore and aft, and the cloth began to claim him. The outfit made him part of another trade as surely as did a railroader's overalls or his fine floorwalker's suits. Captain Stewart was standing next to the steps leading up to the pilothouse, surrounded by men also in uniform. He spoke curtly to one young man, who turned away and ran to a stairway, his shoes clattering down toward the water. To the next he said, 'Well, tell him we want squirrel-nut coal. With the current so stiff we can't use that damned Birmingham slag he's so hot to sell us.' Another man peeled out of the group, and the captain turned to the third. 'If the concession man doesn't like our Negro band, tell him to put on blinders. They'll save us twenty dollars a day in wages, and the dancers like their music better anyway.' To the next he said, 'Look at the sky, man. It's going to be hot, so run all the ceiling fans and put more steam to our generator engine. It don't take a genius to figger that out.'

The last man, very old, short, wearing a neatly ironed uniform and bow tie, looked down as the captain put an arm over his shoulders and said, 'Look, she's a crackerjack pilot and she's caught up on all the channel between here and St Louis. She's good up to Cincinnati as well.'

The old man shook his head. 'She's a lady, and I don't know if she can think like a pilot's got to think.'

'Her husband was Denk Benton.'

'I know who she is, all right.'

'She took a contract for a little more than half what you make,' the captain said, his voice more respectful. 'Rafe, she worked on the *Blazer* with oil barges up the Ouachita.'

'She could handle the *Blazer* on that drainpipe of a river?'

'Yep.'

The little man shrugged off the captain's arm. 'Well, it's all right with me if you want to risk turning your dance boat into five hundred tons of stovewood.'

'That's the ticket, Rafe.' And the captain looked back at the stern, where a man was coming on carrying a big Stillson wrench. He glanced at Sam. 'Now, who are you?'

'Sam Simoneaux.' He pointed to his hat. 'Third mate.'

Captain Stewart stared at him, deadpan. 'Remind me, son.'

'Elsie Weller asked you to hire me.'

He nodded. 'Yes, that's right. Walk the boat and meet everyone. Every last man. Keep your hat clean and drink your coffee.' He turned away when the smudged fellow carrying the wrench walked up and began complaining about his salary.

Since he was already on the roof he stepped up into the gingerbread wheelhouse, curious to meet this lady pilot. He was surprised to see Nellie Benton, the woman he'd delivered the horses to in town, standing behind the steering tillers wearing a navy polka-dot dress, a whorl of gray hair flowing from under a pilot's cap.

'Well,' she said, 'it's the wagon master.'

He swallowed hard and knew he must be showing his surprise. 'Hello, ma'am.'

'Hello yourself. I saw you wandering around down there. You ever see a lady pilot?'

'No, ma'am, I guess not.'

'Well, now that your curiosity's settled, get on down to the engine room and ask Bit Benton – that's the engineer on watch now – if he's finished working on the steering engine. If he is, tell him to let me know through the speaking tube.'

'Yes, ma'am.'

'Sam, is it?'

'That's right.'

'I heard you kind of backed into the steamboat business.'

'I seem to back into most things.'

'Don't your wife feed you?'

He looked down at his stomach. 'I like being light on my feet.'

'Well, if you're a real steamboat man likely the kitchen'll fat you up.'

He went down to give the message to a testy and red-faced Bit, and coming out of the engine-room door he bumped into Charlie Duggs. 'Hey. I'll see you later. I'm supposed to be introducing myself around.'

'Pleased to meet you,' Duggs said to Sam's back.

He met busboys and waiters on the second deck, several members of a large black orchestra, the concessions master, the chief cook, the head steward, two white musicians standing around listening to the black men practice, and the Wellers, who were coming down the starboard staircase from the Texas deck. With them was a big-shouldered boy of about fifteen, composed, wearing a sport coat, one hand in a pocket. They walked together to the end of the enormous dance floor. Sam looked back over the glossy planks. 'How's it going?'

Ted Weller pulled a handkerchief and mopped his head. 'Not so good. The captain let most of the white orchestra go and picked up the black fellows over there to play the main night trips. He said he had to go with what the dancers liked.'

Sam looked back toward the bandstand. Earlier that year, he'd heard, Captain Quincy had taken the *Moonlight Deluxe* out on a harbor cruise downtown. He put a good white hotel orchestra on the main dance floor, a first-class group in tux and tails, and a Negro jazz band upstairs on the dim, open hurricane deck.

Halfway through the cruise everybody was dancing up in the open night, and the main dance floor was nearly empty. That pretty much said it all. 'The sound gets in your feet, all right.'

'Captain says if we hit some towns that won't listen to colored music, we can slap together about seven boys for a dance trip. But the whites will only play the afternoon runs when nobody dances much anyway.'

Elsie settled one hip against a bulkhead. 'Ted can play piano for the black band if the captain lets him. He's figured how they cut the melody loose from the time signature.'

'What'll you do?'

She shrugged. 'I could sing with the day band, you know, and even with a black band if it was okay. I'd sing with them steady if it was up to me, but in some of these towns, you know how it is. Nowadays I'm doing laundry and setting out tablecloths on deck three.' She put a hand on the top of the boy's head. 'Our son here plays a mean alto sax, but now he's in the boiler galley passing coal.'

At the mention of his name, the boy stuck out his hand. 'Hiya. My name's August.'

'Hey, bud. Stay away from those boilers.' Sam looked in the boy's eyes and saw that he was smart, maybe the kind of kid who breathed in knowledge and exhaled accomplishment.

'Aw, I'll be up on the bandstand again someday.' He ran a hand over his slicked-back blond hair.

'You play with the big orchestra?'

'They've let me sit in a few times a week. I can sight-read real well.'

Sam raised an eyebrow. 'In your spare time maybe you can teach me.'

At the midship bandstand the orchestra struck up an embroidered rendition of 'Frankie and Johnny,' mostly in a straight dance rhythm but with the beat and melody disconnecting in the repeat. The music was good. Sam could feel the notes ride up his shinbones into his hips. It made him think of the barrel houses next to Storyville, which more than once he'd stopped into for a beer and a lookaround. The band warmed up like an engine, getting better at what they were doing with each measure, the big piano holding everything together. 'Some stuff. Kind of snappy for the excursion trade.'

A boat whistle sounded in the canal and Ted pulled out his watch. 'Nowadays most dancers like whatever's hot stuff. Ten years ago it was ragtime and cakewalks. Makes you wonder what they'll like in fifty years.'

August's eyes lit up. He reached over and popped his father's left gallus. 'It'll sound like a thunderstorm in an oil drum.'

The engineer was warming up the machinery on a slow bell, the paddlewheel treading water, the boat doing a dreamy two-degree wallow at the dock. Then a big deep groan of the whistle rattled the dance-floor windows, the lines were cast off, and the *Ambassador* ascended the canal's flat greasy water toward the Mississippi River locks. By early afternoon she had come out into the chocolate chop below Algiers Point and was stretching her legs against the current, paddling in toward the Esplanade Avenue wharf. Mrs Benton maneuvered around, brought her in slowly next to the dock, the hull sliding to a stop without a bump, the deckhands scrambling to catch the bollards with their lines before she drifted back out.

The boat's advertising had announced the point of departure for the night's trip, a hard-to-reach landing instead of the more popular wharf at the foot of Canal Street. The captain had called it a shakedown, a trip to make sure the machinery was up to the big river.

Sam was sent down to watch the first customers hustle up the wide stage plank. The captain drew him aside on the main deck around six o'clock.

'Son, these New Orleans crowds aren't so bad. It's a good-time town. But if someone tries to come on with a baseball bat, a belt knife, or you spot a pistol in someone's waistband, you tell them you've got to borrow it until we land again.'

'What if they won't turn it in?'

'Then you kick the son of a bitch into the river.'

'What about if I see someone bringing on liquor?'

The captain leaned close, frowning. 'Hell, son. That's what we sell setups for. Once we leave the bank we're sort of a separate country.'

'I got it. Anything else?'

'Keep a lookout for that woman.'

'What woman? Aw, you think she'd be crazy enough to show up?'

The captain looked away. 'You don't think she's crazy to begin with? Stealing kids and all? Maybe crazy and stupid to boot.'

'I'm kind of forgetting what she looks like, already. I just saw her for a couple seconds.'

'Keep your eyeballs rollin'.'

And he did, trying his best to remember the old woman in the fitting room, fixing the brief observation in his mind, the missing tooth and unwashed hair, the shears poised over the child's scalp. He had to remind himself that his memory was part of the reason he was on the boat to begin with.

Late in the day it was still hot. Sam stood on the wharf and directed jostling couples up the stage plank to the ticket booth on the main deck. The calliope began gargling, the high notes singing flat until the whistles warmed up. Fred Marble, the pianist with the black orchestra, wearing a slouch hat and gloves against the flying steam, tickled out 'Ain't We Got Fun' on the roof, the instrument's wincing notes sailing upriver over the French Quarter. Couples in their twenties and thirties began showing up, then what looked like a small men's club, everybody in seersucker and straw boaters. For the most part, people were well dressed, the young women in thin, drop-waist dresses, the men in summer suits. One older man dressed in khaki shirt and pants carried a sheath knife on his belt, and Sam relieved him of it, promising he'd get it back at the ticket booth when the boat landed. One boy carried a sort of cane as thick as a chair leg, which he gave up grudgingly. The calliope music stopped with a yodel, and out of the long curving line of open windows above him the band began to pour a thumping-loud rendition of 'When My Baby Smiles at Me' in a rattling-good dance tempo, the music coming down on the crowd like peppery candy for the ears. Customers began to back up on the broad stage plank, and as departure time drew close they were stacked three abreast, grinning and craning their necks at the big white apparition. Sam palmed a nickel-plated counter, and when he checked it read 1,255. Four deckhands shuffled down to stand by their bitts and the boat's steam whistle let out a deep, river-filling chord. Ralph Brandywine would pilot the *Ambassador* through the city river traffic, and he leaned out the wheelhouse window holding a megaphone and yelled down to Sam to hustle the last customers on board. The paddlewheel began to turn slowly, the half-ton deck bell banged three times, and a crush of customers bunched up on the stage as though afraid of being left behind on the wharf – the worst thing that could happen to anybody, to be left out of the steamy cloud of music and fun. Sam began to enjoy paddling the people on board, calling out for everyone to step up, thumbing his little counter device, getting lost in the excitement and the smell of vanilla, witch hazel, jasmine dusting powder, and Sen-Sen. Two minutes later the steam capstan sputtered the stage plank aboard and the mob of latecomers jammed against the ticket booth on the first deck as the boat backed away in earnest, steam spuming from vent pipes in the hull, engine-room gongs cracking alive like fight bells, and above it all big mossy gouts of coal smoke roiling from the stacks. Sam looked back across the wharf and saw, two hundred yards off, three teenaged girls running in heels through the falling light, hands on hats, purses flying out from their elbows, the hems on their short dresses shimmying with the white reciprocal blur of their knees, but it was too late, and he didn't want to think about what was in their girl hearts as the big boat turned out under the early stars: an image of romance, hot dance music, or just dumb human fun based on the necessary mystical imagining that things in general just ain't so bad all the time.

8

His job for the night was to roam the decks looking for signs of trouble, everything from fistfights to fires. The forward area of the lower main deck behind the big staircase was an open-air lounge of sorts, a bullpen of wicker furniture and potted plants, and he noticed that mostly older people were sitting here, served by four waiters bringing out ice setups in sweating silver buckets. The boat doddered downstream, threading through the anchored freighters in quarantine at the same speed as the current, and a breeze rose off the water like a blessing, for as much as passengers craved the music and drink, they came to get out of the overheated pavement of the city and their oven houses that wouldn't cool down until midnight. At eight-thirty he went upstairs and the long ballroom seemed like a broad wooden railway tunnel filled with music, each ceiling arch hung with dim yellow, red, and blue lights, and the band was settling into a medium-tempo fox-trot embroidered with clarinet improvisations. The breeze steeped in and matched the flow of music, giving the swaying four hundred couples a lift from their humid life that normally left their dancing shoes green with mildew in the back of the closet. Through the windows the doubled shore lights sparked in the river and everyone felt the watery motion under their sliding feet, the turning of currents melting into the horns' urging; the couples quick-stepped and careened, navigating the dance floor under the colored lights. Sam remembered this deck as a closed-up and creaking static mess, but now it was a moving cloud in dreamland, soon to be a memory for the dancers, who would outlast the boat itself by many years.

He walked over where the second mate watched the crowd. 'Hey,' Charlie called. 'This New Orleans crowd can dance.'

Sam looked over his shoulder. 'I guess they can. What's that fellow doing?'

Duggs yelled over a rising trumpet riff. 'The Texas Tommy. If too many of them start up that hop dancing you have to stop it or at least spread 'em out. The bracing under the floor can't take too much of that. A two-step's worse. The whole deck goes up and down like a fight ring when everybody takes a step on the downbeat.'

'Shake the place apart?' He thought Duggs was making a joke.

Charlie shook his head. 'Last year an excursion steamer upriver had the whole dance deck cave in. Sent thirty people to the hospital.'

'Hell of a way to end a good time!'

'You go check the café.'

'Right.'

The band stopped and the girls returning to their tables across the floor were smiling and fanning themselves, their dresses hanging limp.

'If you see Weller, cheer him up.'

'What?'

'The captain's got him waiting tables on the hurricane deck.'

'I bet the musicians' union will gripe about that.'

'He asked for it himself. His salary was cut now that he's just playing the day trips.'

On the third deck was a long, roofed section open to the night, dim except for a glowing backwash from bulbs outlining the several decks. Here couples were lounging at tables, some mixing drinks from bottles they'd brought from shore, some at the dark edges of the deck kissing, telling lies, making promises. The restaurant on the rear half of this deck was packed with people eating sandwiches or cheap steaks. A door at the rear spewed a stream of white-jacketed waiters serving the whole boat. Everyone forward was well behaved so he turned his attention to the rear of the deck, where Ted Weller was taking an order at a table. He met him at the kitchen door, before he went in.

'Moonlighting?'

'Got to do some damn something to squeeze a nickel out of the old man.' Ted Weller's eyes were red, and Sam wondered if he'd been drinking.

'Hey, I'm on your side.'

'The more I work, the less I have. First my little girl, and now they're trying to starve me out.'

Sam put a hand on his shoulder. 'Your little girl? That's what I'm here for. When we get upriver, I'll start asking around onshore.'

Ted wrote something on his pad and glanced up. 'She would kiss me at bedtime and say "*Gute Nacht.*" I was teaching her German.'

'Yeah?'

He leaned close and Sam could smell the whiskey. 'You don't know what it's like, not to be able to take your kid in your arms anymore.' He turned at once and banged through a swinging door.

Sam wanted to follow him through and remind him that he wasn't the only man in the world to lose a child, but he held back, watching the door swing in and out with waiters and busboys, giving a sliced-up view of Ted Weller arguing with a sweating cook.

Around ten o'clock, the boat swung into a dreamy turn at the Violet locks and was steaming upstream at three-quarters speed. The band broke into an uptempo version of 'Everybody Step' and emptied the tables. When Sam came down the stairs Charlie Duggs was dragging a big young fellow by the collar out toward the forward rail. He broke loose and swung, punching Duggs in the jaw. Charlie's face rebounded wearing a grin, and he slapped the man openhanded, the percussion cracking above the thundering band, the customer plunging sideways under a table. Sam went over to help but the second mate waved him off.

'I can handle this one. He just wants to dance a new step is all. A waiter came up a minute ago and said things were getting testy downstairs.' He grabbed the man by the ankles and hauled him back out into the music.

On the main deck Sam spotted two old men arguing, their faces crimson, one holding a cane by its bottom, the curved handle rising toward a big Emerson ceiling fan, which jerked it away, and carried it three turns before flinging it across the lounge, onto a table, where it knocked drinks in the laps of an overdressed and tipsy foursome. Sam at once understood several things about a dance steamer: people felt safe getting drunk since there was no proper law on board, nearly everyone was drinking, and any cruise was liable to turn more unstable as the trip wore on.

He stepped in front of two men advancing from their dripping table. 'Easy,' he said, holding up his hands. 'It was an accident.'

'Oh yeah?' One of them raised a fist, a short fellow with an ice cube rising out of his vest pocket. 'Where have you been? These old bastards have been carping back and forth for the past half hour. This was supposed to be an enjoyable ride.'

'We want our money back for the drinks,' the other man said, swaying and then taking an extra step to the side.

'I'll see that the waiter brings out another bucket of ice and some glasses.'

'What about an apology?' the little man said.

The larger of the two old men came over. His eyes were small and his nose was a huge overripe strawberry. 'I'll take my cane, thank you.'

'Don't you have anything to say?' the little man snarled.

The old gentleman pursed his mouth, and Sam knew by looking at his face that he was going to say something that would result in the breaking up of a quarter of the wicker furniture in the lounge. 'I see,' the old man began, 'that you would like for me to make you feel better. You want me to apologize for the actions of an electrical contrivance.'

Here the little man's friend stepped up. 'You don't have to get smart with us.' He gave the old man a halfhearted shove in the vest.

A tiny, well-dressed, middle-aged gentleman stood up across the room and steadied himself against a plant stand. 'You just watch who you're shoving around,' he chirped. 'That's my father-in-law.'

Two women were flapping ice off their dresses, and one of them picked up the cane and tossed it at the old man, hitting him on the forehead and knocking his glasses off. 'You trashy people,' he roared, 'ought to be thrown overboard!'

Sam looked around at sixty or so passengers and saw that they were nice people, well dressed and mature, not some unimportant kids he could bully into behaving. He tried to get between everybody at once and found himself in the middle of a jabbering cloud of alcoholic breath. The polite air was turning sour when the son-in-law, who was four tables over, tried to get to the argument by stepping on a wicker-bottom chair, but his foot went through it and he danced three hops and fell onto another couple's table, his hand getting stuck in a small metal water pitcher. At this point everyone started to laugh, except the son-in-law and the old man, who slowly bent over and felt the floor for his cane and spectacles. Sam called over a waiter to dry the tables and chairs and get everybody reseated and supplied with fresh glasses and ice. The steam whistle blew a warning, followed by a rising, shrill signal from the starboard side as a ferryboat cut its engines only twenty-five feet away, its yellow running lights shining angrily, its boiler's fire door a blinding orange star traveling sideways in the night. The passengers calmed down, distracted by the fact that the ferry had come out from its landing without waiting for or even seeing the *Ambassador* at all. Sam watched the ferry slide astern, hoping that everyone would realize that a couple of spilled drinks or a rude remark was nothing compared to a midnight collision spilling hundreds of folks in deep river, but then the son-in-law began throwing punches and it took him ten minutes of pulling and pushing to break up the fight.

Upstairs, the band members were running with sweat, thumping out a shimmy number as five hundred dancers stepped and turned in a massive wink of patent leather and sequins, silk ties and hair oil, good New Orleans dancers who knew what to do with a downbeat making the old deck jump. The waiters were skating around the edge of the action, sliding their shoes on the dance wax, delivering sandwiches and mixers to the people at the double layer of tables lining the walls. The expressions of most of the dancers seemed overly happy, and Sam scanned the faces of the band members, who were too busy selling the tune to exhibit any worry, and indeed no one showed a negative thought, caught up in some kind of capsule of delight, at least while the music kept everything in motion. And then he saw a still silhouette sitting at the stern end of the dance deck, and he walked over because her presence contradicted the motion-drunk room. It was Elsie, sitting alone at the last table, her hair wound in pigtails above her ears, wearing a plain dark dress.

'Hi. You on break?'

'In case you don't know, the staff can't join in the fun. We'll be at the dock in ten minutes and as soon as the lights come up, I'm to start stripping the tables.'

She looked tired, and he wanted to say something to cheer her up, but all he said was, 'Work you to death, don't they?'

'Well, let's just say I need to keep busy.'

'Ted still waiting on 'em upstairs?'

She nodded. 'I was waitressing with him but they cut me loose a few minutes ago. It'll only take a half hour to clear everybody off. This is a pretty mild crowd.'

The whistle moaned out a landing signal and the band began to play 'Home, Sweet Home.' Sam felt a tug on his arm and he turned to face a thickset man also wearing a mate's cap. He introduced himself as Aaron Swaneli, the first mate.

'How'd I miss meeting you?'

'It's my bidness to lay low,' Swaneli said. 'That way I can keep an eye on things, you know?' He made a sideways motion with his head.

'You're the power man. Got a blackjack on you.'

Swaneli put a hand on Sam's shoulder and squeezed it. 'Look, right now I need you to go topside. The hardlegs up there are smokin' and all in love this time of night. Walk the rail and look for cigarettes they've tossed. Every butt you see, lit or not, put your toe on it and twist three times, okay?'

The lights came up on the last note, and the band began to take down music and pack their instruments. People crowded the stairs, and Sam walked up through them and toured the deck, first the open area, then the café, which was hot and nearly empty. He stepped out into the night and looked forward to where Mr Brandywine then ascended a little filigreed bridge on the hurricane deck. He raised a megaphone and called directions out to a man standing by a steam capstan. The big boat seemed asleep in the water at that point, waiting for some type of decision the current was supposed to make. Finally, Mr Brandywine turned the megaphone up to the pilothouse's dark windows. 'Mrs Benton! Give her a nudge.'

A bell jingled in the engine room and two snoring chuffs jetted from the escape pipes as the boat leaned into the wharf and tapped a piling right where a deckhand held a hemp fender against the hull. The fore and aft lines went out and a stop-engine bell rattled as the boat drifted in snug.

It took an hour to clear the last passengers off, a too-jolly batch of overweight young women. Sam did indeed stamp out a dozen lit cigarettes, and also woke up a drunk boy in the men's toilet and walked him ashore. Several people lingered under the dock lights, staring at the steamer as though they couldn't quite believe their ride was over. Their faces showed they'd just been exiled back to their ordinary selves, and they didn't seem to like it one bit. He walked to the end of the loading stage and surveyed for himself the many lights jeweling the decks, the tired porters sweeping the dark upper walkways, the kitchen staff wiping the third-deck tables and chairs, turning them up to make room for a mop-down of spilled drinks, food, trash paper, and smashed candy. He thought of the cooks swamping down the giant ranges in the hot night, the tobacco-smudged and sticky dance floor, the piss-fouled bathrooms and damaged main-deck lounge already prowled by the ship's carpenter. It was all fun for somebody, he guessed, but his back and legs were killing him from the night's climbing and scuffle.

About one-thirty he rolled into his bunk, jammed against the ceiling of his cabin, and a minute later Charlie Duggs came in, stripped down to his drawers, and hung his clothes on two sixteen-penny nails. 'Oh, man,' he said in the dark, 'I feel like I fell through the paddlewheel.'

After two minutes, Sam sensed that he was already falling asleep, and gratitude to whatever controls man's slumber flowed through him like a medicine. Then Charlie yawned and said, 'Don't forget to roll out, wash your armpits, and buck up for the ten-thirty harbor tour.'

At eight the next morning the two of them were eating eggs, fried potatoes, and onions with the rest of the crew. The musicians had gone drinking in town after the boat docked and were eating out on the open part of the deck, moping about like wounded soldiers. Charlie folded a piece of white bread in half and waved it in the air over his plate for emphasis. 'On the way down from Cincinnati we stopped at an odd little town in Indiana, I think, and ran an afternoon trip. I was nailing down new chocks for the piano during the break, and then Elsie and Ted did a number with the little girl and some of the lady passengers gathered around the bandstand and got this look in their eye like they was ready to start bawlin'. I don't know why. It was a happy little song. Maybe they thought she was a come-alive baby doll or something.' He took a heaping bite of potatoes.

Sam straightened in his chair. 'Where was the town, exactly?'

'That was a busy trip. It might have been in Kentucky, now that I think about it. Every time she sang, the mommies would come up to the bandstand. Maybe they were imagining what kind of life she might have in front of her. Everywhere she sang her two little numbers, she got the same reaction.'

Sam finished his eggs and shoved away his plate. 'Some people think a lot about the future and screw up the day they're walking around in.'

'I hear that.'

Sam did a slow pan of the café and frowned. 'You think someone might want to save her from a musician's life? I got to admit, they bring home about as much as a fry cook. My sergeant in the army sang on some phonograph records. Big labels, too. He was paid ten bucks for two sides of the record and never got a penny royalty.'

Duggs drained his ironware coffee cup and put it down, his head bobbing. 'Brother plays in the Orpheum orchestra, and that don't even pay the food bill for his family. He's got to do Sunday band-stand work and Elks club dances and all that kind of bullshit.'

Sam tossed his napkin in his plate. 'I play a little piano.'

'Pick up some extra scratch that way?'

'People tried to hire me for about a penny a key, so I said the hell with it.'

Charlie threw back his head and laughed.

Captain Stewart walked in and stood in the doorway, which everyone took as a signal to get to work. Before long, the boat was swamped by a special charter for middle-school children. The white band played for the chaperones and a few tourists as the boat eased up along the docks toward the grain elevators, the mates and watchmen keeping the children from walking the rails and swinging from the ceiling fans.

Two days later the boat ran a moonlight trip out of Donaldsonville, and two days after that the *Ambassador* docked in Baton Rouge to run three trips. The advance man had come up in his little Ford two weeks earlier, placed ads in the paper, put up posters on three hundred telegraph poles and in every store window, and talked a Presbyterian church group into a two p.m. trip. The captain gave the Wellers the morning off to go to the police station and report their daughter's abduction and provide a description. The morning orchestra wasn't taken too seriously, so Sam took Ted's place at the piano and played the guitar parts off the chart, smiling at the few couples choosing to box-step next to the bandstand. He was surprised to remember how good it felt to have someone dance to his music. He studied the customers and after the set stood ashore by the stage plank to watch the morning riders file off the boat, looking carefully into each face.

He was going up the main staircase when the Wellers caught up with him, Elsie racing past, saying she needed aspirin. Ted mopped his face with his handkerchief and leaned against the rail. 'The damned cops here aren't interested in lost children from Cincinnati. They wouldn't call other jurisdictions unless we paid the charges, and we're about flat broke.' He pulled off his straw and wiped the hatband mark on his high forehead. 'The desk sergeant took our description and threw it in a drawer. We asked him a bunch of questions, if there had been any child stealing that he knew off. You know what he told us? He said he had a few kids of his own he wouldn't mind someone taking off his hands.'

'Sounds like you ran into a jughead. Probably the chief's brother-in-law.'

Ted glared at him. 'That supposed to make me feel better?'

'Look, I'll lay off the two o'clock trip if the captain gives me the okay, and I'll see what I can do.'

Ted cocked his head. 'What makes you think you can do better than we did?'

'I know an old boy on the force – that is, if he hasn't quit by now. We were in the same detachment in France.'

He crossed the railroad tracks in the heat and climbed the long hill into town. At the police station the sergeant told him that Melvin Robicheaux was directing traffic at Florida and North. Sam walked out and half an hour later spotted him standing on a side street under a drugstore awning, smoking. His uniform was wrinkled and greasy, his badge pinned on crookedly. Sam called out his name.

The officer blinked. 'Lucky! Where the hell did you come from?'

'The real city.'

They shook hands.

'You get a indoors job like you said you would?'

'Got it and lost it. I'm working on an excursion boat right now.'

'No cop work? Most boys got on the force.' He took a hissing drag on his cigarette.

'No. Not that. Not official, anyway.' He then told him what he was doing and who he was looking for.

Melvin spun his cigarette into the street and laughed. 'You really are a lucky son of a bitch.' He looked down and laughed again.

'You want to share the joke?'

'You just walk up and get what you want, just like that.'

'What?' He bumped up his shoulders. Melvin Robicheaux seemed angry that the world was taking it easy on everyone but himself.

'I ought to hit you up for a few bucks like I do the pimps.' He looked up and down the street. 'But I'll take it easy. There's a bunch of raggedy outlaws live way up on the river, right before the Mississippi state line, I guess. The Skadlocks. The old woman of the clan is Ninga, and she fits your description.'

Sam looked at him and then down the blinding street. 'So do a lot of ugly old gals. This one ever steal somebody's kid?'

Melvin looked over and watched an Oldsmobile run a stop sign. 'She or any one of them that lives with her would carve out the pope's eyeballs and bring 'em to you in a coin purse if you was to pay enough.'

'The world's got no shortage of cutthroats. Why'd you think of her so fast?'

'Dogs.'

He took a step back toward the street. 'Come again?'

'She steals dogs. Prize hounds, bank-guard dogs, yapping nuisance dogs. Don't know how she makes off with them or who hires her. Last year I found her driving an old Dodge Betsy with three German shepherds in the backseat asleep in sacks. Purebloods from the damned army, no less. The car stunk of chloroform.

We took her in and she had bail in her purse. Never seen her since.' Melvin put his tongue in his cheek and rolled his eyes. 'Then I heard she got pinched for the same thing down in Orleans Parish. Same results, too.'

Sam put a hand in his pocket and leaned against the plate glass out of the sun. 'It's worth a shot. You can go out with me and we'll talk to her face-to-face.'

'Lucky, my authority extends about five blocks from where we're standing. I'm just a city cop.'

'Well, a parish deputy, then.'

'Her place is two parishes away, and that sheriff tolerates the Skadlocks like they was kin. I think they give him his liquor. If you want to talk to her, you'll have to go into Gasket Landing yourself.'

'Where the hell is this place? Maybe I can take a train up and meet the boat at Bayou Sadie. Our advance man set up a moonlight trip out of there for the townspeople.'

Melvin pulled his watch and wound it, shaking his head. 'Gasket Landing isn't really a place anymore. Long time ago there was a plantation in there, but everything's mostly fallen apart, I hear. It's gone back to horse country. A car can't get back in there through the slop.'

'Can I get there by boat?'

'You gonna sneak up on somebody on an excursion steamer?' He laughed and pulled out the papers for another cigarette. 'If you got some wood sense from when you was a kid, there's still one livery in St Frank where they'll rent you a horse.'

'The hell you say.' Sam remembered riding to grammar school with his cousins down in Calcasieu Parish, three of them on one rough-riding plug named Slop Jar. 'I haven't been aboard a horse but once since I left the farm.'

'It's the only way to get there, Lucky. Bring a cheap compass and ask directions from everybody you see.' He put the cigarette in his mouth and gave Sam a sideways look. 'You got a gun?'

He shook his head. 'Don't want one.'

'I'd bring a Colt .45 if I was hunting up a Skadlock.'

'I don't even own a pocketknife. I just want to find this woman and talk to her. Then I'll know what to do, I guess.'

A truck rumbled into the intersection and stopped. Two women in a REO approached from the far side, and the driver squeezed the bulb on her horn.

Melvin blew his whistle and waved the truck on through. 'I'll tell you everything I know, bud. *Vive la France* and all that. You just have to ask.'

'Well, then. Here goes.'

9

After the moonlight cruise the boat steamed all night to Bayou Sadie, little more than a mud landing and a few plank stores connected by a thread of road to the nearby towns. At seven the next morning the purser gave Sam an advance against his salary and told him to get back for the eight-thirty cruise or he'd be docked two dollars. He walked all the way into St Frank and found the livery on the north side of the main street. The owner, a fat man wearing a cut-down pair of overalls held up by green suspenders, didn't know him, so he took all the money he had as a deposit on the worst horse in the pen, a small, nervous-looking animal the color of a stained mattress. Then he tried to explain where Gasket Landing might be. 'You have to go down this here lane and then ford the bayou, but it's pretty shallow this time of year and it's got a hard bottom. Then you head west into the stickers for a while and you'll get into a big swamp that's dry right now and pretty clear of brush. Those big trees cut back on the undergrowth. Keep the horse moving through there, don't let him stop and look around too much. If you keep an animal busy he won't get spooked.'

'What's to spook him?'

The fat man looked up thoughtfully as Sam swung into the saddle. 'Best not tell you. Just keep going a few miles till you hit the riverbank, then you'll ride up to some ruint houses. That's where the Skadlocks stay. You related?'

'No.'

'I figured that. You don't have the look.'

Sam motioned toward the woods with his chin. 'You know if Ninga Skadlock lives in there?'

'She couldn't live nowheres else.'

'How many miles am I lookin' at?'

'I don't know.'

'No idea at all?'

'Somewhere between ten and fifty. It's crazy country back in there.'

'What's his name?'

'Who?'

'The horse.'

The livery owner scratched the yellow hair on his chest where it boiled up out of his undershirt. 'Number 6.'

He got the animal out into the road, and when a lumber truck went by, Number 6 whinnied, reared, and clambered down into a twelve-foot ditch. He sat the horse in water up to his stirrups, petted it, and coaxed it up the bank and back into the lane, where it commenced a pelvis-hammering trot, weaving from side to side. Sam stopped it, rode it several times in a circle to the right and then to the left, as his uncle Claude had taught him, and when he set the horse forward it seemed to remember that it was supposed to travel in a straight line, and its gait evened out. After a few miles they arrived at a place where the road sloped down into a broad bayou. The horse would have none of it. As soon as the water went over his pasterns, he kept turning upstream. Sam got off, stripped down to his drawers, and walked in ahead, tugging the reins. The water was only up to his waist, but the bottom rose in stinking clouds as he pulled across. He sat on the bank in the heat to dry off, then pulled on his khakis, debating whether he should just give up and cross back into town. He closed his eyes a moment to see if the girl child was still caught behind his lids, and her image came up glowing, but beside it was another face, that of his son losing consciousness, slipping away in a fever. He was the type of man who didn't want the bad things that happened to him to happen to anyone else; maybe somebody told him things when he was three or four years old that landed like seeds in the furrows of his character. However he was formed, his tendencies were costly ones. He mounted up with a yodel and kicked Number 6 in the flanks, the horse barging into a hummock of blackberries, scattering dust and dead stalks, wasps flying behind its hooves like red sparks.

Number 6 labored on, now and then hanging up between saplings. In a tight spot it raised a hoof, put it through a fork in a trunk, then pulled it back and wedged around the tree, lowering its head and rooting through the trash woods like a hog. Four miles into the maze, a ropey wisteria vine caught the toe of Sam's shoe and flipped him off like a playing card. Number 6 didn't even look around and cantered west. Fighting the brush, Sam ran after it for a hundred yards in the smothering heat, finally leaping for the saddle horn and pulling himself up. The horse stopped then and looked back at him.

'You ugly son of a bitch,' Sam rasped. 'You thirdhand hook rug pulled from a privy.' Here the horse bucked once, and Sam came down on its neck. After gaining his breath, he slid down and led the animal to a deep puddle of clear water and let it drink. 'All right,' he said, pulling out his compass. 'Eat some of that grass there and we'll move on.' The horse rolled its ears away.

Soon they entered a low-water cypress swamp, the treetops closing off the sky. The red-bark trunks were the size of factory chimneys, and everywhere their roots rose from the soppy mud like stalagmites. He checked his compass and headed across the weedless, canopied land. Everywhere he looked he saw the stout windings of water moccasins, and he felt the horse go rigid with fear. Sam put heels to its flanks, keeping its mind on movement, not on the flint-scaled multitudes boiling in the dim mud.

He was four hours beyond the bayou when he saw bright light between a mossy picket of trees, and he rode through a tussle of brambles into the open air. Reaching into the saddlebag, he pulled out a Mason jar of water and a cheese sandwich and sat, eating and staring at the Mississippi, sensing what de Soto must have felt when he stumbled out of the brush to wonder at this wide arm of water.

He rode down under the bank until he saw sun-lavendered bottles on the mudflats and then turned the horse up a washout that led past a roofless cabin. He turned right into a trash woods that forty years before was a pasture and followed a leaning barbwire fence beyond a weather-flattened barn and into a sudden green rush of old magnolias, sycamores, and ground-hugging live oaks. He glimpsed a chimney top through the greenery and stopped the horse, stepping down and tying it to a low oak limb. After ten steps he was standing in the rear of a three-story house with two encircling galleries and tall stuccoed pillars on four sides. It was invisible to the world, warped and paintless, its windows smudged or broken out, daylight pouring through holes in the upstairs gallery floors. The brick porch was strewn with rags, broken chairs, desiccated watermelon rinds, and a cow skull. He knew better than to present himself at the wide front entrance, and what could he say when someone opened the door in his face holding no better greeting than a cocked pistol? He stood and thought and then went back to the horse, leading it slowly away, but in a circuit so that soon he was going along the riverbank as though traveling through to somewhere else. There was no road, just an area too sandy to support more than weeds and thistle. When he got opposite the woodsy patch where he thought the house was hiding, he talked to the horse in a big, good-natured voice. Number 6 wouldn't look at him and turned his head away, engaged in patient urination. Sam picked up its rear hoof and caught it between his legs, pretending to examine the frog for an injury, but after ten minutes, no one came out to ask what he was about. Finally, he said loudly, 'Well, let's us just go in and ask for what we want, like the dunderheads we are.'

He spied above the branches a paneless belvedere, walked toward it, and was soon through the woods at the front of the mansion, where he tied the horse and walked up the flagstones. He took a breath, then knocked on the weather-scoured door.

From around the corner of the house stepped a man of at least fifty years, wearing a misshapen straw cowboy hat and dressed in denim shirt and pants that had been worn sky blue. 'What you need?'

'I'm looking for Ninga Skadlock.'

The man walked up, followed closely by an all-black German shepherd that slowly and almost reverently gathered a mouthful of Sam's pants leg in its mouth and held fast. 'Excuse Satan here. He just wants to hold you still.'

Sam looked down into the monstrous dog's amber eyes whose depths radiated primal obedience. 'All right.'

'What you want of Mom?'

He swallowed twice. 'I want to hire her to go get a dog for me in Baton Rouge. I heard she was good at it.'

The man touched the shepherd and it slowly drew back. Sam felt its saliva cooling against his calf and looked down again into eyes trained to see things differently than he did. 'I don't know what you're talking about,' the man said.

'Just let me see her.'

The man slowly rubbed his knuckles on the animal's head. 'She's in the kitchen.'

Sam felt light-headed among the soaring pillars. 'This is your big place?'

'It was here when we come along,' he growled.

They walked through a leaf-sodden yard to a small gray-wood clapboard building separate from the main house. Stepping up inside, he saw the walls first, for they were freshly whitewashed. A thick-shouldered, clean-shaven man was seated at table writing in a ledger, and an old woman was working at a kerosene stove, frying onions and bell peppers in a stamped iron skillet.

'Man wants to see you.'

She looked up and he knew at once it was her. The man at the table closed his ledger and watched Sam passively. He was about forty-five, dressed all in khaki, even to his baseball cap.

The old woman wore glasses and didn't have to squint to size Sam up. 'You come in a boat?'

'No, ma'am. I have a horse.'

Glancing at his town shoes, she said, 'You sure didn't walk here in those.' She banged a spoon on the edge of the skillet and dropped chunks of cut-up rabbit into the vegetables. Then she smiled and he saw the gap in her teeth. 'Excuse my manners while I keep working. We don't exactly get much company out here. What can I do for you?'

He looked at the two men, the first still standing in the doorway behind him. Sam was a fair teller of unimportant lies and thought he might fool people like this. Then he looked down at the dog, who watched him as if he were game. 'I have a nice house down in Baton Rouge, on Florida Avenue,' he began unsteadily, 'where I live with my wife and two young kids. A man next door owns a chow. The dog's attacked my kids twice, and all night he keeps my family up with his yowling. I've tried to deal with the owner for a couple years, but he won't get rid of the dog.' He paused for effect here, scratching his ear, glancing across the room. A door was opened halfway, revealing a large indoor still under a metal cowl that vented through the ceiling. 'He seems to get pleasure out of the trouble he's caused me.'

'I never knew a chow to bark much.' The woman lay the spoon down on a dishcloth and motioned to him. 'Sit down, mister?'

'Sam Simoneaux.'

'Well, a coonass.'

His face remained fixed; he couldn't afford anger here. 'Yes, ma'am.'

'And you live on Florida Avenue down in Baton Rouge?'

'Yes.'

'What block?'

'Ma'am?'

'What's your house address?'

A brief surge of panic ran up his backbone. 'The 1900 block.'

'All right.' She pulled a chair out from the table and sat down, then introduced him to her son Billsy, who had crossed his arms over the ledger and was leaning forward, regarding him with distant amusement. 'And that other one's Ralph. Anyway, how can we help you with this dog?'

'I hear you're pretty good at gathering them up.'

'And where did you hear this?'

'I have a friend on the police force.'

Here the man at the table laughed, stood up, and poured himself a cup of coffee out of a porcelain pot sitting in a warming pan on the stove.

The woman tilted her head and looked at Sam directly. 'Everybody's got friends on that police force.' She raised a hand and let it drop. 'Some even have relatives in the sheriff's office.'

Sam looked around the room. 'I don't guess you see much law back in here.'

'Son, if we needed the law I'd have to write a letter, but then somebody would have to build a post office for me to mail it in.' Her voice was fine-grained. Close up, her skin seemed smooth and light. 'What color is this dog's tongue?'

He looked toward the door, where the shepherd sat, its mouth closed, its big ears up. 'I don't know.'

'Hot days, a chow's tongue is always out,' Ralph said, leaning against the door frame.

'Simoneaux, do you have a telephone in your house?' Ninga asked.

'Yes.' This, he sensed immediately, was a mistake.

She got up and went to a high beaded-board cabinet and swung open its door. Inside he could see lines of books and her quick hands flashing through a stack of what looked like magazines. She found the one she wanted and thumbed through it with her back to him. Then she came back and sat at the table, spreading her hands out on the oak.

'We don't have a phone, but it's good to have a phone book anyway. Funny thing is, you don't seem to be listed in the latest directory.' She raised her head and looked him in the eye. 'Now, you can tell us what you really want.'

'I want a dog picked up, that's all. Now if it's a matter of price—'

'As I remember, the 1900 block of Florida is completely occupied on both sides by a cemetery.' Her gray eyes were as constant as facts, and he knew his lie had failed.

He looked over at the men, who were smiling smugly in admiration of their mother. The dog let out its tongue and panted, as if thirsty for the truth. 'All right. I'm from New Orleans and—'

'And somewhere south of there before that,' she added. 'We could hear New Orleans in your talk. But you still say those funny *a*'s the way those dummy Frenchies do. Where were you born?'

'A place you never heard of, over by the Texas line.'

'Lake Charles?'

'Troumal.'

Ralph snorted, then walked up to the table. 'I know where it is.'

Sam gave him a quick look. 'You been there? Nobody's been there much. It's just our families.'

'Your family – it's still there, is it?' he asked.

Sam studied his face, then its hard features. 'My family was killed off by outlaws.'

A brief flash flew through the man's eyes. 'I think I heard about it, long time ago.'

The woman suddenly tapped him on the shoulder with her spatula, and her face began to darken. 'Are you some kind of law? At least tell that much of the truth.'

'No.'

She looked up at the denim-clad son. 'Ralph, do you recognize him?'

'I didn't at first, but now I do.'

Sam turned around. 'How is it you know me?'

'We never been innerduced from the front,' Ralph said, showing a rack of yellow teeth.

A phantom pain rose in the back of Sam's head, and he stood up. 'You about killed me.'

'If I'd wanted you dead you'd of been that way.'

The woman moved a hand as if she were shooing a fly. 'Look, sit down, Simoneaux, or whoever you are. Ralph, you and your brother do a walkaround, make sure he's alone.'

Once they had left, he decided that he might as well ask her, and he did. 'Why'd you take that little girl?'

She stood and tended the little stove, which smelled of kerosene. 'What exactly are you doing out here? Somebody payin' you?'

'I got my reasons.'

She adjusted the sickly flame under the skillet and stirred the contents slowly. 'You don't see a little girl around here, do you? Any sign of one?'

'I work with that child's parents. They're excursion-boat musicians, and they're sick with worry about her.' He looked at the back of her head as if there might be a little window there that his thoughts could climb through. 'You're a mother. Can't you think about how that lady must feel?'

'I'm seventy-some years old, too old to fall for crap like that.' She shook the skillet over the flame. 'You know, sometimes people seem one way on the surface. But inside, they're different.'

'What?'

'Musicians? Those fine parents might be musicians, all right, the drifter kind that think they're better than everybody else just because they can read squiggles on a set of lines. You know what I'm talking about. Rummies in the vaudeville orchestra, whorehouse bands, saloon singers.'

'The Wellers aren't like that.'

She turned her doubtful face on him. 'You really know them?'

He blinked. 'Well enough to know you been told wrong if you think they're trash.'

'Still, where will they be in ten years? They're music players. If they can't keep up with the tunes, they'll be as out of work as a broke talking machine.'

'Well.' He leaned back in the chair and looked through the screen into the weed-choked yard. 'And where will your boys be in ten years?'

She bristled. 'Ralph and Billsy's already there, mister. And you don't have to know exactly where, neither. We come over from Arkansas with nothing, and now we're doin' all right. That kid's parents, if I had to guess, can't give her a thing except how to grow up singin' dirty songs to dancing drunks.'

'Look, I'm not the law.'

A half-smile formed over the sizzling skillet. 'I was worried you might be one of those Chicago boys hired to make some law on the side, if you know what I mean. But you ain't nothin' but a coonass that learned all his words.'

Sam glared at her. 'Just tell me what you did with the girl.'

'I don't know what we're talkin' about.' She raised the lid on a pot that was chattering on another burner and stirred the rice. 'There ain't no little girl around here.'

The two men came back into the room and sat with him at the table, leaving Satan on the other side of the screen, his eyes like two hot coals caught in the mesh. 'You got vittles yet?' Ralph asked.

'Watch this one off the property. He's just leavin',' the woman said.

Sam remained seated. 'I might stay around to sample some of that rabbit.'

The one named Billsy ran a hand through his iron-colored hair and looked worriedly at the skillet. 'What's he want, anyways?'

The woman sighed. 'Hush up.'

'If you won't talk to me, I'll go back to the excursion boat and saddle up the Wellers and bring them in for a little chat.'

'If you can sober them up, you mean.'

'They aren't drunks. Somebody's filled your head full of lies about those people. The same somebody that paid you to steal their girl.'

'If you send anybody back in here, after we deal with them, we'll come after you.' The woman turned off the stove, and a kerosene stink began to fill the hot kitchen.

Sam folded his hands on the table. 'If someone was hired to steal a child, I'd bet it was by strangers who rode up from nowhere with a good story.'

'Nobody came back in here.'

'It might be faraway strangers, too,' he continued.

'Why don't you just get on, Frenchie,' Ralph said, arranging his knife and fork next to his plate.

'He talked better than you do,' Billsy said.

Quick as a snake his mother rapped him twice on the skull with her spatula. 'You are a ringtailed dumbass if ever there was one.'

Billsy raised his forearms above his head. 'I didn't say nothing.'

Sam could see how scrambled his thoughts were by looking at his eyes. 'What did this nice-talking man look like?'

Before his mother could hit him again, Billsy blurted out, 'He just had a little mustache and talked about his wife a lot. Rode a horse in a suit.'

Sam made a face. 'A horse in a suit?'

Ralph suddenly pulled a big sheath knife and banged it on the table boards. 'You about ready to leave, ain't ya?'

'What do you know about the killing in Troumal?'

'I'll tell you about a killin' right here in a minute. Now get out.'

Sam glanced at his eyes and stood up. 'Can I get past that dog?'

'You can get past him goin' out,' Ralph Skadlock told him. 'But I wouldn't try it comin' back. He'll eat you like a meat grinder.'

10

It was one o'clock when he climbed on Number 6 to ride back to St Frank, a slow trip through the spiders and snakes.

The shadows were long when he reached the bayou, and he was so hungry and stuck up with briars that he galloped Number 6 into the water before the horse could think about it too much, hollering him across and up the bank toward town.

The man at the livery stood watching as Sam rode up and tied off.

'Here's your animal. I'll take my deposit.'

The man looked at Sam's clothes. 'Looks like he got his money's worth out of you.'

'It's hard to keep him in a straight line.'

'Well, I guess you did good to even get back.' He grabbed the reins and began to lead the animal.

Sam gave him a hard look. 'Say.'

The man stopped and let Number 6 roll on like a shoved wagon.

'Some time ago, maybe two months, did you rent a horse to a little man wearing a suit?'

'No.'

Sam looked down the road toward the river. 'How come you can answer so quick?'

'I ain't rented nothin' to nobody wearin' a suit coat in five years or better. Nowadays, if you wear a suit you got a Ford.'

'Somebody was up there wearin' one.'

The liveryman crossed his big arms and spat. 'Could of rode in from Woodgulch to the northwest. They's more than one point on the compass, you know.'

He started walking in the direction of the boat feeling not

only tired but thick-headed. More than one point on the compass. He wasn't cut out for the wilderness, was damn lucky he hadn't got lost or killed. And if he could help it, he'd never climb on another horse.

He got to the stage plank five minutes before the boat cast off and was squeezing through the crowd when the captain grabbed him by the arm.

'By God, Lucky, you smell like a sardine. Get cleaned up and out on deck in ten minutes. We've got a load of country boys on with the rest and I don't think some of 'em have ever seen electricity.'

Sam put a hand on his lower back. 'I'm about half dead, Captain.'

'Well, the half that ain't dead better work twice as hard.' He gave Sam a shove toward the stairs, and he went up to wash and change into his uniform. The upper decks and companionways were reeling with excursionists, some well dressed, some in khaki cotton work clothes, a few wearing blue jeans belted with strips of blond leather. Up on the roof he checked the fire buckets, then opened the pilothouse door.

Mr Brandywine, who seldom used the new steering levers, was standing on a spoke of the ten-foot wheel, waiting for castoff, and he turned halfway around. 'Knock before you come in here.'

'I'm looking for the Wellers.'

'Mr Simoneaux, I am not in charge of the musicians.'

As Sam retreated down the steps, Mr Brandywine hung half his weight on the whistle cord and set the big three-bell chime to roaring. The deckhands cast off lines and the boat backed out full speed, the decks shaking as the paddlewheel beat down the water.

The café was jammed, and Ted Weller was pinned at the back of the room by a party of eight dandies examining the one-page paper menus with exaggerated care. The sun was going down and young couples were thronging the open area on the hurricane deck, most of them good natured, smoking and sneaking sips from their pocket flasks. He checked in with Charlie Duggs, who was blending with the crowd at the edge of the dance floor, where perhaps a quarter of the paying customers stood in awe of the black orchestra, of the bounce and surprise of the music, the sass of the trumpet. Most of them had never heard anything like it, but knees began to bend, hips to slide, feet to rise like boats lifted on a freshet of notes. Sam moved downstairs and found the main deck jammed, people tossing cigarette butts in sparking pinwheels across the wooden floor and ordering tableloads of ice and soda.

He walked to the rail and saw that Mr Brandywine had brought the *Ambassador* out into a skein of dead water and was letting the boat loaf with its bow upstream, more or less staying in the same pocket of river. The point of the trip, he realized, was not to go somewhere, but only to seem to go somewhere. It was a sad passenger who knew what was happening outside the vessel on a night cruise. The whole point was to stay in the breezy bubble of comfort and music and forget the dark and airless shore.

The cruise brought three fistfights and a bad screaming match between a woman and her boyfriend. One man refused to quit fighting, and Sam had to drag him down to the little brig in the engine room and lock him in. He banged the man's head with the door when he slammed it shut because he was angry at his own exhaustion. There were still unpulled stickers in his legs, and the insides of his thighs ached from the saddle.

Passing through the main-deck lounge, he watched the bracing of the dance floor jounce over his head, as if an army were doing jumping jacks, and the captain, who was rushing through to the engine room, stopped and listened to the rumble. 'Lucky, run up and tell the band to slow their tempo ten beats per minute on the fast numbers if they don't want the damn boat to fold in half.'

At last came the race of unloading and policing the boat, and he worked asleep on his feet, moving people along, killing cigarettes, counting deck chairs to see how many had been thrown overboard from the dark upper deck. It wasn't until he'd climbed into his bunk that he thought of the Wellers, and he let out a groan.

'I hear you,' Charlie Duggs said. 'Tired as I am, I got the headache so bad I can't go to sleep.'

'What's up for tomorrow?'

'We're pullin' out in a bit, bud.'

'Where bound?'

'Natchez. I expect old Brandywine will run on a full bell all night and have us there by eight o'clock.'

He put an arm over his eyes. 'God, not a morning cruise.'

'It's Sunday. First run is two-thirty. Captain Stewart lets anyone who wants to walk to church get sanctified. You a churchgoing man?'

'Catholic.'

'Well, then, I'll walk up the hill with you.'

The next morning he washed up, brushed out his clothes, and they set off for ten o'clock Mass, walking in a group with a fireman, Captain Stewart, two white porters, Nellie Benton and her nephews, the engineers. At the top of the hill one group split off for the Methodist church while Sam and Charlie walked straight for a spire in the distance. He stopped on a street corner and looked back.

'What's up?' Duggs asked.

'The Wellers ever go to church?'

'I don't remember. Don't start looking down your nose at folks for not goin' to church. Both of them pulled double shifts yesterday and likely won't knock off till midnight tonight.'

'That right? And all I did all yesterday was sit in a bubble bath running a silk brush between my toes.'

Duggs made a face. 'Maybe they ain't as tough as you French boys. Come on, we'll be late.'

'For a war veteran, you got a soft heart,' Sam said.

Duggs stepped into the street. 'Sure.'

'Did you shoot anyone?'

'None of your business,' Duggs said. 'Are you really a Catholic?'

'So, you don't want to talk about it.'

'Just answer my question.'

They both turned to go up the church steps. 'Well, "*Introibo ad altare Dei.*"'

Duggs pulled open the arched oak door on incensed air, stood aside, and bowed. '*Ad Deum qui laetificat juventutem meum.*'

They sat in the rear of the echoing church, and after the priest sang the Gloria, Sam heard the door open and turned to see Mr Brandywine and two busboys come in, one on each side, watchful, as though they'd been propping him up all the way there. Sam prayed for the Wellers and their little girl, and for the old pilot's judgment. He then questioned his own reasons for going out on the great river grasping at straws. What propelled him, he wanted to believe, was the awful diminished feeling he suffered whenever he thought of his dead child or of his taken family. If he could make another family whole, maybe that would help. Help whom, though? Then he remembered that if he found the girl, he'd get his job back and once more cruise along the gleaming floors of the finest department store in New Orleans. Was that the main reason he was doing this? Was he just along to retrieve his floor-walker's salary? On the walk down the hill to the boat, he shared these thoughts with Charlie, whose only response was, 'Lucky, self-interest is better than no interest.'

11

Vessy cleared the dishes after the noon meal and then brought the bedsheets and covers upstairs in her wiry arms. She was a mountain girl and used to steep walking, so at the top of the stairs she wasn't winded at all. Mrs White, in her bedroom pulling on fine gloves and checking items in her purse, didn't look up when the cook came through the door, just said, 'Mrs Hall won't be able to tend Madeline today. You'll watch her for us.'

'Yes, ma'am.' Vessy had wanted to go to her rented one-room house to boil her own laundry in the yard. Usually she was off between one-thirty and four, when she came in to start supper.

'Did you hear Madeline singing with the music teacher this morning?'

'I was out back stackin' stovewood.'

Mrs White's gloved hands worked like mourning doves as she picked at a spray of pills on her dressing table and placed them one by one into a little nickel-plated box she kept in her purse. 'Well, this morning Mr Stover said she sings just like a little bird and has a natural sense of timing.'

Vessy pursed her lips and slid them to one side of her face. 'That so? Like she already been taught.'

Mrs White gave her an appraising look. 'Well, I'm going into town to shop at Welford's.'

'Yep.'

'Listen for her when she gets up from her nap. Don't let her oversleep because she'll be hard to put down at eight.'

Vessy placed the sheets in the bedroom armoire and listened to Mrs White's slow tread on the stairs. When the car started up in the drive and backed toward the street, she bent to pick up a cream-colored pair of gloves discarded in the wastebasket and pulled them on. They were a short style that betrayed her freckled skin. Vessy was twenty-seven years old, had taken care of herself, and still had her teeth, except for a molar knocked out when her father punched her for leaving a saddled horse in the rain. She'd wanted to get married more than anything, but being a bit plain and more than a bit plainspoken, it took her a long time to get someone to court her. She might have stayed in the eastern Kentucky mountains forever, but one Sunday her mother served an old, undercooked pork roast and killed the whole family with food poisoning, except for her, and she lay on the back porch and puked for two days before a neighbor found and rescued her. The man courting her stopped the relationship, believing she was a bad-luck woman, and that had hardened her outlook on life. Vessy admired her hands for a moment, then pulled off the gloves, dropping them back into the can. She might ask for them later but couldn't bear Mrs White thinking that she'd been stealing out of the trash. Then again, what need did she have of dress gloves? To handle stovewood? She spat into the can and went down to wash the dishes.

At two she walked into the child's room and frowned at the ruffled bed, the expensive small furniture, the assembly of dolls lined up against the wall. Pulling a chair next to the bed, she studied the girl, narrowing her eyes at the flawless pink fingernails that showed no splits or coarse cuticles, no signs of roughness. She turned the sleeping child's palm into a beam of sunlight and examined the skin. She woke up and pulled her hand back to rub her eyes.

'Little miss, you want to put on your nice new sundress?'

The girl sat up and smiled at her. Vessy pulled off her short stockings and ribboned pinafore. The child's knees were what she wanted to see, and the skin there was smooth and white as milk. She dropped the sundress over her easy as a lampshade and then sat her on the bed to buckle on a pair of brown sandals, cupping the feet in her rough palms and feeling the soft bottoms.

'Let's see those toes.' Vessy flashed a playful smile and the girl giggled, drawing back her feet and sitting on them.

'I bet you want Vessy to play little piggy with them tootsies?'

'No,' the girl said, but she still held out her feet for the sandals.

Vessy wiggled the big toe and saw not a callus, dirt stain, or crookedness. She examined her ankles for scuffs and little scars. She held and turned the feet the way she would examine sweet potatoes at the market. Then she put on the sandals and led the girl downstairs for a glass of milk and a slice of sugar bread. They sat at the little porcelain breakfast table set by a window, where Vessy usually enjoyed the view down the hill toward the river. But now her eyes took in every detail of this child, sensing that something was badly wrong. Suddenly, she jerked up her right arm and feinted at the girl's head as though she would strike her. Madeline looked up at the open fingers, but did not flinch.

'Orphanage my foot,' Vessy said under her breath. She knew orphans, white and black, and every one would jerk back and cower if anybody raised a hand to them. Orphans wore no shoes, or wrong-sized shoes in which their feet grew crooked. Their feet bore calluses, craters of sores, bite scars, toenails stobbed black, orange dirt stain, ankle meat clipped to white bone. Knees were crosshatched from working in crops or playing in common dirt, fingers stretched out by bucket or firewood chores. When Vessy rested her hand down on the fine hair, the child leaned into her touch and smiled. 'Sweet Jesus,' Vessy whispered. 'Where'd they find this baby?'

12

Sam found the Wellers outside their cabin and explained what he had learned from the Skadlocks and what kind of people they were, how they lived, that he was certain of their guilt.

As Ted Weller listened, his face turned to match the hard red surface of the shore pavings. 'Why in hell didn't you tell us this yesterday?'

'You know how it was. We had twenty-five hundred passengers last night.'

He raised both arms from his sides and let them drop. 'Why didn't you threaten them? They're criminals.'

'I wasn't exactly in a position to put any pressure on them. As far as the law is concerned, these people own their own country.'

Ted grabbed him by the arm and wedged him against a bulkhead. 'You tell me how to get back in there and they'll tell *me* something.'

Sam read his eyes and found them a mix of rage and fear. 'Ted, I think they'll kill you.'

His eyes flew wide and Elsie turned her face away. 'They didn't kill *you*!' Ted hollered. 'You think I'm just big soft Ted the dumb German who all he can do is pound a piano. Let me tell you, I'm plenty tough. I grew up in a saloon.'

Sam pointed downriver. 'Back in there where I went ain't Cincinnati. There's no law at all.'

'I don't need law when my baby's missing.'

Sam looked south along the bank understanding that Ted was going to do something stupid, and the sad part of it was that he agreed with his feelings. 'You don't know how to get back in there,' he said softly.

'I got a mouth to ask.'

Elsie put a hand on his shoulder. Sam imagined she was going to try to calm him, but instead she said, 'I'll get you money from the boat and you can ask directions at the station.'

'This is a bad idea.'

Ted glowered at him, his mustache blooming under his red nose. 'You tell me where this place is. Right now.'

'No. I won't be responsible.'

Ted slammed him against the bulkhead, hard. 'Tell me or I'll break you open like a dollar fiddle, damn you.'

Sam stared him in the eye. Ted was hoping for at least a chance of finding his family's future, of gathering in his blood, but Sam remained silent, to keep him from getting hurt. He himself had been called Lucky so many times that he was beginning to believe the name fit, but Ted might not share his good fortune. Then he remembered the child's face, floating in the folds of his brain like an ivory pendant. A child alive. Out there somewhere. His thoughts changed course, and he decided that luck couldn't manifest itself unless a man took a chance. Feeling sad to the bone, he raised his open palms above his waist. 'Well, to start with, there's this murderous dog.'

Ted walked to the Y&MV station, bought a ticket, and boarded a mixed train going out at four to St Frank. It was a bone-rattling ride in a wooden coach through cut-over land and weed-wracked farms. Two hours later the train jammed on its brakes at a dusty board-and-batten station and he stepped off into the still air and asked the agent for directions to the livery.

The little agent sized him up. 'This here's the last train tonight, so if you wait a bit I'll give you a lift in my flivver.' He waited under the station overhang until the agent came out in the slanting light and turned the oily crank on his Ford. At the livery Ted got the owner up from supper and asked to rent a horse.

'Well,' the liveryman said, 'I like your looks so I'll let you have my wife's mare, Sooky.'

Ted shook his head. 'No thanks. I want the one called Number six.'

The liveryman fished a set of spectacles from his pocket, put them on, and looked at Ted more closely. 'That's not a good horse for a big fellow like yourself.'

'A man who rented it before says it's what I need.'

'You can suit yourself, but that horse will try to gallop through a parked locomotive, it's that stupid.' The man stalked off toward his sun-bleached barn.

Ted rode across the stream before full dark, then sat the horse on the far bank, reading a compass by the light of a match. The liveryman had explained where to go and to wait for the moon to come up, and after half an hour it began to rise above the line of cypresses, shining like a communion wafer. Ted put the horse forward, keeping the moon between the animal's ears. He carried his pistol in one pocket, his big folding knife in the other, and his little girl in his thoughts. In the swamp he lost sight of the sky and became lost. He spilled his matches into the mud and couldn't read his compass, but he kept moving, hoping he would blunder his way to the river, deciding that nothing could stop him. Number 6 brushed against a locust tree and Ted felt the thorns rake his calf, but he didn't so much as turn his head at the pain.

The next day Sam was rushing through his lunch before the loading of the two o'clock crowd when Captain Stewart walked up to the table and asked, 'Have you seen Mr Weller?'

'I thought he'd asked you for the day off.'

The captain's white eyebrows seemed to double in size as he leaned down. 'He sent me a note to that effect but evidently did not wait for a reply. Who's supposed to play for the two o'clock trip?'

Sam swallowed slowly, looking at his fingers. 'Aw, I'll cover it for him. It's a church group, isn't it? How much dancing are they going to do?'

'No offense, son, but I've heard you play. You've got to practice to get the stiffness out of your wrists.' He went upright, his back straight as a broom handle. 'But go down and get ready while Fred Marble plays everybody on board with the calliope. And I'll keep an ear on you.'

After a minute Elsie came over and refilled his coffee cup. 'Is he awful mad?'

'He ain't happy. When's Ted coming back?'

'He told us he'd return on this afternoon's train.'

'I hope he finds out more than I did.'

'Who's going to cover for him, the colored pianist?'

'Yours truly.'

'Oh.'

He smiled at her. 'Don't worry. I'll play like it counts.' Up on the roof Fred began to run scales of weeping notes, the whistles rising in pitch as they warmed in the blasting steam.

About one-thirty he got down to the hot dance floor and put up the lid on the piano, a six-foot-eight George Steck, a tough, loud instrument tolerant of the river's dampness. As the first ticket holders began to roam the big boat he warmed up, playing 'Nola' at a moderate tempo and nodding to the five other band members as they walked up: Zack Stimson, the banjo player; Mike Gauge, the clarinetist; Freddie Peat, drummer; Felton Bicks, cornetist; and tuba player Jackie van Pelt. The men fell into the song one at a time and swapped the lead around for fifteen minutes, letting Sam have the fancy ending to himself.

The band checked their instruments, getting ready for the long haul. Zack leaned over and asked politely, 'Where's Ted?'

'He's laying out today. Going for some information on his little girl.'

Zack shook his head and bent down to tune his banjo. 'We could use her right about now.'

Sam frowned at the remark. 'Well, how'm I doing?'

'Doin' okay, but I can tell you mostly play by yourself. No offense. Ted and us, we're used to each other.'

The big whistle hollered up the Natchez bluff, and four young couples walked up, looking expectantly at the band, so Zack started strumming 'Nobody but You' and the others landed on the melody like bees on a daisy. Captain Stewart skirted the edge of the dance floor, listened to three measures, and kept walking. When Sam had to fake a section, he heard Freddie Peat laugh out loud. He remembered the melody and what was coming up and relaxed, glancing now and then through an open door at shoreline willows flowing past along with the smokestacks of tugboats and ferries. When Mrs Benton blew the whistle again and turned out for the main channel, the breeze began to pour in through the dance floor's many windows and this, too, was what the customers were here for, escape from the soul-melting heat onshore. Twelve couples danced right in front, and a steward walked by sprinkling dance wax at their feet. Soon more dancers came out, the shy ones and the young ones, their steps melding with the music and the scenery passing by in the windows as if it were all part of the same song. He watched the back of a woman who'd begun two-stepping by herself, but when she turned Sam spotted the three-year-old she was holding, his arm high in his mother's hand. He dropped a beat when he saw that and heard Zack call out, 'Steady.' It's what parents did, teach their kids to dance. He shouldn't have been surprised. But for much of the song his timing was imperfect as he kept his attention on her, an ordinary-looking woman made distinctive by her eyes as she watched the boy feel her movements and learn that music and motion belonged together. He wondered if his own son would have learned to dance or sing, and he guessed probably so. His wife would've taught him, and at the thought of Linda he was filled with longing for the feel of her in his arms on a big dance floor. This pained him but the music moved him on, his fingers climbing an arpeggio so hard to execute it hurt him out of remembering and drew him back into the song. He turned his head, and Zack nodded.

* * *

For the night trip, the black orchestra wore new tuxedos. Some dancers who'd never heard the New Orleans sound stayed back for a few tunes, leaning on roof supports or window frames trying to figure if it was all right to have fun with the band's efforts. But the younger ones, or those who'd gone out on excursion boats earlier in the season or last year, they knew what to expect and stretched their steps. Pulled by the music, they walked on the notes, the women turning and shimmying, throwing the spangled tassels on their dresses straight out until their youth sparked like struck flint on the rumbling dance floor. Sam kept watch at the edge of the crowd, shaking his head at how much better this band was than the daylight group. When the clarinetist went off the page into his own riff some dancers stopped to listen and bounce in place, it was that good.

Elsie came down to check tables for burning cigarettes and brushed by him, pulling at his coat. 'Lucky, he didn't come back.'

'What?' He took her arm and walked her to the outside rail just as the boat shaved by the point of a big island.

'Ted told me he'd come into the station on the three-thirty train. August went up the hill to meet him, but he wasn't on the coach.'

'Was that the last train?'

'Yes.' She balled up a fist and held it against her lips.

'That country's slow going on a horse. The trip just took longer than he thought it would, that's all.' He could tell she wasn't fooled, and wished he were a better liar.

'We're pulling out for Vicksburg after this trip.'

'He'll know that. He'll come up there on tomorrow's train.'

'You think so?' He saw in her worried eyes how much she loved Ted.

'Aw, yeah. Now you go walk those tables on the other side before the captain comes along.' He watched her push through the doors and then looked down the roiling river, thinking about the Skadlocks, the dark woods, and the dog. 'Lord,' he said aloud. The dog. He tried to imagine what experience in

Cincinnati would prepare the musician for Louisiana swamps and the Skadlocks. He wished he had gone back with him, for Ralph Skadlock in particular had seemed a maimed soul capable of anything. He remembered that the outlaw knew where Troumal was, that speck of a place down on the Texas line. Was the slaughter of his family some sort of legend among the cutthroats of Arkansas?

Lucky walked down to the main deck and back toward the boilers, where he found August in the dim coal galley, backlit by angry yellow fire and shoving a long clinker rod into a firebox, poking up the flames. Sam grabbed a pair of black cotton gloves off a crossbeam and held them out to him in the dust-choked companionway. 'Put these on and don't let me catch you working without them. You can't play saxophone with burnt-off fingers.'

August smiled, his blond hair lit with a bituminous glow. 'Hey, they put me to firing full-time just this morning. Another half-dollar a day.' As he pulled on the gloves Lucky saw that his nostrils were black with coal dust. 'Why'd you leave all the swells to come done here?'

'Just to check on you. You worried about your dad?'

August pulled out the cherry-red hook, hung it next to the fire door, and grabbed a shovel out of the chute. 'Naw, he can take care of himself. He's gonna find my sister, you know.'

Lucky watched him throw coal and tried to remember himself at fourteen, when some days he knew for sure that everything was going to turn out well, that nothing else bad could possibly happen to anyone he was close to, that life would treat him fairly. He'd felt this way up until his son died. And then there were the sorrows of France, where he finally understood that the family stories weren't legends, but reports of real killings. He watched the boy labor, almost envious of the mindless work. 'Hey, you want to sit in tomorrow with the day-trip band?'

August didn't break his shoveling rhythm. He was counting

loads, as someone had taught him that morning. 'Sure,' he said through his wide smile. 'That'd be great.' He slammed the fire door, set the ash vent, and moved away to the next boiler, sliding further into the hissing darkness.

13

The *Ambassador* set down her stage and let the crowd off at eleven. A messenger was sent up the hill to get a policeman to retrieve two drunks from the engine-room jail cell, and Sam turned them over. Mr Brandywine blew the whistle, the giant note chasing the spent dancers up the road to town as the chuffing hoist raised the stage and the boat began to back out into big river.

After cleanup, Elsie stopped Sam as he was leaving the café. 'Have you seen the captain?'

He glanced at her face and looked away. 'Not for an hour or so.'

'I heard we might bypass Vicksburg for a Moose lodge convention in Greenville.' She had her fists balled in the pockets of her uniform, nothing more than a well-cut apron, and she looked harried, tired unto desperation. 'Ted won't be able to find us.'

'I didn't hear about Greenville.'

'I've been asking everybody. Cap must be down in the engine room.'

'The pilot, ask him.' He gave her a little smile.

'Brandywine? You're teasing.'

'All right.' He pulled his watch. 'He gets a cup of coffee right about now. I'll bring it up myself and ask him.'

On the stairs to the dark pilothouse he tried not to slop coffee out of the stoneware mug. He started to turn the knob but remembered to knock, and Mr Brandywine's chicken voice cracked through the glass. 'Enter.'

Sam approached the steering wheel but the pilot kept his head toward the night. Farm-size plots of fog were skating over the river, and the boat had just plowed into one. There was as little light inside as out. 'Here's your coffee, Mr Brandywine.'

'By God, I could smell it when you were halfway here. Put it on the stool.'

He did, then stood quietly and watched the fog take away the stars. 'Are we still going to play Vicksburg?'

'I don't know about you, boy, but that's where I'm tying up.'

Sam craned his neck forward, staring at the fog boiling in the window. 'How can you run in this?'

'Hush. I don't know exactly where I am.' The pilot closed his eyes. 'Hush, now. Don't even leave.'

The pilothouse silence drove home that every nail and plank in the three-hundred-foot steamer could break apart within moments if old Brandywine's mind faltered. He was the pilot of everyone's future. Reaching out, he slid back the big side windows on port and starboard, then pulled from the whistle a chop of sound, a quick musical rasp of steam sailing out into the blackness. Sam heard an echo to the east; nothing came back from the west.

Mr Brandywine's back straightened and his eyes opened wide. 'You can leave now.'

'Where are we?'

'A thousand yards off Magnolia Bluff.' He turned his head sideways to the oncoming fog, as though listening to it sluice over the breast board.

'I can't see a thing.'

'I wouldn't imagine that you could.'

Sam put a hand on the doorknob, but the pilot stopped him with a question. 'The little girl that sang with the band, last trip. You hear anything about her?' As he spoke he reached up and pulled a big copper ring that sounded a bell in the engine room, and after a moment, they could feel a gentle surge of speed.

Sam looked ahead into nothing, wondering what the pilot was seeing other than his storehouse of recollections from ten thousand trips in the dark. 'Somebody hired people to steal her.

We found out who the thieves were, and Ted's gone to handle things.'

'He can't law them?'

'Louisiana.'

'I see.' Mr Brandywine let go of a spoke and the wheel spun slowly before he stopped it with the foot brake.

'Don't like those new steering levers?'

'There's a time for 'em.'

'Good night, then.'

'Duggs tells me you were in the war,' the pilot said, with sudden animation.

Sam stopped with his hand on the knob. It was late, the fog was beginning to lift, and he wondered if Mr Brandywine just wasn't ready to be left alone.

The boat finished crossing the river and straightened, or at least Sam felt it did. 'Just missed the fighting. I saw what was left over, though.'

'I wish my oldest boy had missed it.' He reached up and pulled one glass-rattling note from the whistle. Sam peered out of the window to the left and after much concentration could barely make out a running light a half-mile off, dim as a cigarette in a dark hallway. From across the river came the vessel's hoarse salute. 'The *Nellie Speck*,' Brandywine said to the night.

'How can you tell?'

He could just make out Brandywine's shape, slowly turning to him. 'A steamboat's whistle is its name. That other pilot knows what boat we are. Everybody's whistle is made to sound different, my boy.'

'You must have some ears.'

'Why, can't you tell a family member's voice even when you can't see them? Your good friend's? Your wife's?'

He didn't answer for a long time. 'I guess so.'

'That's right.'

'What outfit was your oldest boy in?'

'He volunteered in Missouri.'

Sam didn't want to ask the next question, and Brandywine perhaps knew this, that there would be several questions leading to a black answer, so he went ahead and gave it.

'He got his eyes burned out,' the old man said. 'And what a loss that was to him. When he rode cub pilot with me, he could see a green running light a mile and a half away, and now he's at home making brooms.'

'I'm sorry.'

'Sometimes, late at night when I'm tired and waiting for first light, I feel like he's standing right here to the side of me. I'll turn to him and there's nothing there, just this hole in the darkness.' He gave the wheel a nudge to starboard. 'It's hard to explain.'

'Yes,' Sam said. 'It is.'

On the way downstairs Sam watched a fog patch crossing the river. Two or three stars spun overhead, and a navigation light burned yellow above the western batture. A steam towboat came breathing heavily down on the starboard side, escape pipes woofing, running lights no more than sooty fireflies above the velvety stream, its sudden-rising whistle an organ note driven like a nail into the delta night, audible for ten miles where a farmboy hearing its hum might decide to drop from his bedroom window and join a world of wanderers. Sam imagined such a boy and wondered what would happen to him, if he'd wind up shoveling coal all night or sleeping above Charlie Duggs's torturous snoring, a dull life going in a straight line. No wonder so many songs were about going back home.

Passing by the café, he saw Elsie cleaning up, her long waist bent over a checkered oilcloth. Everything would go on in a straight line tomorrow, all right, unless Ted returned with world-changing news. Or unless he didn't return at all.

Ted squatted in the dark guessing when dawn would come, lost in a timeless ocean of blackness where ten minutes seemed an hour. It had taken two days to find the Skadlocks, and now, in a tangle of reeds behind the big house, he crouched and waited for movement or sound. The moon was long gone, and a barge of cloud had moored in the sky. A wind came up and rattled the stalks around him and he thought of his daughter, gone now too many weeks. He saw himself as a shrinking spark in her mind and knew that time was the enemy, an old cliché as true as anything else he might think. Each day cost him more of his little girl's voice, her sense of perfect pitch, her baby teeth shining above her laughter, the touch of her hands on his big ears as he hoisted her up to sing in his arms. All he could do during this dangerous wait for the sun was think of her, and he feared it would distract him from the task at hand. He shook his head, hoping again for light since he could see nothing at all. He had scouted the house and its outbuildings before the moon lay down in the trees, but now there was nothing before him except his dark imagination of a house, a brush-swamped, gigantic thing of nibbled chimney tops and grass-spiked roof gutters. Looking off to the right, he saw nothing. Turning left, he thought he saw – what, distant fireflies? Two amber lights from a far-off boat? As he stared, the color came up in intensity and the glowing rounds grew larger – closing in from a mile away? With a shock he realized they weren't far at all, but floating in midair right beside him, fixed in the warm, silent breath of an animal.

The blood drained from his chest, and though he knew he should remain as frozen and quiet as a stump, he understood that an animal's nose couldn't be fooled. Against his will he rose and his left hand floated up in defense just as a dark fury of indeterminate size struck it like a hungry fish, pain streaking up his arm at once. His hand was crushed and shredded by a huge invisible animal and he drew his pistol and pumped one detonation toward the dark pull, guessing at what had hold of him since he could see only phantom movement in the crashing reeds. The growling power on his hand turned him loose, and he tried to lurch away and find his stride but was seized in the back of the neck by a set of steel-trap fangs that shook him like a rabbit, trying to snap his brain stem. He raised the pistol again and fired once over his shoulder and then something metal banged his skull and a shower of sparks rained down in his eyes. A gruff cry that might have been for the dog's benefit rose behind him. Ted was down on his knees when he felt a second blow and then the crush of wet, sulphurous swamp grass against his cheek.

Mrs Benton was in the wheelhouse when the *Ambassador* drifted up against the foot of the bluff in Vicksburg, and she laid the boat against the pilings as gently as she'd once put her baby in a crib. Down in the boiler room, August cleaned his fires. Getting off duty, he washed up, combed his brassy hair, and hiked the steep redbrick street to check the train schedule at the Y&MV station. The agent told him that passengers coming up from St Frank would arrive in two hours on the eleven o'clock train from Harriston. The boy went out on the platform and sat on a bench under the overhang, just out of the sunshine, looking down the track. A switch engine chuffed by, pulling two flats of lumber, and he watched it hiss and smoke off toward the upriver end of town. Half an hour later a passenger train of three wooden coaches creaked up to the station, thirty or so people getting off. One portly man in a straw boater kissed his wife and two daughters who had come to the station to meet him. August watched their shiny Ford chatter up the hill. His father had told him that they'd buy a car as soon as they finished up the season and went back to Cincinnati, that they'd have a better place for the winter, a flat with hot water and more than two rooms, a ground-floor place that would support a substantial piano and have room for them to play music and sing. He began to pass the time going over arrangements in his head, fox-trots he'd picked up on the way downriver. When he got stuck figuring which way to go with a note, he pictured his father's fingers on the keyboard, rolling up, skipping down, showing the way to the melody. Those same fingers had stung his legs as a child, pulled back at his thick hair when he disobeyed. His father was pretty much all business, and his business was music. So no matter what, they were the same in that.

At ten he heard Mrs Benton pull the whistle ring for the Moose lodge trip as he was meditating on 'I'm Just Wild About Harry,' the way the white band played the melody, then how the colored orchestra played *around* the melody, going in and out of it, and he came to the revelation that there were more notes around a song than in it. He closed his eyes and began to hum and pat his feet on the cindery brickwork.

At 10:58, August lifted his chin toward the whistle of a passenger train, three blended notes rising toward A-sharp, D, and F-sharp. A well-maintained ten-wheeler pulled a train of six coaches into the station, and two conductors lowered step stools to the apron the moment the wheels stopped turning, getting off in their sharp black uniforms and pulling bright watches from their vests. August waited at the first coach, watching down the line toward the third in case his father came out of that vestibule. After every passenger had left the train, he approached the head-end conductor.

'My father was supposed to be on this train, but he didn't get off.'

The conductor pulled his watch again and looked toward the engine. 'Could be he's asleep in his seat. I got to do a walk-through anyways.' He went up into the first coach and five minutes later August saw him come out of the last car, wave, and then shake his head. The agent had told him this was the only train from St Frank today, but August was not yet at the age of worry, and what would happen tomorrow was for his mother to fret about. He left the station and walked through town looking in shop windows and wondering what it would be like to have any money at all.

The Moose lodge trip was back at twelve-thirty, and he wanted to find his mother before he ate and went to sleep. The crew was racing to clean up the spilled root beer, popcorn, hot-dog chili, puke, tobacco spit, and stepped-out ready-mades. His mother was in the kitchen, helping the cooks make sandwiches for the two o'clock general excursion. Her hair was half down, her apron smudged with ketchup. He could smell the morning's sweat on her.

When she noticed him at her elbow, alone, she grabbed his arm hard and pushed him through the swinging door into the restaurant. 'Where's your father?'

'I met the one train he'd be on and he wasn't on it.'

She dug a fingernail into his biceps. 'You must've missed him.'

'Ow.' He pulled back. 'That train was empty when it left, Mom.'

She dropped her hands against her apron. 'He must've run into trouble with those people.'

August couldn't imagine what kind of trouble she was talking about. 'Can I turn in?'

She looked at him as though seeing him for the first time. 'Sure, sure. You go back on at eight?' She ran a finger through his hair and saw the cinders peppering his scalp. 'How's your back?'

'All right.' He pulled in a notch on his belt. 'The second engineer said he'd find me a short-handled coal scoop that I can swing better.'

'I can tell it hurts.'

'It's not nothing. The worst part is the sweating.'

She lowered her voice. 'You have any more loose bowels from the heat?'

He rolled his eyes. 'No. Engineer told me to drink a spoonful of coal ashes in a glass of water.'

Elsie seemed alarmed. 'Did it work?'

'Dried me right up.' He gave her a smile. 'Now quit worrying about everything.'

Some of the Moose lodge men had come on board already drunk and eager to fight with members of their fellow lodge from across the river. Sam shoved four men apart for twenty minutes and spent another half hour wrestling two of them into the brig. By the end of the run he was tired and his shoulder was sprung, but the captain told him to play for the two o'clock trip. He barely had time to sew his vest buttons back on before climbing the bandstand and catching the downbeat from the drummer. The first tune was 'Japanese Sandman,' jacked up in tempo, and he felt he was an eighth beat behind everyone else, playing uphill into the alto sax and clarinet duel in the middle. Several young Vicksburg couples began dancing badly, tripping, kicking shins on their turns, and Sam hung on. The next tune was a waltz, and then he got on top of the following fox-trot and stayed there. As the dance deck heated up, sweat began to sting his eyes; then the boat pulled out and the breeze came through, fluttering the bleached tablecloths. Between tunes he watched the floor, looked at faces, tried to read minds, studied the men lurking against the white-enameled stanchions, hoping to see Ted, maybe a Skadlock, or just someone whose face showed inexplicable guilt or longing. He imagined that by now the little girl could be anywhere on the boat's downbound route, because that was the one connection he understood, that someone saw her and had to have her, someone near the river's fogs, within reach of the big boat's whistle and the pull of the blasting calliope.

At the break, Elsie Weller came up next to the keyboard and told him that Ted hadn't been on the train. Her eyes were red and she was twisting one of the boat's cloth napkins into a rope.

'Aw, he's probably coming up to Greenville. We'll be there tomorrow.'

'He would've sent a telegram, Lucky.'

The drummer gave a rim tap and he turned to a new piece on the piano's music rack. 'Maybe the office was closed. There's all sorts of reasons he might be late or didn't send a wire.'

'That's what I'm afraid of.'

He began an intro to 'I Used to Love You but It's All Over Now,' sorry that this was in the rotation. It was a new song, and he hoped she didn't know the title. She adjusted her little waitress crown and walked bravely out a starboard door with her back straight, and he remembered that she was a better musician than he was and deserved more than a kitchen job, that she was missing two pieces of her life, and he was missing one. His fingers struggled up a knoll of unfamiliar notes and behind him the cornetist frowned. Sam began to think of the day his son died, how Linda was inconsolable, and no matter how much he comforted her, she continued to shake with the loss. He sometimes forgot that she had as big a hole in her life as he did, and suddenly he missed her very much. A strange thing began to happen under his fingertips: he was paying less attention to his music, and his timing improved. He began to feel the notes instead of just reading them off the page. Tilting his head, he listened to himself get better as he went on, feeling sad enough to cry while making the dancers step and spin, and smile.

14

For the moonlight trip he counted the gate at the stage plank, earnestly checking faces, watching up the bluff for Ted to get out of a cab. After loading everybody, he patrolled the dance floor. The Vicksburg people were pretty well behaved, though suspicious of the black orchestra, but a group from the big sawmill in Yokena had brought in an intolerable number of half-pints of 150-proof moonshine, and in midriver several rattling fistfights broke out. There was something wrong with their liquor, and toward the end of the excursion people were vomiting over the deck rails and under tables on the dance floor. One balding man wearing overalls went berserk, and it took a waiter, Charlie Duggs, and two busboys to restrain him from jumping into the paddlewheel. By the time the boat returned to the dock, Sam, Duggs, and Aaron Swaneli had to turn their uniforms over to a maid to be sewn back together for the next day's run in Greenville.

That night while the boat was under way August helped load coal for three hours, pushing a wheelbarrow up and down a narrow plank to a dark coal flat tied to the side of the boat. He was ankle deep in black dust and shoveling in the light of a guttering kerosene lantern, humming a new piece the black orchestra had played twice in a row because the dancers wouldn't quit hollering for it. When the bunkers were full, he threw a few shovelfuls into the firebox and saw that the coal was terrible stuff, half dirt, and he and the other firemen could raise barely enough steam to operate the engines. He fought the fires all night, trying to break up clinkers and get enough air through the coal so it would burn hot, and by the time they landed, before dawn, when his mother came down to tell him where the railroad station was in Greenville, he was too tired to stand, able only to lean on his shovel handle and listen, his eyes the only bright spots on him.

Sam was in his cabin matching Charlie Duggs snore for snore when he was awakened by a knock. He found Elsie outside, teary eyed and begging him to go up to the station and check the schedules because August was dead on his feet and needed an hour's washing besides. She was already late for the kitchen, and receiving his nod, ran down the steps. His shoulder was aching and he was so exhausted he swayed like a drunk. Pulling on mismatched pants and shirt, he stepped out on the wet deck. The boat itself was snoring steam into the gray dawn as he crossed the levee into town.

The night agent was at the end of his shift, and his eyes were bloodshot under his visor. He glanced at Sam's clothes and made him wait at the ticket window a long time before coming over and telling him that the connecting up from St Frank was due in at one-thirty.

Sam made a face and looked over the agent's shoulder at the regulator clock.

'Something else?' The man had a nasty sneer.

Sam took a breath. 'You hear of anybody in town bringing a three-year-old girl into their family?'

'You from down in French country?'

'I might still sound like I am but I live in New Orleans. Off Magazine Street.'

'One of my brothers lives in New Orleans, but he don't like it. What kind of little girl you mean, like a orphan or something?' The fat agent snorted. 'Like people around here need another mouth to feed.'

Sam blinked himself more awake. He had to think straight. 'I bet everybody in town goes through this station. We had a baby girl stolen from a musical act on the excursion boat on the trip downriver. I was hoping something might have caught your eye.'

The agent cocked his big bald head in the little barred window.

'Everybody's got some big tragedy to deal with sooner or later. Are you not old enough yet to know that?'

'I don't know. Maybe not.'

'And why are you even interested in these other folks' kid? You owe them something?'

'Mister, it's a long story, but I'm sort of responsible she got stole.'

The agent looked him over carefully. 'You just trying to get rid of a little guilty feeling, maybe?'

Sam didn't know what to say to this. He already suspected that most human action was self-serving but now wondered if there wasn't something beyond the selfishness, a possibility that interested him. 'That and maybe something more.'

The agent stared at a wad of waybills in his hand, but he was not reading them. 'I'd like to wipe my ass with these things.' He took a long breath and let it out, sounding like a man who'd come to a hard decision. 'You say it's a little girl?'

'About three years old. They cut her hair short to disguise her, but some weeks have gone by.'

'So she'd look like a boy, maybe.'

'I guess so.'

The agent met his gaze and looked away. 'All I can do is keep my eyes and ears open.'

'I'm a mate on the excursion boat, the *Ambassador.* If you find something, anything, send me a wire and I'll pay for it.'

From under the window, the agent picked up a hook stuck full with waybills. 'In the unlikely event that I do, it'll be from Morris Hightower. That's me. But nobody I know would steal somebody's kid.' He wet his lips with his tongue. 'Now, if it was a boy, some mud farmer might be after making him a hand. But who'd want a girl?'

Sam bent at the knees to look under the man's visor. 'She was pretty and could sing like a bird.'

Morris Hightower frowned and pulled the paper bills apart angrily. He was tired, sedentary, probably wouldn't be alive in five years and knew it. 'Partner, there never was a bird that made a nickel off a song.'

The ten o'clock trip was a field day for several grammar schools, and no music was required, so he haunted the railings, keeping the children from falling into the river and away from the hot smoke-stacks on the upper deck. After lunch, the boat landed and he walked back to the station to wait for Ted, who wasn't on that day's train either. He sat down on the long bench and stared south along the tracks. The Skadlocks were dishonest in all ways and coldhearted as well, but he didn't know if they were killers. Throughout his life people had accused him of never suspecting the worst of people, but he didn't see any need to without reason. The Skadlocks had let him leave safely. But then, he hadn't threatened them, had tried to deal with them on their own level. And he wasn't the desperate father of a child they'd stolen away. Down at the landing a donkey engine's whistle went off like a woman's scream, bouncing away from the buildings in town and spreading west over the Arkansas wilderness. He hoped more than anything that Ted hadn't done something stupid.

After he walked back to the boat, he went to the kitchen and asked Elsie if Ted had brought any weapons with him. She told him about his knife and pistol, and he looked at the floor and shook his head.

'You didn't expect him to go off without so much as a penknife, did you?' She picked up a crewman's order and headed for the out door. Then she stopped and studied his expression. 'You think he's been hurt?'

'No. Not that. I bet he went ahead to Memphis. The train I met was packed full of Confederate veterans coming in for the two-thirty trip. He might've been forced to ride the main line all the way up. I wouldn't worry until tomorrow, or whenever it is we get to Memphis.'

She set the plates down. 'You checked for telegrams?'

'Yes.'

'I don't suppose we could call the law down there and see if there's been any trouble?'

The calliopist on the roof began to belt out 'Camptown Races,' the whistles calling out over the county.

'The law down there isn't real law,' he told her. 'And the Skadlocks live where hawks couldn't find 'em at noon.'

She closed her eyes. 'I'm so scared.'

'I know. We'll talk after I go down and play some Stephen Foster for the veterans.'

She shook her head, roused herself. 'All right.'

'This time I'll let the right hand know what the left hand's doing.'

She didn't smile. 'Okay, Lucky.'

There was no one on the dance floor for the afternoon trip, the old soldiers staying as far away as possible from the music so they could retell their legends. Sam saw many one-legged fellows crowing about in long white beards. Some of them drew maps in the air with their crooked fingers to bring old battles back; in their brittle memories they rode horses dead so long their bones had gone to powder in the deep clay fields of northern Virginia.

The band knocked off, the musicians set free to wander with the customers, and as he walked along the starboard rail, Sam noted the missing arms, the eye patches, the nervous twitches. Most of the men were animated, wore their old uniforms or some version of those gray markings, but he wondered about the ones who'd stayed at home, who wanted nothing of the remembering, who'd gotten in the mail a two-cent postcard announcing the veterans' excursion and thrown it in the stove and then maybe looked out the window, gladdened by the fact that people weren't shooting each other down in the street. Charlie Duggs had been to France and had killed a few Germans, and twice Lucky had to drop down out of his bunk in darkness and shake him out of a nightmare. The first time, Duggs was calling out, 'Not that, not that,' one leg thrashing out of his bunk, his body vibrating in the memory-stoked heat of despair. Sam had put a hand on his chest, feeling the spasms die off like the vibrations of a departing train.

'What?' Charlie had gasped.

'Bad dream, bud?'

He was quiet for a moment, gulping deep breaths of the stale air in the little cabin. 'The worst,' he'd said.

The moonlight carried eight hundred, and Sam studied faces at the stage plank, not sure what he was looking for, maybe nothing, maybe Ninga Skadlock stumping up the ramp. Later, on the dance floor, he saw a surly crowd stand well back from the bandstand and regard the black orchestra with bovine mistrust. No one from the scowling, slouching group danced for two numbers, and then the musicians seemed to size them up and began 'Down Yonder,' played straight hotel-style but with a subtle African jounce that drew out first the young dancers and then, pair by pair, some of the others. The captain ordered the lights turned down, blackness receding into blackness, the mood of the deck graying out, rhythm, for a time, overcoming hate.

15

Ted's flesh shrank back against his bones like cooked meat. He was lying in the half-light on what felt like a wood floor. An old woman was pressing a bandage on the top of his head and he smelled the cooking on her, the coal oil, and the sweat. It occurred to him that he might have been unconscious for days.

A man appeared above him. 'He's coming around,' the unshaved face said.

'Leave him be.'

'He can hear me.' Ralph Skadlock bent down. 'Hey, son of a bitch. You shot my dog in the hip. I ought to tie a sash weight around your neck and throw your ass in the river.'

Ted was astounded by the pain in his head, back, and hands. He raised his left and found it to be a throbbing thing crusted in blood. Blinking, he tried to remember the reason for all this hurting. 'Where's my little girl?' His voice sounded as if it were coming from under the floor, and his vision began to fail again.

'Listen,' only a voice close to his ear said, 'I'm going to bring you to the damn train. If we ever see you again, I'll cut you like a October hog. You understand me?'

His sight brightened, and he looked at the beaded-board wall, at the cloudy windows. He could hear the rasp of wasps in the room. Next to him was some type of copper device and a burner, a still. Outlaws. He was among outlaws. 'Where's Lily?'

'Come back here again and I'll fix you good.' Ralph Skadlock looked up at the old woman. 'You know, they'd never find him back in here.'

'How many times I got to tell you, we got to send him out. Otherwise somebody might come lookin' for him.'

Ted parted his lips to say something, then even his ears failed, and he passed out.

When next he opened his eyes, he was on the freight platform of a tiny board-and-batten railroad station out in the woods next to a single set of buckled tracks running through broom sedge. He turned his head to study the gray wood and found sitting next to him a man of about twenty wearing a straw hat and overalls.

The man folded up a piece of paper and stuffed it back into the opening of Ted's shirt. 'Hey, I come up a few minutes ago to catch the local and here you be with a note stuck in your shirt.'

Ted opened his mouth but nothing came out. On the second try he said, 'I hurt.'

The man held up a forefinger and bobbed it. 'Judging from the sight of you I reckon that's a fact. This here note is to the Fault agent to put you on the baggage coach for the Memphis hospital. Says you got money in your wallet.'

'Fault agent.' Ted thought it a mystical phrase.

'He ain't here yet. This station's called Fault. His name's Toliver and he don't come to work but two hours a day, morning train and afternoon.'

'Which one is this?'

The man looked around as if to verify this for himself. 'Afternoon.' He nodded. 'What happened to you anyways, get stomped by a bull?'

'Some people named Skadlock—'

Suddenly, the young man stood up as though he realized he was near grave contagion. 'Well, my granny used to say if you lie down with dogs you get up with fleas, but I believe you been lyin' with the alligators.'

'Where am I?'

'Fault, Louisiana. Used to be called No Gun Switch, except they took out the switch five years ago.'

Raising his head a bit, Ted glimpsed only a poorly graveled lane crossing the tracks. 'Can you get me some water?'

'I'm sorry, old son, ain't none around here.' He pulled out a nickel silver watch, fobless, from his yellow pants. 'Toliver'll be here in a minute.'

Shortly, a Model T's aspirate spitting sounded at the edge of Ted's hearing. The station agent appeared in an open pasture adjacent to the one-room station. The middle-aged agent, bald, wearing thick glasses, got out and stepped up on the platform, standing over Ted and looking him over. 'You get blowed up in the sawmill?'

The younger man leaned against the wall. 'I think he's about dried up. Can you fetch him a cup of water?'

'I brought a pail in the Ford, and there's a dipper you can get him.' The agent pulled his switch key and removed an outsized brass padlock from the door. 'You going to a hospital down the line, are you?'

'I feel terrible.' Ted wanted to say more, but felt as if a brood sow were lying across his chest.

The telegraph sounder began to clack in its box, and the agent went in to listen and to open his key and answer.

The younger man came up with a dipper of water and raised Ted's head.

The agent came out. 'Number forty-three's on time and we'll see engine smoke in a minute.' He bent down and tied a freight tag around Ted's left ankle. 'Sidney, what happened to him to black his eyes and mash his hand like that?'

'He tangled with some Skadlocks, he said.'

'He did? Who brought him out of their territory?'

'He was laid out when I got here.'

The agent read the note stuffed halfway in his shirt and pulled out Ted's wallet, removing several small bills. 'They want you sent north.' Half a mile away, the locomotive began blowing its out-of-tune whistle, and through the woods the men could hear the arrhythmic cough of a badly regulated engine. The agent got his flag, held it aloft, and the train pulled in, its two wooden coaches squalling to a stop on the flaking rails. An overweight clerk wearing a vest threw open the sliding door to the baggage coach, handed off six rocking chairs, two spools of barbed wire, ten sacks of feed, and a wooden box with the illustration of a clock on its side.

'You got a patient,' the agent said.

'Aw,' the clerk said, turning to pull down the coach's stretcher, a stout wood-frame apparatus with short legs. The three men lifted Ted onto it and then into the baggage coach, laying him down in a clear area against a side wall.

The young man in the straw hat crouched next to him. 'You need some more water, feller?'

Ted opened his eyes, glad to be inside anything, but said nothing.

The whistle hollered and the clerk slid the door closed. The train moved perhaps fifteen miles an hour, and he took pleasure in moving toward a better place where dogs didn't crush and tear your fingers or men beat on you with the flat of a shovel as they would a snake. The train moved in a shuddering, unsteady motion with the sound of much loose metal in rattling distress. The baggage clerk got down on his knees and put his hand on Ted's forehead, then gave him a drink of ice water, which went down like a blessing.

'Oh, thank you,' he rasped.

'You need something, you let me know.'

'All right.'

'Eventually we'll get up to the main line at Harriston, where we meet the northbound train. You'll get on their baggage car.'

'All right.' The rail was unmaintained and the joints hammered his back when a wheel passed over them.

'I hate to see you down among the cinders and husks there,' the baggage clerk said. He had pulled up a deck chair and was sitting near his head. 'I hear you run into some bad folks.'

'The Skadlocks.' His head cleared for a moment and he looked up at the man, who was somehow motionless in the swaying coach. 'They kidnapped my little girl and won't tell me where she is.'

The clerk stood up. 'They got your kid back in there?'

'No. I don't know where she is. They were paid to do it.'

'If you'd caught 'em with her, then you'd have something.'

'To show the law?'

The clerk ran a finger crossways through his waterfall of a mustache. 'Well . . .'

'What would you do?'

The clerk looked blankly through a window. 'If they did run off with one of my brood, I'd round up ever Salser with a trigger finger and ride out.'

Ted closed his eyes. 'I don't have folks like that.'

The big clerk's voice grew low and mean. 'We'd chase 'em in that big house and set fire to it. When they run out smokin' we'd knock 'em down like deer before dogs.' He kept scanning the dull woods, and Ted knew he saw no longleaf pine, no honeysuckle, no swamp iris, just visions of killing, legends of hate passed down from poor, shot-up, unread forebears.

Two hours later, the undersized locomotive poked out of the woods at Harriston. The baggage clerk opened the door on the other side of the car and his counterpart from the northbound was there to help with the stretcher. They loaded him onto a larger baggage coach and set him down on a well-swept floor between a safe and an upright piano. The new baggage clerk was used to handling the poor sick as freight and gave him a shallow pan in which to urinate, then bent to check the tag on his ankle. 'We telegraphed ahead for an ambulance at Memphis.' He was a slight man with wrinkles running across his forehead like threads on a pipe. 'I got some aspirin. They don't let us carry liquor no more, else I'd offer you a shot.'

The thought of aspirin made Ted smile. 'You have four of them?'

The baggage man got an enamel dipper of water scooped out of a canvas bucket and handed over the pills. 'You get in a real good poker game?'

'Can you check the back of my neck? It feels like hamburger.'

He got down on his knees and adjusted his glasses. 'Well, I haven't seen a bandage job like that since I fought in Cuba.'

He gently examined the wound, and Ted wondered if he might have become a doctor had he been born in a more civilized part of the country. 'You got a knot and a cut on top of that, but nothing they can't fix at the hospital.'

'Thank you.'

'That hand's busted up pretty good. Want me to look at it?'

'No. It hurts just to think about touching it.'

'When you get hurt?'

'Yesterday. Some time ago. I don't know.' The train was taking the well-tamped high iron at seventy, and the car's springs imparted a jouncing thrust to the world around him.

'We don't carry many emergency cases, but there's been times when somebody fell out a tree and waited a week to get to the hospital and have bones set.'

'That makes me feel better,' Ted told him.

The baggage clerk looked surprised. 'Well, I'll let you get some shut-eye. Can I bring you anything right now?'

Ted swallowed slowly. 'I have a question.' It was hard to get the words up the elevator of his throat.

'What say?' The man bent at the waist and leaned a hairy ear close.

'You think I should go back after the man who did this to me?'

The clerk scanned him theatrically, head to toe. 'Sure enough,' he said. 'If you want him to finish the job.'

The train began to rock him to sleep, and ahead he heard the engine's whistle singing up and down the scale a frantic and operatic warning. Ted imagined that some dunderhead was trying to get his loaded wagon across the tracks half a mile away, a farmer willing his mules to beat a speeding locomotive, as if his pitiful will alone were enough to accomplish anything.

16

The pilots fought the tricky channels around Greenville and after the day's last trip told the captain they were too tired for a night trip toward Memphis, so the boat laid over. The rest of the crew was worn down as well, and it was late morning before the *Ambassador* turned out from the landing.

The captain came in and found the three mates at the same table and completed the foursome. He put his cap next to the salt shaker and wagged his head. 'You gentlemen get the news?'

Aaron Swaneli stopped buttering his toast. 'What kind of news?'

'The advance man sent me a wire. There's money to be made this trip between here and Memphis.'

Charlie put down his coffee cup. 'Not Bung City.'

The captain put up his hands. 'I know, I know. It's sawmillers and creosote workers, but that's a spending town.'

'It's a gravestone-and-crutch kind of town,' Aaron said. 'I don't think it has electricity.'

'We'll put Sam at the stage plank with the three baskets.'

'Three baskets?' Sam cocked an eye at the captain. Every day brought surprises.

'One for pistols, one for knives, one for blackjacks and things like that. All the dance boats do it at rough towns.' The captain replaced his hat. 'Charlie and Aaron, check with me later today. I've got some new pocket slapjacks that can knock down a horse.'

Sam laid his napkin on his empty plate. 'I never heard of Bung City.'

Charlie looked out at a steamboat passing on the starboard side. 'Shit. How're those hillbillies going to take to a colored band?'

'They won't see 'em,' the captain said.

'How's that?'

'I told them to stay in their bunk room down on the main deck. The white band can play such junk as the Bung City folks want to hear. "Turkey in the Straw," "The Letter Edged in Black."'

'How'm I going to watch the plank and play piano both?'

The captain stood and began walking backwards to the door. 'Fred Marble is kind of light, so we'll unscrew the bulb over the piano and he'll wear a little ladies' face powder.'

Sam shook his head gravely. 'What's he think about this?'

'Hell, he thought it up. It's costing me an extra fiver for his trouble.'

'I could play that junk.'

'Son, he can play it better.'

The boat made slow time up to Bung City. The poor coal made a floury smoke, and flaky cinders rained from the stacks like infernal sleet. The cabin boys swept the decks and wiped down the chairs every thirty minutes, beginning at the forward rail, walking toward the stern, and then starting over. The dance trip was scheduled for eight-thirty and the *Ambassador* approached the bank at half past seven, the calliope blasting 'Dixie' to announce to the stragglers in the hills that the boat's advance man and his thousand nailed-up flimsies had not lied. Sam came out of his cabin when he heard the landing whistle and saw a big sawmill rack yard and a water-tank factory. In between the businesses, a single unpaved street led down to the river and was jammed with people, their faces lit by kerosene streetlamps. A few men by the waterside were carrying torches, their shadows writhing on the yellow mud, the smoky glow held above their heads reminders of the first flaming knots thrust aloft by cave dwellers living hard by a lightning strike. Mrs Benton nosed the bow up against the bank, the *Ambassador*'s old broad hull sliding over a mudflat, and Sam started down.

The stage plank set, two deckhands brought down a long table and three deep baskets. Sam followed and announced to the crowd that weapons had to be turned in, and could be retrieved at the end of the excursion, that anyone caught armed on board would be put in the boat's jail until landing. A deckhand set up a carefully painted sign announcing the weapons policy, and Bit Benton, the engineer, six-four and built like an oil drum, stood next to Sam. 'I'm just out here for show,' he said, his mustache following the contours of a frown. 'I wouldn't waste my time tangling with these jugheads. Some of 'em would kill you for a nickel.'

Sam stood next to the table and Bit crossed to the other side of the stage, staring at the men who began to move past. The third fellow in line was with an emaciated woman dressed in a homemade frock. She elbowed him sharply and he tossed a huge buck knife into the second basket without a word and walked on toward the ticket window. Ten passengers later, a hulking, stoop-shouldered man wearing a rain-drooped felt hat pulled a .32 revolver from behind his vest and put it in the first basket, read the sign, then dropped a blackjack in the third. A woman in an outdated red dress opened her pocketbook and fished out a .25 Colt automatic, and then there was a quiet run of fifty people before Bit Benton reached out into the stream of passengers and lifted a man's coat.

'You could leave us the pig sticker.'

The man pulled a Bowie knife with an eight-inch blade from his belt and threw it, pinning the second basket to the table. 'Hit better be thar when I git back.'

Sam took a set of brass knuckles from a tubercular man who could have been twenty years old or forty. His jeans were belted with sash cord and the woman at his side was barefoot. As the crowd filed by, he noticed that the night's passengers were dressed ten years out of date; some of the men wore derbys or cheap felt planter's hats or moth-drilled Stetsons. The women wore a little of everything, but mostly long, broad-paneled serge skirts and brocaded blouses. Some of their hats were enormous dyed-straw disks garlanded with screaming cloth flowers, and a few wore old tiered crinoline dresses with petticoats. Men wore no coats, just suspenders over checked shirts choked with polka-dot four-in-hand ties. One grim, toothless fellow turned over a pitted Scofield revolver, a weighty relic that in its time had probably dispatched Indians to the next world. When fifteen hundred riders had been loaded, the baskets were nearly topped off with skinning knives, big barlows, and three-dollar mail-order pistols.

A barefoot child stepped up to the table, a telegram pinched between two greasy fingers. 'Your name Sam?' He made a simian motion toward him with the back of his hand.

'That's me.'

'This here telegraph's fer ye.'

Sam looked at the boy's eroded fireman's cap and string suspenders, then up the street that snaked along a dark hill. 'Where's a telegram come from in this place?'

'Hit's a railroad station three mile yonder,' the boy said.

Sam took the paper, saw that it was from the station agent in Greenville, and felt the blood flush up the back of his neck.

'Some folks gimme a pennyertwo for my trouble.' The boy put one galled foot on top the other.

Sam dug in his pocket and found only lint. He turned to the engineer. 'Can you loan me a nickel?'

Bit frowned. 'We ain't exactly long-lost friends.'

'Damn it, don't you know where I live?'

The engineer pulled from his pants a change purse much like one an old lady would carry and fished out a nickel, giving it straight to the child.

By eight-fifteen only a few stragglers were coming on board. Sam and Charlie Duggs took the weapons to a locker between the boilers and the engine room and padlocked the door. In the transverse gangway between the main-deck lounge and the boilers, eight dime and nickel slot machines had been set out on stands, and the gamblers had already found them. Sam stopped here under a hanging light and read the telegram. SIX MILES

NORTHWEST OF BUNG ON FERRY ROAD MAN NAME SMALLY PROCURED SHORTHAIRED CHILD. OVERHEARD TURPENTINE BUYER IN WAITING ROOM. ADVISE OUTCOME. MORRIS. He imagined the overweight agent engaged in his newfound art of purposeful listening, turning an ear toward his customers, concentrating between the clacks of his telegraph for hints that might bring someone rescue. When Sam first laid eyes on Morris Hightower at the station in Greenville, he didn't judge compassion to be his long suit, so the surprise of the telegram wasn't the message as much as who sent it.

A backing gong struck in the engine room, the whistle roared out into the dark, its echo returning from the western hill, and the paddlewheel drew the *Ambassador* into the night-wide river. He heard a shout and ran toward a pushing match in the main-deck lounge, where two men were already arguing over a chair. Both of them reeked of creosote and a bilious home brew akin to the essence of mildewed rag. 'Hold on, damn it!' Sam yelled at the larger one. 'We've got two hundred extra chairs down here. How many do you need to keep from killing one another?'

The smaller man spat on the deck. 'Git him three 'cause he's fixin' to be laid out.'

Sam grabbed the larger man by the shirt front and banged him into a bulkhead. 'You calm down and enjoy the ride or I'll set you afloat in a skiff.' He waved over a waiter. 'Give them some free ice to cool down on. And a chair.' For five minutes he watched their bad nature recede and then pulled himself up to the next deck, where the orchestra was banging out a twenty-year-old one-step, sounding like a park band playing in a gingerbread stand. No one in the crowd seemed to know how to dance, or they hadn't drunk enough yet, so he climbed up to the hurricane deck and watched out for smokers. He saw the captain and went up to him at the restaurant entrance. 'When are we pulling out for Memphis tomorrow?'

'We're running a one o'clock here for just about every church on both sides of the river.'

'Can I lay out again?'

'Boy, you're off as much as you're on, ain't you? Is it about Lily?'

He nodded. 'I've got to go up the country a little ways.'

'All right. How much trouble can a church trip be anyway? But look sharp tonight. These folks are drinking paint stripper.' The captain moved off among the passengers, clapping men on the back, telling everybody to have a good time, buy extra sandwiches, not to forget the slot machines by the boiler room. Sam had heard he was part-owner of the boat and presided over the avalanche of money that went out daily for fuel, ice, supplies, and wages. After everyone else had collapsed in their bunks at night, the captain stayed up working with the purser, adding up a thousand figures to budget for the next trip.

By ten o'clock Mrs Benton had worked the boat into the slack water behind Chicken Neck Island and held her there on a half-bell to save coal. It was then the belt on the engine-room generator broke and all lights went dark. In five minutes the waiters were pulling lanterns from lockers and hanging them on the gingerbread braces above the dance floor and anywhere else light was needed. The band kept playing, sounding even worse in the dark, snoring along with a waltz while Sam walked the slick floor. Most customers were sitting and generally hollering at each other to overwhelm the piano and trombones. Sam wasn't sure what everybody was drinking, but it all came from the same pint bottles and probably from the same moonshiner tending his fires far back in the hills. He wondered if anyone would sell him a jar. After a while, the lanterns heated up and began to smoke. Throughout the evening the music waned in the sooty light, and the smudged and toothless people seemed less and less happy.

He went out on deck and stood behind the ship's big bell, trying to clear the bad playing from his head. The Mississippi side was bereft of light, the bank a dark intimation of trees. On the Arkansas side, a place he'd never been, he saw the faint rectangle of one window on a ridge, and he wondered if whoever lived behind that glass had ever heard of the people who had killed his family. The few shards of information he'd learned suggested the murderers were from Arkansas. He might be close to where they were, and he studied the black ghosts of the far rises to the west. It had been twenty-six years. Where were the killers, each of them? Did they ever think about what they'd done, about the effects of their revenge? For a moment, he felt sorry for himself, but only for a moment, because if being raised in the presence of lost parents and siblings had taught him anything at all, it was not to look back, that the view was unthinkable. And as Linda had told him time and time again, what good would brooding do?

He walked across the dance floor and saw two groups of men pointing fingers and complaining loudly that the band didn't know how to play any reels. Zack Stimson studied his abusers and tentatively began to strum 'Under the Double Eagle.' The band fell in behind him, and nearly a hundred and fifty couples started to dance three hundred different ways. The water-tank-factory workers, mostly in hobnail brogans, tried to form two lines for a clomping Virginia reel, while the creosote workers, many in pressed overalls, were dancing deluded buck-and-wings, clog steps, or lunging polka stomps deadly to their partners' toes. Pinwheeling dancers broke through the Virginia reel lines like crazed mules spinning out of a flaming barn. By the middle of the tune half the dancers were capsized on the floor and a general stomp-and-gouge had broken out. Charlie Duggs, Sam, and Aaron waded in and began pulling scuffed and screaming women out of the fray; then they began shoving apart the fighters and getting knocked around for their trouble. The biggest waiters waded in next, pulling hair and kicking, and the orchestra kept playing, as if trying to remind everyone what they were there for. A little man pulled a knife, and Charlie slapjacked him on the top of his head. Someone knocked down a tin lantern and a big fellow fell on it, crushing open the fuel tank, and women shrieked as he caught fire, then leapt up and ran, a flaming cross flying down the middle of the dance floor. Men stopped fighting to knock him over, everyone suddenly mad to get at him, a flurry of sympathetic hands rolling him like a barrel across the dance floor as he hollered and cursed. A man in overalls dumped a pitcher of water over his length, and suddenly the battle was finished. People from all sides grabbed the smoking man's singed hands in congratulation and hauled him to a chair. Most of his hair was gone, and his face was blacked, but a woman came down from the café with a stick of butter and when a water-tank worker handed him a full glass of whiskey, the victim gave the room a bald-faced grin. Couples re-formed, a few started to dance again, and there was a general search for hats and eyeglasses. Waiters found two brawlers unconscious under the piano and propped them against a bulkhead near four women who were sitting drunk and weeping at their tables. Sam told a waiter to bring them sodas and then surveyed the room, walking from bow to stern scanning the floor for broken glass and dropped cigarettes, wondering how much time was spent in the world protecting people from one another, folks who had no cause to fight, no reason at all.

Charlie examined a tear in his jacket as he walked alongside. 'You know, these ain't bad people. They're just uneducated, unsophisticated, untraveled, immoral, and uncivilized. Plus stupid.'

'It's kind of scary tonight, all right. All these lanterns stink to high heaven.'

'I'm glad for the light, though.'

They heard a single gunshot and stopped at a window to listen. After a half-minute the boat's whistle began a series of short yelps, the fire signal, and both men bolted for the upper deck, making it halfway up the stairs only to be bowled over by an avalanche of people running from a smoky bloom of flame under the roof of the skylight deck. Then another shot went off, and they ran back in and across the dance floor to the starboard stairs. Up top they saw two men facing off with pistols.

Sam pulled a full fire bucket from its rack and yelled at Swaneli, still at the bottom of the stair. 'He shot a lantern and set the damn bunting on fire. Come on.' They rushed at the armed men, considering the gunfight of little importance compared to a fire. The underside of the roof was hung with drooping panels of striped cotton material to give the spindly construction a plush appearance. These had ignited, the flames licking at the thin pine lumber. Cooks and waiters began running up onto the roof hauling fire buckets, flinging their contents and stumbling off for more water. Shortly a line formed with Sam and Charlie at the head, heaving one bucket after another up to the flaming stripes. Swaneli came forward with a fire hose and pulled the lever on the nozzle, soaking nearly everyone on the open deck as he knocked down the fire.

Soon Captain Stewart appeared at the top of the stairs holding a lantern and stared at the blackened roof. 'Now who the hell started this?'

'Those two.' Charlie pointed at the men, who had gone down to the dark outside rail of the lower deck and were looking up at the smoke, still holding their pistols. A waiter came up and pointed out the man on the right as the first to draw and shoot.

The captain passed Sam his lantern and thundered down the steps, and one of the men stumbled backwards. He was dressed in a bibbed cowboy shirt frayed through at the neck. 'Hey, now. Ain't no reason to go crazy,' the man said. 'Ah'll buy you a new fuckin' lantern.'

Even in the dark the captain's face was terrible to see. He jerked both revolvers away and threw them over the rail, then grabbed the man who'd fired his gun. 'Can you swim or are you too drunk?'

The little man was bucktoothed, stubble-faced, and round-headed. 'Ah kin swim faster'n this here garbage tub you the captain of.'

'All right, you undernourished squirrel, start stroking for land.'

Captain Stewart grabbed his triple-stitch shirt with one hand and his crotch with the other and hurled him over the rail into the blackness next to Chicken Neck Island, the only sign of his landing a brief white flash as he broke water.

The captain turned to the customers coming back out on deck, now that the fire was out, and through the wayward tendrils of smoke, he screamed, 'Who's the next son of a bitch wants to swim back to the landing?'

The other man in the gunfight said out loud, 'Old George was just a havin' some fun.'

The captain took a deep breath, then grabbed the man's overall straps and shook him and hollered in his face, 'If your idea of fun is turning a three-hundred-foot pineboard boat into a flaming coffin of fifteen hundred people, then you're a thirty-second-degree asshole and the dumbest donkey turd in Arkansas!'

The electric lights came back up and the man blinked, looked over the rail, and said, 'Who's gonna pay fer my pistol?'

The boat came into the landing at midnight. Though he nursed a bruised forearm and bleeding shins from breaking up three fights late in the cruise, Sam still had to go down to the stage plank and hand back weaponry. Charlie Duggs, who'd had some experience as a medic in the war, spent twenty minutes sewing up a busboy who'd been gouged with a bottle, then came down to help return the last of the knives and blackjacks.

'How's the boy that got cut?' Sam asked.

'I think he'll do fine. Sure thing there wasn't no infection alive in that whiskey bottle.'

'What about the old gal who lost her dress overboard?'

'She's passed out on the Texas deck. The maids'll drag her down directly. Nobody can find her beau. I swear we come back with several less than we went out with.'

Sam handed over a rusty revolver. 'You're tempted to laugh, but if you think about it, none of it's funny.'

Charlie handed the large Bowie back to its grim owner. 'The things you laugh at never are funny. That's why you just got to laugh.'

'I'll think about that.'

'If you figure it out, explain to me what I said.'

17

All night the crews dried the skylight roof with a wood-alcohol wash, then wiped, scraped, and repainted it. They turned on every light and washed soot, cinders, tobacco ash, spit, snot, chili, beer, moonshine, popcorn, and chicken salad off of everything, and either repaired the broken furniture or threw it overboard.

Sam got up for breakfast and sat with August in the restaurant for the morning potatoes and eggs.

The boy looked at Sam's denim shirt and frowned. 'You going somewhere?'

'Just want to check out something onshore. Where's your mother?'

He rolled his eyes. 'In bed with the headache. A woman she was waiting on last night didn't like the food she brought and punched her. Knocked her down.'

'I didn't hear about that.'

'You hear about the man chased the woman through the firing gallery?'

Sam grabbed a hot biscuit and pulled it apart. 'Ah, no.'

'She picked up that hammer we use to bust apart the big coal pieces and laid him out. He was asleep in the coal pile till an hour or so ago. I've never seen such people.'

Sam slathered butter on the steaming biscuit. 'Well, I'm about to meet some more of them.'

The town of Bung City had no automobiles for hire but still supported three liveries. Sam held the reins before a mellow, listing mare and resigned himself to another ride. The animal was long legged and he let her walk up the hill as he read Morris Hightower's telegram again. He put it back in his pants pocket and surveyed the two blocks of gray storefronts faced with cupped pine boards bleeding nail rust. Behind these sat a line of whitewashed houses faded to the color of wood smoke. The street was full of animals, and his mare stepped on a chick, leaving behind a yellow hoofprint in the hot dust. At the edge of town he went into a swaybacked store to ask where Ferry Road was, and the proprietor took ten minutes to make sure Sam wasn't a revenuer, bounty hunter, deputy, or Northerner before he answered.

He found the unmarked turn in the cottonwoods that was the start of Ferry Road and several miles later he saw a shiplap-siding farmhouse in the back of a field of green beans. The man at the store had told him that this was where Biff Smally lived. The thought occurred to him that he might have brought a pistol along. He sat the mare and looked for someone in the field. The place had good wire fences, he'd give him that. The roof was of painted iron and the porch had rails. He turned in at the gate and wished himself luck.

Before he could dismount at the front porch, a woman about thirty years old came out. She wore a sunbonnet and was smoking a pipe. 'You come to bid on our beans, mister?'

'I was looking for Smally.' He saw twin girls around ten years old come out from behind her to stare at him.

'What for?'

He didn't know how to explain and just said, 'It's about the new child.'

The woman let out a puff of smoke. She was not unpleasant looking, what he could see of her. She raised a rawboned hand over her eyes and peered to the west. 'They're off in the barn yonder, loadin' stakes in the dray.' She stepped off the porch, the girls following like ducklings as she walked to the pump.

He touched the animal up and rode to the barn and got down. A man came out and took off his straw hat. 'You come about the beans?'

'I ain't after your beans, Mr Smally. I'm trying to help some folks find their young child that was taken from them, and I heard one showed up here.'

Smally was a young man and fair skinned for a farmer. 'Who told you I brung in a child?'

'A friend in Greenville. I was already in Bung City and decided to see about it.'

Smally threw a thumb over his shoulder. 'Well, this here child wasn't lost from nobody. He come off the orphan train that stopped in town from New York City. You know, they line 'em up on the station platform and you can take your pick.'

'He?'

'Yeah.' He turned to the hayloft and called, 'Jacob.'

A dark-eyed boy who looked about seven stepped tentatively up to the loft gate, his head bristling with a two-inch growth.

'When we got him his scalp was buggy, so we had to shave his head.'

Sam touched his chin. 'I was looking for a little girl,' he said absently. He looked up at the child. 'You doing all right?'

'Yes,' the boy said. 'I have my own clothes.'

'All right, you can start throwin' down those sticks into the dray,' Smally told him. The child backed off into the dark loft. 'Where was this little girl took from?'

Sam told him the story, and the farmer listened to all of it patiently. He motioned for Sam to walk over a few yards by a heart-pine corncrib that might have been sitting there for a hundred years. 'Unless you foolin' me, you look like a good feller and I don't talk to no other kind. My daddy was a peace officer got shot out of the saddle for doin' the right thing. He raised me to not let the bad stuff go on.' He looked behind him and lowered his voice. 'What I'm gettin' to is that I didn't fetch that boy off the orphan train myself. A old boy three mile from here you don't need to know the name of got him off that train some time ago and brought him home like a bought tool and made him chop firewood till doomsday. Beat him when he fell out.' Smally looked right into Sam's eyes. 'At night he'd come get in the bed with the boy and fool with him. His hired man told me that because he saw what was goin' on.' Smally's eyes drew up tight, and wrinkles blossomed around his eye sockets. 'Men in these parts don't mess in each other's business, but we know what's happenin' just the same. Most of us work like a pump handle all our lives, hard and hot work all of it, but we never forget those five years or so when we're kids. When we're looked after, I guess. Not hurt by our elders unless we do somethin' to deserve it.' He looked back to the barn, and Sam thought for a moment that Farmer Smally was about to shed tears. 'When we're little shavers we don't think there's nothin' bad in the world, and nothin' that can make us hurt. If we do get a little pain we kin put our face on our daddy's shirt or momma's dress and it'll go away, sure. I hope that's what it's like again after I die.' He turned back. 'Them that takes that from children are robbin' heaven from earth.'

Sam looked up at the barn loft. 'How'd you get him away?'

'Some of my neighbors paid that man a visit, and I understand he pulled out a shotgun from behind his door.'

'What'd he say?'

'I don't know. He don't say much of nothin', anymore.'

Sam watched a crow light on the edge of the bean field. 'They ran him out of the country?'

'You could say that,' Smally said softly, but in a way that told Sam not to ask further.

He looked over at the rented mare, which was cropping grass by a fence where he'd tied her off. The boy came again to the loft opening and looked out at them. Here was another one with no parents or siblings. 'They just give those kids away like calendars at the drugstore?'

Smally turned and followed his gaze. 'Yep. Some of 'em go to bad folks all right, but Jacob, he's safe now. He'll make a good hand in a few years. He just does chores now. I wouldn't put a little bitty like that in the field.'

'You say your daddy was the law?'

'He was. Dollar a day and all the trouble you'd want in a lifetime on Saturday night.'

Sam took a breath, and the air came in as heavy as mercury. 'When I was a baby, as far as I can tell my whole family was killed by a clan from south Arkansas.'

Smally acted as though he'd heard such news every day. 'Your family must of kilt one of them.'

'I guess.'

'All rode down there together and did everbody in, did they?'

'You ever hear of something like that?'

'More'n I like to. There's no lack of wild clans in this or any other country. There's even whole families that'll give humans in general a sorry name. There's the Kathells and the Blankbulls just to start with. It was Blankbulls killed my daddy.' He shook his head. 'The Luthlows specialized in killin' preachers. But about forty, fifty mile from here's a bunch by the name of Cloat. They're worse than worst.' He spat next to his boot. 'My daddy used to tell me they thought ridin' horseback two hundred miles to kill somebody was like goin' to the state fair. They just lived to get angry. I hadn't thought about 'em in years, but if you wanted to find a murderin' bunch from around this part of the world, I'd start with them Cloats.'

'Do they live near a town?'

'Not hardly.'

'How do people find them?'

Smally gave him a long, baleful look. 'People don't.'

Riding back to the boat, he spotted the railroad station, more of a raw pine booth with a semaphore bolted outside and telegraph wires running in through a gnawed hole. He sent a note to agent Morris Hightower at Greenville: THANKS FOR LEAD. CHILD WAS BOY. KEEP EARS OPEN. THANKS. SAM SIMONEAUX.

The *Ambassador's* calliope started up as he was turning in the horse, and by the time he got to the landing Mr Brandywine was hanging on the roaring whistle. Sam jumped aboard across five feet of muddy water, ran to his cabin for his uniform, and turned out for the one o'clock ride.

He met August coming forward, an alto sax under his arm and a grin on his face. 'The captain said I could play this trip.' He had scrubbed the coal dust out of his hair, and Sam turned him around, wondering how he could get so clean.

'Hey, knock 'em dead, kid. The captain payin' you?'

'I guess not. Experience is like money, he said.'

Sam bit his cheek. 'Well, there might be something to that.'

'I'll have to make up the time I missed in the boiler room, but that's all right.'

'Captain tell you that too, did he?'

'Did you find out anything about Lily or Dad?'

He shook his head. 'I heard about a kid, but it was a boy. You go on and join the band. Keep your ears open. If Mr Gauge has been drinking, he'll be slow an eighth beat or so. Don't get ahead of him and he'll be your friend for life.'

The boy's feet were dancing when Sam waved him off, watching him run, trying to remember the last time he'd felt that excitement boiling in his own feet, so happy at fitting in and doing well that the future seemed to promise just one long, ecstatic performance. He went back into his cabin and found Charlie Duggs's quart of Canadian whiskey, poured a shot into a tall glass and a couple slugs of warm pitcher water on top of that, and took it down like a purge, then had another, rinsed his mouth, and bit a nip of Sen-Sen.

He found the captain walking the restaurant with his hands behind his back, and he went up behind him. 'Hi, Cap.'

'Lucky. Glad you made it back.'

'How'd we do last night?'

The captain leaned toward him. 'Son, we made the money. It was rough going but those chuckleheads had silver in their overalls.'

'You make enough to give August a couple bucks for playing this trip?'

The captain pulled back, then studied the deck as though checking the quality of its varnish. 'He ought to pay me. I'm training him.'

Sam took a breath. 'To do what? Be a slave?'

Captain Stewart let a waiter breeze by. 'I have to watch every nickel, you know that.' He hazarded a glance at Sam's face to see what he thought of this statement, and after a moment threw up his hands. 'Damn it, all right. You're holding me up, but I'll slip him something. Now check out the main-deck lounge.'

Sam gently pinched the captain's left lapel between thumb and forefinger. 'He'll tell me what you gave him.'

'I said all right. You trying to make me feel like a crook?'

They took on a flat of new coal better than the last, and after the sober church excursion the *Ambassador* escaped Bung City running on a full bell upriver toward Memphis. Plowing through the afternoon, the old boat followed the channel in Mrs Benton's brain, working hard through Sunflower Cutoff, then around Island Number Sixty-three, and fighting upbound for Miller's Point. The riverside was all of it a grit-banked lowland of bleached sandbars and willow brakes too flood-prone even for wild animals, land passed over by early explorers and Indians alike, who knew it for the dangerous fen that it was. Meanwhile, the crew waxed the monstrous dance floor and hung new broad-striped material under the skylight roof. At dusk Mrs Benton pulled the whistle ring, letting it slide out of her fingers. Sam heard the short whoop and intercepted the porter bringing up a cup of coffee. He found her in one of her thin, dark dresses, sending a half-speed bell to the engine room and squinting over the breast board to starboard.

'Gonna cross the channel?' he asked.

She didn't turn around. 'Captain demote you?'

'Elsie was just curious about when we'd get into Memphis.'

'Captain Stewart thinks this stretch can be run in jig time, but the water's down a little. Can't take a chance with this old chicken coop.'

He watched her read the water's surface, saw her steer the boat away from lines of ripples. When, after five minutes, she turned to him, he handed her the mug of coffee.

'Y'all hear from Ted?'

'We're hopin' he'll show up next stop.'

'And you didn't hear anything about his little girl?'

He shook his head, and she turned back to the river. 'Maybe Ted's found out something,' he said, desperate for a cheerful statement.

Mrs Benton squinted and pressed a hip against a steering lever. 'It's a terrible thing to lose one of your own. That way, especially.' She took a long swallow of coffee. 'When they pass away from us, we believe they've gone somewhere good, don't you know? But the way little Lily's gone, you hate to think about it.'

He moved up beside her and studied the long shadows arrowing from the west bank. The deep water she was following was in her fingertips, for it all looked the same to him. 'I'm doing the best I can.'

'Are you?'

He met her glance. 'I lost a boychild myself. I kind of know what people go through.'

'Sickness?'

'Yes.'

'I lost two to scarlet fever and one to diphtheria.'

'Good lord, I'm sorry . . .'

She gave him a sharp glance. 'It's not a contest, you know, to see who's got it hardest. Everybody's got it hard. If they don't, they're not alive.' She drained her cup and swung it out to him, hitting him in the chest.

'Were they young?'

'Old enough that every time I walk into a kitchen, they're at the table.' She threw the levers over to cross the river and reached up to pull the whistle cord. 'Dead or alive, they never go away. But if I had a living child out there I couldn't get my hands on, it'd drive me crazy.'

* * *

The boat paddled in to Memphis the next morning in time to board two thousand Masons lined up on the levee for the eleven o'clock ride. As soon as the *Ambassador* bumped the dock, the advance man leapt aboard with bills, a few pieces of mail, and several telegrams, and when Sam came down he saw Elsie standing at the forecastle rail opening a note. Her mouth slowly fell open as he walked up.

'What is it?'

'It's Ted. He's up the hill in the hospital.'

He looked down on a group of rousters struggling to place the balky stage. 'Let's find the captain and lay off the eleven o'clock. You want to take August?'

She began to tear up. 'Oh, I don't think so. We don't know how badly he's hurt.'

They walked up into the city through the hot morning and found the hospital, a broad marble-faced building roamed by smells of ether and alcohol. They found Ted in a small, stuffy room on the fourth floor. He was bruised all over and didn't answer Elsie when she touched his shoulder and said his name. Sam had seen a survivor of a boiler explosion once, and he'd looked like the bandaged form lying crookedly on the thin bed.

Ted didn't even turn his head to speak. 'I've been here since yesterday,' he told them, his voice like a dry hinge. 'They cut on me twice and set the bones in my hand.' He held up a mittenlike bandage with three drain tubes snaking out of it.

Elsie kissed him on the small patch of unbruised skin below his nose. Sam took in the bandages, the casts, the wormlike black rubber tubes. The Skadlocks hadn't seemed the type to hurt a man this badly, but he'd misjudged them.

Ted explained what had happened, as much as he could remember. Looking at a long drain leading into a bottle on the floor, Sam thought of riding again to the Skadlocks' place.

For all of Ted's trouble he had found out nothing. He'd called his relatives in Cincinnati that morning, and as soon as he could travel he would go to his aunt's. The doctors told him his left hand might regain strength, but it would take a year and a long regimen of exercises.

Elsie placed a hand on the bandage covering his forehead. 'August and I, we'll go with you.'

Ted shook his head, and it cost him to do so. 'No. You both need to work and save every penny. I've run up a bill here, and I pay my bills. You know that.' He turned his head again to bring Sam into view. 'I want to talk to you alone for a minute.'

'Ted?' Elsie put a hand on his arm.

'Go on. It'll just take a minute.'

When she closed the door behind her, Ted asked for a drink of water. Sam helped him with the glass straw swinging in the hospital tumbler. 'Lucky, I've been thinking. I have to talk to you about Elsie.'

'What about her?'

'I know you'll keep an eye on her for me, won't you? I mean, she's very good-looking, don't you think so?'

'Hey, I better not answer that one.'

He coughed and Sam helped him take another sip of water. 'Sam, I know you miss your missus, and Elsie will miss me. She'll be lonely.'

Sam placed the glass on a side table. 'You don't have to worry about me.'

'Lucky, she's comfortable around you. She relies on you. I don't want to make you angry about this, but I know how things go sometimes.'

'I told you. You don't need to worry about me.' But as he said this, he knew why Ted was concerned.

'Lucky, you know the way she looks all dressed up.' Ted rolled his eyes upward. 'I know how I'd feel about her if I was some other man. You're not being honest if you tell me you don't find her attractive.'

'Now, look—'

'You don't have to say anything.' He tried to raise his right hand, then realized that arm was in a cast. 'I'm asking you to watch yourself is all. Try to think of her as your sister, I guess. Remember you're a married man.'

'All right.'

'Don't get close to her, Lucky. And for God's sake, if the captain lets her sing with the band, don't watch her.'

'All right.' He knew Ted didn't trust him, and he looked away toward the window.

'Don't get sore. You're helping us with our little girl. I can't tell you how much I appreciate that. You're better at finding than I am. Look at me, busted up like a run-over dog. I won't be able to turn a nickel for a year. You think a woman wants to put up with that?' His eyes began to fill. 'What if they can't fix this hand? I won't be able to work.'

'Those Yankee doctors'll fix it.'

'But if they don't?'

'Just tell her, and she'll help you figure it out.'

'Tell me what?' Elsie swept into the room along with an orderly.

'How to hit a high note,' Sam told her, edging past into the echoing hall.

18

Willa White felt a duty to please her husband any way she could. She hired Vessy, the best cook she could find, and though the girl was coarse and simple, Acy enjoyed her meals. Willa considered herself two or three pounds overweight, so she traveled to the nearest big city to purchase exotic-colored foundation garments with brocaded straps and buckles that camouflaged her lushness and made Acy breathless with the effort of getting them off her in the dark. She wanted to entertain her husband with bright talk, so she subscribed to many magazines that digested the world's complexities for her. Acy liked a dustless and orderly house, so she hired an excellent maid, the daughter of a woman that worked for the Calhoun family. The one thing she couldn't supply Acy with was a child.

Usually Willa took a drink of wine after lunch and supper, along with an olive-colored pill the druggist, her first cousin, had given her. It was a cure for opium addiction in the old days, he explained, and would merely calm her nerves. She took another drink or two about eight o'clock, then another at bedtime, a whiskey, for her digestion.

One night around two o'clock she heard a sound like a mosquito whining in her ear and sat up, dizzy, to realize it was her Madeline crying in the next bedroom.

She sat in a brocaded chair next to the child and could see in the glow of the night-light that she was sweaty under the fine sheets and coverlet. 'Here, honey, let's get all this off of you. It's okay to sleep just under a sheet when it's warm.'

'Where's my mommy and Gussie?' the child cried, her voice sleepy and thick.

'You're just confused, Madeline. Your family got sick and passed away, remember?'

'No, they didn't.'

'You were in the orphanage just one day when we picked you out to be our own little girl, precious.' She leaned over and began to stroke the girl's hair. 'I saw right away you were talented and pretty, not like those dirty, snotty children. Oh, you could sing like a bird.'

'My mommy taught me songs.'

'Well . . .' Willa straightened her back. 'Didn't I hire a trained musician to teach you better ones? He cost lots and lots of money, Madeline.'

'He didn't like the song I sang for him.'

Willa looked toward the window and frowned. '"Cleopatra" is a nasty New York song from one of those tawdry revues.'

The child began to whimper. 'Vessy said she liked it.'

'Vessy is an uneducated servant who barely knows how to wear shoes. She probably sleeps with hound dogs back in the woods.'

'I like her,' the girl said.

'Bless you, there's not a thing you know about how people are. I'll teach you, Madeline, the difference between good and bad people. All you have to do is listen to me and watch me.'

'Can I have a drink of water?'

Willa let out a sigh. 'All right. I probably won't get back to sleep anyway.'

Down in the kitchen she fumbled around in the cabinets for a common tumbler. She started to draw a glass of tepid water from the mop faucet, which still ran to the old rainwater cistern, then remembered Vessy saying the water had things in it. What things? She would have to ask. She remembered the girl's hot face and chipped a little ice for the glass and drew water from the city tap. What a bother it was to raise a child! But as she stood in the dark hall outside the girl's door, holding the sweating glass, she felt somehow ennobled. The child sat up in the dim room, barely visible.

'Can I have the water?'

'Can I have the water, what?' Her heart nearly stopped beating with the expectation of her answer.

'Can I have the water, lady?'

The *Ambassador* stayed several days in Memphis. No big excursion boats had come to town for months, and the men's lodges, church groups, trade unions, and general crowds kept the steamer running three outings a day at full capacity. The passengers on the night trips were mostly couples, very well dressed, fairly good dancers out for a civilized time, and the crew was able to relax.

Ted Weller, when he could walk on crutches, decided it was time to travel to Cincinnati to another hospital. After Elsie and August said their goodbyes before rushing off for a two o'clock excursion, Sam helped him into a cab and rode with him to the station, bought his ticket, and handled his trunk. He sat a long time next to him on a bench and waited for the train, noting the hurt in Ted's face and wondering if surgery could put the rhythmic lightning back in his fingers.

'God, Lucky, I feel awful. This whole left arm is throbbing.'

'You feel too bad to travel, we can catch a hack back to the hospital.'

Ted took a long breath. 'No. I'll be all right once I get on board.'

Sam reached over and stuffed the long ticket into Ted's inside coat pocket. 'I'll watch out for August.'

He moved and his face showed a bolt of pain. 'What do you think about Lily? That maybe we've lost her for good?'

'You can't think like that. We can find her if we believe we can. Maybe that sounds dumb, but if you expect something to happen, sometimes it does. Kind of like my piano playing.'

'Stop, it hurts too much to laugh.'

Sam put his hands together and hung them between his knees. 'I'll keep looking.'

Ted turned slowly toward him, bones popping in his back. 'I expect it of you.'

Between trips Sam stayed busy and spoke to the police sergeants, showed a picture of Lily around at the various precincts, journeyed to the city's rail stations, and spoke with telegraphers, telling everyone that he'd pay for the telegram if they learned anything that might be useful. Twice he called home and spoke with Linda, telling her how much he'd missed her, asking if any messages for him had come to their house. She seemed to sense a sadness about him that he himself was unaware of, and she was overly cheerful, unlike her usual steady self. She told him she was glad to get the money he'd wired her, that she was eating so much good food she was getting fat. Though he knew this was a lie, it delighted him.

The night before the boat was to pull out, he was leaning against the starboard smokestack ignoring the heat running up his back when Captain Stewart came down from the pilothouse and handed him two revolvers.

'What's this?'

'Two new Smiths I got in town. Give one to Duggs. We're playing Stovepipe Bend tomorrow, and I want you to wear them in your waistband out on the stage.'

'Same setup as Bung City?'

The captain shook his head. 'Bung City's like a Sunday school compared to this place. Watch out. These things are loaded.'

He found Charlie in his bunk, suffering from a dizzy headache, and he tossed a revolver onto his stomach. 'What's Stovepipe Bend?'

'The advance man told me, but I didn't believe it.' He put a forearm over his eyes. 'Oh, it's just a bad place, Sam. We'll live through it.'

'You got a sick headache or the alcohol flu?'

Charlie gave him a look. His eyes looked like a copper sunset, and Sam reached over and felt his forehead. 'Oh, I'm all right.'

'You got a little fever there.'

'It's just being tired. My back hurts from wrestling those slot machines on the late-night run.' He closed his eyes. 'Just let me be, and I'll get up or I won't.'

Sam removed the revolver from Charlie's bunk. 'I'll put this on the washstand so you don't roll over on it and shoot us both.'

'Obliged.'

Sam looked at the shiny revolver, a .38 Special with checkered walnut grips. 'You ever shoot anybody?'

'You tryin' to be funny?'

At once he realized his mistake. 'Sorry. I forgot you really were in the war.'

'Yeah, really,' Charlie groaned.

The boat backed out and would steam north all day through empty territory. Between Memphis and Cairo only a few small towns withered on the bank and between them was uninhabited shoreline, short hills, slick and panther-haunted lowlands, sandbars, and willows – a gravelscape fit for nothing but avoidance. Mr Brandywine told him stories of outlaws still living in the unpoliced backwaters, some making whiskey in factory quantities, of revenuers who went in but never came out. Swaneli told him of one Arkansas lawman's skeleton found shackled to a drift log, pulled out at Vicksburg.

As he turned in, Sam listened to the engines' escape stacks sending big gasps up into the night sky. The engineers were using steam full-stroke to make good time, and he knew the firemen were suffering for it as they fought to keep pressure up. He wondered if August was holding his own, if the more experienced firemen were helping him out. He was a child, really, and had no business being down there in the heat and soot and leaking pipes. When Sam was a boy he'd worked all day digging potatoes with the sun rolling around on his back like a hot rock, but he'd been stronger than August. Thinking about it, he was glad to leave a place where he had to get up in the sleeting December dark to cut sugarcane all day wearing only a thin shirt, eating only a cold sweet potato in a tin cup for lunch. He smiled in his bunk as he thought of getting away from Uncle Claude's farm. He smiled again when he remembered Krine's department store, the broad aisles, the glowing salesgirls in their stylish dresses, Maurice playing waltzes on the mezzanine pipe organ.

The boat labored under a hot, empty sky, Mr Brandywine at the wheel except when he sent for Nellie Benton to run the disorienting crossing at Poker Point. The busboys cleaned up from the night before and found a drunk in a life-jacket hopper. After the man was wide awake, Charlie and Sam put him in a skiff and rowed him to shore at a place called Rowel while the steamer treaded water midriver, sending up restless spirals of coal smoke. When they got back, the captain told them to strip off their shirts and mix buckets of soap and bleach. The whole boat was graying over with soot, and it was time for a washdown. Customers didn't want their summer skirts or shirt cuffs or seersucker pants smudged as soon as they boarded.

Sam was working over the bulkhead outside the engine room when Elsie came by wearing a paint-stained smock.

'Been gambling?' she said.

He thought a moment. 'I get it. I lost my shirt.'

'I thought you were a ghost when I first walked through the door. You better stay out of the sun so you don't burn up.' She seemed almost cheerful, and he guessed she was relieved that Ted was still alive.

'The captain said we're playing a rough town tomorrow. You ever heard of it?'

'No.'

He tossed his brush into the pail of bleach. 'So you didn't stop there on the way down?'

She shook her head, her straight blond bob swimming. 'The advance man nailed up some flyers about the northbound trip and the new boat, but we didn't stop on the down trip. From what a couple of the waitresses say, though, the last thing Stovepipe Bend men are interested in is babies. It's not very civilized.'

He lifted the brush from his pail and continued swiping down soot and mildew. 'The captain gonna hide the black orchestra again?'

She shook her head. 'He said each landing's different. He didn't think a black band would matter at Stovepipe Bend. Captain Stewart knows his towns, I guess. He asked me to sing ten songs, and I told him I didn't really want to because there might be trouble.'

Sam looked at his wall and dropped another flurry of soap flakes into his pail. 'But he offered you good money.'

'Two bucks a song.'

'Man. So you're singing?'

'Practicing all day. Haven't you heard?'

'Been busy.'

'You know, the next big city's Cairo. I've got a feeling about the place. Lily sang in two shows there with lots of women crowding the bandstand.'

'You told me some time ago.' He looked at her. She was a nice woman, pretty and talented, but he could tell by her eyes that she was incomplete. She was lonely. 'You taking good care of yourself?'

'Sure. But when I sing at Stovepipe Bend, I don't know what'll happen. Might be a riot.'

'Show business!'

She laughed at that and picked up her pail, walking past him into the engine room.

The next day he watched the cabin boys and cooks roll out bunting left over from a July Fourth trip and drape it over the rails. The captain told him to pull out all the slot machines and space them around the lower deck. Ten miles out from Stovepipe Bend, the leader of the black orchestra, Fred Marble, came onto the roof, pulled on kid gloves, opened the steam valve wide, and warmed up the calliope with 'I Found a Rose in the Devil's Garden,' the notes screaming out to five miles around. At two o'clock Sam buttoned up his uniform and did a walkaround, spitting on hot cinders on the upper decks. They were to play two moonlight trips, nothing during the day, because this was a fairly new and hard-nosed factory town with no clubs, church groups, or schools that might take a day trip. When Nellie Benton pulled a short rasp from the whistle, Sam headed up.

She was leaning on a steering lever ringing a slow bell when he tapped on the door, and she waved him in. 'Lucky, go down and tell Bit not to let idlers hang around in the engine room tonight. I understand this is a squirrelly bunch we'll have on board.'

'I been warned.'

'Watch yourself, son. You're a good fellow, and the Wellers need you.'

'Well, I survived Bung City.'

'Stovepipe Bend might be more of a challenge.' Suddenly a little tugboat slid out past the point of an island right ahead and stopped in the channel as if its pilot were unsure which side of the *Ambassador* to pass, and Mrs Benton pulled the whistle valve wide open, the big glass panes of the wheelhouse vibrating like harmonica reeds.

Late in the day the boat slid around a muddy bend, and there on the west bank rose a long series of iron smokestacks like spines on a poisonous caterpillar, little coal-burning factories spewing smoke and unworldly smells into the damp afternoon. The river-bank was without vegetation except for balding willows dying behind the mudflats. A gravel slope two hundred feet long served as the landing. Sam watched a smelter spew orange smoke; at the river's edge, discharge pipes from a creosote plant pushed out gouts of ebony foam. A cottonseed-oil mill, a broom factory, and the Gettum Rat Poison plant huddled behind the levee. Painted on the water tower above the last factory was a giant rodent writhing on its back. Tiers of company shacks, each like the other, sweltered up the naked hill toward where somewhat better houses with broad sagging porches were skylighted on the ridge.

Sam couldn't see a proper street, but down the cinder-strewn trails streamed men and women drawn by the squalling calliope. The black orchestra was on the foredeck playing a jacked-up version of 'Ain't We Got Fun' as Mrs Benton eased the *Ambassador* against the landing and the deckhands lassoed two cypress stumps. The captain mounted the little flying bridge on the hurricane deck and through a large megaphone announced the schedule for the next two nights. Sam scanned the crowd, the mismatched boots, patched overalls, chemical-slathered aprons, and flour-sack dresses that made Stovepipe Bend seem more beyond the news than Bung City. It looked to be a town where there would be child thieves or any other kind of criminal in abundance. He noted the square yellow flyers stapled by the advance man to every fence and porch post and imagined they were tacked up in the poor neighborhood above the factories as well, and even out along the mud road coming into town that threaded through the hookworm-haunted farms of the region. He hoped the milling workers would go home and wash before the first evening trip, which cast off at seven. Hundreds of men stood around with their thumbs under their overalls straps staring at the only white thing in their smudged hamlet. The women were dressed mostly in old shirtwaists and long full skirts, though some wore washed-out housedresses and no shoes. One woman came out of the back door of an abattoir wearing a blood-soaked jacket, stopped dead, and stared at the *Ambassador,* her open mouth a toothless hole.

By six Sam and Charlie were standing by the gangplank, pistols in belt, asking each patron if he or she carried any weapons, and for a while only pocket knives dropped into the baskets. But then gaggles of younger couples began to show up, some men in reblued overalls or their fathers' patched suit coats, and then straight razors and dollar pistols began to weigh down the long table. Skiffs from the hamlet of Yunt, a cluster of crooked smokestacks across the river, started to land and tie up, each boat bearing four or five contrary, hollering folks dressed in gay, cheap clothes.

The first of these that Sam stopped pulled back his arm when asked if he had any weapons. 'Yeah, what's it to you?' He was drunk and sweating and his straw boater was cracked in two places already.

'You can't board with a weapon. Hand it over, whatever you got, and we'll give it back after the trip.'

'Hell, they's five or six on that boat want to kill me. I need my little six-gun.'

Sam grabbed his lapel. 'We've taken everybody's weapons, sport. You'll be safe as in church.'

The man frowned. 'If I went in a church the place would prob'ly ketch on far.'

Charlie Duggs slipped up behind and slid a hand into the man's pants pocket, fishing out a Colt with the barrel hacksawed off. He tossed it to Sam. 'Here you go.'

'Hey!' The man lurched for his gun.

'Aw, go on and have a good time.' Charlie gave him a shove up the stage. 'When you get off we'll let you kill as many jugheads as you want.'

The man continued to holler, but the crowd pushed up against him and he floated toward the ticket window. 'My name's Buxton, and I better get the same gun when I come back,' he called.

The second engineer was helping them look for weapons, but they could only do a patchy job of it, checking the customers with coats or lumpy pockets. The people were wrinkled, sunburned, generally thin, coal stained, thick voiced, and bent, a hard-used population with limps, eye patches, bad breath, casts in the eye, crooked teeth or none, missing fingers. Sam looked at the smoke-stacks of the town, now just giving off mild waves of residual stench, and knew that most of the workers had some money but nowhere at all to waste it, until now. He turned and spotted the captain surveying the crowd from high up on the Texas roof. He was smiling.

Several other skiffs landed ahead of the *Ambassador* and tied off to anything that would hold them. One carried a single man wearing a dark coat and an old-fashioned shirt without a collar. He mixed in with the crowd and gravitated toward the stage like a dark spirit, seemingly carried not by his legs but by the motion of others. Sam didn't study him, but at some point while counting, touching, and questioning the crowd, he felt a lull, an absence of light, something that connected him to the worst possible world. He took a blackjack from a man and turned to receive, without having asked for it, an antique throwing dagger with an ebony handle and a carbon-steel blade, a knife invisible in the dark. Its owner was the lone skiffman, and when Sam looked at his face he felt each bone in his spine line straight up.

It was Ralph Skadlock, who said, 'I come to talk to you, Simoneaux,' and then looked behind him. The crowd, which had been pressing up toward the stage, stopped for a moment under his gaze. 'You load these chickens and I'll find you aboard.'

Sam was stunned and could think of nothing to say. He watched the man's dark back as he drifted through the crowd and onto the boat.

At that moment, Charlie and the second engineer began struggling with a large Indian who'd showed up in the heat wearing a long canvas duster under which he'd concealed a sawed-off eight-gauge hammer gun. 'Good God,' Charlie began to shout, 'give us a hand, Lucky – this fellow's stark raving!' They all boarded him like terriers on a mastiff, knocked him down in the mud, threw his gun pinwheeling into the river, and handed him over to a local constable, who broke his nightstick atop the Indian's huge head before he agreed to go along. And when Sam leaned on the table, caught his breath, and scanned the boat, Skadlock was nowhere to be seen.

They cast off fifteen minutes late, the boat wallowing low in the water with over two thousand excursionists walking her decks like so many fire ants inspecting a slice of wedding cake dropped on their mound. A good deal of moonshine was brought on board, and the waiters and busboys were running to keep up with demands for ice and setups. Before the boat hit midriver, a platoon of Yunt men began a bite-and-stomp fight with rivals from Stovepipe Bend that took both slapjacks and pistols to quell.

The captain walked up to the skylight deck to see how the contest ended and called Sam over. 'Lucky, you're bleeding already. Can you handle them? Tell me if you can't, and I'll give the order to head to the bank.'

He thumbed blood from his nose. 'I guess so. Good thing you asked us to pick the iron off 'em.'

'Hang on. Just hang on. They're spending money like water at a whorehouse fire. On the main deck they're fighting over the slot machines already, and I don't think most of these people have ever seen popcorn.'

19

It was a warm night and Mr Brandywine decided to run on a full bell upstream to keep everyone cool. Sam took the exterior staircase down to the first deck to do a walkaround. He passed women whose lips bulged with snuff, but the men were smoking hand-rolled, and he reminded every waiter he saw to step on the dropped butts. Then he climbed to the dance deck.

Up there, the floor was dark and the band was heaving itself into 'Avalon,' Fred Marble leading the way with the big piano. Sam walked up to Charlie Duggs and yelled over the horns, 'You got a feel for the room yet?'

'It was dicey for a couple tunes. It was a good thing the old man had them out playing in the open when we pulled in so nobody was surprised.'

'Good music is good music.'

'That's the ticket. None of these goobers have ever seen a Negro in a suit before, and they were bristling about that, but once the band set everybody's toes a-tappin' all they want to do is dance.'

Sam pointed his chin toward the crowd. 'I guess you could call that dancing.'

'Looks like five hundred couples having a thousand fits.'

'Have you seen a big fellow in a dark coat and white shirt? Sort of a flat-brim cowboy hat?'

'As you sometimes say, "Been busy."'

When the band landed on the last note, half the couples returned to their tables and the rest stood in the windows to dry themselves off. Sam turned his head as a spotlight fired a circle on the bandstand and Elsie stepped into the powdery glow. He remembered Ted's warning about not watching her sing, and in a second he knew why, because now she was neither a worried mother nor a waitress but a smiling blonde in a richly beaded burgundy silk crepe de chine dress, and from her oval collar lined with glistening rosettes to her matching satin high heels, she was the real thing, an expert singer swaying her hips to the intro of the new song she'd taught the band. She leaned into 'Am I Blue?' and the band followed her, leaving out nearly all the wandering jazzy notes and lining up behind her voice, playing to the motion of her swaying dress. The dance floor crowded up for the slow song, but Sam noticed many rough men propped on the window jambs, smoking slowly and just imagining what it would feel like to hold a woman like that. He was surprised at the power she projected into the room, and by how much larger she now was than her real self.

Charlie gave him a nudge. 'She's got it.'

Sam touched his chin. 'She sure does.'

When she finished the song, drawing the first applause of the night, Sam went out to check the upper deck, and as he passed through the door a pair of bearlike hands jerked him into a pocket of darkness next to the port smokestack.

'Where's that damn Dutchman?'

Sam could smell the river on him, and something else: liquor and a scent of angry dog. 'I don't know what you're talking about.'

'That piano player.'

'Ted Weller? You should know. You about killed him.'

Skadlock leaned into a shaft of light, and his face looked like something made out of fieldstone. 'I aim to set him back a bit more. He owes me money.'

'What?'

'He shot my black dog. I thought he'd get better but he got the infection and died on me.'

Sam pulled free and stood away. 'The way I understand it, your dog was trying to eat his hand off at the time.'

Skadlock pulled a glossy automatic pistol out of his jacket and pressed it against Sam's temple. 'You think this is funny? Some kind of joke? Tell me where that man is.'

Sam looked at what he could see of the gun, then back at Skadlock. 'You hurt him so bad they sent him on the train to Cincinnati. He's got to have about five operations to straighten him up.'

Skadlock seemed to realize something all at once and his expression took on a blue heat as he pressed him against the stack. 'You the dumb shit what tole him where we was.' He began to curse and ramble, and Sam wondered what he'd been drinking and for how many days.

'I was just trying to find his little girl,' Sam told him, yelling into his face, but Skadlock didn't seem to care.

'You led him to us. I ought to kill you. I wish they hadn't left you alive down in that shithole town so you could come back to haunt us.'

The statement was like a jolt of electricity. 'What did you say?'

Skadlock strengthened his grip on the pistol and raised his elbow high. Sam closed his eyes and for an instant started praying, but then there was a bony pop, the kind of noise the blunt side of an ax makes when it kills a steer, and Skadlock hit the deck, slack all at once. Sam looked and saw Charlie pocketing his slapjack.

'Friend of yours?'

He straightened his coat. 'Pick up his pistol and let's get this bastard in the brig before he wakes up.'

'Better hurry. Trouble's a-brewin' below.'

They dragged Skadlock down the stairs, his riding boots banging every step and the people from Stovepipe Bend cheering them on. They'd just clapped him into the engine-room brig when August came back from the firing galley.

'Who's that?'

'Nobody you need to know.' Sam pushed him along roughly and he and Charlie headed to the main-deck lounge, where they found a scuffle between smelter workers and sawmillers from Yunt. When they got among the tables they noticed ten different poker games were going on, and at one of them five men were standing and hollering back and forth.

Charlie spread his coat, showing his pistol. 'What's the beef here?'

A cross-eyed man wearing patched suspenders pulled his cigar. 'This feller checked a bet and I raised and he raised me back.'

'So?'

'That's sandbaggin'. We don't play like that in Stovepipe.'

The man from Yunt put his finger in the first man's face. 'That's how you play the game, chickenshit. That's poker.'

'That's ambushin', you mean, and it would take somebody with sawdust for brains to play like that.'

The other man straightened his back and strutted two steps sideways like a rooster. 'If they hadn't of took my Smith I'd see what was in your fool head. Prob'ly lead sinkers.'

'Aw, sit down and just call dealer's choice if you want to sandbag,' Duggs told him.

'Or what?' the man from Stovepipe Bend demanded, drawing a pearl-handled straight razor from his coat pocket.

Everyone at the table turned toward the sound of a pistol being cocked. Sam had pressed the muzzle of his revolver behind the man's ear. 'Or you'll get a hot pitchfork in your ass in about half a second.'

Charlie took a step away from the table. 'Easy, Sam.'

'Let's have the razor,' Sam said, and the man handed it over his shoulder, his arm the only thing moving at the table. 'We gonna have any more trouble out of you?'

'No,' the man said, but even from the one syllable Sam knew that for the rest of his life he'd better never find himself in Stovepipe Bend past dark.

In ten minutes the area was again filled with hollering and the stink of homegrown tobacco. Sam and Charlie leaned against the capstan, looking back into the lighted area of gamblers and drinkers.

'You scared me for a minute back there.'

'I kind of scared myself. I should've hauled his ass down to the engine room.'

'Well, maybe it was that other fellow got you excited. We all tend to go downhill when someone sticks a pistol in our face. Who the hell was that?'

'One of those Skadlocks I told you about.'

'Half man, half weasel.'

'The weasel part might be right.'

For the next hour they kept in motion on the dance floor, showing their pistols and palming slapjacks. Elsie appeared again and sang 'Leave Me with a Smile,' her sweet alto taming down the room and calming Sam as well. Her voice was a drink of cool water.

Toward the staggering, glass-breaking end of the trip he went back to the engine room and saw Ralph standing above two passed-out drunks, holding on to the bars, staring at all the heaving machinery.

'We'll get to the bank in about ten minutes, and I'll escort you off.'

'Where's my pistol?'

'Part of my salary for a hard night.'

Skadlock's eyes showed several worlds of pain. 'You gonna law me?'

Sam put his hand on one of the bars, tempted to say he wasn't worth the trouble, but that would only make things worse. His uncle had taught him that for some people, hard words were the same as bullets. Finally he shook his head. Then he asked, 'What do you know about the trouble down in Troumal?'

'I was livin' in Arkansas them days.'

'Do you know who did it?'

Skadlock looked away, feeling the lump on the back of his skull. 'Coulda been anybody.'

'You know.'

'Why would I tell you? You couldn't touch 'em, even nowadays.' The big backing gong went off like a detonation above his head, but he didn't flinch.

'How did you know somebody survived?'

'I didn't till you hauled up in our kitchen.'

'Who did it?'

Skadlock stared at the port engine as though he envied its untouchable heat.

Sam cocked his head, imagining what he could say to make Skadlock talk. Finally, he said, 'Maybe I could pay them a visit like I did you.'

At that, Ralph Skadlock's eyes rolled sideways into jaundiced thought. After a long time he said, 'It was Cloats what did it.'

The name went through him like a chill. 'How do I find them?'

'Everbody around Bung City has a opinion.'

'You're just a fountain of information.'

'Go to hell. If I was you I'd grow some eyes in the back of my head.'

Sam heard the engine bells jangle for the landing. 'Who'd you sell that little girl to?'

'The devil.'

'When I find her, I'll do my best to send the law after you. Maybe some federal law.'

'I ain't got her. They can't arrest me for havin' thin air.'

'But I got a feeling you're worse than the ones that do.'

Skadlock looked away as if offended. 'I don't know about that. I ain't the start of your troubles. And I sure as hell didn't deserve no dead dog.'

When the landing whistle began roaring, Sam unlocked the brig and walked him to the stage.

Skadlock pushed out the dent in his hat and settled it back on his head. 'I ain't forgot about that Dutchman.'

'That's your trouble. You don't forget much of anything.'

'Keep a lookout, coonass.' He started down the plank with the rest of the tipsy crowd.

Sam faked a friendly wave. '*Manges la merde,* Skadlock.'

The second moonlight trip was worse. Among the eighteen hundred people dawdling at the landing, two hundred or so had been drinking while they waited. After they frisked the crowd and the boat slid off into the river, the generator failed again. The band kept playing, but after a few minutes a blind volcanic brawl broke out that took half an hour to stop. The mates and several waiters and even the cooks had to wade in to separate the fighters as best they could, and the captain showed up with a megaphone and shouted that there would be no more music if the crowd didn't calm down. The crew brought up the coal-oil lanterns and hung them, and under the smoky yellow aura the band continued playing for the reeling dancers. Sam was still breathing hard when someone called out 'Fire,' and he and the first mate ran to quench a smashed lamp in the men's toilets at the rear of the boat, beating it down with sacks until an oiler coaxed the fire hose alive.

Sam sat down on a stool by a sink, his mouth open, and watched the muddy water knock down the flames. 'Son of a bitch. If that had got away from us this tub would've gone up like a haystack in July.'

'Get up, bud,' Swaneli told him. 'I just heard a gunshot.'

On the first deck several men had started shooting at the ceiling-fan blades, and one had his arm broken by a ricochet. The three mates fought them and then hustled the banged-up men to the brig, stacking them in with five others already there.

The café ran out of food halfway back to the landing, and the cooks began to fill any pot that had a lid with oil and made tubs of popcorn they salted and sold cheaply to staunch the angry hunger of the drunks. The café register was so full of money it wouldn't close, the people wild to buy anything, even extra salt. When Sam stepped through the door he was hit across the chest with a chair, and before he could get up a woman began screaming into his face that her friend was being raped up on the Texas roof. He took the stairs two at a time to a dark open area where passengers were not allowed and saw men in overalls hoist a yowling, half-naked man over their heads and throw him off the boat. Sam looked down and saw a white scissoring motion in the water, headed aft.

A middle-aged woman was sitting on the roof tarpaper adjusting her long skirt. He looked at the skinny man next to him, whose hair was longer than the woman's, and tried to make out his features in the dark. 'If he was raping that woman, you should've held him for the sheriff.'

The man bent over laughing. 'Her? We don't give a shit about her. She's just a old whore he hired to ride with him tonight.'

Sam looked at the other men, trying to understand. 'Why'd you pitch him overboard, then?'

'Hell, we'uns just wanted to see could he fly.'

The men standing at the rail started laughing, coughing up popcorn, punching each other, cursing the whore and the six other men they said they'd thrown off the boat that night.

When they gave back weapons at the end of the trip, two pistols and five knives were left over. He considered the weapons in the glow of the deck lights, and then lobbed everything into the river.

The general cleanup was unending, the boat filthy in every way. During the hour that the restrooms were closed, several people had gone up on the rear promenade and squatted in the dark. Three hours before sunrise, Charlie and Sam climbed shaking into their bunks, and neither could fall asleep.

'I saw you waltz Skadlock off the boat. What was you talking about?'

'He showed up to bother Ted Weller and then got real focused on me. I told you about his dog, didn't I?'

'Yeah. That boy's been in the woods too long.'

'He was drunk.'

'Why didn't you turn him in to the law?'

'He'd maybe just kill that little town constable.'

Charlie seemed to think about this. 'What else did he tell you?'

'He was whelped in Arkansas. He knows who did what they did to my family. Some people named Cloat from around Bung City.'

Charlie leaned out of the lower bunk and looked up at him. 'You don't exactly sound excited about that big news.'

'I'm still thinking about it.'

'Think, hell. Don't you have folks you can round up to go find these people? At least try to tell the law about them. Man alive!'

At once a wave of fatigue swamped Sam. 'Charlie, it's been around twenty-five years. I never knew my parents or brother or sister. Don't have pictures, nothing. Just some wooden markings in the churchyard. My uncle never raised me to be big on revenge, you know? Most French people on the bayou are like that. Too poor to afford a grudge.'

Charlie seemed amazed. 'Well, you're a little pudding if I ever saw one. You don't try to find out about these outlaws, I hate to say this, but I'll be ashamed of you.'

'What? What would you do?'

'What do you think? If I found out for certain they'd killed my folks, I'd go to the sheriff. If he was bought off or scared, I'd dump my bank account and buy as many pump shotguns I could afford and a case of high-brass goose shot.' He began waving his arm toward the low roof. 'I'd get my cousin Buck, who was with me over in France, my brother Maxie, my uncle Dick Agle, who was with Roosevelt in Cuba, and that big Eyetalian who married my sister. We'd wait for asshole-hunting season to open and go find 'em in their nest.'

'With bad luck, you'd all get arrested. With good luck you'd all get shot up. I'm wondering if that's why Skadlock told me, thinking these Cloats'd swat me like a mosquito. And maybe they didn't have anything to do with it at all.'

Charlie rolled on his back. 'Some things you don't worry about.'

'If I did get some kind of revenge, you can bet one of them would get away and show up at my house one night two years down the road, squattin' there in the bushes, a knife between his teeth.'

The cabin was quiet for a long time; then Charlie's voice came out of the darkness, sleepy and yawning. 'I still think you're chickenshit.'

'Maybe after I find the little girl, I'll think about all this. First things first.'

'Chick-en-shit.'

'You think shootin' up a yardful of folks is the right thing to do?'

'Kill a snake, and the next man on the trail won't get bit.'

'Not unless another snake gets him.'

'Boy, I can see you ain't never been shot at.'

Sam put an arm over his eyes and let out a long sigh. 'Not in a good while, anyways.'

The next night drew sizeable crowds again. A logjam of denim-clad sawmillers and their women came over the river from Yunt in skiffs, and the captain hired the local constable and three men he deputized and armed with shotguns to ride and help break up fights. Sam took four aspirin and patrolled constantly, the pistol gleaming in his belt, but generally the crowd was subdued, a fact which didn't improve his opinion of human nature, that it took a show of hardware to teach people how to have a good time. Elsie sang her beautiful songs, August played in the band for both trips, and Sam listened to them as he made his rounds, wishing he were at the piano.

One o'clock in the morning found the *Ambassador* digging river for Cairo as the crew fire-hosed the upper decks of the crowd's sediment. The ship's carpenter began replacing balusters kicked out of the upper railings, and the waiters threw ice on the main deck to chill blood off the wood.

That night, Charlie Duggs carried a pint of his own, and by the time he crowded into the cabin he was fueled up with malevolent energy.

Sitting down on the stool beside the lavatory, he looked up to where Sam lay in his bunk.

'You goin' after the Cloats when we come back downriver? I'll go with you.'

'Been too busy to think about them.' Sam saw only an outline of the man seated across from him.

'If I was you I couldn't think of nothin' else. They killed your whole family, bud.'

'I'm turnin' in.' He was unable to think about anything.

Charlie stood up. 'Think I'll bed down on the Texas roof.' He lurched toward the narrow door. 'The air smells better up there.'

Sam folded an arm over his eyes and tried for sleep. He thought of his uncle and of his aunt, who'd always treated him as their own son. Still, he remembered feeling at times that he was not totally theirs. The cousins were the whole children, and he was loved as much, but still not of the same house, born somewhere else out of someone else. He tried to remember anything, a touch, a flash of light, the timbre of an owning voice, but there was nothing at all. When they had been killed, the part of him that made memory had not yet come alive. Like a sudden foul cloud, what the murderers had done began to envelop him, and he understood with a shudder what they had taken away. He began to cry quietly in the sour bunk, wondering what was wrong with him. Maybe he was changing, approaching the edge of that age where for the first time he would begin to look back on things, and he realized dimly how sad a change that was.

20

Acy White lounged in his parlor listening to the girl sing 'The Letter Edged in Black' in her pure bell tones. Now and then she would end a line with a blue note, and Acy would stop her. 'No. How many times do I have to tell you not to do that? It sounds trashy.' He'd taken to overseeing her practices and even her playtime. He made sure she didn't sing to herself while she dressed her dolls, because inevitably she would come out with something improper – probably, he thought, written by a New York Jew for some lowbrow vaudeville theater.

The girl would listen to Acy's commands because she sensed she had to, obeying him because there was no one else to obey. She was a child with no options. Sometimes she cried, and this was always in some way connected to her mother. Lily had no notion of death and didn't know what to make of this nervous couple who told her five times a day that they were her mother and father. She was a baby, disoriented in a baby's world. But she was smart.

Acy ran a finger along his thin mustache. 'Sing it right, will you?'

'Where's Vessy? I'll sing it to her.'

'Vessy's at her shack.'

'What's a shack?'

'It's a nasty little place where stupid people live.'

The girl came up to him and put a hand on the arm of his chair. 'Is Vessy stupid?'

Acy pulled his watch and frowned at it. 'She's an untrained gal from up in the hills. Her people are dirt poor and we had to train her to wear shoes.'

She looked at him, unblinking. 'Did you give her shoes?'

'What? Why, yes. Otherwise she'd be tracking up the house.'

She walked over to the grand piano and pressed down two notes of an A chord. 'Thank you for giving her shoes.'

He went to her, got down on his knees, and put his face next to hers. 'Look, remember that the last person in the world you want to be like is Vessy. She's bad. Don't forget that Vessy is a bad person and you shouldn't trust her. She's hardly a step above a nigger.'

The girl put a finger in her ear and yawned. Acy stood and looked out the window where Willa was haranguing the gardener next to the cast-iron fence, the old man's head bobbing under the storm of her words.

On the trip up to Cairo, Sam shared a meal with Elsie in the café. He thought about her singing and had to admit that he was a little bit infatuated, though he couldn't reconcile the image of her extraordinary presence in front of the orchestra with the woman seated across from him at the cheap wooden table. She had the buttermilk skin of a healthy midwestern girl, and he admired Ted Weller's luck in matching up with her. August walked in and joined them, looking from one to the other before sitting down tentatively, as if worried he might be interrupting something. A stranger watching them eat and talk and laugh might have mistaken them for a complete family. It was a pleasant meal that Sam would remember for years, probably because it would be the last such meal for a long time.

When the boat tied up at Cairo the dapper advance man was there with the new schedule and an armload of mail. The weather was windy and a rainstorm was building in from the west, so he brought the mail to the central staircase to give it out. Among the envelopes was a telegram he'd been given that morning at the Western Union office, where he was sending precise schedule times upriver. He shuffled the mail and called out names, announcing that the telegram was for Elsie. Sam got a long envelope from New Orleans, a letter from Linda, and sat down on the staircase to read it. She told him the family news, then neighborhood tales, said that she wasn't feeling all that well, that perhaps it was the heat and dampness. She let him know she missed him around the house and complained that she'd had to fix the gas range herself, but he saw that as her way of saying she needed him. The letter was four pages long, and he read it twice. Several crewmen were leaning against bulkheads or seated on coils of rope, reading slowly to make the letters last. He looked around for Elsie and saw her standing by the capstan, the buttermilk color of her face gone gray, the winsome expression missing as if scraped off by a surgeon. When she put her face down into her hands, he walked over.

'Bad news?'

She didn't look up. 'Go find August and bring him to my cabin. Then leave us alone, Lucky.'

He turned toward the rain-stippled water, afraid to look at her. 'Is something wrong with Ted?'

She put down her hands and looked past him, up the stairs toward the dance floor. Her voice was flat and tired. 'He got blood poisoning from the first operation. He died yesterday.'

'God. If there's something—'

'Go get August.'

On the trip back to the boiler galley he thought of how the boy was about to be delivered, with just a few of his mother's words, to the land of adult sorrow. He stopped at the entrance, not wanting to take the next step, but then raised his foot over the sill. August was on a stool in the companionway reading through a smudged arrangement for a De Silva fox-trot.

He looked up and smiled. 'Hey, Lucky. Get a load of these licks.'

Sam felt like a black cloud, drifting close. 'Your mother sent me down to get you. Go on up to your cabin.'

'Sure. Did you hear me play the other night for those hillbillies?'

'You played like a champ.'

August hopped off the stool. 'She got that new music for me in the mail? I saw the advance man on the dock.'

'I don't know.' He pretended to study a steam gauge. 'You'd better get up there quick.'

The boy ran through the furnace room and out into the sun. Sam walked back by the engines to let the Bentons know they'd have to take on another fireman for August's shifts, then climbed to the restaurant and dawdled a few minutes at a table until little Mr Brandywine saw him.

The pilot walked up stiff-legged and slapped a folder of papers against his chest. 'Bring these up to the pilothouse, young man, and lay them out on the liars' bench for me.'

He took the papers and looked at them dumbly. 'What are they?'

'Well, if you have to know, they're the channel reports up to Pittsburgh. Off with you before you forget where you're going and lose them.'

He walked up to the Texas deck, and as he turned for the steps leading to the pilothouse, he passed the cabin that Elsie shared with August, and coming from inside was the thing he most feared hearing: the bawling, incoherent voice that signaled August's fall from childhood into a wild, uncharted, dead-serious place cut off from fathers and all things those fathers teach and give. For a moment Sam stopped and shared the immeasurable and growing loss.

The next day he helped carry their bags up the hill to the streetcar that would bring them to the station. Elsie had drawn their pay and figured they'd have enough to bury Ted and begin installments on his medical bills. Beyond that, she didn't know what they'd do. When the streetcar appeared far down the street, she grabbed his lapel and shook it.

'Lucky, you've got your own life to live. I appreciate what you've done to find Lily, coming along with us and all. But it's not working.' She began to cry. 'She's out there in the world somewhere, but it's too big a place. Just too big.' She put her forehead against his shoulder for a moment. 'If I ever get some money I'll hire someone to look for her. I really don't know what else to do. I don't have a cent. I don't know if I ever will now that he's gone.'

He looked up the long street at the stone and brick buildings, wondering how anyone ever put together the money to build them. No one he knew had more than a few dollars saved. 'I'll ride out this circuit on the boat. It might look like I haven't done much, but I've put out feelers all along.'

'If you hear anything, you have my mother's address in Cincinnati.'

'That's right.' He gave August a pat on the arm. 'So long, bud.'

'Yeah.' The boy stared blankly down the street, his shoulders rolled forward in the wind like an old man's.

The Greenville station agent, Morris Hightower, dozed in his chair next to the telegraph sounder. The room was hot as an attic, the next southbound wasn't due for an hour, and the local switch engine was out in the country switching the lumber mills. He had a headache, and each eyelid felt as if it had a lead sinker glued to it. The sounder came alive in its box, and he reached for a Western Union pad. Dr John Adoue of Memphis sent a message to the husband of Mrs Stacy Higman telling of the outcome of her operation for female problems. He copied several lines of medical descriptions and the statement that Mr Higman would call at the station for the telegram at five p.m. Morris sent a 73 on his bug, folded the telegram, and placed it in a window envelope. Settling back into the bay window of the station, he looked with one eye down the track to the south. He was feeling worthless and burned out in several ways, old, sickly even. Surely there was something he should be doing with his life other than sitting here sweating. Slowly, his head drifted back, his mouth fell open, and his upper plate floated down with a click.

Some time later, two cotton buyers barged into the waiting room complaining to each other about the market, and the bigger one bellied up to the counter. 'Wake up there 'fore you catch a fly.'

Morris lifted one eyelid. 'Do for you?'

'We need tickets to Graysoner, Kentucky.'

'What class?'

'We can stand day coach if there's a parlor car for a good poker game.'

'There is.' He pulled out his guide to see what the connections were past Memphis and told them it would take a while to set up the tickets as they involved three different railroads. While he worked, the men chattered around their cigars about cotton prices and the damned bankers not wanting to loan money on signature anymore. The voices were just noise; some of it went in his ear, some of it didn't. Then one of them mentioned a banker in Graysoner who'd demanded a whole cotton shipment for collateral on a small loan.

'I went to grammar school with Acy. He knew me when I still peed my pants, and when I asked for enough to ship eight thousand bales, just the shipping, mind you, he wanted to put the whole crop subject to duress in a contract.'

'You don't say.'

'Sure enough. And I've been a guest in his house, made small talk with that odd wife of his.'

'I know her. She ever do anything other than walk around and shop?'

'When I was in his office she came in there with a sweet, crop-haired little girl, so I guess he finally put a bun in the oven.'

The other buyer pulled his cigar and looked at the soggy end. 'Well, maybe that'll sweeten his disposition.'

The men stepped out into the sun to look down the line and tell a joke. When they came back into the waiting room, a heat-drunk Morris Hightower was at the window with their tickets, his red face against the bars. 'So Acy has a little girl?'

One of the cotton buyers looked at him and made a face. 'You from Kentucky?'

'Agents know everybody up and down the line. She's not a baby, is she?'

'She's about three years old.'

'Cropped hair, you say?'

'Yes.' The buyer looked at him hard.

'Did they tell you how good she could sing? About all those songs?'

At this, the cotton buyer smiled. 'Why, you do know the Whites!'

Morris Hightower laughed for the first time in a long while. 'It's a small world.'

The crowds at Cairo were moderate in size and well behaved, so the order was not given to check for weapons. After an easy night trip, Sam was washing up at the little lavatory and inspecting his two uniforms, which were not holding up well.

'I told the captain I needed another jacket,' he said over his shoulder to Charlie, who was in his bunk holding an unlit cigarette under his nose.

'What'd he tell you?'

'Said I'd have to buy it out of my salary.'

'What you think about that?'

'I don't know. It'd take two or three days' wages to get one that'd last through the fights.'

'It'd be nine dollars or better, anyway. The boat raked in a fortune at Stovepipe Bend. The purser like to got a hernia haulin' the change bags up the hill this morning.'

'Sometimes I think I'd be making more as a waiter, with the tips and all.'

'You could get into that late-night game down in the galley.'

'I gave that stuff up.'

'Then hold on to your pennies.' The cigarette traveled slowly under his nose. They were not allowed to smoke in the cabins. 'You still thinking about that young'un?'

'I walked into town and spoke with the police captain. Went by the station and talked to the agent. He was full of information but mostly wanted to sell me some raffle tickets.'

'What'd he tell you?'

'About another boy they gave off the orphan train. I called this farmer up on the phone and sure enough it was a boy.'

The cabin door was open, and Charlie hopped down and walked right out to the rail to light up and watch the stars. 'You give any more thought to the Cloats?'

'Not enough to ruin my day.'

'Damn, you're worthless.'

'I'm thinking about it. You got to give me that.'

The *Alice Brown* passed downbound pushing a big raft of coal barges, the glow from her furnace doors sparking up the water. Her carbon-arc light raked the *Ambassador* and moved over the channel like a wand of ice.

'What'd Elsie say when you walked her to the streetcar?'

'Not much. Said she couldn't even imagine he was dead. That she had to hold off thinking until she got up there.'

'I can't believe old Ted's gone myself. It'll be a tough row to hoe for the both of them. The kid's too young to play in the union bands. You say she'll be living with her sick mother?'

'Starving is more like it. Her father's too old to work anymore.'

Charlie drew in a lungful of smoke and let it out slow. 'At least she's got that boy with her. It could be worse.'

'Don't say that. For God's sake, don't even think it.'

Above Cairo the *Ambassador* steamed into more populated regions where people in the civilized river towns looked forward to the new dance music promised by the flyers posted on every cottonwood by the advance man. Radios, the few there were in these rural areas, didn't play New Orleans jazz, and record companies weren't promoting it either. But the *Ambassador* had the real, rare commodity, and over the next week the boat did good business at Mound City, Metropolis, and Paducah, though at a mining town called Potato Landing, all three mates and six waiters were injured in a huge café brawl between baseball teams from opposite sides of the river. The boat was left in such a sorry condition that Sunday's afternoon run at Evansville was canceled, and Captain Stewart gave the crew as much time off as possible. Sam went up to town to attend Mass and then find the railroad station. The agent looked at his bruised face and wouldn't answer any questions, so he walked back to the river, stopping several times to let a leg cramp die down. He'd been kicked by a drunk woman after he'd pulled her away from a slot machine she was hammering with a high heel. Hobbling up to a corner bench, he sat and rubbed his calf, feeling silly and useless, a fool matched with a fool's errand. He thought again longingly of his wife and his lost kingdom at Krine's. A long vista of cottonwoods rising up from the Kentucky side made him feel solitary, small, and a long way from the house.

But when he returned to the boat, the advance man, a vest-wearing glad-hander named Jules, buttonholed him on the stage and handed him a telegram. 'Here you go, bud.'

'Where's it from?'

'Can't you read?' The advance man jumped off the stage to the mud and headed for his idling Model T.

It was from Greenville, Mississippi, and the very paper felt crisp with possibility. He tore it open. THIS A GOOD LEAD. ACY WHITE AND WIFE. GRAYSONER KENTUCKY. LET ME KNOW. MORRIS.

He ran across the forecastle and asked a deckhand if he knew where Graysoner was.

'Don't know, Cap. The chief steward upstairs, maybe he knows.'

He raced up the big staircase and walked back to the restrooms, where he saw the man talking to a janitor. 'Can you tell me where Graysoner is?'

The chief steward looked at his face and winced. 'Rough time last night. Graysoner the new man what replaced that old Jenkins boy with the broke leg?'

'No, it's a town in Kentucky.'

'It's a town.'

'That's right.'

'Go see Mr Check in the kitchen. He's from Kentucky.'

Mr Check, the head cook, was scraping down a stove top with a firebrick. 'Naw, I ain't from Kentucky. I was raised in St Marys,

West Virginia. The steward's thinking of that Meldon feller who cooked for us two years gone. Go ask the captain. Maybe ten minutes ago I saw him kicking cinders off the skylight roof.'

He walked forward, but the captain was nowhere to be seen, so he took the stairs up to the Texas deck and found the first mate in his cabin. Swaneli was propped in his bunk reading a week-old newspaper from Chicago. 'Lucky, what's up?'

'I need to know where Graysoner, Kentucky, is.'

'It's up ahead somewheres.'

'On the river?'

'Or close to it. Ask someone in the pilothouse, if anybody's up there.'

He ducked into the companionway and went up the steps to the Texas roof and saw Mr Brandywine's cap moving about. He tapped on the narrow door and the old man waved him in with one crooked finger. He was leaning down over a river chart.

'Mr Brandywine, can you tell me where Graysoner, Kentucky, is?'

'We'll play there in a few days if I can get this boat in among the rocks.'

Sam leaned back against the door and caught his breath. 'Is it another pigpen?'

'Well, it's not a big town, but there's five little burgs right around it, and all in all it's a decent place to play. The people there know how to behave themselves.'

'Nice place to live?'

Brandywine leaned down over his channel map and pursed his lips, slowly placing a finger on a blue line passing between islands. 'Paved streets. Electric lights. Good stores. Right now you can go down and get me a mug of hot coffee.'

'You heard about Ted Weller.'

'Of course. The captain gave his wife an extra fifty dollars when he paid her off. Told her she could come back and work the end of the season if she wanted. But you know she can't.'

Sam reached over and gathered up two empty mugs. 'Her life's pretty much wrecked.'

'That's a good way to put it, all right. She'll be starting from scratch, I imagine.' Mr Brandywine looked at him sharply. 'Were you sweet on her?'

'I'm a married man.'

'I hope you plan to stay that way.'

He motioned at him with the mugs. 'I'm very happy with my wife.'

'Don't take offense. I've seen you sitting with Mrs Weller at table with her son.'

'And?'

Mr Brandywine's eyes narrowed at some problem on the map. 'And would you please get me my coffee?'

21

The Evansville wharf boat had an excellent telephone connection in a little private room used by freight brokers. Here Sam sat in a chair and called his wife, collect, and after three operators made the links, she picked up the receiver on their candlestick phone in New Orleans.

'Hello?'

'Hey, it's me.'

'Oh, Sam, I'm glad to hear from you. How are you?'

'I'm fine. I'm in Evansville.'

'Where is that?'

'Illinois, right above Kentucky. How are you? Your last letter said you were kind of sick.'

'I've been feeling so bad I had to go to the doctor. It got so I couldn't work for a week.'

He moved closer to the phone and felt a rill of fear run up his arms and across his chest. 'The doctor? Is something wrong? What kind of doctor?'

'Dr Duplessis, the one you go to.'

He felt a pain rise in the pit of his stomach. There was so much bad luck going around, he wondered if he was in for his share. 'Did he give you some medicine? What did he say?'

Her voice was thin but musical, even over the wire. 'He said we're going to have a baby. I feel so stupid because here I thought I was sick all summer and it turns out I'm over three months along. Are you happy?'

'Yes!' He made a punching swing with his left hand. 'I'm more than happy! Do you need me home?'

There was static on the line, and then her voice came back.

'I know you want to look for that little girl and I want you to keep on. I don't want to make you mad, but I've got to tell you that the money you've been sending home isn't quite enough, honey.'

'It isn't?'

'We'll have to get set up here and pay the doctor, you know. The furniture people haven't ordered much of my needlepoint this month.'

'Maybe I can figure something on this end to make a few extra bucks.'

'Sergeant Muscarella called and said the bank on Baronne needs a superintendent of its bank guards there. I think it pays what you're making now, but with no expenses.' There was a brief pause in her voice. 'And you'd be home.'

He told her they could discuss that soon. He wanted to talk for a long time, just to hear her voice, but she reminded him the call was expensive. When he came out of the room he realized he hadn't even told her about the Wellers. He saw Charlie Duggs, and they climbed the hill into town to celebrate with a beer. In the back room of a speakeasy they got into a poker game and Sam lost over three dollars, and later, walking back down into the coal smoke of the dock area, he cursed the jack of hearts that did him in. 'I can't figure what I did wrong,' he complained.

Charlie spat next to the *Ambassador*'s stage as they went up. 'I think it's called playin' poker. Lucky in cards you ain't.'

'Three dollars. Linda could've paid the light bill with that.'

Charlie stopped to set his watch under a deck light. 'Or you could've bought a little Cloat-killing pistol with it.'

In late summer the Ohio River is a hazy green, and Sam watched it slide under the bow of the steamer like an endless watery lawn. After six hard days of day trips for veterans' conventions, Elks lodges, and high schools, night trips for mostly easy crowds intent on practicing their new steps or proposing romance on the dark upper deck, the boat pulled in one morning to the landing at Graysoner. Sam leaned on the Texas deck railing, his bruises driven inside where they banded together and roamed his burning shoulders and lower back. He stared hard at the town, watching it develop out of a fog as Nellie Benton drifted the boat in, and after the docking he hiked up to the main business section, several blocks of well-maintained and amply stocked brick stores fronted by paved streets with curbs and electric streetlights. Water oaks had been planted twenty years before, and the lanes above the business district were shady and lush. Upriver he saw the masonry smokestack bearing the name of a furniture factory, and judging from even the modest houses, everyone here made more money than he did. He was out of the Deep South and could smell the money and comfort.

He left his uniform behind in his cabin and wore his best shirt, which needed ironing and mending at the cuffs. Going into a drugstore, a place with marble counters and waxed-oak display cases, he asked to see a phone book. Sure enough, he found an Acy White at 653 Lilac Street. He grinned in spite of himself.

The woman behind the counter took the book back, and he asked where Lilac Street was.

'Why, it's up the hill three blocks and to the right.' She smiled at him and became a template for the rest of the population, people with something to smile about.

He left the store and began walking through a neighborhood of big, well-kept houses, some of them made of stone inset with transoms of stained glass. It occurred to him that he'd never imagined who had the girl – that is, what kind of people. If he'd had to guess he would've said outlaws, or sick-minded people who wanted a lightning rod for their electrical meanness, or just someone who wanted a kid to train up as a serving girl. As he walked deeper into the fine neighborhood, he realized that Morris Hightower's lead was another fool's errand, that there were no child thieves living in houses like these. People who hired thugs to steal little girls didn't live in fine mansions with copper trim and beveled-glass entries, with sunrooms and carriageways, wrought-iron fences and belvederes.

He reached 653 Lilac Street and stood at the fence, his head cocked up at the three-story Victorian soaring into the Kentucky sky. Seventy-five feet of billiard-table lawn stretched to the marble front steps that led up to the leaded glass door. Another dead end. He would walk back into the business district and find the railroad station and leave his usual plea with the agent. Suddenly a woman who seemed to be in her late twenties opened the front door and put a milk bottle out with a note in it. She was thin and ordinary-looking, but under her brown bangs were a set of intense eyes, and she fixed them on him for a long moment before turning inside. She actually looked at him. Noticed him. And there was connection in that look, as though she might somehow be on the same page as he was. He could have turned and walked back to the boat, but after standing there for a full minute he decided instead to walk to the far corner, and when he arrived there, he saw that an alley ran through the middle of the block, parallel with Lilac Street. He entered it and walked along the rear of the great homes, casually inspecting their garages and wash houses and flower gardens. Behind 653 he stopped alongside a low iron fence and saw a young girl in the yard with short golden hair sticking up at all angles, idly nudging a rubber ball through the grass. Seated on a bench next to a marble birdbath was the woman he'd seen out front. He waved at her and smiled, trying to control himself. He glanced at the girl to see if her face matched the cameo burned into his brain.

'Hi,' he said. 'This your little girl?'

She looked at him as though she suspected he were dim-witted. 'Naw. I just take care of her sometimes. I work for her folks.'

'She looks like a happy little thing.' He wondered what he could say that would keep the conversation going. 'I've got a niece at home looks exactly the same.' Then the child turned toward him, and with a thrill he knew it was her. 'Is she happy, too? Cheerful, I mean.' He fought to steady his voice.

Vessy took out a handkerchief and blew her nose, looking at him with suspicion. 'You not from around here, are you?'

He gave her a laugh. 'No, I'm visiting an army buddy who lives up the hill a bit. I left a prescription at Baumer's and decided to take a walk while they filled it.'

Vessy nodded. 'That druggist is the slowest old man. Rolls them pills one at a time.'

'What's the little girl's name?'

'Madeline. They tell me she's a orphan and as far as her being cheerful is concerned, I don't know. I sure would be if the man who calls himself my daddy was the richest man in town and I had somebody waitin' on me hand and foot, plus a free-spendin' momma and music teachers and all.'

He looked up and down the street and could smell the wealth of the neighborhood. Even the dirt under his thin soles seemed rich.

'She's young to be taking music, isn't she?'

'She can sing like a Victrola, that one. She's liable to perform in a opera house somewheres when she grows up.'

'Nice people, the ones who adopted her, I bet.'

'Sometimes they ain't too nice to me, but that one there, they spend like a princess on her.'

He looked at the girl's yellow dress, at the silk bands running through the hem. Her shoes looked to be new strap-on flats and her barrettes were banded with garnets. Parents who bought her such things would send her to the finest schools and provide for her in a manner he could never imagine. He caught the girl's eye, but her expression was unreadable. To her he was only a stranger in wrinkled clothes. 'She looks like a princess in the making, anyway,' he said at last.

Vessy stood up and grabbed the child's hands, raising her arms straight up and wiggling them. 'Are you a princess yet, sweet thing?' she crooned.

The child looked at him boldly, as if to ask, 'By what authority do you want to change any of this?'

'I better get down to Baumer's,' he said, moving on.

Vessy began to swing the child in a slow circle, chanting 'Sweet thing's a princess,' and the girl giggled brightly. He listened to their playing voices as he walked down the alley.

Sam ate lunch by himself in the café and sleepwalked through the two o'clock trip. That afternoon he lay in his bunk and drank from Charlie Duggs's bottle, wondering what to do, whether or not to rob the girl of a good life and cause her to live in a freezing flat in Cincinnati while her mother scrambled to buy what poor food she could, what cheap clothes, what cheap life. The fact that he had survived well enough without natural parents settled on him. Had they not died, he might have been living barefoot in a muddy cane field in south Louisiana. But he couldn't miss what he never possessed, and he knew that the girl had a better memory of her folks. He squeezed his eyes shut, trying to decide what to do, and in the course of the afternoon he changed his mind a dozen times.

The *Ambassador* cruised that night and Sam watched the people from Ohio and Kentucky behaving themselves, people who seemed to be cut from a different bolt of cloth than he was. He thought he might wire Elsie, even though she would be in the middle of suffering through the awful transition caused by Ted's death. He doubted that the local sheriff would take his word that Lily was abducted, and knew that a stranger would never be believed in this town, not against a man living on Lilac Street. Mostly he worried about what he was taking from Lily. Isn't that what parents wanted most for their children? A better chance at living a prosperous life? Especially a single parent with a teenager to feed and raise, an unemployed single parent who would never in her life have more than ten dollars in her pocket-book at one time.

When the band played 'Home, Sweet Home' and the boat rubbed against the shore at midnight, Sam helped stack tables and started with the sweepdown and kept working, finishing up the Texas and mounting to the roof to go after pigeon droppings and cinders in the dark, sweeping the tarred surface by memory as the big bell banged and the whistle ripped through its departure song, the stars swinging above as the boat turned upriver, its escape pipes sending long breaths of steam up against the night sky. He walked to the stern and leaned on his broom, watching the lights of Graysoner slide backwards on the dark Ohio. Behind him he heard a pilothouse window slide open and Mr Brandywine's nasal question, 'What's wrong, son?'

That word, 'son,' hit the back of his neck like a stone. Any man could be anyone's father, was that it? He turned in the dark. 'I'm just trying to wear out this broom.'

'You can't fool me. I can read you like a book.' The old man was hollering over his shoulder now, stepping on the spokes of the great wheel.

Sam took a swipe at the dark deck and said, under his breath, 'Turn the page, old man.'

After the last cruise at the little town of Aurora, he quit, telling the captain his wife needed him at home. He knew the boat would wind up in Cincinnati, and he couldn't face seeing Elsie or August. After he was paid off, Charlie found him in the cabin, packing.

'Givin' up?'

'I guess so.'

'I know what you'll do. Go after the Cloats.'

'That's not it.'

'But you don't want to say it, so you can tend to things on the sly.'

'You're reading too many of those detective books.'

'Well, if you need a hand, I'm your man.'

He snapped his cardboard suitcase shut and turned away from the bed. 'I appreciate it.' He would let him think what he wanted.

'What about the little girl?'

He shook his head. 'Some things you can't do anything about. Or maybe I'm not the man to do 'em.'

Charlie seemed to consider this. 'Well, you gave it a good shot. Look me up after the season. I'm in the book, as they say.'

He walked out as the calliope began caterwauling up on the roof. He stopped and said goodbye to several people, waiters and mates who'd helped him civilize the crowds. On the first deck he walked back to the engine room to say goodbye to the engineers, who were working the condensate out of the engines, the big piston rods slowly paying in and out. Bit Benton came over and asked him to check on their house in New Orleans, and he told him he would.

Bit took off his gloves and reached out his hand. 'Hate to see you go. You're a good egg.'

He didn't know what to say to that, so he shook hands soberly and walked out the gangway. On the riverbank he turned and watched the two o'clock excursion head out, the black band playing hot and heavy for the high schoolers and their parents, 'I'm Just Wild About Harry' simmering and kicked ragged with a hard downbeat, Old Man Brandywine ringing bells for more speed and blowing the whistle, the *Ambassador* wearing the hymning plume of steam like a feather in its cap. The music pulsed out from under the gingerbread rooflines and sailed above all the scrubbed white paint, the fresh enamel cooking off the hot stacks, the black smoke rising like a sooty prosperity. For a moment he was tempted to join up again after Cincinnati for the few nickels the job paid, for the music and the friends. Then came the thought of Linda and what the next year was going to bring for them, and he became excited about having his own child again, being with Linda in New Orleans, eating good food, getting work that paid, a job where he didn't have to war with drunks and dodge vomit.

He walked to the station and paid his fare south, purchasing his way over various railroads, different trains, boarding the first with a streamer of tickets in hand that would take him away from defeat and toward the rest of his life. And later, the locomotive breathing hard upon the long Kentucky hills under endless spoolings of steam, he dozed against a window, dreaming of nothing at all until the image of the girl's bright face drifted back to him, but diminished now, muted like the glow of a jellyfish dying in silty water.

22

Linda found him skinny and pale. 'Were they starving you on that boat? Not only don't they pay anything, they can't fry you a nice pork chop once in a while?'

'Steamboat food. Flour and grease.' They were looking out the back window at the rain, and he patted her behind. 'But you'll fatten me up.'

'After you get a good job I will.' She enjoyed teasing him, and he was drinking in her attention like a cold glass of water on an August afternoon.

He closed his arms around her. 'You know, *chère,* you look good pregnant. Like peaches and cream.'

'Oh yeah? Want a bite?'

The next morning he entered the office of Crescent Security Division, a company that provided bank guards for the Gulf Coast region. Franco Crapinsano, the manager, was a first cousin of Sergeant Muscarella.

'Ay, Frenchie, I'm glad to see you come down here for the interview. Nice suit.'

'Thanks. Where will you send me to train?'

Franco laughed and put up his feet. 'Lucky, you don't need no trainin'. I can tell you what you need to know in fifteen minutes, tops.'

'I don't know. I've never been a boss before.'

'Look, I been talking to the folks at Krine's. You got brains. You big enough to be, how you say, formidable.' Franco smiled broadly, proud of this word.

'What exactly do I do?'

'You in charge of the twelve-man crews at the Louisiana Bank. You do the schedules, you figure the hours. Nobody's gonna give you no crap because the guards are all over sixty, just making enough to pay their rent and buy enough pork and beans to keep 'em fartin'. I'll tell you in a minute how to handle the Wells Fargo pickups and deliveries, how to proceed when they close the vault. It's a snap.'

'I was wondering if you could tell me the salary.'

'It's four dollars twenty-five cents a day.'

He sat back in the oak chair. 'I made five seventy-five at Krine's and was about to get a raise.'

Franco turned over a hand, palm up. 'You had a good job there at Krine's. We give you the uniforms and a pistol. You can work overtime for the restaurants.'

'I have to carry?'

'Yeah. You'll be out on the floor with the geezers. The gun's chambered for .38 New Police, the short cartridge. Real hard to kill anybody with it. You know, we had troubles a couple years ago about robberies.' Franco gave out a hearty laugh. 'Shot three customers and no robbers.'

'I heard. You had trouble before, too.'

'Whatever. Just remember rule number one. If a robbery happens, everybody shoots. The bank got to feel we're protectin' their money. If they don't, they gonna hire another agency.'

Sam looked at his left shoe. 'The lobby at Louisiana Bank is all marble, as I remember.'

'So?'

'Ricochets.'

'Lucky, these guns is so weak a ricochet won't hurt nobody too much. When we wing a customer, it's just part of the business.'

'I see.'

'If you have a robbery, look at everybody's gun after it's over. If they ain't at least one empty shell in a gun, you fire that man.'

He wanted to walk out, but he wondered what else he could do to make a living. He thought only of drinking smoke all night in a whorehouse lounge or watching his fingers disappear in the midnight clash of railroad couplers down in the freight yards. 'All right,' he said quietly.

'Now, here's what you do when the Wells Fargo wagon pulls up. The pump shotguns are stacked in the vault . . .'

The next day was Sunday and he and Linda went to early Mass. They sat sixteen rows back, and the priest began an incomprehensible sermon about the meaning of the Trinity. Sam started to wonder if he would have to go to confession if he shot someone at work. It then occurred to him that he could be shot himself, and with a better gun than he carried. Would it be immoral to expose himself to this danger? Then he thought of old New Orleans bank guards in general and couldn't name one that had been killed.

After two weeks in the lobby of the Louisiana Bank, he began to get the hang of things. He walked down to Baronne Street to do the paperwork on that branch's crew, then walked back to the main office. The crew he worked with was composed of Mr Almeda, a soft-voiced seventy-year-old Isleño from down in St Bernard Parish; Aren, a fifty-eight-year-old albino gentleman; and sixty-five-year-old twins, Charlie and Jerry Boudreaux. The bank had been held up three times that year, and all of the men had fired their weapons, though only a relief teller had been wounded. Two gilded chandeliers bore bullet holes; there were graze marks along the marble counter facings; and several holes had been puttied up around the mahogany entrance to the lobby. There seemed to be more thugs in town every month, from Chicago or New Jersey, and they needed money to operate, so each year the number of bank robberies in the city had increased.

The job went smoothly. Two men, usually Charlie and Jerry, patrolled the lobby; two others walked the varnished wooden rails of the upper gallery, where the safety deposit boxes were; and Sam sat behind the main counter watching the teller gates and reading. Lately he'd been checking out westerns from the library, staying lost in illusions of gunfights. In the background he heard the chatter of customers, the echoing of high heels as the women stepped across the marble. He had an oak chair and desk almost as tiny as a phone table, and for hours he sat there, shoehorned in beside a water cooler, reading or writing down the arrival of armored-car deliveries and departures or the guards' hours and schedules.

That winter in New Orleans was its usual mild self, but his house was drafty, and during the evenings he worked in the baby's room, painting or tightening up the seal of the windows. He would read to Linda, and she would recount gossip from her side of the family gleaned from telephone calls. Once every two weeks his uncle Claude phoned from west Louisiana and spoke with him for half an hour, mostly in French. Sam pictured him standing next to a crank telephone in Letillier's general store, in the back by the bins filled with dusty mule harnesses and kegs of horse-shoes. The old man usually went through the catalog of cousins, telling what was happening with each of them. Sam would ask about people on the surrounding farms, nodding at the answers.

During one of their calls his uncle said, 'Some time ago, you told me about a little girl you was looking for. You find her?'

He had never lied to his uncle before, and words began to stack up in his throat. 'She's all right.'

'Ah, good. You found her. I bet her parents were some happy.'

'She's all right,' he repeated, with a slightly different inflection.

'Good. Most times, blood belongs with blood. Don't forget that.'

To change the subject, he told him about the Cloats.

There was an astonished silence on the other end of the line. When the old man spoke, he sounded breathless. 'For true? You know where they are?'

'I think I can find out.'

'It been twenty-six years they been suffering.'

'What? I didn't understand what you said.' He thought some wires had crossed somewhere in the connection, that maybe he'd heard a fragment of another conversation on the line.

'It's what the priest says, Sam. Sin is its own punishment. They got to live with what they did.'

He snorted. 'You think they even worry about that?'

'Baby, what they did is who they are. It makes them cripples. Half-people.'

He thought for a long moment. '*Nonc,* do you think I should do something about them?'

At once, his uncle said, '*Mais oui*. Dust you hands together *comme ça – pop pop,* and forget about those people.'

Again he pictured his uncle, pinning the receiver between cheek and shoulder and striking his palms together in sliding, glancing blows. *Pop pop.* 'Not worth the trouble?'

'Not Sam Simoneaux's trouble. Who they are is trouble enough for *them*.'

'I don't know. Maybe I ought to try to bring them a little extra grief.'

'Oho! So now you the grief man, eh? Look, stick to getting rid of a little grief, like you did for that child in France you told me about. Like that little girl you found for her parents.'

He looked at the floor and put a hand on the top of his head. 'Yes.'

'That's a great thing you did. You can look back all you life and say that. What can you look back and say about a killing? Especially one you didn't have to do?'

He looked over at his wife, who was raising the flame in the gas heater. 'I don't know, *nonc*.'

'Yeah. You'll be glad you don't know.'

It was a few days before Christmas. The bank closed for lunch that day, and Sam and the other guards were at an oyster bar down the street. Mr Almeda removed his cap and put it on the table and ran his fingers through his white hair. 'Lucky, I need tomorrow off. My wife, she needs me to help with the holidays. It's a big deal at my house.'

Sam put a dot of hot sauce on a small oyster and sucked it up off the shell. 'Okay, I'll call up Rosenbaum.'

Mr Almeda nodded his gratitude. 'All my kids come over with their kids. You got some kids, right, Lucky?'

'One on the way.'

'Somebody told me you had a little boy.'

He was reaching for another oyster, but his hand paused and then drew back. 'He got a bad fever and died.'

Mr Almeda made a face and pulled his head to the side. 'I didn't know. There's nothing like losin' a kid.'

'I'll call Rosenbaum when we get back.'

Charlie Boudreaux put down his sandwich. 'My brother got drownded swimming off Algiers Point maybe thirty-five years ago, and my old man never got over it. He didn't live two years.'

Jerry, the other twin, never said anything unless asked a direct question and always agreed with what his brother said, perhaps thinking that to add anything would be redundant. But now, he said something. 'The week after he drownded, Mother was ironin' his clothes one afternoon, and when she realized what she was doing, she sat down and stared at the ironin' board like she never seen it before. Then she put her head in her hands and cried for the first time. I remember her sayin', "I used to have a boy in these clothes."'

The waiter came and began banging down ironware cups of coffee on the table. 'Hot stuff,' he called.

Charlie frowned and turned to his brother. 'How come you never told me that?'

'I just now thought of it.'

Sam looked at the old guards. They were trying in their awkward way to tell him something about loss. Maybe they thought he was too young to know how serious it was to lose someone. Maybe they were right, for as time passed, he thought more of his son, how the baby felt when he held him twisting in his hands, twisting away even then. When it happened, he didn't realize what it meant. His son was now more real to him than when he was alive, and this thought made his fingers shake as he lifted the coffee cup. He felt a hand on his back.

'Lucky.' It was Mr Almeda, his gray eyes worried. 'Let's head back. This time of year. It's bad in our line of work.'

'What?'

'Christmas. There's almost always a robbery.'

'At our bank?' He put a hand on his badge.

'Somewhere in town. A branch bank in Gentilly went down yesterday, I heard. There's usually a couple more. Just keep your eyes open.'

A half hour after the bank opened, on a Friday, Sam was reading a novel about a lady piano player in a western saloon. He was in his little space to the rear of the water cooler, behind the tellers' counter at the end. On his desk, a little red light ignited. It was a lens the size of a dime, sitting in a nickeled bezel, and he furrowed his brow, trying to remember what it was for. And then he did. The silent alarm had been tripped. Instead of poking his head out and around the cooler, he looked at a mirror positioned to show the counter. In the reflection he saw all three tellers bailing money from their drawers. Three men, each wearing the same type of soft cap, were bellied up to the cages, and on the counter in front of the nearest teller, an older woman named Irene, he could see a crumpled note. He put down the novel and tried to think, but only the hum of instinct was buzzing through his nerves. He wasn't wearing his cap or uniform coat, so if he stood up with a bunch of papers in his hand they might just think he's a clerk. And then what? Would he shoot someone? He undid his belt, slid his holster off, and rebuckled. The little Police Positive revolver he stuck in his waistband, in the small of his back. Gathering up the week's duty logs, he stood and walked out of his cover, turning right, away from the tellers, as if to go out from behind the counter into the lobby. As he approached the gate leading to the open floor his mind was running like an express train toward a storm-weakened trestle. What would he do? Walk up to the three robbers, pull his gun, and threaten to kill them? Here was some type of chasm to be leaped, and it occurred to him that such an extreme act might not be his job. His mind shut down completely. As he stepped around the end of the counter, he suddenly visualized his piano and hoped he wouldn't be shot in the fingers.

The man nearest him drew a pistol from his coat pocket and leveled it at him. 'Guard, sit down.'

He couldn't help saying, as he bent his knees, 'How did you know I'm a guard?'

The gunman snickered. 'Nice stripe on your pants leg, sheik.'

In the edge of his vision he saw Charlie and Jerry looking out from behind the open brass doors of the bank's entrance. The robbers backed away from the counter together, holding their bulging canvas bags. From above came an echoing click, and then the pop of a revolver. Mr Almeda was lying on his oyster belly on the upper gallery, firing from between two balusters. He missed. For the next six seconds gunshots rattled through the lobby like a pack of fire-crackers as the robbers blasted away at Mr Almeda and then at Aren, who drifted like a cloud at the opposite mezzanine rail, squeezing off shaky two-handed shots. Charlie and Jerry stuck only their hands from behind the heavy doors, firing blind, pumping a round every second into the center of the lobby, the tellers screaming, plaster dust and wood chips raining down and the robbers slipping on the glossy marble floor as they blindly emptied their revolvers and ran toward the doors. Sam sat on the floor, his arms crossed over his head, and when the shooting stopped he heard the hysterical tellers and the hollering of a middle-aged man in khaki shirt and pants sitting in a potted plant and holding his left shoulder. The robbers had run out into the sunlight, and he heard their shoe leather clapping sidewalk down toward Decatur Street. One of the twins, Jerry, walked over to him, and Sam thought he was going to lay a comforting hand on his head. Instead, he pulled Sam's revolver from his waistband, walked out in front of the building to an enormous cast-iron planter, and fired the gun once into the dirt. Back inside, he handed Sam the Colt. 'You know the rule, don't you?'

He looked at the gun. 'I know the rule.' And then he stood up, wondering about every rule in the world. 'Three of 'em. Man, we were lucky.' He raised his eyes. 'You guys up there all right?'

'Yeah,' Mr Almeda called. 'I think Aren peed his pants, though.'

Aren hung his ghost of a face over the rail. 'Did we hit anybody?'

'Well, somebody winged Mr Halloran over there.' Sam pointed to the gentleman seated in the plant, now being tended to by the assistant manager, who was packing the wound with a handkerchief.

At the end of the day, he rode home on the rocking streetcar wondering what his wife would do if one day he were killed. He knew what emptiness his child would face if he were never in its life. And there are times when robbers don't get away, when a lucky shot knocks out their brains on the bank steps, and then what void does that death cause, what unopened front door, what cold side of the bed, what raised and empty arms of a child uncrossed by shadow? Do people ever think of such things if they've never been forced to greet the phantom waiting in every room, to long for the ghost in the kitchen chair? He closed his eyes and wondered what his father had looked like. He could picture his uncle's features, and taking these for a pattern, he tried all the way home to imagine a face to fit the loss.

23

On Christmas morning, Acy and Willa, he in a brocade smoking jacket and she in a fur-lined housecoat, opened the door to the girl's bedroom and watched her sleep, the scene bearing a likeness to any number of sentimental illustrations found in Willa's magazines. Acy walked over and picked her up out of the covers but she straightened her legs against him, and he let her slide down.

'I have to pee-pee,' she said.

Willa reached down and gave her a little shake. 'Don't say that. It sounds nasty. I've told you to ask to go to the bathroom.'

'I have to,' she said, rubbing her arm.

Downstairs the girl came into the presence of the tree, a tall, aromatic spruce loaded with etched glass balls ordered from Chicago and strings of bubbling electric lights. 'Go ahead, Madeline,' Willa coaxed. 'Open your presents.' She led her to a box wrapped in shining red paper embossed with silver bells. The child stood stock-still, then looked up at the two adults, then past them, surveying the room for something. 'Go ahead, dear. Aren't you curious?'

The girl slowly tore the paper away and opened the box, revealing a doll with blond hair and blue eyes, dressed in green lederhosen with red piping and wearing a felt hat topped by a cocked feather. 'Hey,' she said, smiling and sitting down on the rug. She pulled the doll free of its wrapping and examined its joints and clothes, moved it into sitting position, and fingered its eyeballs open and closed.

'Do you like it?' Acy asked. 'It's the best money could buy.'

'I like it,' the child said.

Willa leaned over her, and the girl frowned at the shadow. 'What do you say?'

'What?' She looked up into the cumulus of Willa's hair.

'Thank you?'

'Thank you, Santa Claus,' the girl murmured, pressing her thumbs gently against the doll's eyes.

Acy lit a cigarette. 'Don't you think your doll deserves a name?'

'Like what?'

'Whatever you want. She's yours.'

'I'll call her Lily.'

Willa shot her husband a look. 'Why not Mary, isn't that a pretty name?'

'Or Sue. How about Sweet Sue?'

'She's Lily,' the child repeated, embracing the doll as though she'd just recognized it. '*Ein alter Freund.*'

'Look at your other presents,' Acy said quickly, wedging a sparkling box between her and the doll.

She unwrapped a painting set, a tin mechanical jumping dog, a little Limoges tea set, a new frock, a bright yellow child's umbrella, a musical top embedded with red and green stones. She looked at each gift calmly, smiled at the jumping dog, though she was not strong enough to wind it up. The last of the gifts was a tin piano with two connected minstrel figures. When Acy wound the key, a tin woman jittered before the piano and a tin man in blackface wiggled as though playing his banjo, while the music box inside played 'Camptown Races.' Acy sat on the floor. 'You like this, Madeline? See, the little niggers move in time to the music.'

The child looked at him appraisingly. 'They're not playing, silly. It's a trick.'

Acy scowled. 'Well, I think it's damned funny.'

The girl began singing the lyrics, all of them.

Acy stood up and handed Willa a box, which she quickly opened. Inside was a ring bearing a rectangular-cut diamond. She smiled and slipped the ring on next to last year's gift. 'I love it, Ace. The shape is so different. I bet it's the only one in town.'

She gave him a watch, an expensive Hamilton pocket model, and he set it and slid it into his jacket pocket.

Down next to the tree, the girl was singing, almost under her breath, 'Gwine to run all night, gwine to run all day . . .'

Throughout January, Sam worked at the bank with the empty shell corroding in his gun's cylinder. If there was another gunfight, he'd show the spent casing and be done with it. He told Linda that he didn't know if he could kill a criminal. He wasn't sure why not, though he thought about it a great deal. The robbery returned to him in dreams, and upon waking, he would imagine all the bad things that could have happened. He became nervous on the job once he understood that any day, another group of pistol-wielding men could appear in the bank's broad doorway.

On an icy day in early February, Mr Almeda was on one side of the entrance and the ghostly Aren on the other when Nestor Cabrio walked in. Every policeman and security guard knew him as a thug's thug who specialized in robbing jewelry stores and didn't worry about who he had to shoot down to escape. He'd do a job, then disappear for a year. But a few months after his picture appeared in the *Picayune* and in the post office, people would begin to forget. He'd been robbing stores and banks in New Orleans all his life, more or less once a year.

As soon as he walked in, Cabrio drew a big break-action Smith & Wesson revolver from his pocket and turned toward Mr Almeda, who was chatting with a customer. Aren knew who he was at once, stepped out from behind the door, and shot him in the back before Cabrio's gun arm could straighten out. He twisted and fell, yelling with pain and ripping off shots at random. Aren stood over him and shot him in both shoulders, the left side of his stomach, and twice in the gun arm, placing the shots carefully as though Cabrio were a skiff and he was trying to sink it.

Sam was filling out his duty log for the week when the first shot went off. He stood up and watched the old albino looming over a man and firing at point-blank range. When Aren ran out of bullets, Mr Almeda crab-walked closer, stepped on Cabrio's bloody arm, and took the pistol away. Sam ran over to a phone and called the closest precinct, then the nearest hospital. The robber was hollering something in a foreign language, arching his back and rolling in his own blood. Sam didn't want to study the gory mess at the door, so he drew his gun and sidled past the scene to check the street for an accomplice. Outside, the air was crisp and breezy, the sky blue. It was a nice day, and he decided to stay out in it forever. Somebody had to do this job, he decided, but not him. It took forty minutes for the mud-spattered ambulance to arrive, and when the attendants got to him, Nestor Cabrio began to curse them in Spanish with great gusto and creativity while Mr Almeda translated for the other three guards, who laughed and put up their weapons.

When he saw Linda waiting right inside the door of their house, he blurted out, 'I quit the job.'

'That's nice.' She pushed him backwards onto the porch.

'I'm sorry.'

'Right. That's nice.' She pushed him again toward the steps, harder.

'Linda, I'm real, real sorry.' His voice began to rise in pitch, and for a moment he thought she wanted to push him across the street and out of her life altogether.

'Yeah. Let's go now.'

'Go?'

'My water's broke.'

For a moment he glanced at the house, wondering if she meant a pipe had burst. Then he knew. He put her in the ratty Dodge, noting that she'd loaded her bag in already. It took five minutes to start the engine, but eventually they got to the hospital. At eleven o'clock that night she delivered a boy, and by twelve they were in a ward curtained off from other women in the room. They named the child Christopher, and Sam took him, looked at his features, and saw a chin that was his, eyes that were Linda's, and a nose he didn't recognize. The nose would probably change over time, but it was prominent for a newborn's, almost like his uncle Claude's. With a thrill he understood that part of this baby would be his father and mother. For much of the child's life, he would wonder where his ears, cheekbones, feet, angers, inclinations, and talents originated, whether from the killed folks in Troumal or from hundreds of years back in Nova Scotia. The baby writhed in his arms, a wailing package of history.

Though her mother and aunts were clopping around the house all day, and everybody related to her plus the neighbors came by to see this new Christopher, Sam stayed home in the chaos and helped Linda with the baby. In the nights, after feeding him, she would hand the boy over and go back to bed. Rocking the snorting infant against his belly in the dark, he would feel how warm he was, like a soft little engine slowly burning up the milk.

One night, very late, at the beginning of April, Sam got up with Linda, and while she fed, went to stand on the back steps. He looked up at a rare clear sky graveled with stars and thought about going to work on the railroad, about buying paint for the hallway, about discovering that Christopher was another part of his own body. He couldn't imagine being without him. He wasn't feeling mushy-hearted; it was just a fact that if anyone took him away, it would be like losing a part of himself. As improbable as it seemed, he now missed his first boy even more. He closed his eyes and saw the ghosting of galaxies on his retinas, and a frightening patch of paleness drifting in his imagination among the real lights. He knew what the cloudy image was – though amorphous and faded, he knew. Going into the house, he took his son to rock and tried to forget what he'd just remembered. But that night he couldn't sleep.

The next morning at the breakfast table, taking his time, haltingly, he told his wife the truth. She was furious.

'Sam, how the hell could you do that?' She sat back hard in her chair and banged her hands on the table.

'Like I said, these people were so well off—'

'Since when is being well off a license to steal children?'

He winced, her words going in like pins. 'I'm going to let Elsie know right now.'

She folded her arms. 'Sam, you of all people.'

He looked away, stung to the heart.

'You had to hold your own child before you could understand what the Wellers were missing? I guess I can grant you some understanding there. But only some. Honey, what were you thinking when you walked away from that girl?'

He rolled his head back and stared at the ceiling. 'Again, I thought she'd be better off.'

Linda began to speak with her hands. 'Maybe you'd do what you did if Elsie and her boy were murderers or some other kind of terrible people. But they're like us, for God's sake, just struggling to get by.'

He turned his face toward her. 'So what do I do?'

She shook her head. 'I wouldn't want to be you for all the chicory coffee in Orleans Parish.'

'I've got to come up with a good story.'

'Baby, you're a fool if you think a lie will fix things between you and them.'

'I guess I'll have to go up there and tell them face-to-face,' he said.

She narrowed her eyes. Her voice was low and matter-of-fact. 'And how will you buy the train tickets, and how will you pay to feed yourself? And what about hotel bills? My family's helped us out too much already.'

'Well, what can I do?'

'Write a letter.'

He tilted his head. 'A letter.'

'A good one. If I was Mrs Weller, I'd rather have it laid out in print than look at your bumbling face trying to gild the lily on this one.'

He pulled close to the table as she stood up and got a tablet and an envelope. 'I know you've got her address.'

'Somewhere.'

She left the room, and he wrote one full page, then tore it up. He began another, and then a second page began to flow under a freshly filled fountain pen. He got up and drank a tumbler of water from the tap, sat down, and wrote three more pages.

The sunlight was slanting through the kitchen window when Linda returned holding the baby. 'You have it all worked out?'

'I think so. I'll need an extra stamp, though.'

The next day he started for the post office but stepped into a tavern on Magazine Street for a beer, sitting under the moth-eaten deer head at the end of the bar and watching the silver chains of bubbles rise in his mug like bad ideas. Though he wondered if he was condemning Lily to a hard, dumb life by sending his letter, he was ashamed to acknowledge the chief reason for his worry, that Elsie and August would hate him body and soul for not telling them at once when he'd located the girl. He had a second beer, then walked into the poker game in the back room, sat down, and won thirty dollars playing spit.

He never made it to the post office and hid the letter in his sock drawer. Another day to think things over might help. Maybe events had gone too far for a letter to do any good. In his little parlor he played piano for an hour, working on embellishments, on forgetting.

The next morning there was a rude rapping at the front door, and on the porch he found a ruddy, birdlike man, vaguely familiar, a blunt stuck in the corner of his mouth. He wore a seersucker coat but no tie, and his straw boater was sliding off the side of his head in the sunny breeze. He made a motion with a stubby finger. 'You the excursion-boat man?'

'I was.'

'My brother called me up and said you lived about four blocks away from me. Damned if you don't.'

'Who's your brother?'

'Station agent in Greenville. He sent you a telegram up to Evansville and wanted to know did you get it.'

The notion that someone else was concerned about his search made him take a step backwards in the door frame. 'Yeah. I should've sent one back to thank him.'

The little man eyed him harshly. 'Morris wants to know did the message help you any? He don't burn much daylight helping folks out, you know. It's not his nature.'

'Yes,' he said. 'It helped a lot.'

'You find the little girl, did you?'

Sam looked at the brother, who seemed a bit concerned himself over a lost child he'd never seen or heard of before getting a phone call from the wilds of Mississippi. 'Yeah, sure. Let him know she's been found safe.'

The man removed his cigar and shook Sam's hand. 'All right, then. I'll tell him that. Nice to meetcher.'

'Tell him I'm sorry I didn't write him back.'

'That's all right. He's used to sorry.' He threw his cigar into the street and headed up the sidewalk at a brisk walk, his bright seersucker flapping in the breeze.

Sam went out to the end of his walk and watched Morris Hightower's brother striding under the oaks, his jacket winking white in the sun. He decided it was a scary visit – that he'd somehow been called to accounts.

That was a Tuesday, and he mailed the letter about noon. As soon as it whispered into the brass slot at the post office, he began worrying about the response, when it would come and in what form. He dreaded it until Saturday, when his phone rang with a collect call from Cincinnati, Ohio.

'Mr Sam Simoneaux?' The voice was Elsie's, sounding as flat as a skillet against the head.

'It's me, Elsie,' he muttered.

After a pause, she said something that sounded much rehearsed. 'I read your letter several times with all your reasons, and I've got a question for you.'

'What's that?'

'You told me once you had a child.'

'Yes. I've got a new one now. A new baby boy.'

There was no congratulation in what she said next. 'And of course you're rich as can be and can give him everything in the world?'

It was as though she'd read his insides from across the country, knew him better than he knew himself. 'No.'

'And you've got this big job, making maybe five hundred dollars a month?'

'I don't have any job right now.'

'So, you must have this grand inheritance, and with it you're going to send this boy to Harvard and Paris, or at least a private school somewhere.'

'Elsie, all I can say is I'm sorry.'

'You are. You really are. If you'd just done your floorwalker job like you were supposed to, none of this would've ever happened.' She began to cry now, and accusation began to pile on accusation until he took the candlestick phone off the table and sat on the floor, his legs drawn up, his back against the wall. Linda came out of the bedroom holding the baby and looked at him with no particular expression. Elsie ended her long recital with 'And if it weren't for you, Ted wouldn't have died.'

'How's August?' he ventured, his mind reeling with shame.

'How do you think?' she cried. 'He's not the same person. He never will be.'

'What do you want me to do?'

The response was quick. 'I'll tell you. I have no idea how to handle this, so I want you to figure out how we can get to that hick town and take my baby back from those people. You've got to come with me. All *my* relatives work for a living.'

'I can't even afford the train ticket. I'm making a few dollars at odd jobs, but I can't leave my family without any money in the bank.' He looked up at his wife. 'It might take two weeks to straighten things out.'

The voice came back thin as a needle. 'I don't want to hear it. This will never be straightened out. Me and August have been eating potato soup and shivering for months. At least down where you are the river doesn't freeze over.'

He closed his eyes and reached deep inside himself for the words. 'Well, maybe we can try this.'

The phone call lasted ten more minutes. Later that afternoon, she called back. The *Ambassador* was coming out of winter quarters above Cincinnati and would run down to New Orleans light, making no stops, to get dry-docked, stocked, and take on crew and musicians before starting her initial upriver excursion schedule. Captain Stewart said she and August could deadhead free down to Graysoner and stay at the Wilson Hotel on the boat's account if they promised to work the season. She would be there in seven days, waiting for him.

Sam hung up the phone and walked to his piano, a glossy red-mahogany Packard, a stolid instrument with bell-like upper notes and a booming bass. He opened the sheet music for 'When My Baby Smiles at Me' and played it as written, but when he was finished he played it again, adding ragged filigree to the plain arrangement, then jazzed it up on a third run-through. He played ten other pieces in a row, feeling the ivory slide under his fingertips, and afterward he sat a long time staring at the fine wood until he saw his face reflected in the French polish. He got up and called a furniture store on Dryades Street, and in an hour the dealer arrived and bought his piano for seventy-nine dollars.

24

Some time in March, Ralph Skadlock had been hired by a Louisiana state legislator to steal a specially engraved and gold-inlaid Parker shotgun from the home of a plantation owner in Braithwaite. The day after he stole it, he pulled the double out of its gun bag and looked it over while sitting in his mildewed front parlor. The sidelocks showed bird dogs jumping a covey of quail, and he ran a sooty fingertip over the razor-sharp checkering on the swirling walnut stocks. He noted how it snapped shut, as though barrels and receiver suddenly became one piece of metal through the cold welding of expert craftsmanship. Still, to him, the piece was ridiculous. A gun was a wrench or a hammer. It did a job.

The next day he rode horseback to the depot and took the southbound to the Baton Rouge station, where he handed a smudged cardboard box to a corpulent, florid man dressed in a tailored suit.

'I think you'll be happy with this here item,' Ralph told him.

The legislator gave him a look, paid him, and turned away without a word. Ralph held on to the envelope and watched him walk out into the sunlight, knowing for a fact that this fool couldn't hit a quail exploding out of a dewberry bush to save his soul and probably not even a dove sitting on a branch outside his bedroom window. But he could show off the gun to men gathered in his parlor for drinks, the weapon suggesting how much better he was than they.

Skadlock went home and brooded about their meeting, how the man's little sharp eyes looked at him, how he'd refused to give him a single word. He remembered the envelope coming over with a nasty flick of the wrist. Men had gotten killed for such manners.

A week later he crossed a long, apple-green lawn and climbed through the window of a many-columned house northeast of Baton Rouge. He stood under a high ceiling and smelled the furniture oil, the floor wax, the fresh paint of the place. The gun was conspicuously displayed in a leaded-glass case, and he took it, fading back out into the night, knowing that when the theft was discovered, the legislator wouldn't report it, wouldn't send any lawman against Ralph Skadlock, who might tell who had paid him to take the gun in the first place, along with a few other items he'd been hired to steal in the past. He walked two miles to a highway and crossed it into a stand of sycamores where his horse was tied. He wondered why he hadn't thought of this double thieving before. On the long ride back, he made a mental list of all the haughty, weak men he could revisit, taking back animals, clocks, jewelry. It was then that Acy White came to mind.

He and Billsy were looking the gun over the next day in the big kitchen house, debating where they could sell it, when they heard a spatula hit the floor. Their mother, cooking breakfast, had slumped down on the floor planks with a wheeze, and they went and stood over her, nudging her arms with their brogans and then kneeling down and trying to talk her upright. Ninga would have none of it. One eye rolled toward the window and the other toward the door, signals that everything in her had suddenly quit, muscles turned loose, breaths escaped, thought gone out like a wick. After ten minutes of staring and cajoling, the men understood that she was dead, but could not imagine what might happen now. A vast emptiness grew up around them, and Billsy stood to turn off the aromatic stove, not sure which way to twist the valve handle.

They laid her out straight on the floor, so she would cool in a decent posture, and stood around outside the kitchen eating slices of white bread, wondering what to do next. Neither of them had been to a family funeral, and they couldn't remember what had been done to their father after his still had exploded when they were four and five years old. They weren't sure where any relatives lived over in Arkansas, as the clan tended to move around.

There was a magnolia-haunted graveyard a hundred yards to the rear of the mansion bearing several humpbacked markers and a stone cross crenellated with lichen. The men scratched out a vacant space at the rear of the highborn dead and dug her hole. Wrapping her in her own quilts, they set her in the ground and covered her up, then stood looking down at the soppy mound. Ralph felt a thickness in his throat he thought might be some words coming up, but he didn't say anything. No one in the family had ever read a Bible or stepped foot in a church one time, and both men were too primitively formed to deal even in the clichés of Christianity, having no more notion of a hereafter or its price of admission than lizards stunned asleep in the noon sun.

Billsy looked around at the other weed-wracked headstones bearing inscriptions in French. 'She needs her a marker.'

Ralph looked up. 'Like what?'

'Just a second.' He turned back to the kitchen house. Ralph walked the dirt down around the edge of the grave until his brother returned holding a stamped skillet with a long handle. 'This here's the ticket.'

Ralph took it from him, turned it front and back several times as if he were inspecting it for purchase, then stuck the handle in the earth at the head of the grave. 'That there about says it, all right.'

They ate potted meat and sardines, then rode several miles toward a ferry landing upriver. Turning onto a road leading to the water, they rode against automobiles coming off the boat. Near the bank they reached a roughboard roadhouse fronting three mildewed tourist cabins strung out along a raw red ditch. Upstairs, the dark, low-ceilinged bar served skin-peeling moonshine in jelly glasses, and after an hour of it they both were ready for whores.

Ralph leaned over the counter and put a hand on the ample arm of the barmaid. 'Is Suzy servin' tonight?'

She fixed a lead ball eye on him. 'Ruttin' season, is it?'

'Is she still three dollars?'

'Ralph, a good-lookin' man like you, I'm surprised you ain't married.'

'Costs more than three dollars. Is she seein' fellers?'

The barmaid put a finger in an ear and scratched. 'In cabin two, at the back.' She slid her gaze past Ralph's dark bulk to round-shouldered Billsy, who'd been here dozens of times but was still shy about it. 'You want a good pokin'?'

'I reckon so.'

'Who you want?'

Billsy thought for a moment. 'This time I want a gal with teeth.'

The door to cabin two swung open to reveal Suzy Kathell, long-waisted and long-faced, fifty years old with orange hair. Swaying in a lime green negligee, she held a drink and a cigarette in one hand and tugged him into the light with the other. 'Hello, opportunity,' she said, and laughed like a horse. 'How the hell you doin'?'

Ralph stared at her bodice. 'All right.'

'How's your bashful brother?'

'He's all right, I reckon.'

'Is your mother still kickin'?'

'Naw. She died.'

'She did? When was that?'

'This morning.'

She turned her head at an angle. 'Well, damn it to hell, you need some cheerin' up,' she said, shucking her negligee.

Ralph was near senseless from the moonshine, and it took a while for the woman to get finished with him. After it was over, he said, 'Would you come live with me on salary?'

She gave his face a playful slap. 'Hell, that almost sounds like a proposal. Or will I have to do Billsy too?' She guffawed at this, blowing smoke in his face.

'Do us or not, we need a woman out at the place.'

Suzy Kathell took a sizzling drag on her Picayune. 'Lambchops, I don't think you can afford help like me. Plus I done tried domestic bliss before and it didn't work out. I like my fancy drawers and my automobile I can drive anywhere I want. You got a automobile out at your place?'

Ralph admitted that he didn't even have a road.

She gave his stubbly cheek an enormous pinch. 'Sweetie, you straight in the back, you got all your teeth, and you got that scary look that drives dumb women off their nut. You look around good and you'll have that old cookstove hot in no time. Now if you'll put your clothes on and excuse me, I got to call my next case.'

The brothers sat in the bar and drank from the same jar of shine. 'I think my eyeballs is switched sockets,' Billsy said.

Ralph reached over and jerked a button off his brother's shirt pocket and threw it at him. 'Wake up and listen.'

Billsy looked stricken. 'Who's gonna sew that son of a bitch back on?'

'How much is that racehorse worth you took over in Carencro?'

'I got no idea. I think they said a thousand dollars.'

'That LeGrange man paid you to take it?'

'Yeah.'

'Could you grab it back?'

'Hell no, that black devil bit me six times. It was like dancing with a wolverine evertime I fooled with him.'

'But you could just steal it back, and he wouldn't say nothin' because it's stole by him in the first place.'

'Then what, sell it?'

'Yeah. Back to him.'

'That's crazy. Who'd buy something that was his in the first place?'

'That's the beauty of it. It never was his.'

Billsy took a sip, hoping the drink would clear his head. 'Why not just blackmail the son of a bitch?'

'There's something about havin' that physical thing in your own hands. Something you want that somebody else could wind up with. That's what drives 'em up a wall.'

'Well, I ain't going after that horse. I couldn't sleep for a month after that job. Thought I had rabies.'

'Come on.' Ralph batted him on the shoulder, knocking off his fedora.

Billsy bent down to pick it up. 'You want to resteal something, you ought to think about that kid.'

The chair under Ralph cracked its knuckles. 'I done thought about it. Just don't know how to make that deal work.'

'That job was good money.'

Ralph bent over the table and took another drink. He spread his arms out onto its surface as though it were a giant wheel he was trying to stop from turning. 'That job cost me my dog.'

Billsy straightened up and composed himself, as if he knew he had to be careful. 'That was some dog.'

'I took a step, that dog took a step. We'd sit out in the woods, he'd come up and bite the flies out the air if they was buzzin' too close to my head. He'd eat bees before they got a chance to sting me.'

'He was the only pureblood in the family.'

'Sometimes I'd wake up in the night and look around the bed. If the moon was in the window I'd see old Satan's big eyes in the room lookin' my way, kind of the color of pine sap, keeping watch on me.'

'I remember him killin' that pit bull that come at you.'

'That Cincinnati son of a bitch,' Ralph mumbled into the table. 'How many policemen you reckon they got in Cincinnati?'

Billsy squinted over at the barmaid, who was wiping glasses with her shirttail. 'I'd bet a thousand. They got paved streets and automobiles. Telephones on ever street corner.'

'Damn telephones. If it wasn't for them, a man could get away with most anything.'

The barmaid called over. 'If he's about to puke, haul his ass outside.'

Billsy looked around for the voice. 'He ain't sick. He's my brother.'

She didn't laugh. 'Billsy, you drunker'n a rat ridin' a ceilin' fan. If he pops off, you got to clean it up.'

'Aw, he's all right. Give us another drink.' He felt his shirt pockets. 'And we out of cigarettes.'

'Don't sell 'em.'

'Aw, sweet thing, you don't want us to smoke in here? Scared it'll make you smell worse than you do?'

The barmaid spat in a glass and rubbed it hard. 'You'll smoke enough after you're dead,' she told him.

The next morning they woke up and stumbled around in the sunshine outside the big house trying to detoxify, hungry as refugees, smelly and stunned with headache. Ralph fired a big heater in the house and warmed up water for a bath in the galvanized tub. After, he found some tins of sardines in the cupboard and a block of moldy cheese, and at table his head began to clear.

'Tell you what,' he said to Billsy, who was seated across from him in the kitchen with his shirt off, little horns of hair rising from his shoulders. 'You stay here and tend the still and keep an eye on things. I'll go up the country and check out that kid.'

'Leave me money for some eats.'

'All right. That bundle of shingles we fished out the river you could nail up on the roof. It leaks pretty bad.'

'You never complained before. Said it sounded like a waterfall in your sleep.'

'Well, we never found them shingles before, did we? Everything's getting slimy with mold and the floor's warped up.'

'I'll take a look at it.' Billsy pinched up a sardine out of the tin and ate it, sucking his fingers.

'I'll pack my glad rags. Them light wool pants we got from that laundry in Scotlandville. White shirts and a string tie.'

'Scrape the horse shit off your shoes.'

'I'll use them new brown boots we got out that house in McComb.'

'Whoa. Nobody'll know you.'

They rode to the little station in Fault, and Billsy took both horses back. In two days, Ralph was walking the neighborhoods of Graysoner, Kentucky, his thumbs under his suspenders as if he owned the place. It was after nine a.m., when most men were at work, most women busy getting the day's shopping done before the heat set in. He'd spent an hour down at the farrier's, getting the information he needed from the old-timers hanging around the forge who told about the trails of ten or fifteen years before, when the automobile had been a thing unknown. He listened to what they said about the hatchet-back ridge south of town and the passes that threaded over it. The next day he walked down the alley behind Acy White's house and saw what looked like a hired girl in poor clothes and the child rolling a ball in the short grass. When he passed the fence, he tipped his hat and smiled as best he could. The woman, robust-looking with a narrow back straight as a kitchen chair, smiled back at him, and he moved down the street. 'Well, now,' he said to himself. 'Gray eyes.'

Skadlock went down to a hotel where steamboat men stayed and washed up in the restroom at the end of the hall. He slicked his hair back with oil and put on a fresh shirt. He got a haircut in the shop in the lobby and passed small talk, gradually sliding the conversation around to the woman who worked in the middle of the block on Bonner Alley. He didn't want to use Acy White's name. Ralph understood that local barbers knew everything in a small town since chitchat was their stock-in-trade, more so than bartenders and whores. The barber snipped his scissors three times in the air and looked into the middle distance. 'That gal lives somewhere down the hill in Ditch Street. I've seen her walking that way after seven when she's finished up at Mr White's house. Damned if that ain't a place for the rats. The tannery leaves its slops out in the canal, and they're all over in there, up and down.'

'She's married to that foreman at the tannery, ain't she?' Skadlock held up his boot and pretended to look at it.

'If she is, I don't know it. Mr White says she lives alone in one of those red tarpaper shacks this side of the boiler house.'

Realizing that his hair was being cut by the only barber in town, he changed the subject. 'You know, I ate in a café the other day that put sugar in its cornbread.'

The barber quickened to the comment. 'I know it. I guess somebody in New York thought it was a good idea. Me, I like the old pie-shaped cornbread with bits of crackling in it, salty as sweat.'

'Yessir. How about dodgers?'

The barber spoke solemnly for five minutes about his grandmother's corn dodgers and blackberry jelly while Skadlock figured the schedule for the rest of the day.

From where he stood between two willow saplings half a block to the north, he saw her leave the backyard gate and enter the alley. He slipped out onto the sidewalk and affected a lazy saunter down the hill in the direction of Ditch Street and soon heard her come up behind him. He imagined she'd want to hurry home and put her feet up after working for the rich folks all day. When she came alongside, he pretended to be startled. 'Hey,' he said. 'I saw you somewheres today, didn't I?' Her face was fairly narrow, her chin small, but a tough smartness hid deep in those pale eyes.

She gave him a quick glance, the kind of look she'd normally give a big strange dog, but she slowed down. 'I was out behind the house where I work, and you was traipsin' up the alley.'

'That's right. You was playin' ball with a kid had too much clothes on for this heat.'

She began to match his gait. 'Ain't that the truth. Missus ain't happy less she's got a week's salary on that kid's back mornin', noon, and night.'

'You her nursemaid or something?'

Vessy raised her chin a bit. 'I'm rightly the cook. But I watch the girl some.'

Skadlock stopped walking. 'Cook, you say. You cook everday?'

'Yeah. I believe that's what a cook does. It's what I'm cut out for, anyway.' They started out again down the hill, walking slower. 'You in town lookin' for work? I heard some old boys say they heard the tannery's hiring.'

He shook his head. 'Naw. I just come to buy somethin' for one price and sell it for another.' He practiced a smile on her.

What she saw was on the border of frightening, but she ignored his expression. 'Like a horse trader.'

'Somethin' like.'

'Well, my brother, when he was alive, he traded in mules and always went barefoot.' She gave him a longer look, noted his boots.

'I usually trade to advantage,' he told her.

He walked with her to the start of Ditch Street, a narrow lane of greasy dirt shooting off from the cobbles of the respectable street they'd come down. 'So long, miss. It is "miss," ain't it?'

'Yep,' she said ruefully. 'Miss. Or maybe "missed."'

He lay on his single bed that night and looked at the ceiling, sipping from a pint of his own white-hot stock and thinking where he might run into her again. He was hungry and tired of the food he'd brought from home, bread he could drive tacks with and cheese that smelled like feet. Longing suddenly for his mother's skillet-fried marsh hen with garlic, he was stunned by the thought that she would never cook for him and Billsy again. 'Well, damn,' he said to the ceiling. Ralph never felt sentimental about one thing in his life, but at the present moment he felt heart pangs when he remembered the old woman pushing around a cut-up bird in a smoking skillet. He wondered long why she did it.

The next afternoon he met Vessy at the head of Ditch Street and spoke with her for another ten minutes. He noticed powder stuck to the sweat on her face and thought he detected the smell of violets or Sen-Sen. Later that night he showed up at her place, where they sat on her teetering porch in dry-rotted wicker chairs.

They talked for an hour or so before he offered her a pour out of his flask. She sniffed at the inch of liquid in her cloudy water glass, then took it all down in a slug. 'All fire and no ash,' she said approvingly. 'Sure ain't no singlings.'

'I figured a east Kentucky gal would know a good sip.'

She looked at him. 'What exactly you do for a livin' there, Ralph?'

'Oh, people hire me out to do things. Find things. Make things.'

'I bet some of them things flow in a bottle.'

'Could be.' He poured her another sip, and with this, she took her time, staring at him over the glass.

The third day was Saturday. That night he took her to a café and they each ate a plate of chops and vegetables. Walking back to her place, he asked about the child and she told him what she knew. They drank a pint between them sitting at the rough wood table next to her bed, and he leaned over and gave her a lasting kiss that she took as though it were a long-awaited letter from the mailman. Then she said, 'Well, Mr Ralph, that's all right, but just to get things straight, you can kiss on me all you want, but I ain't spreadin' my legs for no man. I seen too many left with a big belly watchin' a feller's back walkin' away.'

He lit a cigarette and looked past her at the bed, then he kissed her again as if he liked the taste of it. He straightened up in his chair and gave her his cigarette and watched her take a drag. 'All right. You tell me how you think they got that little girl.'

'It's somebody else's, I know that much. Probably hired somebody to steal her away from her parents.' Her eyes narrowed. 'You a detective or something?'

'No,' he said. 'I'm the man got paid a thousand bucks to steal her.'

Vessy gave him back the cigarette and reached for the bottle. 'Well, ain't you a jack-in-the-box.' Her mouth formed a straight line. 'What you want now?'

'I aim to steal her back.'

She stopped before taking a drink. 'Excuse me, but that don't seem too bright. The sheriff's in Acy's poker club.'

He pointed a finger up the hill to Lilac Street. 'They can't report me, not without admittin' to a crime themselves. And I'll sell that kid right back to them again, but this time for a cool two thousand.' He got up and put the cigarette in the trash burner, then turned to look at her. 'Could you use five hundred of it?'

She glanced rapidly around her shack, every surface jaundiced in the kerosene light, as if she might never see it again. 'What I got to do?'

'Can you ride a horse?'

She made a face. 'What you think? I was raised ridin' a mule to school, all five grades, then I come home to plow till dark.'

'I need you to help with the girl down to my place in Louisiana.'

She stuck a tongue in her jaw and thought about this. 'And then what?'

He was not used to smiling, but smiled now and straightened his back the way a gambler with the winning hand does before he lays down his cards. 'Sweetness, then you can do whatever the hell you want.'

He stayed at her place talking with her long after the streets were empty. The next day he laid low at the hotel. The following night, he walked over to Ditch Street, ignoring the aromatic fog rising from the steaming runnels flowing downhill from the tannery. She let him in and told him at once that Tuesday Acy would be away from the house early for sure, and that Mrs White was leaving on the morning boat headed upriver to Louisville to shop. Neither would get home until five-thirty at the earliest.

He wedged back in the spindle chair and its joints popped like caps in a toy pistol. 'You got pants you can wear under a dress?'

She nodded, sitting across from him at her table. 'You got horses?'

'I got two set up to buy.'

'Neither one of 'em bite?'

'The ones I'm lookin' at might not have teeth.'

She grinned, and a trace of a blush formed above her cheekbones.

He smiled back, his expression mysterious, the way some mean men smile at people, with the suggestion that he might bring her as far as he needed her, then leave her in the woods somewhere with a knot on her head. If Vessy read these notions on his face, she gave no hint of it. Taking his flask, she poured herself a small drink, hoping the taste would burn the tannery stench out of her nostrils. She smiled delicately into the glass.

25

On Tuesday at a quarter to six Acy walked home from the bank. His fine burgundy Oldsmobile stayed in the carriage house on the alley because he liked the exercise the uphill route gave him, even when he was tired, as he was today. When he opened his front door, the quiet was palpable, and at once he knew that something was different. No cooking smells. He looked at the floor, wondering if he had forgotten some event, perhaps a recital or music class for Madeline. Nothing came to mind. He went into the kitchen and put a hand on the stove, which was cold. Upstairs, everything seemed in order and the beds were made, which meant that Vessy, who did the housework when the maid was ill, as well as the cooking, had been in.

He decided to take the car down the hill and eat at the Wilson Hotel. At the restaurant, while waiting for his food, he studied his ironstone plate. Had Vessy taken ill? His wife, he knew, had caught the *Galeno* upriver to shop, and there were all sorts of reasons the old boat might be late getting back in. Perhaps Madeline had gone along, and Vessy as well, to help with the packages. Two young lawyers came over to join him, and soon he was talking of tax laws and thinking about the night's steaks. He would have enjoyed a glass of wine, as in the old days before the war when drinking was legal. But the steaks arrived plump and running with hot fat, so he was happy.

The *Galeno* had indeed developed boiler trouble and was limping downstream two hours behind schedule. Willa liked riding a boat upriver, imagining against fact that the dowdy, short-trade packets still running were grand floating palaces, but after dark she always wished she'd taken the train. She was tired, and the ladies' lounge at the rear of the main salon had lost its gilt and gloss, the chair seats threadbare and smelling of coal oil. Two dour spinsters were returning from a doctor's visit, and all they wanted to talk about were the limitless female problems they'd suffered. She passed the time by going through her two large bundles of purchases, one of which held even more shifts and pinafores for the girl. She was anxious to return and show her Madeline the new things, though the girl seldom reacted much to gifts of clothes. That would change as she got older and learned more about style and fashion. Willa had taught her many things already, although the girl still refused to call her Mother, or to wave at people properly, or to refrain from certain unruly expressions. The times she tried to feel close to Madeline, when the girl was in her lap and she was brushing her hair, the child would turn suddenly, staring at her as though Willa were a complete stranger. Then she would feel hurt and denied, but she was always able to cheer herself with the knowledge that at last, at long last, she possessed a child.

The *Galeno* landed after eight o'clock, and Willa called the house from the wharf boat and asked Acy to come down and get her. When he arrived, he helped her with her packages. 'I guess we'll have to drive by Vessy's to pick Madeline up.'

'What on earth for?'

'She must've brought the child home with her. They're not at the house.'

'I don't understand.'

'Nobody was home when I got there after work.'

She waited for him to close her door and walk around the hood. He was moving quickly and jumped into the driver's seat like a boy. 'I hate for Madeline to be in that neighborhood, it just smells so awful,' she said, waving a perfumed hand before her nose.

He put the car in gear and drove up the hill, turning down Ditch Street and driving past a row of narrow, tin-roofed houses, their windows yellow with kerosene light, until he stopped in front of Vessy's. The house was dark, but he still got out and knocked.

He sped a little as they rolled on toward home. Willa put a gloved hand on his arm. 'What is it?'

He motioned with his chin. 'No lights on at home, either.'

They went in and searched for a note, a clue.. Willa went to a drawer in the walnut breakfront and retrieved her bottle of Canadian whiskey, pouring herself a long swallow into a cut-glass tumbler. A tremor ran through her hand as she drank.

Acy came back from the old carriage house and sat down, taking her drink and downing it. 'They're not here.'

'Maybe Madeline became ill and she took her to the doctor.'

He let out a sigh. 'That's got to be it.'

But after an apologetic phone call, he came back into the dining room and said the doctor hadn't seen them. By this time it was nine o'clock. He went to the neighbors on either side. Mrs Spurlen hadn't seen Vessy or Madeline all day. Mr Scott, who owned several farms but had retired to town, brought his great gray eyebrows together and asked if there was any trouble.

'No, nothing at all,' Acy told him, backing off the old man's broad stone porch. 'We've just got our schedules mixed up, and we don't know where Vessy brought our little girl tonight.'

The old man checked his outsized pocket watch. 'It's late, but if you want I'll go and check somewheres. You ask the doctor?'

'Yes. It's all right. I'm sure she'll turn up shortly.'

'Oh, Acy?'

'Yes?'

'Are you going to have your back fence painted?'

'What? Oh, sure.' He was walking backwards toward the street.

'I know it's just the alley, but we have to keep it looking good, what with the automobiles using it as a shortcut and raising the dust. There were even horses early this morning.'

'I'll have a man get on it next week.'

'Thanks.' Mr Scott closed his door and turned off the porch light.

When he got home, Willa was crying, and he sat next to her on the divan, attempting to calm her. He made them both cups of tea, which they drank at table, saying nothing. Waiting. For the first time he missed the girl's face, the bright newness of it, even her pert refusal to grant him much in the way of affection. The child-noise she'd made was a beating heart in his house. For a brief second he wondered how the girl's parents had felt, but he killed that thought as quickly as he'd slap a mosquito.

At ten o'clock, he had an idea and found the new battery-powered flashlight and walked down into the backyard. At the gate he shined the light in the alley and saw the apple-shaped leavings of a horse. Perhaps two horses. He walked next door and knocked on Mr Scott's door until the old man came downstairs and appeared in his pajamas, blinking through the partially opened door. 'What is it?'

'Sorry to get you out of bed, Jess, but you mentioned horses were in the alley?'

'Horses? *Where?*' He looked out over the lawn into the blackness.

'This morning. You told me.'

'Oh. Yes. Two of them.'

'On a wagon? Was it the lumber company?'

Mr Scott paused a moment. 'No, a man was leading them. I was on the way to my garage and I saw him. I started to call for him not to let the animals dawdle and smell up the neighborhood.'

'Just him?'

'That's all I saw. Has your little girl come home yet?'

Acy liked for things to be orderly, liked for them not only to fall into place, but also to stay there, and now someone had broken the order in his life. 'We're doing what we can. This man, can you describe him?'

'I don't remember. I just saw a man.' Mr Scott put two fingers on his chin. 'He was big. Wore a pretty big hat, and not a bad one. Probably a Stetson. Certainly not trash.'

'Anything else?'

'I just glimpsed him. He was just walking the horses, holding the reins.'

'What time?'

'I beg your pardon?' Mr Scott put one bare foot out onto the porch floor.

'What time of day was all this?'

'Oh. It was early. Maybe eight or so.'

'Thank you, Jess.'

'Do you need for me to do anything?'

But Acy had already gone out to the street and was feeling for the gate in the moonless dark. A moment later, Willa heard him come up the steps and let him in.

'Does Vessy have any friends who come by on horses?'

'I don't know. She's so cross I don't know if she's made any friends at all since she's been living here.'

'Someone was in the alley with saddle horses right after we left the house.'

'Do you think she planned an outing and something went wrong?' Willa stood up and clenched her fist, but it occurred to her that she didn't know who she was angry with and sat back down. 'Should we call the sheriff to look for them?'

'Does Vessy have any man friends?'

'How could she? Have you smelled her? Just the essence of pine oil and kitchen smoke.'

Acy looked at her, trying to smile, but failing. 'I'll call the sheriff. But you know, we'll have to be careful what we tell him.'

Her eyes grew wide, as if she'd just remembered where the child had come from. 'Could her parents have—'

'Her parents wouldn't make off with her like that. They'd come straight up the hill.'

'Oh God, Acy. Do you think someone found out? And where's Vessy?' She stood up quickly and put a hand against a daffodil in the wallpaper.

'It doesn't make sense. But if we don't call the sheriff tonight, he'll find it odd.'

The sheriff arrived at their house at ten-forty-five. He was middle-aged, a politician of sorts, ambitiously dressed in a suit. Acy held a thirteen-thousand-dollar mortgage against his new house, so he took off his fedora, came in politely, and listened politely. Then he told them that Vessy probably took the girl off and would have a good explanation come morning. Just to be sure, he'd drop by the train station and the wharf boat and ask if anyone had seen something they all should know about.

Acy started to tell him about the horses, but something – perhaps his most fearful suspicion – made him hold back. 'In the morning, then.'

He lay awake all night, thinking about the girl, while his wife roamed the house from bed to bed, finally settling on the divan downstairs. Before the sheriff drove up in the morning, Acy had already told Willa what he thought. 'The Skadlocks have taken her back. That's the only thing I can figure.'

They were seated at the kitchen table drinking tap water. Willa looked at him, incredulous. 'Why? We paid them what they asked, and it was a lot of money.'

They both were quiet for a long time before the sheriff came, hat in hand. He stood in the dining room, studying the china cabinet, and said he'd searched Vessy's cabin and found nothing out of the ordinary. Her few clothes seemed to be there and not a thing had been moved out that he could see, but then, the furniture came with the place, even the cheap enamel pots and the rusty knives and forks. She owned almost nothing.

'When are you going to start looking for my child?' Willa said, glancing at her husband.

The sheriff explained what he could do and left as quickly as he could.

Acy stared through the front window as his Ford chattered away down the hill. 'I can't even leave to look for her,' he said. 'Not right away. I couldn't explain my absence.'

'If Skadlock does have her, you can't lead the sheriff to him.'

He continued watching the lawman's departure, as though

envious of his motion and freedom. 'But where's Vessy? That's the part I don't understand.'

'Maybe he bought her off and she left for the mountains.'

He looked long at the bare dining-room table, the empty chairs. 'I don't have any idea.'

'Are you going in to work?' She was twisting a handkerchief in her hands.

'I don't think it would look right.' His stomach rumbled and he glanced at the kitchen door. Looking down, he saw that his shirt was wrinkled, but there was no one to iron it. Most days he felt his life was on schedule like a crack passenger train, but not today. Now all he could do was wonder where his little girl might be.

26

Graysoner was on a branch line, the track so buckled that Sam fought off seasickness in the rocking coach. He checked into a hotel near the river, washed the cinders off his neck, and walked back down to the desk, where he found that the Wellers hadn't come in yet. About five o'clock that afternoon he heard the *Ambassador*'s whistle upriver and walked over to the wharf, striding along a line of spindly Ford trucks and mule-drawn coal wagons awaiting the boat's arrival. He was already red-faced, not from the heat of the day but from his shame.

The boat came in bearing the soot of her last season, and a coal gang came off and set planks from the fuel galley to the wharf. After a minute Elsie and August appeared on the main deck and crossed onto the dock as soon as the main stage had been set down. Neither would look at him as they approached; instead, they looked beyond him, studying the town they now had to go against. She was thinner, her face without color. August had grown taller in the intervening months and was as thick as a man. When they stood next to him, August dropped his suitcase and wheeled. Sam felt the percussion of an open-handed slap that nearly knocked him over. His mother grabbed the boy's arm and stepped in front, pushing him back.

'I'm not going to hit him again,' August said. 'But I wanted him to know what I think of him.'

Sam staggered in a circle and blinked at the fire dancing in the left side of his face. 'I thought I was doing the right thing when I did it,' he said, holding a hand to his cheek.

Elsie dropped her arms and looked at him. 'You decided we weren't good enough for our own little girl.' Her voice was without anger, yet without the least of kindness. 'I know what you did and why you did it, and it makes me feel like trash.' Her accusing eyes drilled into him. 'Do you think people down on their luck don't deserve their own children, Sam?'

He stepped back and looked down at the tarred wharf. 'I wrote you that I was ashamed.'

She bent down to her suitcase and August did the same. 'You wrote a letter.'

The way she said this sounded as if she had practiced it for days, and the color rose in his face again.

August switched hands on his suitcase. 'You can tell people you're sorry all you want. But what's that compared to what you did, what you're sorry about.'

The hotel sign was visible up the hill, and the Wellers started toward it, Sam following and anxious to get the whole day over with. It could only get worse, he thought, considering what they had to do next.

He talked to the middle-aged hotel clerk and discovered that Graysoner, though a small place, was the county seat. He got the location of the sheriff's office, and at eleven o'clock the three of them walked into the courthouse through a rattling twelve-foot-high door made of carved and varnished hardwood. Up two flights of curving stairs, they found a deputy who told them the sheriff was out on an investigation and would probably be back at one o'clock. Sam stopped Elsie when she began to tell why they were in town.

'We'll come back then,' he said, taking her arm.

Once on the street, she asked him why he'd cut her off.

'You don't play much poker, do you?' He guided them into a café across the street where they sat in a booth and ate breakfast. At the end of the meal Elsie looked across the table at him and said, 'Do you think we'll need to get a lawyer involved in this? I'd hate to have to pay one.'

'I don't know. We're in another man's henhouse here. Nobody knows who we are.'

'I'll have to trust you to handle the talking.'

He shook his head. 'I'll do my best.'

August made a disapproving noise in his throat.

'Son, you've bulked up some since I've seen you. Been lifting weights?'

'I found a job loading wagons with sacks of stove coal.'

'You can't get away from that soot, can you?'

The boy said nothing to this.

The sheriff was late, so they waited in his echoing outer office in hard chairs until they heard a door open somewhere inside, then the deputy motioned them to come forward.

The sheriff, his hair neatly combed and parted in the middle, gave them a brief introductory smile, showing his straight rank of teeth. His scan of evaluation raised the hair on Sam's neck. 'What can I do for you people?'

'It's a long story, but this woman and her son are my friends, and this lady's baby daughter was stolen from her in New Orleans.'

The sheriff leaned back in his spring-loaded chair. 'A stolen baby girl,' he said airily. 'So why aren't you looking in New Orleans?'

'I've seen her here in town.'

The sheriff did not seem surprised. 'You have? And when was that?'

Sam looked at August and swallowed, then explained how long it had been.

'Why'd you wait so long to see about this?'

'That's neither here nor there,' Sam said. 'We've come to claim her and bring her back into her family. This is Elsie Weller, her mother.'

'That right?' The sheriff's question carried a note of disbelief.

Elsie drew a photograph from her purse and placed it on the desk. 'Yes, I'm her mother and this is Lily. She was three when she was abducted, and now she's four.'

The sheriff looked at the photograph without picking it up. He pursed his lips. 'Where exactly did you see her?'

'In the yard of a man named Acy White. I talked to some maid about her in the alley.'

'And why didn't you come to me then?'

He glanced at a bookcase filled with leatherbound volumes. 'She looked well off. Mr Weller had just died, so I made a mistake and kept quiet about it until recently. When I realized I was wrong.'

'About what? The girl's identity?'

'About not telling Mrs Weller right away.'

The sheriff came forward decisively in his chair. 'This sounds a little fishy to me, all of it.' He turned to Elsie. 'You say your husband's dead?'

'Yes. He died from—'

'I'm not interested in his health problems. I'm just trying to figure out who you are. How do you support yourself?'

'My son and I work on the *Ambassador*.'

'That the excursion boat? What, might I ask, do you do?'

'My son plays the saxophone, and I do some singing. Mostly I waitress.'

'So you're musicians,' the sheriff said, as if this explained something. 'You live on the boat, do you?'

Elsie sat up straight. 'We keep rooms in Cincinnati.'

The conversation went back and forth like this for fifteen minutes, until the sheriff stood up and pulled down his vest. 'I've known Acy White for a long, long time, and I know he's a fine man who would never do anything unethical.'

'We know the girl's here,' Sam told him. 'I saw her. I met the people he hired to steal her away.'

The sheriff waved him off. 'Two things you have to know. Even if this child was stolen, which I'm rock-hard sure she wasn't, it happened out of my jurisdiction and I can't have anything to do with it.'

'Can't, or won't?' Elsie asked.

'Have whichever word you please,' he said. 'Do you want to hear the second thing?'

She nodded, casting Sam a sour look.

'The Whites reported to me a few days ago that their daughter, Madeline, has disappeared. Along with their cook, Vessy.'

There was silence in the office, and then, after a few moments, a burst of explanations, accusations, and denials, all leading to an outright argument.

The three of them stood on the sidewalk, confused and angry, and Sam felt the anger turning against him. Looking up and down the long, clean street, he could smell the café but nothing like the stench of New Orleans. The storefronts were spotless, bright awnings fending off the heat, windows filled with merchandise. 'I feel like jumping in the damn river,' he said.

August spat on the curbstone. 'Where do they live?'

Sam looked up the hill, wondering where the boy he'd known last year had gone. 'Way up there, at the top.'

Elsie began walking. 'Let's go, then.'

They went to the front gate and opened it. Elsie rang the bell. The house loomed, quietly. Then she knocked. After a long while, August stepped around her and pounded on the door with his fist, then tried the knob, but the door was locked, and as he rattled it they all sensed the heaviness of the wood, the wide bolts thrown into the frame.

Elsie stepped back into the yard and looked up at the broad windows cinched with squares of colored glass. 'Are you in there?' she yelled. 'We need to see you about our little girl.'

To her right a neighbor, an old woman wearing an alarmed expression, came out and stood on the steps, but Elsie yelled again, 'We know you took her, and we want to get her back.'

Sam stepped out next to her and checked all the windows himself, but they showed no faces, just recently cleaned glass, blank and facing west. One broad pane captured a cloud like a picture frame, but besides this, there was no movement. After a while they walked around back and tried there, knocking and yelling until a city policeman drove up and told them to please leave, that they were disturbing the neighbors. 'They've left home,' he told them.

Sam walked over, and seeing that he was bright-eyed and young, not a small-town thug in a uniform, he asked him a question. 'What do you know about the Whites reporting a little girl missing?'

'Her name's Madeline. It's been a few days now, but they think their cook made off with her.'

'Vessy?'

'That's right.'

'Vessy what?'

The policeman pushed back his cap. 'I don't recall hearing.' He glanced over at the Wellers, who were still watching the doorknob. 'It's a funny thing about cooks and gardeners,' he said. 'Hardly nobody ever knows the last name of one. Why do you think that is?'

Sam leaned a hip against the short fence and shook his head. 'I guess some people think it only takes one name to call a dog.'

The next afternoon August stayed at the hotel with a headache, and Sam and Elsie caught the sheriff in the hall of the county building. When they approached, he put his palms out in a pushing motion.

'I've got nothing to say to you.'

'We'd just like to know what you're doing to find my daughter.'

'We're doing a great deal to find the Whites' little girl,' he said, then turned and began to walk off.

'I can't believe you won't go after kidnappers just because they're your friends,' she called after him.

'I resent that.' He was still walking away. 'I've already told you that the little girl was taken by the cook, I don't know why. We haven't had a ransom demand.'

'What kind of lawman are you?'

He stopped and looked at her. 'Mrs Weller, what kind of waitress are you?'

Sam took her arm and led her out into the sunshine, for her

face had gone bone white and she was shaking with anger and fear. 'Can you afford to hire a lawyer?' he asked.

'Not and eat too,' she whispered.

He looked up and down the pleasant street. 'This isn't good. I don't have the money to hang around and track this Vessy character. The desk clerk says she could be in eastern Kentucky somewhere. From what I hear, the people up there back in the hills and hollers can't even find each other.'

'How will we know,' she began, swallowing with effort, as if keeping down nausea, 'if they find her? I'm nearly out of money myself.'

He looked up in time to spot the young policeman who'd shown up in the alley behind the Whites' house. He was coming down the courthouse steps, looking in their direction.

Sam raised a hand. 'Excuse me, Officer.'

'Do for you?' He walked over to them.

'I believe you're the only man in town that would do a favor for that little girl.'

'Oh, I wouldn't say that.' He grinned, and Sam could tell he hadn't been a policeman long.

'If she's found and brought back to town, how about sending me a telegram?'

'I reckon. Where you want me to send it? And I'll need a buck, won't I?'

Sam had a railroad ticket stub in his pocket and borrowed the policeman's pencil. He fished a limp dollar out of his billfold and put it in the policeman's palm along with his address in New Orleans. 'If it costs more than this, let me know and I'll send it along.'

'All right, then. I'll be glad to.' The policeman touched the brim of his cap and turned away.

They did what they could, spoke to whoever would speak, but next day the three of them were on the local train headed out through low alluvial hills toward the main line, where they would switch to the Illinois Central. Sam had used the hotel phone and found that the *Ambassador* was laying over downriver for boiler wash and coaling. On the ride down in the old varnished coach, they'd run out of things to say, and Sam was worried about the boy, who sulked against the window in the manner of an old man pained by some vast inner hurt.

'You going back to play with the band?'

'My coal-passing days are over, that's sure.'

'You're keeping up with the tunes?'

'I'm keeping up. What's hard is I've got to teach myself technique. Since Dad's gone, I don't have any help.'

'Well . . .'

The boy turned and gave him a challenging look. 'You know, I think I might have to kill him.'

Elsie looked up at the coach's curved ceiling. 'August, not now.'

'Kill who?'

'That man. The one who beat Dad up. The one they hired to get Sis.'

The locomotive whistled for a crossing, a sorrowing rise and fall of sound, and Sam glanced out the window at the engine, visible on the curve ahead. 'He'd be a hard one to find, much less kill.'

'I've been to the library and studied maps of where that murderer lives. There are maps of every square inch of this country in the library, you know.'

'When it comes to killing, I believe he's got the upper hand.'

'All I need is for him to walk in front of a gun.'

'And you have a gun?'

Elsie leaned toward him. 'No, he doesn't. Haven't you ever been fifteen years old?'

'You better not let him think like that.'

'He's entitled,' she said, sitting back. He again saw how thin she was, how pale, strikingly older. He didn't think being alone could take that much out of a person.

By late afternoon they were in Paducah and caught a cab down to the waterfront, where the *Ambassador* was raising steam, pillars of black smoke going straight up from the stacks. Captain Stewart was in the purser's office on the main deck wearing a new uniform, the creases ironed in with so much starch the cloth gleamed like silk.

He looked up. 'Lucky, I hope you've come to work this trip with the Wellers.'

Sam shook his head. 'I can't afford to work as third mate.'

The captain put a hand on his shoulder. 'We lost Swaneli in Evansville. Fell down a flight of steps and broke his left leg in two places. What say we put you on at second mate and you can sit in with the day orchestra a bit. It'll be seven dollars extra a week over your old wages.'

He thought of his new baby, his lost piano. 'I guess I can phone my wife and see what she says.'

'That's the ticket. You stay the whole season, there'll be a bonus in your last pay envelope.'

'If I come on, I'll take it a week at a time.'

'All right. You'll bunk with Charlie, then? He's the new first mate.'

'I guess so.'

The captain laughed. 'So putting up with Charlie's snoring is better than breaking in a new bunkmate.' He turned to the purser. 'Put Lucky back on.'

The Wellers took their cabin assignment and left without a word.

He walked up three decks to the Texas and found Charlie reading his missal. 'Hey, you must be dying, because you're saying your prayers.'

'I just run out of reading material. I killed off Zane Grey and a half-dozen *Review of Reviews*. Figured I'd fish around in my prayer book for some Old Testament wisdom. You back on with us?'

'Looks like it.'

'You got any news on the Wellers' little girl?'

He sat on a backless stool and told him what he knew. 'We're just hoping for a telegram at this point.'

'You say a cook stole the child?'

'I don't know who stole what at this point.' He watched Charlie's face sag into a suspicious frown and remembered he'd been a beat policeman.

'I'll have to think on that one, yessir. Something's not right.'

'Same crew as last year?'

'Yeah, but old Brandywine's getting addled, so Mrs Benton spends as much time with him as she can stand.'

'How addled?'

'Runnin' fast, like in his mind he's on the old *City of Memphis* on the mail schedule or something. We come through that bend north of Evansville and the river was all whitecaps for twenty minutes after we were finished with it. We must've turned over twenty rowboats in that stretch.'

'Bit can't cramp his bells down in the engine room?'

'Won't do it. Says when he gets a bell for full ahead he don't know who's ringing it, so he just delivers on the throttle. I keep Brandywine supplied with coffee every chance I get, and you can have that job. He cusses me down the steps once a day.'

'Well, if I ever go up on the roof, I'd better have a uniform on.'

'Go down to the laundry door and draw one, then.' Charlie lay back in his bunk and opened up a detective magazine.

27

The boat ran past Cairo, leaving the green Ohio for a dun Mississippi made of the flushed-out topsoil of half a million farms. Most of the day orchestra was on board, so he and August sat in with them, learning the season's new tunes as the boat steamed past the empty lands above Tennessee and down into the intestinal bends approaching Caruthersville and beyond, the engineer working the engines hard and the boat pulsing ahead with each piston stroke. After one practice session Sam went up to the pilothouse with a cup of coffee for Mr Brandywine, who was standing on a spoke, bringing the boat around the head of an island using the old steering wheel.

Sam froze and watched the coffee surge with the push of the big engines. 'Still don't like those new steering levers?'

'Hush, boy. This is a touchy spot. I'm tryin' to feel what the river's doing through my feet.' He reached over and rang a stop bell. The escape pipes ceased their intermittent rasp, and after a moment Sam felt the boat turn like a drunken head and yaw to starboard as the current steered her. When the tip of the island went past, Mr Brandywine rang for half ahead and Bit Benton answered the bell, the boat regaining its southbound steps. 'Now let's have some coffee and a report on Elsie's missing girl. I heard she was restole.' He reached back for the cup.

'Yes, sir.' Mr Brandywine did not acknowledge the fact that Sam hadn't been on the boat for months, as though it made no difference to him who showed up with his coffee.

'Who took her?'

'If I knew, I'd be trying to run them down.'

'I didn't ask what you knew, but who took her.'

Sam stared at the back of the pilot's head. 'Oh. The sheriff says it was the housemaid.'

At this point Mrs Benton came in and sat on the lazy bench. 'Hi, boy.'

'Mrs Benton. We were talking about Lily.'

She nodded and sat up and pulled at the shoulders of her customary black dress, which she wore to conceal the soot. 'I heard you talking when I was coming in.'

The foot of the island went by on the left and the eastern light came up in the pilothouse. Mr Brandywine looked at her. 'Mrs Benton, he says kitchen help stole the little girl. Now, I have no notion what goes on in a lady cook's mind, so what do you think?'

'Well, how old was this cook?'

'I'd guess around thirty or less,' Sam told her.

'Where was she from?'

'I hear she was from eastern Kentucky.'

'Mountain girl?'

'I'd say so.'

Mr Brandywine snorted. 'Well, then that settles it. She'd be more likely to make off with a jug of coffin varnish than a singin' baby girl.'

'I'm inclined to agree,' Mrs Benton said. 'My lady instincts tell me she won't make off with a child and take on a world of bother that's not hers to bear. A poor girl won't do that, most cases.'

Sam placed a hand against the cold stove. 'Well, who would?'

'A thief is what steals things,' she said. 'Rafe, are you answering a hail?'

'No, by gosh.'

'Why're you going to the bank, then?'

'There's deep water here, I'll thank you to know.'

Mrs Benton looked at the bank sliding by. 'I'd just as soon stay on top of it.'

'It's all right.'

'Sure it's all right. But I think your head must itch and you're planning to stick it out the window and scratch it on those sycamores coming up.'

Mr Brandywine stepped back from the wheel and turned the steering levers hard to port. 'What were you sayin' about a thief?'

'Wasn't somebody hired to take this girl in the first place? To my way of thinking, that's who you ought to look up.'

'The same people?' Sam shook his head.

'How many times does a person get stolen in her life? I'd bet the original thief has something to do with this. Look 'em up, I say.'

'They ain't too fond of being looked up,' Sam told her, taking the empty cup from Mr Brandywine's back-stretched hand. One thing he knew about crooks is that they believe if they do the opposite of what people expect, they're harder to catch. That's why most shoplifters in Krine's, the experienced ones, dressed in nice clothes and smiled at the clerks. They carefully stole in the middle of a crowd of shoppers, everybody else intent on their own purchases. He gazed out at the deserted riverbank, land not unlike that inhabited by the Skadlocks, a weed-infested, eroded clayscape showing scars of its annual submersion in the river's spring ravage. Skadlock and his mother would figure how to blend into Graysoner, and, knowing them, they'd get out on horseback. But he doubted the old woman would travel so far, and he guessed Ralph would be helpless with a four-year-old girl. All at once, the missing cook made sense.

'You can't call the local authorities on them?' Mrs Benton asked.

'No, ma'am. There ain't a lot of law where they're at.'

'You could try.'

'Well, maybe. You might be right about checking them out, anyway.'

The *Ambassador* paddled up to a wooded point and Mr Brandywine was swinging the levers farther to port to get to the deep water in midriver when a loud whistle sounded twice around the bend. 'Try your ears on that one, Mrs Benton.' He grinned meanly, as though he'd finally trumped her skill.

She put her head down and adjusted her hemline. 'It's the *MacDougall* blowing her three-bell chime.'

He wagged his head. 'Golly, Ned, I thought I had you.' He rang a stop bell and blew one glass-rattling blast for a port-to-port passing. 'I wonder how they knew we were up here. Must've seen my smoke.'

'More likely they're runnin' with all the windows open and heard your exhausts.'

Coming up around the point was a one-stack steam pushboat behind two oil barges, *MacDougall* painted on its bow. It crossed over to the east side and Mr Brandywine yanked a bell cord for full speed, the old boat beginning to bob with each piston stroke. Pulling the plug out of the speaking tube, he blew into it, and when Bit's pipe-strangled voice hollered up, Mr Brandywine called through the funnel, 'Quit dragging your feet down there. Throw the cutoff lever all the way in the corner.' Shortly the escape pipes began to bark, the smokestacks dumped out twin black tornados, and the sliding windows shuddered in their frames.

Mrs Benton rolled her eyes at Sam. 'Rafe, you must think you're coming down from Cincinnati and delivering the governor on the big old *City of Louisville*.'

Mr Brandywine arched his back. 'Ha. One time they docked my pay for shaking china off the tables down in the main cabin on that boat. Yes, ma'am, coming downstream on a full bell over nine foot of water, that *City of Louisville* was one rattling load of lumber.'

The next day, after morning practice Sam got up from the piano and walked over to where August was sorting his music into an accordion file. The boy didn't look up and kept thumbing through a sheaf of papers. Sam saw that some of them were maps. 'You doing all right?'

The boy still didn't look up. 'Mr Simoneaux, I've just about got everything under control.'

Elsie walked over and stood between them, her arms folded. 'Sam?'

'Listen, I've been thinking about those Skadlocks. They might have something to do with Lily's disappearance.'

'That's pretty foolish thinking,' she said.

'When we get into New Orleans, I can take a train up there and maybe find out. Maybe give the local law a try.' He knew he sounded desperate.

She turned her face away. 'Lucky, that Vessy person has her.'

'What state is the local law in?' August looked at him for the first time that day.

'What do you mean?'

'If the Skadlocks live where you say, they're on the Mississippi–Louisiana line. Does anybody really know where that line is back in the woods?'

'You've been reading too many maps. It's in Louisiana, and I'd bet money on it.' But he was less sure of this as he spoke.

The boy got up and stepped off the bandstand. 'Maybe you ought to do some map reading of your own.'

'He's not too happy, is he?'

Elsie watched after him as he passed through a door to the open deck. 'It's been rough on us both.'

'But it's given him a hard edge.'

Elsie sat on a maple folding chair, and her voice came out dreamy and tired. 'One day he had a father who could teach him anything, and the next day he didn't.' She looked up at him. 'We've both lost a lot, but you know that. Sit down and play that last song again. I've got to sing it sometime on a night trip.'

He opened up his music and began to play a lively tune. 'Make it bounce more,' she called, and on the next breath she was singing. Her voice was good, but there was something missing in it. She was merely singing the notes, and last summer she'd tackled the song and thrown it to the ground.

South of Memphis the *Ambassador* lay up, blinded by fog, tied to willows for twelve hours. The next day Mrs Benton put the boat through the strangulated loops of river switchbacking down toward

Helena and Greenville, deep into the land of dampness and heat. The river slowed and widened below Vicksburg, and the river birds that showed up were long-legged and moved like ghosts. Sam propped open his cabin door and watched the misty air below Natchez bear clouds of mosquitoes chased by buckshot patterns of cycling martins. The boat landed briefly at Zeneau, a hamlet that seemed to be falling house by house into the river that undercut the sandy bluff on which it festered. Here a fireman and an oiler who'd worked the previous two seasons got on with their sacks of clothes, and Mrs Benton backed the boat out and aimed its bow toward Fort Adams light. The night settled down like wet velvet, and Sam went to the empty dance deck to practice. He was bumping up the intro of 'Grandpa's Spells' when a door opened and Elsie walked in. He kept playing, thinking she was just taking a shortcut over to the port side, but she came up and stood by his treble hand and spoke over his music. 'I'm looking for August.'

He thought for a moment that her voice was part of the song, but looking at her eyes, he stopped. 'Haven't seen him. You try the café?'

'Yes.'

'Maybe he went down to the engine room.'

'I've checked. Will you look?'

He nodded into her worried face, understanding what was unsaid. There were places she might have passed over, like the big room where the musicians stayed, the firing galley's grit and hiss, the deckhands' tool room where men played cards and spat. He got up and walked the boat, hoping the boy was talking music with the night-orchestra pianist. Fred Marble was nattily dressed as usual when Sam spotted him at the rail. He was deadheading back to New Orleans to join up with the new group the captain had just hired. But Fred hadn't seen August.

'Naw. That boy came around yesterday and we talked about his saxophone.' Fred flicked a cigarette over the rail into the river. 'He's getting good. That little Dutchman can make that thing talk like a parrot.'

'Yeah, but he's not so little anymore.'

'I hear that. He's getting his growth for sure. Big as his daddy was.'

Sam looked past him into the tiny room, its floor littered with arrangements. 'He talk much about his daddy?'

'Yeah. That man trained him from a baby. And that boy's mad deep inside, like only a boy can be. He can't think about it. Not old enough to think. He can just be mad.'

'Any idea where he is?'

'Check the banjo man. They was talking yesterday.'

But Zack Stimson hadn't seen him either, nor had the captain, whom he found running deckhands out of the tool room, nor had the pilot on watch. He went into the café and saw Elsie sitting at a table, a forefinger lifeless in the handle of a coffee cup. She was staring out a night-blackened window.

'I couldn't find him.'

'I know.'

'What's that mean?' He sat down next to her.

'Mr Brandywine was coming through and stopped in for some pie. He told me he saw August get off the boat at Zeneau and thought he'd been sent to a deckhand's shack to roust him out. I asked him how he was dressed, and he was wearing his fireman's overalls and boots.' She began to tear up. 'Lucky, he's going after that man.'

Sam sat back, his mouth open. 'Why, he can't get to him. He's just a kid.'

'August had a little money saved up, and when I checked his bunk just now, it was gone.'

'Where's the next stop?'

She shook her head. 'You say he's just a kid. He *used* to be a kid.'

'He's graduated all the way to fool.'

Her head jerked up, her mouth a hard straight line. 'I heard Charlie say your whole family was murdered and nobody was ever arrested. He said you weren't even interested in finding those people.' She focused on him, her jaw rigid.

‘It happened before I was . . .’ He couldn’t find the words to finish the sentence. Maybe there *were* no words for not being vengeful. Would vengeance matter to an infant so glad to get out of a stove and into his uncle’s arms? It occurred to him that maybe he should have learned along the way that something like vengeance did matter. But of what use was it? Setting old scores right? Paying back a son of a bitch? He wasn’t trained to think that way. His uncle had told him many times that revenge didn’t help anybody and that the punishment for being a son of a bitch was being one.

28

Vessy woke the girl and told her they were going on a long horse ride and having a picnic in the woods.

The girl clapped her hands and sang out, 'I can wear pants.'

'Yep, you can wear those little overalls things.' They were the smallest pair Vessy had ever seen, and she thought Mrs White liked them because they mocked working people. 'Here now, lets us get dressed and hurry up.'

They left by the back door and walked to the alley. Vessy lugged a cardboard valise with her left hand and a two-handled picnic basket under her right arm. 'Would you like to meet Vessy's friend?'

The girl pulled at her hair, which had grown out the color of polished brass. 'Yes.'

'Yonder he is.'

Ralph Skadlock stood by the carriage house wearing a new pair of jeans, a black preacher's shirt, and a big Stetson.

The child saw him and walked boldly up, studying his face a moment before looking past him. 'Horsies!'

'Hey there, missy,' Skadlock said, as though addressing a miniature barmaid, for he had little notion of how to treat a child. 'Would you like to take a ride on this here animal?'

The horse he motioned to was a big five-dollar horse, swaybacked and standing on splayed hooves. The smaller one picked one back leg up as if the ground were too hot to stand on and wagged his fiddle-shaped head. His saddle was cracked to dissolution and the one on the large horse was painted with brown enamel. They were disposable horses, good for a day's work, if that.

Vessy mounted the small horse and pulled the child out of Skadlock's hands and set her in front. He tied her suitcase on the animal's rump and bound the picnic basket alongside his mount. They started up the hill away from town, rode into an empty field and out the back of it into a graveled lane, crossed the drain flute on the hill side of the lane and took a path up into a section of red oaks, the forest floor crackling with last fall's leaves. Soon they were on a trail through the hardwoods, climbing. Within two miles they came out of the woods into someone's backyard, passing behind the woodpiles, then slipped among the trunks again, going higher, Vessy pointing out things for the child to look at all the while.

The girl was a good traveler but got tired around eleven o'clock and started to fret, wanting to stop. Vessy called to Skadlock and he pulled up and looked back. 'What's the matter with her?'

'She's just tired and a little hungry.'

'Can't you get her to stay quiet? There's farms all over these woods.' He slouched back on the swayback horse, which was blowing hard as a bellows.

The girl began to cry, and Vessy got down. 'Give me that basket.'

Skadlock stayed on his mount. 'We're on a schedule here.'

She just stared at him, and after a moment or two he sighed and passed down the basket, then got off.

The girl sat on a rock, and Vessy gave her a cup of milk and two cookies. The child ate as if she expected the service. After a while, Vessy said, 'You want to get up on the horsie again?'

'Is this our picnic?' She looked around, still chewing. The trees were big boled and full headed, so there was little underbrush.

Skadlock led the horse up and slapped the end of the reins in his hands. 'We're havin' fun,' he said in the tone he might use to announce a death in the family. The child looked up at him and squinted, hard. Fearing for a moment that she recognized him, he turned quickly and walked off.

They mounted up and went on, across a wide clearing and back into woods, a pine belt this time, and the ground grew rocky. After an hour of this, stopping three times to let the poor horses blow lest one of them drop stone dead on the grade, the girl began to cry out with boredom. The little lame horse rolled back his ears and craned his neck to look at her.

Skadlock rode back to where they sat the horse, a minor urge to slap the girl flying through him like a bat through a chimney hole. 'Shut her up, will you?'

Vessy gave him an evaluating glance. 'Haven't you been so upset you just wanted to holler out?'

'We're comin' up on a farm. I can near see the house. Keep her quiet!'

'I can't.'

He reined the horse around sharply and plodded ahead into a small open area of pine stumps. When the child wailed out, 'I want to go back, go baaack,' Skadlock stopped and wondered how hard he would have to thump her in the back of the head to knock her out. Her skull was about the size of a raccoon's, and he figured for a full minute, thinking of animals he'd stunned and what they were like when they revived. He dismounted and walked back to them, taking the halter of Vessy's horse as it stumbled up. 'Get down a minute and let me see her.'

Vessy misunderstood and tilted her off the saddle toward him. He put up his hands and the girl jumped, throwing both arms around his neck to keep from falling. Her soft bottom found his forearm and next thing he knew, he was holding a soap-smelling child who was looking him straight in the eye. He turned around to scan the woods, then looked at her closely. 'You . . . uh . . . can you be quiet now?'

'Let's have a picnic.'

'You just ate.'

'You play games on a picnic.'

He stepped back from the horse and almost fell over a broad, flat-topped stump. He examined the dry surface and put the girl down on it, then bent and brushed away the pine straw. Pulling himself up straight, he focused on her small, perfect features, her smart eyes. 'You know your numbers?'

'I can count to fifteen.'

'Which is bigger, six or seven?'

'Seven, silly.'

He walked over and dug into the rotten pair of saddlebags the horse's owner had thrown in, the leather split, the copper rivets green with verdigris. The saddle maker's name was pressed into the decorative tooling, proclaiming his location in Saginaw, and for an instant Skadlock thought of the old boy who rode horseback through the snow all the way from Michigan. It toughened him up to consider this. Then he dredged out a deck of cards.

He sat the girl on the picnic basket on one side of the stump, and he dragged over a bucked-off pine top and sat across from her. He dealt out the whole deck. 'Leave 'em facedown,' he said.

'Is this a game? This is a game!' she said, clapping her white hands.

'It's called battle.' He turned up one of his cards – a four. 'Now you flip a card.'

She pushed a sprig of hair from her eyes with the back of a hand and rolled her top card with the other. 'Nine.' She looked at him.

'Which is bigger?'

'The nine.'

'You done won my card.'

'Good.' She clapped once, reached over, and picked up his four.

His next card was a queen, and the girl turned a six. 'Which is bigger?' he asked.

She shrugged. 'The lady card?'

Vessy, standing behind her, snorted.

'This gal might have a head for cards,' he said. 'That's right. That's a queen and it's higher than your six, so I take your card.' After a few plays the jack and king came out, and he explained the hierarchy. Then she tried to claim a queen with her jack, and he stopped her. 'Say, "Jack, queen, king, three in a ring."' The child repeated this twice.

'Where'd you hear that?' Vessy said.

'Mamma taught me.' All at once he remembered the old pack

he'd learned on as a child, a deck of forty-six cards so old they had only the spots on them and no numbers. They lived in a thin-board shack in Arkansas so cold that they played cards to keep the blood from freezing in their fingers. He'd sat in his mother's lap and learned his numbers that way. As he grew, she taught him every type of poker there was and, once he got his growth, what kind of knife to carry to the games.

The girl turned her cards faster and faster, and soon the game was over. Skadlock then made a show of counting the piles. 'You got thirty and I got twenty-two. Who done won?'

'Me!' She threw up her hands.

He gathered the cards, shuffled, and handed them to her. 'Now you deal. Give me one and then you one till they're all gone.' He watched her bright little fingers struggle with the cards, and finally reached over and formed her hands in his. 'Look, damn it, you deal like Billsy. Hold the deck in one hand like this and lick your thumb to push the top card off on the table.' She did as he said and dealt the deck onto the rings of the stump. He reached into his pants and drew out a coin and placed it on the wood.

'What's that for?' she said.

'You don't play cards for nothin'. You got to bet. I bet a dime, so what'll you bet?'

'I don't know.'

'You got money?'

She shook her head and turned her first card, a seven.

'Well, then we got to stop playin'.'

'Aw, no!' She balled a fist and put it up next to an eye.

'Can't play without no bet.'

'Oh, please!'

He rubbed his two-day beard. 'Tell you what. See that big open hayfield?' He pointed ahead to a mile-wide opening, and she turned and looked. 'If you promise not to go cryin' when we ride over it, well, I'll take that as your bet.'

She spun back to him, smiling as if he were joking, but when she saw his eyes she knew he was not. The child glanced at Vessy, who was standing patiently off by the horses, holding the reins. 'I'll be quiet,' she whispered.

'It might could take us a good fifteen minutes to ride through. Promise you won't cry?'

'Your card, mister.' She began bouncing on the basket.

His eyebrows went up, and he flipped an ace.

The girl stared at the card. 'High or low?' she said.

'In this game it's forever high,' he said, raking the trick.

He won by two cards, picked up the dime and her promise, and they mounted up and went on quietly, passing through the big farm and on into another band of timber, and then higher, where the animals scrambled for purchase on the mossy rocks. The three of them topped the ridge at last and stopped to let the horses wheeze and shudder under them, the bigger animal leaning against a fat pine for twenty minutes.

The child complained that she was hungry, but Skadlock started his horse.

'Can't we'uns eat now?' Vessy called ahead to him. He didn't respond, though he pulled his watch. In a few minutes they started down the other side of the ridge.

In a clear, level spot he stopped the horse and checked his watch again. 'Schedule says we got fifteen minutes.'

Vessy dismounted, spread a cloth on the ground, and they sat around it. 'Here,' she said, taking a block of cheese from his stubby fingers. 'I'll fix things.' She gave the child milk in a cup and poured water into two others. Opening a box of crackers, she sliced cheese onto several squares and spread potted meat over that. They ate in silence until Vessy, looking around the bald, said, 'This here dirt looks pretty good.'

He followed her gaze, chewing. 'I seen better.'

'Was you a gardenin' man or did your mamma do the growin'?'

He became still. 'She just passed, and this is the first I thought of it.'

'What did she grow?'

He squinted. 'Tomatoes, some sweet potatoes, and turnips. The usual.' He was lying on his side but sat up Indian-style. 'Tomatoes was the best. Ain't nothing better than a big one sliced with salt and a little vinegar.'

'That's the truth,' she said, popping a cracker into her mouth. 'Looks like you're gonna have to get friendly with your mamma's hoe.'

He looked at her and at the child, who was licking potted meat off her fingers. 'You grow stuff up in the mountains where you're from?'

'Aw, no. We just sent all them sarvants we had down to the lowlands to shop for us and haul it back up to our place on their backs.'

He gave her a startled look. 'Ain't you saucy.'

Her expression didn't change. 'I like the garden. One thing I hate about livin' in town's there ain't no place for the vegetables to come up in.'

In an hour they noticed smoke rising up above the trees, and though they could see no houses, he knew they were coming to a town called Cletchy, three dozen houses in a narrow valley threaded through by a railroad. They rode slowly into a cornfield, then came out on a tractor road where the fields changed to cotton. Before long they began making their way past a string of tenant houses. In the first yard, black women were boiling wash, and in the second children were feeding dominique chickens, and on the porches of the third and fourth and fifth old men sat smoking pipes and watching them pass like some dream drifting before them, perhaps the only strange white people they'd ever seen, too rare even to believe much less call out to with a good word.

They found the rail embankment and rode down it to the small gingerbread station. He walked in and woke up the drowsing agent and bought tickets to a connecting station further south, not buying through fares so he would not leave a trail. He also bought north-bound tickets for thirty miles up the line toward Indiana. The agent asked where the people were who would use the extra set, and he said that relatives were coming at this very moment to take the southbound.

Outside, he scanned the long ridges they'd crossed. He would buy new tickets in the first connection and the second as well, northbound and southbound at each, figuring the expense was worth it to make it that much harder for anybody to trail them, if trail them they would.

While Vessy and the girl sat on the long bench on the track side of the station, he walked around to where he'd tethered the horses to a sapling, the old hitching rail too rotten and wobbly to trust. Two Fords passed in the gravel road, and he stood in the sun with his boots gathering street dust until a white man passed on foot. He looked him over and decided he looked wary, and a wary white man would ask questions when somebody tried to give him two horses, even two sorry broken-down nags. Next came a black man wearing a creased and shiny face and riding a mule with no saddle on it, a very old man who wouldn't question anyone's motives, not in this town.

'Hold on!' Skadlock called.

The man pulled up his little mule, which seemed mostly donkey. 'Cap'n?'

'You look like a man what needs a horse or two.'

The black man's eyes were cloudy, and he got down and took off his hat, leaning in to try and recognize who'd flagged him down. 'I wanted this'n to pull my buggy, but he won't get between the shafts, no he won't. My woman can't come to town no more, so she send me everywhere she want.'

'You got any money?'

'Cap'n, I ain't got a cent. Can't get one, neither.'

'Well, I tell you what. We come down from Louisville on these two and they've give out. We got to take the train, so if you want 'em, just haul 'em off to your place and let me have two dollars.'

The old man walked over, trailing the reins of his mule behind, and ran a hand down the neck and along the saddle of the tall horse. He felt all four legs. He did the same with the little horse, which kicked out at him and almost knocked him down. 'Tack go, too?'

'Tack, too.'

The black face froze in thought and Skadlock interpreted the hesitation as meaning nobody would believe that any foreign white man would sell him two mounts and tack for two dollars. He would be charged with stealing. 'Reckon I better not, Cap'n. But I thank you.'

He tried not to show his rising anger and looked around at the town's simple buildings. 'What if I give you a bill of sale? I can't leave these animals in the street.' From three miles away he could hear the whistle of the southbound train.

'I don't know.'

'Look, damn it, if you had all the money in the world, what would you give for the pair?'

The man looked down. 'Well, the big fella old as me and the little one only got three legs. Them saddles feel like oven toast. I guess maybe nine dollars.'

He went inside the station and got a sheet of paper and a pencil, making out a receipt from a Mr Walter Lee Copes, Louisville, Kentucky, for nine dollars, then went back to the road and put it in the man's hand. 'If anybody asks you about them horses, show 'em that paper. My street address is on it and they can write me a letter.'

The man looked at the sheet closely, holding it upside down. 'How I know this paper don't say, "Hang this fella for a hoss thief?"' He smiled to show he was joking, but they both knew he wasn't.

Skadlock set his jaw. 'How far out in the country you live?'

The black man stepped back. ''Bout five mile.'

He reached into his coat pocket and peeled a five-dollar note off his wad. 'You think even a fool would pay five dollars to play some joke? These animals is going to suffer if I leave 'em here. This here's a dollar a mile.'

The man folded the bill carefully and put it down in his shoe. 'Okay, Cap'n. I can take these po' boys off your hand.'

He slowly climbed onto the mule and received the reins of the horses. The mule turned around as of its own will, and the lame animals followed.

Skadlock watched for a while, furious at how he'd been outsmarted, then turned toward the tracks thinking about the train ride, which would involve two changes. He recalled that his brother would leave horses tied to the little station at Fault for the ten-mile trek back to their place. If he didn't have Vessy helping, the girl would be screaming her head off the whole way.

But when he came around the corner of the station and sat on the bench, the child climbed up in his lap. He studied her warily, as though a possum had decided to perch on his right thigh and grab hold of his shirt pocket. The warm child-smell of her drifted up to him again, and he put a hand on her stomach as she leaned out to watch the locomotive smoke its way up to the station. She clapped her hands and leaned farther away when the engine bell rang, the air brakes hissed, and the cylinders bled bursts of steam. He put his other hand around the first and held firm, sharing with her this amazing sight.

29

Gray dawn. Mrs Benton signaled for a tug to come out from the Baton Rouge levee. Sam could see commas of steam spring up against the bank, and a boat came out toward midriver with a coal flat on its hip. He climbed down and jumped aboard the tug, which cast off from its barge and chuffed back in. Crossing the levee, he came up behind the great redbrick expanse of the Y&MV station. An agent sold him a ticket on number 36 for Gashouse, where he could change for the mixed train into Woodgulch, putting him at the end of the line at 2:45.

He made the first connection with no idea of what he would do in Woodgulch, knowing only that it was ten miles from Zeneau, where he could begin tracking the boy. The one passenger car rocked at the end of a string of boxcars and three stinking chemical tankers. On a curve he saw the small locomotive, filthy with soot and forty years old, its mailbox whistle shrieking at a dirt road crossing. He sat next to a white-haired gentleman and asked him how he might get from Woodgulch to Zeneau.

He regarded Sam a long time before spitting over the window ledge. 'Who are you, son?'

'Sam Simoneaux. I live in New Orleans.'

'New Orleans,' the man repeated, inching higher in his seat as if his seatmate were from New Delhi or some other foreign place replete with contagion and unspeakable ways. 'What are you after in Zeneau?'

As Sam explained, an acne-scarred man in the seat ahead turned around. 'This young'un you after, where's he a-headed?'

'South along the river.'

The man snorted. 'Ain't nothing in there. Is he after black bear or something?'

'He's kind of a runaway.'

The white-haired man also snorted. 'His old man take a stick to him?'

'His daddy's dead. I just want to catch him for his momma before he gets into trouble.'

'You say he's fifteen year old?'

'That's a fact.'

'You wouldn't believe some of the crazy stuff I did when I was fifteen. One time on a dare I rode a bull and that devil carried me through a bob-war fence and a quarter-mile into town, where he and me went through a hardware-store window and took out a hundred dollars' worth of sash work. I landed next to a Coats and Clark thread dispenser and the doc sewed me up with navy-blue number three right out the display box.'

The acne-scarred man pulled out a handkerchief and blew hard, three times. 'Look here,' he began, 'when *I* was fifteen I got up too late to milk and my old man told me to stay in our little feed-store and keep the stove hot all day. "Just keep the stove hot," he said. I sulked around and stoked that son till it was cherry red and the pipe was glowin' all the way to the ceilin'. The damper melted and fell down into the firepot and I found some cokin' coal in the back and dumped ten pounds of that in the door. That stove turnt white and run me out the door, and not long after that the attic caught fire. When my old man got back from Woodgulch, all that was left was a square lot of white ash and the stove sittin' more or less upright in the middle of it. He looked at me and said, "Well now, I'll grant you that son of a bitch is hot all right!"'

'What did he do then?' the white-haired gentleman asked.

'Not a thing.'

'That was the punishment.'

'Say what?'

'You'd of turned out worse if he'd a tooken a strap to you.'

The acne-scarred man gave him a startled look. 'I reckon that might be true. I know I felt low as a dachshund's nuts for a long time after that store burnt down.'

Sam leaned in between them. 'I've got to get to this boy.'

'I don't know about no boy,' the old man said, 'but if you want a ride to Zeneau, a truck should be waitin' for freight at the station. Ask the driver for a ride.'

A fat man wearing red suspenders that disappeared under his belly was waiting at the station in a tan Model T truck. The white-haired man got off the train and shambled over, grabbed a gallus strap in a fist and pointed toward Sam, who walked up and introduced himself.

'Cost you a dollar,' the fat man said.

'All right.'

'I'm just joshin' you. Help me get them boxes out the last car and we'll get on down the road.'

There were only six boxes of stove parts and ten feed sacks and a crated Victrola, and soon the fat man was at the crank starting the Ford. He got in with a whistle and asked, 'Can I sing on the way?'

'Sure.'

'Funny. I never could sing before.' He laughed until his face was crimson, then set the truck off across the ruts of the station yard.

They rolled through the six blocks of Woodgulch out into a countryside of washboard hills stippled with gum trees strangled by poison sumac and catbriers. He could see no houses, and after a while the road grew sloppy and plunged into an old-growth cypress forest, the trees fifteen feet through the base skirt, blocky trunks rising like factory smokestacks into a spongy canopy. He looked into these waterlogged woods and hoped the boy hadn't stumbled far into such a terrible place.

The fat man fought the wheel over the bad road and couldn't talk much, except once when a sack of feed fell over the tailgate and they were forced to stop. Sam got out and looked around. 'That's some timber. Damn, that's some timber for sure.'

'Yeah, it's been bought and paid for. A Natchez mill is finally gonna cut it all out next year.'

'How much of it?'

'All of it, I hear. Thirteen thousand acres, out on the river south of here down to the prison and beyond.'

'Down by where the Skadlocks live?'

He loaded the sack and left his hand on it. 'How you know about the Skadlocks?'

'I've run into them.'

'You ain't no kin, are you? I'll leave you here in the road if you are.'

'No. What'd they do to you?'

'None of your business.'

'Fair enough. You know how to get to their place from Zeneau?'

'Boat.'

'Is there a place to rent one?'

'No.'

Sam sighed and shook his head. 'Horse?'

The man walked around to the front of the truck and leaned against the steaming radiator. 'If you go overland, it's about seven, eight miles due south, and you'd have to rent you a gorilla to tote you up and down them gullies. I hunted back in there when I cared about it, and I'm tellin' you it's a miracle I'm standin' here.' He turned the crank, climbed in the cab, and let off the brake.

Sam got in. 'How you know about them at all?'

'I deliver for the sheriff. The west deputy has a office in Zeneau. I seen that biggest Skadlock come in there and talk to him. Him and his dog.' The fat man looked over at him, and there was a sudden longing in his eyes. 'I used to have me a little black-and-white rat terrier rode in the truck. Sat right where you're at. He was smart. Like a little fuzzy person, he was. I was down deliverin' a chair and box of supplies to that one-room deputy office when I seen Skadlock's horse and his dog next to it. I went into the office and didn't think a thing about it, but from inside I heard a squeak. When I went out my dog was dead under the truck and that German police was pissin' on my front tire. I told Skadlock off when he come out, but he just dug in his pocket and give me a dollar. Then he got on his horse and rode off. I was mad as hell, but later I thought, you know, somebody like that can't do no better.'

'You get yourself a new dog?'

He shook his head and geared down for the next hill. 'Naw. That was the one dog.'

'Can't replace him?'

The driver turned slowly. 'Can you replace your mom?'

Sam rolled his head away and looked down the awful road. 'Doesn't seem like the same thing, exactly.'

The fat man shifted gears. 'Bud, the older I get, I think ever livin' thing is one of a kind.'

Zeneau was a store, a deputy's office the size of a big privy, five wood houses, and a mud landing. The driver let him off in front of the unpainted office, and he looked at it doubtfully before deciding to move on through the mosquitoes to the store, breaking sunbaked, puckered mud as he walked. It was after three o'clock, the day's heat at its zenith. Inside the dim store three graybeards were sitting around an unlit stove, their feet propped on the fenders. The clerk was busy on the back landing, taking delivery off the truck.

'Hey, bo,' one of the old men said, a fellow wearing patched overalls and a long hound's face.

'Hi. I'm looking for a big kid, fifteen years old. Anybody seen him?'

'Where you from?'

'New Orleans.'

'You don't talk like New Orleans.'

'I was born in west Louisiana.'

'A Frenchieman,' the hound's face called out. 'Hey, talk some of that palaver to us.'

'Comment ça va? Brassez mon tchou, têtes de merde.'

A red-faced man dropped a foot off the stove skirt. 'Ha, ha, listen to that! Sounds like a monkey with a mouthful of olives.'

'Have you seen him?'

'What you wantin' him for?'

'His mamma sent me after him. He's run away.'

'Oh!' the hound's face exclaimed. 'Whyn't you say so? You know, I run away when I was a kid.'

The red-faced man slapped him on the knee. 'But you never went back.'

'You know, you're right.'

The conversation stalled at that point. Sam looked at the first man and said loudly, 'The boy?'

'Oh. Yeah, he come in here yesterday, said he wanted to hunt turkey. Bought a huntin' vest and some eats.'

Sam looked at him. 'He doesn't own a gun.'

'He didn't when he come up on the porch. Talk to the clerk about it.'

After a while, the bald clerk came back inside, sweaty and sour-smelling. 'Hep you?'

'I'm looking for a boy.'

'Who you, then?'

'Aw, he's all right!' yelled the red-faced man.

'Well, sold him some cheese and potted meat and crackers and a toy compass. And a used shotgun.'

'Aw, hell. I was afraid of that. What kind?'

'A old double-barrel wore-out Parker. Ten-gauge with rabbit ears.'

'What kind of shells did you sell him?'

'Feller that traded it to me give me the shells, and I passed 'em on with the gun. About a dozen.'

'What size shot?'

'Hell, I don't know. They was old goose loads. Maybe number-two shot with black powder under 'em.'

'Good lord.'

'It was none of my business, but I knew he wasn't no hunter, least not much of one. Kind of a city-lookin' kid.'

'Well, when did he leave?'

'I let him sleep on the porch out on the cotton. He left about a half hour after I opened up at six. Give him some syrup and bread for breakfast. I saw him start off due south into the woods.'

'Is there a trail?'

Everybody laughed, and the third man's feet fell off the stove's fenders. 'Not much of one. We all pretty much stay out of the south woods. Louisiana's got a state prison a few miles in there against the river and there ain't no tellin' who you could meet up with, if you know what I mean.'

One of the men said, 'You goin' after him?'

'I guess so.'

'You own a compass?'

Sam reached into his khakis and pulled it out. 'I've been back in there before.'

'You got my sympathy,' said the hound's face.

'I was on a horse.'

'Well, well,' the red-faced man said and spat into a box of sawdust next to the stove. 'You got him now?'

'I'm on foot.'

The man stood up. 'You need to see my brother, then.'

Sam looked at the clerk, who shrugged. 'What for?'

The man lay a spotted hand on his arm. 'Come on, he's down the street.'

Sam followed him half a mile to a dog-trot house, and the fellow who came out had the same sun-botched face as his escort.

'Buzz. Who you got there?'

'Fellow needs a animal.'

'I got a pig he can have.'

'Does it come with a saddle?'

The brothers smacked hands and chucked shoulders and then stood side by side looking down off the unpainted porch to where Sam stood in the chicken-bald yard.

'I don't have a lot of money,' he began. He explained what he wanted to do and the horse trader gave his brother a doubtful look.

'I should of knowed you wasn't bringin' around somebody with cash in his jeans.'

His brother shrugged.

'I can only sell you a animal. I don't rent, there ain't no sense in it. But when and if you get out of that terrible country' – he nodded his shaggy head to the south – 'I'll buy it back less what you skint off him in there.'

Sam tried to remember how much was in his wallet, how much a pair of train tickets would cost to get him and the boy down to New Orleans. 'What can you sell one for?'

'I got an Appaloosa that's tough and is good on short hills and mud. He's thirty-five dollars.'

'God, I can't afford that.'

The horse trader blinked. 'Somehow I thought not. Well, I got a old mare, then, slow, but she won't spook. You can't make no time through those woods nohow. She's twenty dollars cash money.'

'Maybe. What else?'

'I got a couple trained mustangs, but if you ain't a real good horseman, they'll kill you dead, 'cause they'll do what you tell 'em even if you spur 'em into quicksand or off a drop. Now, I got a retired dray horse with heart trouble you can have for fourteen dollars, but once you get in the woods he won't fit between trees.'

'Let me see him.'

The trader looked at his brother and shook his head. 'Let's us go around back, then.'

On the way to the barn, an animal in the pasture caught Sam's eye, an oversized mule a hand and a half taller than most and gray as fog. 'What's the story on that one?'

The horse trader looked everywhere except at the mule. 'What one?'

Sam pointed.

'Oh. That's a hinny. Biggest I ever saw. I got him in a trade last year and done sold him and took him back three times. That one's too smart to ride.'

'How's that?'

'Aw, he just knows better than anybody that gets on him. If you could just figure out how he thinks, he'd be a good animal. But you can't make him do a damn thing he don't want to.'

'He's sort of white.'

'Yeah. Folks around here think that means bad luck.'

'Can I try him out?'

The man turned and looked at him. 'Why would you want to?'

Sam looked out into the field and the mule looked back, rolling his ears forward. 'I rode a mule like him to school.'

The horse trader spat out the side of his mouth. 'This one'll take you to school, all right.'

They got a rain-hard saddle out of the barn, and Sam asked for a thick blanket when he saw it. He cinched it on, leaning against the animal while he worked, rubbing the mule over before clipping a cloth saddlebag on the back. The roller-mouthpiece bridle he passed slowly over the ears, which stayed relaxed, though the mule looked at him carefully. Sam talked to the animal and patted him. 'You got a crupper for this saddle?'

'Naw. I got a old double rig in there somewheres if you're scared of that one.' He motioned to his brokeback barn.

'Let me see something.' He walked to the fence and got a length of mildewed plowline hanging there and tied one end to the saddle horn and walked around behind the mule to the other side, pulling the rope and rolling it up the animal's legs and quarters. The mule watched him but barely moved a hoof. Then he took the line off and put it back on the fence. He mounted up and started the mule off in a straight line, turned him, backed him, and made him trot a bit. Getting off, he left the reins on the ground and walked away. The mule looked at the gate and back at Sam, but didn't move.

Sam climbed on the fence. 'What's wrong with him, then?'

'A man can't get in that animal's head. Some you can beat, some you can treat, but that one don't respond to neither. To be fair, he's done good for me, but everybody else tells me he'll stop sometime and might as well be a stump. Worse, he'll keep going even if you pull his head off. Just won't stop for nothing.'

'Does he have good wind?'

'Oh, hell, yes. He'll climb a tree and yodel at the top, but that might not be what you told him to do.'

'How much?'

'Ten dollars.' He spat. 'Eleven if you bring him back.'

'How about the tack?'

'Now that's worth money. That stuff'll listen to you. I want it all back, and you leave me a ten-dollar deposit.'

'What's his name?'

'Gasser. That's what was wrote on the bill of sale I got. Came from over the river in Pointe Coupee Parish.'

They shook on it, and Sam rode the animal back to the store for a sack of food, a canteen, matches, oil of citronella, and a straw hat with a curled brim. He also bought a box of Quaker Oats. Starting out toward the south, he noticed Gasser's gait was rough when he hurried him along. He slowed him to a walk, and the mule grew soft footed. Then he bumped him up with his heels, and the hard gait returned. 'Damned if you don't trot like you're runnin' on crutches.' In ten minutes they entered the trees at a fast walk.

The country south of the Skadlocks' was a mix of dry and submerged cypress swamp, but this higher northern route showed hardwoods mixed with longleaf pine, the terrain choppy and bent as a run-over washboard. He was two miles south of Zeneau when the forest closed in completely, and the mule stalled against a wall of tallow trees and briars, refusing to budge. He turned the animal around and found a hogback ridge which he followed for a quarter-mile until it came to a point at a gulch full of fallen timber. He sat the animal and looked down into the tangle. Turning the mule again, he backtracked and crossed to the next ridge and rode along it until it also petered out, so he reversed tracks again, sidling west until he found a ridge that sloped down gradually into a mudbottom gorge. He tapped Gasser's flanks to go down, but he just stood there looking from side to side. 'Git up.' After half a minute the animal sidestepped to the bottom and walked south in a narrow ditch full of mudballs washed out of the ridges. Sam dodged vines as big as a man's arm, and after a mile of riding in what felt like a long grave, he tried to urge the mule up a slope onto high land, but he just stopped and drank the opaque water.

'Aw, get up!' The mule continued to drink. He popped him with the reins and found himself carried along the ravine, still in its bottom. Reining to the side made the mule jam to a stop, sideways, his nose in the moss on one side, his rump imbedded in dirt on the other. He cursed the animal for a full minute and then straightened him out and waited in the slow moving current. He kicked his ribs and called out every command he knew, every curse and animal insult, finally resorting to the French of his childhood, calling him a *maudit fils de putain,* at which the mule rolled his ears back all the way, though he didn't budge. Sam noticed the ears and thought a moment, sucking a tooth. *'En avant!'* he yelled, and the mule picked up his head and walked forward. Sam raised his hands and let them drop. *'Eh bien, un mulet qui parle français!'* The animal picked up speed, as if what he'd heard made him comfortable with the work at hand. Sam decided to give the mule his head and let him figure the woods out for himself. The light began to fade and he played with the name 'Gasser,' trying to understand where that might have come from. Finally, he called out *'Garde ça!'* and the animal gave a jump and picked up his step, bobbing his head. *'Garde ça!'* Sam said again, remembering that every village had a *garde ça,* an old rascal who sat in front of a store begging tobacco and telling dirty jokes. *'Regardez ça!'* the women would exclaim, shaking their heads. 'Look at that.'

Garde ça dug up a slope and got on top of a wooded promontory, where he stopped. Neither French nor English would get him going, so finally Sam dismounted and pulled on the bridle. The animal refused to take a step and bent to taste a weed. It was then he saw it, a wink of tin next to his brogan, and he looked out at the woods, knowing what it was before he picked it up: the can with the image of the red devil on its side. He called the boy's name, his voice broken by the matrix of vines and trees. Putting his head down, he listened but heard only the mule's rotary crunching.

He mounted and rode through a clattering brake of wild magnolias, then into a cloud of honeysuckle, and after a mile the mule again stopped dead for a long time, where the ridge started to descend. A good rein-whipping had no effect. He looked over the animal's ears trying to imagine what he saw in the mat of pigweed woven with generations of wisteria and poison oak. He began to suspect a snake and got down to study the woods floor, then looked up to scan the trees for signs of a wildcat. He hoped they weren't near a bear's den, and the thought of a flying comb of claws made him tug on the mule's bridle. *'Allons!'*

The mule closed his eyes and grew as still as a statue. Sam stepped back to give the bridle a jerk – to tear it off the sticker-matted head, if need be – and then he put his foot on something that was not solid ground. He looked behind him and jounced a bit, as if testing a gangplank for soundness, and the whole surface for fifty feet around moved up and down like a taut waxed tarpaulin. He dropped the reins, took another step, and his leg went through into nothing. Scrambling back to the mule's hooves, he understood that a section of the ridge had washed out, leaving the forest floor of vines and leaves suspended over a chasm underneath. Both of them could have been killed had they tried to cross. Turning Garde Ça around, he opened a burlap pack and took out a round box of oats, feeding half of them to the mule in tribute.

Backtracking, he turned south down a trail of sorts. Near dark, Garde Ça stopped and looked off to his left. Sam listened to a hot breeze stir the tops of a line of sycamores, and in the distance saw a watchman crow give three caws and flit off a pine top like ink slung from a pen. Under him, the mule seemed to be holding his breath. Then he heard two metallic clicks and turned his head, knowing that hammers had been drawn back and fingers were tightening on the triggers. A dart of orange fire blasted out of the brush and the mule stood on his hind legs, braying. Sam slid behind the saddle and hung on until the forelegs slammed back down, then Garde Ça bucked and he arced over the long ears, impacting the trail like a mortar round. He lay there, his lungs flattened, his mouth open as if to ask why all the air had been sucked out of the world.

August stepped out of the brush while reloading a mottled double-barrel shotgun. 'I want you to catch your animal and get back out of here.'

He tried to say something for a long time. His shoulder felt knocked out of its socket, and pinwheels of white fire spun through his vision. He wanted to say 'Bastard!' but knew that wasn't right, and that 'Son of a bitch!' was even less true, so when he got a bit of wind he said, 'I'm tryin' to help, you fool.'

August stood over him, expressionless. 'You can't even help yourself.'

'Put up that gun. I didn't come out here to hurt you.'

'I wasn't sure who you were, exactly.' He brushed his hair out of his mosquito-stung face.

'Come on and pull this arm. It's just out of its socket a little.'

August propped the shotgun against a sapling and grabbed Sam's left hand. 'You want me to yank on it?'

'Just turn it right when I tell you.' He took one breath, then another.

'Now?'

He nodded and cried out when the shoulder popped back in. 'Damn it to hell!'

The boy took up his gun and stood in the trail. 'Now you can ride.' He pointed down the trail to the mule, who stood sideways to the track, eating bright-green leaves of marsh alder.

'What you expect to do, boy?'

August's face was still a child's, but his eyes were fixed like a hawk's. 'I'm going to kill Mr Ralph Skadlock, at the very least.'

Sam sawed his left arm gingerly, looking up at the boy, trying to figure how to reason with him. 'I think you've heard this before, yeah, but if you do that, you'll regret it the rest of your life.'

'I've got plenty to regret already, don't you think?' He helped Sam to his feet.

'I'm not going anywhere. You mother told me to get you back safe.'

'Nobody's stopping me.'

'One of the Skadlocks will put the brakes on you.'

August turned his back and walked off into the brush, and Sam tried to remember what he'd felt like at fifteen, when he'd already made up his mind to leave his uncle's farm. Nothing would have changed his mind from the one thing it had focused on. He suspected such single-mindedness was both the best and the worst thing about youth.

Sam retrieved the mule and followed the boy to where he'd been building a campfire.

30

The three of them had arrived at the big house two nights before. Ralph was standing in the yard next to his brother, staring up at the roof.

'Well, I'll be damned,' Billsy said.

'You carry them shingles up to the window for her?'

'No. I guess she found 'em in the yard.' Billsy tilted his head like a dog. 'She damn sure knows how to patch. Look how she's lappin' 'em.'

Vessy was on the roof in a worn pair of corduroys, copper nails stitching her mouth as she swung the hammer lightly to keep from splitting shingles.

Ralph nodded. 'Makes me dizzy just watchin' her.'

The men stood in the yard a long time. Now and then Vessy would call to the dormer window, and the child would put three or four shingles on the ledge.

'This one a whore?'

'Nope, just some kind of housemaid or cook.'

'How long you gonna let her hang around?'

Ralph spat. 'Till we get rid of the kid.'

'I ain't never seen a woman on a roof before. Not wearin' pants, anyways.'

'You ready to hit the road?'

'I guess. You still want me to go all the way to New Orleans?'

'And use a coin phone to call Acy at night. I decided he better bring the money to us in Woodgulch.'

'What if he says he won't pay?'

'Oh, he'll pay, all right. I'll keep that little girl and make a cardsharp out of her.'

'She's bright as a cap pistol, all right.'

Ralph looked over at the tangle of trash woods behind the house. 'We got to keep an eye out from now on.'

Billsy looked up in awe at the woman on the roof. 'Breakfast was terrible good. I never knowed you could do that with cornbread.'

He told the boy to smear himself with citronella oil. They ate cheese and a potato roasted on the coals and said nothing for a long time until August looked at him over the flames, his eyes catching fire.

'Charlie Duggs told me about you.'

'That right? I hope it was an interesting story.'

'He said your whole family was murdered and you never even tried to find out who did it.'

'I think that must be the most interesting thing Charlie ever heard in his life. He never quits telling people about it.'

The boy's face glowed with sullen disgust. 'Well, why don't you look them up?'

'Maybe I don't want them to complete the job.'

'I'm not joking. Don't you take anything to heart?'

'I take plenty to heart, you little shit. I was six months old when it happened. I never even knew anybody I lost.'

'That's pretty heartless.'

Sam looked away from the fire, from the disturbing eyes. 'My uncle told me it was in other hands.'

August tossed a stick onto the fire. 'Other hands? You know, the Bible teaches justice along with everything else. Sam Simoneaux, you're just a coward with all sorts of excuses, and your uncle's next to worthless for not setting things right for your father. All he taught you is excuses.'

Sam stared at his feet, then turned his head sideways. 'Maybe.'

'Tell me. You remember your father's hands on you?'

He settled back against a fallen loblolly and looked up at the fire-coppered limbs. 'I told you, I was a baby.'

'When I was old enough to make a chord on a piano, my father started teaching me. He'd sit behind me and tap my shoulders with his fingers, sort of playing the notes on me while I played them on the piano. I knew if I was lazy and delaying a note, or if I was rushing a run out of time. His fingers guided me in the rhythm, see. When I started the sax, he did the same thing, tapping out an improvised beat, hearing where I was going with the melody and telling me where I should go, where not. It was like he was passing himself into me through those fingers.' He looked up, and his eyes were yellow mirrors. 'You can't know what it's like never to have that again.'

'Your old man made a good musician out of you. He wouldn't want you to waste it.'

'I'm not wasting a damn thing.'

'You're about to. When one of those Skadlocks knocks you down with a rifle bullet tomorrow, where will all that music learning be then? Dead as your smart-ass little carcass.'

'Skadlock's just a hillbilly rummy. I can sneak up on him like I waylaid you.'

'Good lord, August. I'm a department-store floorwalker. These people *live* waiting to get waylaid. They're not three miles from here, I'd bet, and probably can smell the smoke from the pine knots you built the fire with. Maybe even see the smoke. I wouldn't be surprised if they step out into the light right now and do us in.'

August gazed to his left into the dark and smiled. 'I don't think they're as sharp as you think.'

'Listen. If you believe you know more about hurting people than they do, go back to town and talk to some of the locals.'

'I'll do what I need to.'

'Boy, this doesn't have a thing to do with your father. You just want to think of yourself as important. A show-off is all you are.'

The boy stood up and grabbed the old shotgun by the barrels. 'Take that back.'

'That's what revenge is, kid. You'd like to think you're going to help your mamma or provide justice for the world, but you really just want to kill somebody to make yourself feel big.'

'That Ralph Skadlock might kill someone else.'

'I got news for you. I don't know for a fact that he's ever killed anybody. He didn't kill your father, either. Ted got an infection in a Cincinnati hospital and died of blood poisoning.'

August's face convulsed. 'He wouldn't have been there if it hadn't been for Skadlock,' he yelled, his eyes welling with tears.

'If Skadlock wanted him dead he'd of killed him out here and thrown him in the river with a sack of bricks tied to his neck. You're not thinking straight.'

'It's not right,' he cried. 'If people don't get what they deserve for killing somebody, it's just not right.'

'I agree with you. But trying to shoot 'em up with a six-dollar shotgun ain't the way to do it.'

'It feels right to me.'

'Feeling's got nothing to do with it. But what's true does have something to do with it. The truth is, your daddy never taught you to go out and gun anybody down. He taught you to make music for the rest of your life.'

August sat in the dirt next to the fire and let his hand slide down the shotgun. 'Just shut up.'

'After you sprinkle Skadlock with that Parker, what'll you do about his brother?'

'He has a brother?'

'And a mother, who I'm pretty sure is never more than three feet from a pocket pistol. They run a still back in there, and I've never seen moonshiners who didn't have more guns than a hardware store.'

He looked over when he heard a sniff and saw the tears shining down August's face. 'Lucky, for a second I thought I believed you, but just as soon as I did I could feel my father's hands on my shoulder. I've got to make it right.'

Sam nodded once. The matter was past arguing that night. When someone is struck, the first mindless impulse is to strike back. After reflection, sometimes that impulse fades. He knew the boy needed time to calm the notion of revenge. Or an alternative. 'August,' he began, 'once those people see you armed on their place, they're going to protect themselves. They'll hurt you real bad, maybe even kill you, because you've made them believe they have to. I'm not going to bring that news to your mother. No way in hell. If you'll just listen to me, maybe there's a way we can capture Skadlock and bring him to the law in Zeneau.'

The boy lay the shotgun down on a blanket before the fire and stretched out next to it, his hand on the walnut wrist. 'I already talked to the deputy.'

This surprised him. 'The hell you say.'

'Yeah. He's Ralph Skadlock's second cousin.'

That night he lay on a mound of leaves listening to spiders grinding away in the weeds. His arm and shoulder seemed to glow with dull pain. Sometime in the night he fingered citronella into his ears to scent out the keening mosquitoes. He dozed when the fire burned down, but soon woke up imagining how the boy would blunder onto the homesite full of confidence and catch lead like an animal drawn to a baited field. Nobody should let this happen to a child, even one big enough to be a man and already smarter than most. August still lived in the one-dimensional world where he couldn't understand how the irreversible can happen, drawing your final breath or watching someone else do it. In the morning he'd do what needed to be done, even if it meant the boy would need stitches or to have a bone set. First thing, he'd break the shotgun to pieces.

At dawn the temperature came up and the trees began to tick with dew, a glossy magnolia leaf dripping into his face and waking him. The boy was gone. He sat up and whirled around but saw only the hobbled mule, staring at him knowingly. He brushed off his shirt, stretched out his arm, which hurt worse than the night before, and saddled Garde Ça, reining him out onto the narrow ridge. The lead-colored sky revealed nothing of the time, and he stared up as he rode, trying to figure out how long past daylight he'd slept and wondering if the boy was dead yet. The mule shambled along, shaking his head as though Sam had started the whole series of sad events that would end with Elsie's losing the only child she had left.

Inexplicably, he came to a straight, one-lane gravel road running east-west. He sat the mule in the middle trying to comprehend this connection to the known world. Then he crossed over and continued south through the woods. In less than an hour the trail ran parallel to the mile-wide river, and he knew he was close when the mule's hoof clanked down on the lip of an inverted sugar vat, a huge cast-iron kettle shaped like his wartime helmet. In a collapsed shed he saw a litter of dove-colored shingles covering two other kettles, remnants of a *batterie* where slaves boiled sugarcane juice down to blackstrap. He reined into the marsh alder and cattails here, knowing the house was perhaps a mile or less away. When they reached the tree line the going was easier, and he turned south and stopped, keeping the animal's head up so he wouldn't pull and grind grass. Garde Ça's breathing calmed, and he listened. To the southwest a steam towboat was making a racket, fighting upstream in the high river, and the covering noise allowed him to move through the brush up to the house. He tied the mule off and went on foot until he could see the dark planks of the belvedere rise above the willow saplings. Passing through the graveyard, he crept along until he spotted the fawn cloth of August's vest. The boy slowly turned his face as if expecting him, and Sam dropped down on his knees, water seeping through to his skin. Sixty yards or so in front of them was the board walkway that ran between the kitchen and the big house, and a woman stepped out of a door, gathered a small bundle of shingles, and walked back in.

'You don't want to do this,' he whispered.

The boy fixed his wounded eyes on him. 'You don't know what I want.'

'What are you planning to do?'

'I saw him walk into the house. The split second he comes out again, he's a dead man.'

'You'll be nothing more than a murderer. You can think you're a musician all you want to, but for the rest of your life you'll look back on this here with nothing but shame.' Sam saw that the hammers were drawn, the boy's fingers set on both triggers, and he imagined the buck and roar, the stink of smoke and the twin pattern of coarse shot splintering apart the door frame and anyone in it.

'I'm no murderer,' August said, his voice trembling. 'I'm getting even for my father.'

With a glance Sam saw there was no way he could wrest the ten-gauge away without it discharging. 'Look,' he whispered, 'Skadlock's maybe fifty years old. He smokes, he drinks rotgut, God knows what kind of women he goes with.' Sam scanned the rear of the house, deperate to think of the right thing to say. 'He drinks cistern water full of bugs. He probably won't be around another five or six years. You won't be taking much from him, and you'll be giving up a whole lot more.'

'Just shut up,' August hissed.

'And down the line, when he does die, he'll have to pay up then. I don't know what will happen, exactly, but it probably ain't good.'

'I don't care about that stuff.'

'Well, you'd better care, because when you die you'll have to answer for this. You might not believe that, either, but consider if you're wrong, boy. Consider if you're wrong. And you know what else? Whatever you say about Ralph Skadlock, he let your father live after he came here against him with a pistol and knife.' He kept his eyes on the door frame, praying for it to stay empty. 'Another thing, I'll bet Skadlock never hid in a bush and killed another man.' Watching the boy's eyes, he saw something there that made him go on. 'Believe me. You're not doing this for the reason you think you are.'

August turned to him as though he'd suddenly appeared out of thin air, then looked back at the house and down at the shotgun. The plum-brown hammers reared back like snake heads, but he let down the left and then the right, and lowered the gun, defeat he didn't understand showing on his face.

At that moment the side door to the big house squalled on its hinges and Ralph Skadlock stepped through, carrying a child on his right arm as his boot heels knocked along the walkway. The steamboat blew its whistle, and he stopped and pointed in that direction. When the child turned its head to look, both Sam and August could see who she was.

After the kitchen door closed behind them, Sam laid a hand on his shoulder. 'Let's back off a little.' The boy's face contorted toward crying, and Sam pulled him along.

They found the mule and led him north along the tree line, then turned into a blackberry thicket and stopped. The boy was mortified, unable to speak, but Sam finally got him to look up.

'I almost—'

Sam took him by the shoulders. 'Shut up. Knock that out of your head.'

'She would've—'

He pushed him, and the boy fell in a heap. 'You can beat yourself up later. Right now we got to think about this from every angle.'

He tramped down a flat spot and they sat and ate crackers out of the saddlebags, washing them down with coppery water from the canteen. They talked a long time and sweated in the noon sun, trying to understand what Lily was doing here. Sam kept after the boy with questions, not letting him think about what he'd almost done. After nearly an hour, they decided it was all about transit. Skadlock hadn't taken her out of loneliness, and the cook wasn't running off to start an instant family in the hulking mansion. Given what he'd seen in the graveyard, Sam guessed the old woman was dead.

August seemed confused. 'You think he's shaking down the Whites?'

'They're shaking down somebody. Why else would they take her again?' He looked around and lowered his voice. 'When they first made off with your sister, the old woman took care of her. They need that Vessy woman to do the same.'

'The Whites are as much at fault as anybody,' the boy mumbled.

'More. And you just think about that.'

August jerked his head sideways. 'You think they're going to deliver her?'

'Where, and to who, that's the question. I know it won't be in Kentucky. Ralph's liable there, even though the Whites probably won't risk setting the law on him.'

'It could be anywhere.'

'I don't know about that. Let's ride back to Zeneau and hang around the store, maybe find something out by accident.' He stood and looked up at the sky. 'Come on.'

The boy remained on the ground, sitting cross-legged. 'Lucky, I'm sorry.'

Sam studied a cumulus shaped like a horse, a blue hole about where the heart would be. 'So far, there's nothing to be sorry about.'

Doubled up on Garde Ça and backtracking north, they spent the afternoon losing and finding the trail in the vine-tortured gullies. For a whole hour, the mule stood like a steaming boulder in the middle of a washout for no reason they could discern. They dismounted and sat on the ground, watching him shake off flies.

The sun was low in the sky when they broke out of the woods and rode up the one street that was Zeneau. At the store they greeted the same old men and chatted their ears off until they rose one at a time and went home for supper. Sam bought two bottles of soda and pigs' feet wrapped in wax paper, and they lounged on the front landing, eating and looking around at the board-and-batten buildings as if they'd grown up in this sorry place and knew every tick-haunted dog under every porch in town.

The storekeeper came out shortly before sundown and padlocked an iron bar across the slantboard doors. 'You boys goin' to ride the station truck out tomorrow?'

Sam took a draw of soda. 'If the driver'll let us and we can sell the mule.'

'They's no place to take a room here. If you want, spend the night up on these cotton bales like the boy done before. Just don't smoke if you do.'

'All right. Does that deputy make rounds?'

The storekeeper put on his fedora. 'When he's chasin' his tail. He won't bother you.'

'Drinks a bit?'

'A bit.'

'His cousin keep him supplied?'

'You know Ralph?'

'We're not exactly friends, but I've dealt with him.'

'I'm sorry for you.'

Sam was waiting for such a signal. 'Seen his old mom lately?'

The man put a hand against a post. 'She comes in town maybe four times a year, loads up two horses, and heads back south. I was kind of expectin' her last week when the weather wasn't so hot.' He spat and looked them over. 'You didn't get down as far as the old house?'

'We did. Nobody was there.'

'The hell you say. I saw 'em all, even Billsy, plus a woman and some little cousin's child. They rode down there four, five days ago.'

Sam turned his head toward August. 'We didn't stay around there long. When's the last time you saw the old woman?'

'Like I said. Maybe three, four months.' He hitched his baggy pants up over his belly and cinched his belt.

'You see her pass through here last year with her little niece a second time? Comin' out?'

'Cousin's child,' the storekeeper said. 'Told me later it was her cousin's child from over in Arkansas. Pretty kid to spring out of that bunch.'

'Where were they going from here?'

The storekeeper shrugged and seemed aggravated. 'This is last year, and they was headed north to Woodgulch. There's a train there, as you know.'

* * *

They smeared themselves with citronella, Sam slapping it in his armpits and on the backs of his hands.

The boy watched, then took the offered bottle.

'Damned if I don't smell like a sardine,' Sam said, climbing up on the third layer of bales on the broad front porch. He stretched out under the roof tin, listening to it pop in the cooling air.

August lay against the board wall down below. 'They'll take Lily right past here, won't they, Lucky?'

'Only way to the rest of the world.'

'And meet the Whites in Woodgulch?'

'If I had to bet.'

'And we won't be able to do a thing about it.'

He tried to focus on a red-wasp nest a few feet above his head, a dim copper disk promising pain. 'Now you gonna kill the Whites?'

A single pained word – 'Don't' – drifted up from the darkness of the porch. It sounded like the last plea he would make as a child in this life.

'All right. It's all right. I'll try to figure something out.'

Sam tried to sleep, and did, but was awakened by a dim flash on the Louisiana side of the river followed a long time later by a low stumble of sound, a thunderstorm walking toward them on legs of lightning. He wondered how the girl was doing with her third set of caretakers and thought about when he was four, remembering nothing at all, neither face nor hurt or anything else, which maybe was a blessing. The next day they would go to Woodgulch and wait in sight of the little tall-windowed railroad station. Wait for what he wasn't exactly sure, but maybe the Whites would show, arriving on the wobbly train and leaving on the return half an hour later. But what could he and the boy do to the Whites? Take the girl away and ride along with them back to Baton Rouge on the same train? Try to get the law to help? Woodgulch was a Mississippi county seat, where the high sheriff had his office, the man who probably let the Skadlocks sell whiskey and steal whatever they wanted, who hired Ralph Skadlock's second cousin as the Zeneau deputy. There was no chance anyone there would believe two outlanders.

At daylight Sam woke and found the boy grim-faced and sitting with his arms crossed next to the locked door, his legs stretched out toward the west. When the storekeeper unlocked the building, he went in and sold the dew-rusted shotgun for a dollar less than he'd paid for it. Sam bought a tin of Vienna sausages and one of peaches in syrup. They went outside and sat on the porch like useless vagrants of a century before, hanging around to await some accident of good fortune. After he finished eating, Sam counted his money.

'You can sell the mule for something,' the boy told him.

'The old fellow told me he wouldn't take him back. Said it cost money to hang on to it and that the ten-dollar bill I gave him didn't eat. If I keep the animal, I'll keep the tack.'

'Where's that station you were talking about?'

'Woodgulch. Maybe ten miles.'

'We could ride there in two hours.'

'Let's see.' He walked into the aromatic store and offered the animal and tack to the storekeeper, who laughed at him. Back out on the porch he looked down at August, who sat slumped against a post pulling apart a wad of cotton. 'Let's ride.'

They went out back and saddled Garde Ça and got on. The mule stood like a piano bench. They remained still on his back, waiting. Sam dropped the reins on the animal's neck and crossed his arms. After five minutes, Garde Ça looked back at them, then began a drunken walk to the road, where he paused, looked both ways, and turned right toward Woodgulch. After a while, Sam picked up the reins and said, *'Dépêche-toi, lambin,'* and the mule evened its gait, his ears turning like ventilators on a ship's deck.

They met five automobiles on the way to Woodgulch. Sam looked carefully at the faces in the machines, and some stared back at his rudeness. He watched the road in the distance as well, and suddenly he pulled the bit sharply to the right and they rode off a hundred yards into a stand of cypresses.

'Stay here,' he told August, sliding off. Stooping in a berry patch, he watched Billsy ride by on a small horse the color of axle grease. He was wearing a new tan fedora and glossy boots.

'What?' the boy asked, when Sam remounted.

'Skadlock's brother. I'm not sure what that means.'

'He's probably bringing news.'

'What kind of news?' He turned the animal's head.

'I don't know.'

When they got back on the road, he said, 'News?'

31

Woodgulch was a town of seventy buildings, the hub of small farms and two mills that made window frames and nail kegs. There was a brick courthouse surrounded by graded red lanes and the usual small businesses. They rode down the main street to the station, Sam feeling dumb and disconnected from the rest of the world as he tied the mule to a catalpa. It was three-thirty. He was nobody here.

August went in and used the restroom for a long time and came out and looked at him as if to say, 'Now what?' His face and neck were red where he had scrubbed off the dirt and sweat. 'You don't know a soul around here, do you?'

'I'm thinking.'

'Nobody we can trust.'

'A connection,' he said. 'We need a connection. Time to talk to the connection man.'

He found the station agent copying waybills, a youngish fellow with an untrimmed mustache who was quick with his pencil. 'Can I help you?' he said.

'What's the name of the local sheriff?'

He came over to the window and looked at Sam's clothes and unshaven face. 'Kyle Tabors.'

'I might need to talk with him about something.'

'You might?' The agent narrowed his eyes.

'Is he a pretty good fella?'

'Who are you, bud? I saw you come through the other day, but I ain't seen you around here before.'

He told him his name and where he was from as patiently as he could stand to do it.

The agent looked him over again. 'If you want to find out about the sheriff, I recommend you walk down the street and ask him.' He returned to his desk and sat amid the clutter of hand stamps and bundles of paper stuck on hooks.

'I just need a little information.'

'Sorry. I don't know you.'

He walked out on the platform and the boy was laid out on the bench. He looked down the street to where the old idlers of the town sat on the low retaining wall at the edge of the courthouse lawn. He looked down the tracks lined by telegraph wire drooping between poles as if weighted with information and commerce. The lines made him remember the Greenville telegrapher, and he went back in.

'Hey.'

The agent looked up from a desk. 'Sir?' The word was strained.

'Do you know Morris Hightower?'

He rolled back in his chair and returned to the window. 'Yep. Do you?'

'I do. And he knows I'm looking for a little kidnapped girl, helping out her parents. You could telegraph him about me.'

'We get some Greenville freight back in here from time to time, and he contacts me about it. Sends Morse like a mouse runnin' on tin. I used to take train orders from him in Jackson.' He put a pad and pencil on the little counter. 'Write your name here and come back in a few minutes.' The agent opened his telegraph key and began sending an even stream of dots and dashes.

Outside, the mule was rolling the bit with his great tongue, so he sent the boy down the street with Garde Ça in tow to find water, telling him to wait at the station when he returned. By the time Sam went back inside, the agent was waiting at the window.

'You're a pretty lucky man.'

He glanced out the door after the boy. 'I've been told that.'

'Lucky we found him on shift, and lucky the dispatcher handled the relay up to Greenville. Have you found the baby?'

'I have. But I need a good lawman to help me.'

'Well, you know how the law is.' The agent sucked a tooth and studied him. 'I'd suggest you go talk to Sheriff Tabors. I don't know him that well, but I think he's all right.' He bobbed his head. 'You don't believe me?'

'Why'd he hire that drunk down at Zeneau?'

'What? Nelson Watty? Oh, he's all right. Just sick is all. He don't make thirty dollars a month but he stays in that little box of an office and collects taxes and signs permits for folks. It's not like they's a lot to choose from in Zeneau.'

Sam looked up at the Seth Thomas clock. 'What time does the passenger train come in?'

'The tri-weekly you rode in on yourself comes in at two-thirty more or less. It goes back about three. Took off a few minutes early today.'

He looked out into the dusty street and saw August stop a gray-bearded gentleman, who pointed down a side lane. 'You see that boy with me?'

'Yes.'

'When he comes back, will you keep an eye on him?'

'As much as I can.'

'Well, here I go.'

He had to wait for the sheriff. He stood in the hall and watched the lawyers clop in from the broiling street onto the hardwood and take the stairs to the courtroom. A policeman hauled in a handcuffed vagrant and brought him past Sam to a heavy door and shoved him through it. In the rear of the building he heard the clang of cell doors and drunken hollering. He hoped he wasn't making a mistake, that Tabors wasn't a fat rummy who liked the taste of Skadlock whiskey. Or just a mean local who hated outlanders, or Catholics, or people from Louisiana, or Cajuns, or anybody not born inside the county.

The sheriff came in at four o'clock, and Sam stood up. He was in his early forties and wearing a suit and vest of no mean quality, a big star pinned under his right lapel. His blond hair was freshly trimmed, as was the mustache that ran straight across his face, as straight as his teeth.

'You look like you're waiting for me.'

'I am.'

'Been rabbit hunting, have you?'

Sam looked down at his pants. 'It's a long story.'

'Well, come in, then, and have a seat.'

The walls of the office were cream-painted beaded board that ran floor to ceiling. A photograph of a woman unconscious of her good looks rested on the oak desk next to a box of pistol ammunition.

There are important starting points in serious conversations, and he paused a long moment to figure out the best way to begin. 'Do you know Ralph Skadlock?'

The sheriff didn't blink. 'Who are you?'

He patiently explained who he was, where he was raised, why he'd lost his job as floorwalker in New Orleans, how he'd been looking for a child named Lily while working on an excursion boat.

When he finished, the sheriff nodded. 'All right, Mr Simoneaux. As for Skadlock, I know of him, but I can't do a thing about him.'

'You say that as though five people a week ask you to.'

'That's about right. Including my mother-in-law. That place he lives on is probably in Louisiana. We are presently, as you realize, in Mississippi.'

Sam looked down at his dusty shoes and then up at the sheriff, who'd gotten up to take off his coat. He wore a tooled gunbelt and holstered on it was a Colt New Service revolver with pearl grips. 'Nice gun.'

He sat down again. 'Me and all the deputies switched to forty-fives last year. Our old thirty-eights wouldn't shoot through car doors. Times are changing.'

Sam looked at Tabors' eyes, wondering if he could trust him. Ultimately, he had no other choice, and had to take a leap of faith.

'Well, that ought to solve that problem for you. Let's see if you can do something about mine.'

'Let's have it.' Then the sheriff did something that convinced Sam that he'd made the right decision. He pulled a pad in front of him and held a sharpened pencil at the ready.

It took ten minutes to explain the history between the Skadlocks and Acy White, the death of Ted Weller, and why he believed the child would be exchanged in Woodgulch.

The sheriff took notes all along, and after Sam finished, he sat back. 'Son, you probably realize this already, but one crime was committed in Louisiana and the other in Kentucky. My jurisdiction is only this poor little Mississipppi county. Do you think they'll trade money for the child at the station?'

'I don't know.'

'If they did, I'd have reason to arrest everybody and wire for warrants from the other places. That is, if the child recognizes you.'

'She'll know her brother.'

The sheriff put down his pencil. 'She better. I can't turn her over otherwise.'

'You're telling me a four-year-old has to convince you of who she belongs to?'

The sheriff pulled the box of pistol shells toward him and placed it in a desk drawer. 'Seems like she's the one with the most to lose.'

Sam smiled. 'Well, I guess that's fair.'

The sheriff leaned back and pulled a folder from a different drawer, his body movement suggesting that the meeting was over. 'What do you do on the excursion boat?'

'I play piano and bang around the rowdies when I'm not.'

'I like piano music and have a player piano at home. I took music appreciation, two courses worth, in college.'

'College? Where at?'

'Rutgers. On weekends I went into New York for the revues and plays. There's a lot of music in that town.'

'Why'd you come back? Family?'

'Not really. I just came back because it's so bad around here.' He gave Sam a smile and motioned to the door. 'Come Friday we'll help you out.'

He found the boy at the station and together they walked to a two-dollar-a-night hotel on Batson Street, a mildew-smelling place with tall windows covered with storm-belled screens, bathroom down the hall, and an old man somewhere on the third floor coughing deep and long. They cleaned up and walked downtown to a café, counted their money, and ordered ham sandwiches and tap water. The train would next rattle into town on Friday afternoon, and it was Wednesday.

The hotel room held two small iron beds and that night they lay in the hot, breathless room and tried to sleep.

August turned repeatedly, went down the hall to the bathroom, came back and began tossing again. 'Lucky, you awake?' His voice was young again in the dark room.

'Yeah, I'm one hot dog.'

'I'm glad you made me put down that gun.'

He rolled on his back and tried to see the ceiling, which he knew was cracked like a map of desert rivers where the electric wire had been nailed to the plaster. His sore shoulder throbbed with his heartbeat. 'Count sheep, and maybe you'll drop off.'

'I've got to say it.'

'Go on, then.'

'If I hadn't backed off, I'd have killed her.'

'All right.'

'No, I need you to know how I feel right now. I mean, I want to get her, but I'm mostly glad she's alive. It's like it's okay if we don't even find her, just so she's, you know, still somewhere.'

Sam thought about that last phrase, 'still somewhere.' 'Aw, we'll get her back when that old train rumbles in day after tomorrow. The sheriff said he'd sit in the waiting room with three of his deputies and hash it out with all concerned.'

'You sure they'll bring her here?'

'I can't imagine where else. I'd bet a month of piano playing that Billsy was coming back from setting up the meeting somehow. It makes sense they bring her in Friday, since the train won't run again till Monday.'

August was quiet for a long time. 'What if those people talk the sheriff out of it? Didn't you say this Mr White was a banker and his wife a proper lady? You think the sheriff will believe us over them?'

'Oh, maybe she was bred in old Kentucky, but she's only a crumb down here.'

August laughed aloud, and it was the first time he'd laughed since before his father died. 'I wish you could play piano as good as you tell jokes.'

'I'm getting better.'

He talked to the boy a long time, easing him off to sleep. And then the image came to him of armed men waiting in the small depot for the likes of Ralph and Billsy Skadlock, and he thought of the possibility that something could go wrong, a gunfight and pursuit, slugs the size of bumblebees slamming through the flimsy pine walls, with a little girl in the middle of the fracas. Bullets didn't seek out guilt or innocence; they were flying accidents of fate. He eventually fell asleep and began to dream of Lily in Ralph Skadlock's arms, both of them turning to face a boy pointing a monstrous shotgun at them, and when that vision faded, he was in a hospital in France, and his wife was working on a needlepoint chair bottom, at one point holding it up to him and showing an image of a bombed-out house, a girl standing before the smoke and fire raising both hands, each finger made of khaki thread, nine in all, and a stitch of red for the bloody socket.

When Ralph Skadlock got out of bed, Billsy was standing in the doorway scratching and yawning into the new day.

'You smell that?' Billsy asked.

Ralph had begun sleeping upstairs again now that the ceiling no longer leaked and Vessy had dried and turned the mattress. He pulled on his pants with a grunt, and they went down and out into the kitchen.

Vessy had fired the big stove, robbed eggs from the hens that were left, and cut up onions and cheese, making the men an omelette and floating it on a pad of grits and butter. The little girl was at the table penciling mustaches on photographs in an old newspaper. The men sat down and began to eat, their heads low over the plates, staring at the food as it disappeared. The girl dropped her pencil and bent under the table to reach for it, but banged her head when she came up and started crying. The men glowered at her and Billsy said, 'Hey, shut that stuff up.'

Vessy picked up the pencil, gave it to the child, and brushed back her hair, kissing her forehead. She rubbed her back and found her a fresh page on which to draw. The child stopped wailing and began marking dark eyebrows on the image of a Baton Rouge debutante.

The men stopped eating and watched all of it, as if the notion of calming a child with anything other than a peppery slap or a whack with a piece of kindling had never occurred to them. Billsy put an elbow in his brother's ribs and asked, 'You remember the time I sassed the old woman while she was ironin' and she threw that flatiron down on my foot?'

Ralph made a face and took another bite. 'What made you think of something like that?'

'You remember that?'

'Sure I do. I'm the one tended to your foot. Took off your shoe and had to shake it to make your little toe fall out.'

'Took all winter for my foot to heal up,' Billsy mumbled, watching the girl drawing.

Vessy came to the table with her plate and sat down. 'I don't guess you heathen ever say grace.'

Ralph looked at her, chewing slowly. 'Grace who?'

* * *

After breakfast the brothers took a horse that was favoring a rear leg from the little wire trap of a paddock and checked its hooves.

The girl came out and pulled at Ralph's pants.

'Can I ride?'

'Go buy your own horse.' He walked backwards toward the woods, leading the mare and watching its rear legs. Thirty feet into the long grass, he stopped and looked at the ground. The girl walked up and put a white hand on the horse's knee. 'Billsy!' Ralph hollered.

His brother came out and looked at the footprints in the mud. 'Looks like two of 'em.'

'Town shoes. What the hell?'

'Can I ride?' the girl asked again.

Ralph circled her waist with his hands and lifted her onto the animal's bare back. 'Grab hold of her mane,' he told her, planting her hands in the coarse hair. 'Come on.'

The three of them moved off into the brush, where they found animal prints and, off toward the river, the flattened weeds of a resting place.

'You reckon it's somebody after the still or our reserves?' Billsy asked, pushing back his straw hat.

'Naw. None of them rascals wears shoes like that. Shallow heels and broad soles flat as a spinster's backside.'

'Somebody's been watchin'.'

'I don't like it.'

'Giddyap!' the girl yelled.

Billsy spat. 'We best change our plans a little.'

'One thing for sure. I ain't ridin' into Woodgulch in broad daylight with the kid.'

They turned back toward the house, the girl singing in her sweet voice the first two stanzas of 'The Horse That Outran the Train.'

Billsy looked up at her admiringly. 'Do you know "The Girl in the Window Above Alfred's Saloon"?'

His brother reached over and knocked off his hat. 'Damn it, Billsy!'

'Hey,' he hollered, swinging down for his hat, 'everbody knows that one.'

Vessy was waiting for them in the rear of the great house, wearing a housedress she'd found and washed and ironed. 'I figured you boys gone berry pickin'.'

Ralph told her what they'd found, and her eyes raked the woods. 'We still turnin' her over Friday, right?'

'I'll have to do some figurin', but you get her ready.'

'When can I get my part of the money?'

Suddenly, he looked down at the ground. 'I have it and I'll give it you.' He looked up and he was blushing.

Billsy rolled his eyes and walked past into the house, saying 'I'll be damned' under his breath.

'What's that about?' She put her hands on her hips.

'Nothin'. I told him you could buy into the still if you wanted.'

She drew her lips together, vertical lines forming around her mouth as though she were figuring some great sum. 'How much of a cut would that get me?'

'One part out of six.'

She looked at the house and back at him. 'You don't own none of this, do you?'

'We sort of found it.'

'What you really want is a house gal and now and then a free ride on me. Well, I've known women who traded for less.' She looked around again. 'But I ain't one of 'em.'

He looked at her walnut hair, then into her gray eyes. 'What's wrong with that deal?'

'It ain't a deal.' She turned away. When she turned back, her face was composed, the corners of her mouth in their habitual downturn. 'I got used to livin' with electricity and a store down the road where I can walk and buy a pork chop. What you got here's no better than that mountain shack I was raised in. I can't live on saltmeat and sardines ever day.'

'My line of work kind of needs some distance between me and a town.'

'Where at you live before?'

'Arkansas.'

'And the feds busted you out, right?'

He took a step back. 'How'd you guess that?'

'And before?'

'Around Longview.'

'Who got you there?'

He shook his head. 'The Babtist fire department came down on my cooker with their axes. After they finished, you could've drained spaghetti with the thing.'

'How long you reckon before some dollar-a-day feds come through them weeds and chops you out of business? And you want me to invest in that? Include me out.'

He slowly reached for his wallet. 'What you plan on doin'?'

'Goin' back toward the mountains. Maybe over the hump into Virginia. No offense, but it's like living in a croup tent down here, and these is the ugliest woods I ever been dragged through in my life. You got weeds that would poison a wild Indian to death and mosquitoes to carry off his corpse. And if Woodgulch is your example of a town, I seen better-lookin' places drew with a burnt stick by an idiot child.'

He counted out the money into her red palm. 'Like you say, I ain't stayin' here forever.'

She folded the bills and stuck them down her bodice. 'I know you're in the business of turnin' things over for profit. You understand what things is worth in dollars and cents. For about six weeks up in Point Pleasant, West Virginia, I worked in a pawnshop addin' up accounts in a ledger before the owner's wife run me off 'cause I wasn't ugly as she was. Lord, if that wasn't a place that had a license to steal I don't know what one looks like. You ever been in a pawnshop?'

'I sold to a few of 'em.'

'All you got to do is go somewhere there ain't a warrant on you yet, maybe in east Tennessee or North Carolina, and rent a store. A feller walks in with a pistol worth two dollars and you loan him twenty cents on it. If he comes back to claim it you charge him twenty cents interest. If he don't, then it's yourn and you put it on sale for three dollars.'

He put his billfold back in his pocket. 'I get run off from here, I'll consider it.'

She reached out and put a forefinger in one of his belt loops and tugged it. He wobbled as if he suddenly were dizzy, and her voice softened. 'Don't you wait too long. I'll start out in Bristol but there ain't no tellin' where I'll be in six months.' She turned and went into the kitchen, where she'd sent the girl to cut out biscuits with the mouth of a jelly glass.

Ralph went into the house and stopped inside the door, letting his eyes adjust to the darkness. The walls showed flowering spills of mildew and cumulus blooms of lime dissolved out of the plaster by rainwater. The next room was a great hall hung with dangling leeches of paint. Billsy sat in a velour chair with the stuffing leaking out under his legs.

'You pop the question?'

'Shut up.'

'All right, bud. Let's talk business. We goin' into Woodgulch with the kid?'

'I said not, but now I don't know.'

'We could take the skiff across the river.'

Ralph looked through the clouded glass over the broad gallery toward the fungus-haunted live oaks hiding the west. 'Just who in hell was watchin' us?'

The two of them ate breakfast at the Woodgulch Café, a plain-wood room painted from floor to ceiling the gray of a rainy dawn. Sam counted their money together and figured they could afford something for supper but not much else until they got back to New Orleans.

August thumbed his empty plate away. 'Can we trust him?'

'Well, I'm as sure as I can be.' He knew that when outlanders passed through a community like Woodgulch they touched on old biases and blood alliances going back generations, considerations that were complex and far beyond right and wrong. 'He said he'd show up at train time with some deputies.'

'I hope there's no shooting.'

'Look, there's no telling what'll happen. Just try to stay in the clear. Get hold of Lily and stay in the clear.'

'What exactly do you want me to do?'

He took the last bite of egg and stared at his empty plate. 'When you're playing "Sweet Sue" and the trombone gives it over to you to build the song, do you stop the band and ask what they want you to do?'

'No.'

'You just rip into her with that alto sax and play between the notes until it's right with what the band's doing. If everybody's jumping and the dancers are springing the floorboards, you just cut up like crazy, you step all over the clarinet and make him wait for the next turn. On the other hand, if the band is tired and just plugging along, you take your turn and sort of match. It's like that with everything.'

'Keep my ears open and watch the room.'

'That's the ticket.'

They passed the day wandering the aisles of the hardware, walking the town's six gravel streets, sitting on the one public bench in front of the courthouse. They arrived at the bench about two o'clock, and after an hour of watching a few Fords, mule-drawn wagons, two delivery trucks, and one buggy with a rotted top come and go on their errands, the boy shook his head. 'Not much to do, is there?'

'If you lived here you'd be working at something.'

He thought about this. 'I'd be working at moving away.'

A man wearing a flannel shirt buttoned up wrong rode a little quarterhorse past them. Across the street a baker came out and, with floured hands, turned the crank that lowered an awning against the westering sun; he looked at them and dusted his hands one against the other, then turned inside. Behind them, the courthouse door rattled and they turned to see the sheriff come out into the heat and start toward them.

'How are you?' Sam called out.

Tabors walked up and put a foot on the bench. 'I've been on the telephone finding out about your story. Called down to New Orleans and Baton Rouge, and everything checks out. I talked to a Muscarella at the French Quarter precinct and he read me the report.' He looked at August. 'Called a lot of people. I hear you play on a big dance boat.'

'Yessir.'

'That jass music or what?'

'Yessir, we try to make people want to dance.'

The sheriff looked at both of them, as though trying to divine their characters. 'If that little girl shows up tomorrow, I have to be satisfied about her identity. Do you have a photo?'

'I don't.'

'No, sir, not on me.'

'Well, if we wind up with her, I'll have to perform an interview before I can turn her over, you understand. I can't just go around giving away children.' He put a hand on August's shoulder for a moment, and Sam saw how large it was, thick in the palm. The sheriff was a big man, his size partially concealed by his suit, a mild gray pinstripe. He took off his fedora to wipe his forehead, revealing a big, straightsided head, the close-cropped blond hair free of gray. He was built of preventative muscle that would make those he dealt with think about the gravity of their actions and words, or else.

'You have things set up?' Sam asked him.

'Everything's ready,' the sheriff said.

Late that night in the hotel, they again talked across the dark, their voices boxy in the plank-walled room. One side of Sam's bed was against a low window, and a wet breeze seeped through the screens but did little to allay the breathless heat.

'Lucky, you think we should've sold the shotgun? We could have traded it for a little pistol.'

Sam turned over on his side, the springs squalling under his weight. 'Bud, a pistol in the pocket changes the way a man thinks. Without it, he might not take certain chances. With it, he goes where he shouldn't or does something that's not a good idea. He thinks it's a free pass, but it isn't.'

'But it's kind of a life preserver, isn't it? A safety device?'

'If you can't swim, best not go near the water.'

'I can see how sometimes one might come in handy, though. Like when a robber comes at you.'

'Listen, unless you're trained or some kind of natural-born killer, a criminal will get the best of you every time. You're surprised, and he's not, that's all there is to it. He'll shoot you through the heart before you get a finger on your pistol.'

They lay there in silence, the little town as quiet as a shadow. After a while, through the screen came the dull aeolian hum of a steamboat whistle several miles off.

'What about tomorrow?'

'It'll get here, won't it?'

'I mean, do you think everything will turn out all right?'

He knew August understood that in fact things were not that simple. Many things had recently not turned out all right. Sam guessed August wanted what every boy did – assurance, a good night's sleep, someone on his side. 'Everything's going to be fine,' he said, turning his face to the window and looking down to where a black horse stood in the middle of the street, facing west, untethered and lost and asleep.

The next morning they could afford only toast and coffee for breakfast. They washed up and straightened their clothes as best they could, wiping down their shoes with the only cloth in the room. Walking to the edge of town they sold the mule for six dollars and fifty cents to a liveryman who spoke a little French and wanted him as a pet.

At two o'clock they walked through the sun to the station and waited inside on one of three varnished benches. The agent nodded as though he'd expected them. Fifteen minutes before train time the sheriff came in and sat next to the door, wearing a different suit than the day before, no badge visible. After him, a beefy man dressed like a farmer came in and sat by the other door to the platform, a pistol-shaped bulge in his overalls pocket. The sheriff nodded to him, and they both bent to stare across the street where a man sat on a doorstep looking back at them. After a while, he raised his arm, and the farmer waved back.

Sam stood up and walked out onto the platform, looked over at the dusty town, and read the train board. South of Woodgulch were three flag stops named Fault, Lacy Switch, and Stob Mill, then the main line interchange at Gashouse. The tri-weekly mixed train was the only one scheduled. He expected that the train was close and thought of the picture that still flashed in his mind, sometimes in his dreams, sometimes when he was trying to remember why he wasn't with his wife and child in New Orleans. He wanted to fasten in his imagination the little girl's face, and closing his eyes for a moment saw the familiar cameo and next to it the image of his new son, and then from out of nowhere the girl in France whose house he'd leveled with the errant artillery shell and next to her a dim painful image of his first child. He opened his eyes and tried to remember everything Elsie and August had told him about Lily, the pitch of her voice, the precise color of her hair, and then he heard the train whistle, hoarse and foreboding, and his heart stumbled. He walked inside, and the sheriff told him to stand in the back corner.

The locomotive was followed by one passenger car and five red, sun-dulled boxcars. The train stopped and the fireman cut off the locomotive and it pulled ahead past a switch, then backed into a siding and ran alongside the train, where it went through another switch and then came forward to pluck the five boxcars away from the coach, chuffing backwards through town to distribute them on sidings. The conductor opened the vestibule door and put down his stepstool, handing the passengers down to the platform. Twelve men got off, local men, the sheriff nodding to each in turn as they walked down the platform to be greeted by those picking them up in Fords or buggies. After the last man was off, the sheriff boarded and walked through the coach. When he came back into the station, he shook his head. 'Maybe they'll come Monday.'

'We shouldn't have sold the mule,' August said, his voice cracking. 'We're stuck here.'

The man wearing overalls stood up. 'Sheriff?'

'You can go back to the office. I know those hogwashers you're wearing are hot.'

The man jerked a thumb over his shoulder. 'What about Mike?'

'Bring him with you. Tell him we'll try the same thing on Monday.'

Sam walked out on the platform and stared down the track. He could hear the locomotive huffing around in the yard of the window-frame factory. 'I don't know.'

Tabors looked in the same direction. 'What do you think?'

'Once they start something, the Skadlocks don't strike me as the kind that waste time.' Sam turned to the train board. 'What's Fault?'

'Just a flag stop right over the Louisiana line, though nobody seems to know exactly where that line is. There's still two farmers that ship a few cans of milk, and a little shop that sends out a half-car of cypress shingles every week. Plus a little barrel operation. There's just one road that runs through the area and crosses by the station.'

Sam looked down the crooked rails again. 'Where's the road go?'

The sheriff squinted an eye. 'From the prison on one end to

a gate five or six miles miles east of the railroad, where it reaches the highway.'

'I rode the mule across a straight gravel road when I went down to the Skadlocks'. Was that it?'

'Had to be.'

He stared at the board, then walked into the station, where the conductor was taking an order from the agent. 'Excuse me, but did you let off two passengers at Fault?'

The conductor was an old man who arched a thick eyebrow. 'And who might you be?'

'He's all right, Sidney.' The agent shoved his orders at him under the window grate.

'As a matter of fact, we did. A gentleman and a lady.'

'Well dressed? Maybe thirty-five years old?'

'I'd say so. The lady was taking from a flask right on the aisle and I had to ask her to go to the restroom if she wanted a sip.'

Sam glanced at the sheriff and August walked up and stood between them.

'Is there an agent there or what?'

'Yeah,' the conductor said. 'On the days the train comes.'

Sam shook his head. 'Hell, they're down there right now waiting for the train to come back.'

The sheriff crossed his arms and looked at his boots. 'If they are, well, I'd like to help you, but I can't. Not my jurisdiction.'

'Could you telegraph the Louisiana sheriff?'

'It wouldn't do any good. I don't like to talk about the man. Let's just say he's never been to Fault.'

Sam turned to the agent and paid two fares to Fault.

August watched the agent retrieve the tickets. 'You think she's down there, sure enough?'

'I can't take a chance on thinking otherwise.'

The locomotive turned on the wye in the mill and drifted back to the station with three empty flatcars and coupled to the coach.

August boarded ahead of Sam and they chose the first seats

on the left. 'Well, we'll find out soon enough, won't we?' the boy said.

Then Sheriff Tabors stepped on and sat behind them. 'Don't look at me like that. I had the agent write me a pass.'

'How'll you get back to town?'

'My brother-in-law lives at Gashouse. He can ride me up here in his Ford after supper.'

The whistle let out a growl and the train jerked into motion, swaying and rattling over the branch-line track toward Fault, six miles away. Sam counted telegraph poles and figured they were going twenty miles an hour. The train went past a pasture full of milk cows and plunged into a brake of old-growth pine for a mile or so.

August looked up at him. 'How's your shoulder?'

'I try not to think about it.'

'You won't do much in a fight.'

'I don't guess so.'

They passed a clearing and he saw a small barrel factory, nothing more than a shed covering an undulating machine and a mud yard stacked with blond-wood kegs bound with metal hoops. A switch ran into the yard, and two flatcars sat loaded in the sun. A mill hand waved and waved like he'd never seen a train before, but the little engine kept on puffing south, leaking steam and wobbling along the kinked rails.

Snaking out of the pines, the railroad traversed three miles of scrub country, cut-over land crowded with brambles and trash-wood saplings. Soon the engineer was blowing the whistle for the little wooden station, and Sam felt the air brakes grab. He looked at August.

'Showtime,' the boy said.

They got up and stepped off onto the platform. A man wearing a tailored suit was standing next to the bench outside the station, a streamer of tickets in his hand. A woman was struggling with Lily, who was angry at being held and kicking her legs, her face red and running tears. 'I want Vessy,' she wailed. 'Where's Vessy gone?'

'Oh, hush up,' the woman snapped. 'Aren't you glad to see us? What's the matter with you?'

Sam and August walked up, the sheriff dawdling behind as if he didn't know anyone there. Sam looked around but saw only an old Ford and no horses. 'Where's Ralph Skadlock?'

The man looked at him blankly. 'I don't know what you're talking about.'

August drew close and looked at Lily, smiling.

'Get away,' the woman told him, a shining alarm rising in her eyes. 'What do you want?'

'That's my sister. Let her look at me.' And when the child did turn around, she gave him the look of a baby who hadn't seen her brother in many months. She wriggled out of the woman's grasp and stood there on the rough planks. Lily shaded her eyes and peered up at him but said nothing. The sheriff made a clucking noise in the back of his mouth and looked away.

'I know who you are,' Sam said. 'You're the Whites from Graysoner, Kentucky, and that girl was stolen from Krine's department store in New Orleans.'

Acy White looked at the conductor, who had his watch in his hand. 'Will you board us?'

The conductor looked at the sheriff and the child. 'I can't stop you from getting on if you got a ticket.'

'Well, come on, then.' He made a move toward the coach.

Sam grabbed his arm. 'We've come for the girl.'

'Get your hands off me. I don't know what you're talking about. This is our daughter, Madeline.' He grabbed Lily by the hand but Sam pulled him away from the train and the two of them stumbled backwards across the platform and fell against the bench. Lily began to shriek and August kneeled next to her as Sheriff Tabors went over and began to separate the men.

The agent dashed outside, shouting, 'Everbody calm down. What's this all about?'

Sam had banged his shoulder against the bench, but even the

pain couldn't overcome his worry that the Whites would get Lily on the train and slip away with her. He couldn't show up empty-handed in New Orleans and have to tell Elsie they'd lost her again. He got untangled and stood up. 'You're not getting away with this. I know what you did, and I'll follow you until you're both in the jailhouse.'

At the word 'jailhouse,' Mrs White reached into her purse and brought out a nickel-plated revolver and pointed it at Sam, her mouth open and trembling.

'Take it easy,' Sheriff Tabors said. 'Let's sort this thing out.'

She shifted her aim to the lawman's forehead. 'You stay on the platform, whoever you are, or I'll blow your brains all over this godforsaken station.' She was sweating and didn't look at all well, more like a woman who'd made a monthlong journey on foot.

'Damn it,' Acy White said. 'Let's just get on.' He grabbed Lily and took his wife by the arm, and they stepped up into the coach.

Before getting on, the conductor turned around and faced the platform. 'I wouldn't board if I were you.'

'I sort of have to,' the sheriff said, pushing back his coat and putting a big hand on his revolver. His face was flaming, and his eyes showed he was furious.

Sam put a hand on his shoulder. 'Step over here a minute.' He motioned to the station agent to join them. 'Why didn't this crew pick up those two flatcars of barrels about three miles back?'

The agent's eyes moved off, as though he'd been caught in a lie. 'It don't really matter none. They'll get 'em Monday for sure.'

'When we passed the switches, those boys in the yard were waving for your train to stop. Can you cut the crew an order to back to that switch and get their cars?'

The agent pulled his watch. 'I reckon. It ain't like this outfit runs on a tight schedule, if you know what I mean.' He looked at August and the sheriff. 'What's this all about with children and barrels?'

'I think I just figured it out myself,' the sheriff said. 'Just write the order and hand it up to the engineer. It's Ned running the engine today, isn't it?'

'Yes, it is.'

'Never mind the conductor, he's occupied. Come on.' The sheriff motioned them along to the engine and they climbed into the cab. Soon the agent came running alongside and handed up a new flimsy. The engineer pulled the Johnson bar into reverse, tugged three short blasts from his whistle, and began backing the train hard.

The three of them stood behind the engineer, staying out of the fireman's way as he shoveled a thin layer of coal on the boiler's grates. Over the engine noise Sam hollered, 'What you gonna do about her pistol?'

'I think she was just trying to scare us off,' the sheriff told him. 'I'd bet she wouldn't use it.' About three miles from the station, as the barrel mill came into view, he leaned over and hollered something to the engineer above the hiss and chuff of the locomotive. The old man stopped the train, and the three of them slid down the grab irons and walked back to the coach. The sheriff went up first and walked the aisle to where the Whites were sitting with Lily jammed between them, crying silently, her nose running, her eyes cloudy with confusion and grief. He looked around at the five other passengers and told them to stay in their seats.

'Who are you?' Acy White said with the calm assuredness of one who thinks he's in charge.

'These two men say that little girl isn't yours.'

The wife began to stand, but the sheriff held up his hand. She looked at it and kept rising, lifting her chin as well. 'You three men are the abductors.' She turned to the other passengers. 'They're trying to steal my baby,' she said, her voice nearly screaming. The three farmers and two drummers watched placidly, their heads moving from the sheriff to the finely dressed woman.

'We need to talk to the little girl,' the sheriff said, reaching for the child.

Acy White said, 'Don't,' but it was unclear whom he was addressing, and in the next instant the nickel-plated revolver came up in her hand, aimed at the sheriff's head, and went off. An orange dart of fire and rotten-smelling smoke bloomed into the aisle as the bullet went through a clerestory above a farmer's head, and the startled sheriff backhanded the gun out of her grasp, sending it over the next seat, where it clattered to the floor.

'Lady,' he told her, his voice shaking, 'assault with a deadly weapon is a felony in Mississippi.' He spread his coat and both Whites focused on the sizeable badge pinned on his vest.

'But we're in Louisiana,' Acy White protested, his eyes suddenly sick and weak.

'Not anymore. I figure we're a mile inside the state line.' He pulled back his coat on the other side to show his gleaming Colt. 'And you're both under arrest on that charge. Now let me see that child.'

Sam turned to August. 'You're on, boy.'

He stepped around the sheriff and pulled her gently into the aisle. 'Hey, Lily.'

The girl looked at him hard and said nothing.

'Oh, this is ridiculous,' Acy White said. 'Conductor, I insist you get this train moving in the direction it's supposed to. She's our child. She doesn't know this young man.'

'Is your name Lily?' The sheriff bent over her like a cloud of dark cloth, and she said nothing.

August seemed to show his panic. 'Sure it is. Come on, Lil. Tell them who I am.' He stared at her, seemingly frightened by the blankness in her eyes.

The sheriff stood up and frowned. 'If your name isn't Lily, what is it?'

In a small voice she said, 'Madeline.'

'I told you,' Willa White cried.

'Wait a minute.' Sam stepped up and put his hand on August's neck. 'Little girl, do you know what this fellow told me?'

The girl shook her head slowly, on the verge of tears.

'He said he taught you a tune from the *Sinbad* revue in New York and that you could sing the whole thing through.'

'This is ridiculous,' the wife said. 'The child knows proper ballads and some hymns. Do you think she's a little tramp?'

Sam held up a hand and backed the sheriff and August away a bit, creating a little stage in the aisle. 'I told him I didn't believe it one bit.'

'It's true,' the child said, slowly raising her head.

'I don't believe it. Bet you can't sing a single word of "Cleopatra."'

Her eyes flashed over at the Whites; then she held her right arm out, looked at the coach's ceiling, and began singing in a schooled, vibratoless voice:

> *You've heard of Cleopatra*
> *Who lived down along the Nile.*
> *She made a 'Mark' of Anthony*
> *And won him with her smile.*

Her feet began a matching dance step, and the other arm went out.

> *They say she was Egyptian*
> *But I've reason to construe*
> *She was Jewish and Hawaiian*
> *With a dash of Irish too.*

The sheriff was smiling broadly as if he'd heard the tune many times and thought it the best thing ever written. The child paced up the aisle and kept singing, stepping out of her captivity into her gift, no longer in the aisle of a sooty train but onstage in her mind, the one she'd been born to.

When she strolled with bold Mark Anthony
On Egypt's yellow sands
You could see that she was Jewish
By the motion of her hands

She would shake her hands and shoulders off—

Lily gave her shoulders a shimmy, and an old farmer down the aisle guffawed and clapped his hands.

'All right, all right,' the sheriff said. 'Who taught you that Jolson song, little girl?'

She stopped and pointed dramatically at August. 'Gussie. My brother there.'

The conductor allowed the train to back the rest of the way to Woodgulch. The Whites were taken off the coach against their loud, wailing protests and threats, and many townspeople turned out to see the splendidly dressed couple led through the streets in handcuffs.

Before the train left again, a sheriff's deputy boarded the coach and walked up to where the three of them were seated. 'Sheriff said he's calling for warrants in New Orleans and Kentucky both, that whoever wants 'em most can have 'em. After he gets through with 'em, of course. He'll get in touch so's y'all can be deposed down the line.'

Sam relaxed against a window and said, 'Good news.'

The deputy leaned down, smelling of Old Spice and sweet chew. 'Did that crazy woman really take a shot at our high sheriff?'

'That's a fact, yeah.'

'Damn. That'll be a lively trial.'

The whistle blasted a farewell to Woodgulch, and the deputy lumbered down to the vestibule. In seconds the coach jerked forward and Sam glanced over at August and then down at Lily, who was sitting between them eating a sandwich the agent had given her out of his lunchbox. He gazed out the window glad for each foot of travel the train was making toward home. The longer he looked, the more he imagined that he could see his wife and child, and past them Elsie Weller and, all the way downtown, Krine's vast store. He relaxed for the first time in months, but as the engine pulled into the interchange at Gashouse, where they would switch trains, Lily sat up straight, looked at August, and asked, 'Why didn't Father come to get me?'

Her brother turned his head toward the aisle, the finality of the gesture proof that the news would not come from him.

Sam bent over and said, 'Your mother will explain that, darling.'

'But why did you come, and Gussie, but not my daddy?'

He gave her shoulder a squeeze, surprised by how small it was. He'd been looking for her for so long he expected her to be larger than life. She was just a baby. 'Hey, we'll travel down to New Orleans and your mother will tell you everything you need to know. We'll go down to the Café du Monde and eat some of those square doughnuts buried in confection sugar. You'll like that.' He kept talking to keep her mind on the future, but he and August had been so busy in the act of finding her that they'd forgotten what she didn't know. He hoped she was too young to take it as hard as August had. He hoped she was like him, with no memory whatsoever of a father, but he knew that wasn't true. Lily would see an empty chair at her mother's table for the rest of her life, a space lacking words and songs that were her birthright.

They changed trains at the junction, riding to Baton Rouge, then catching another for New Orleans. It was dark on this last leg, and Sam slept with Lily in his lap, the smell of soft coal blowing through the windows and a scrim of cypresses sailing by. In his dream, he himself was in someone's lap, a man, judging from the smell of kerosene and wood smoke and a little gale of beer breathed over his head; his stomach felt full, and a callused hand pressed down on it as though holding a jewel secure.

When he woke up, the conductor was walking the aisle announcing New Orleans. August looked at him closely.

'What is it?' Sam asked.

'Your eyes are wet. Smoke bother you that much?'

32

They walked in the heat down to the ferry landing, taking the boat to Algiers, where the *Ambassador* was having work done to the rudders. The three of them found Elsie, down on her knees, recoating the café floor, her hair half-unpinned, her washed-out blue dress wrinkled. She had the good sense not to charge at Lily all at once, but got up calmly, wiping her hands on a rag. Bending in front of the child, she hugged her, and Lily received her light kisses, but studied this tired woman wearing a dusty housedress sticky with varnish and smelling of turpentine. Sam could tell she was confused about who Elsie was.

Elsie stared into her eyes. 'Lily, I love you.'

'I know.'

'Have you forgotten me?' Elsie's voice faltered and her eyes grew wide, waiting for the answer, which was slow in coming.

'They told me you went to heaven. I didn't know you could come back.'

'No, no, I didn't go anywhere. I know you don't understand, but you were stolen, and we're so happy to have you back.'

'Did Father go anywhere?'

Elsie stood up and looked at August, who shook his head. She sighed. 'You boys give me some time with her.'

The men sidestepped along a strip of unvarnished floor and got into the kitchen, where they fixed sandwiches. August seemed tired to the bone and worried, the kind of worry that tattoos the face.

'Well, she's back,' Sam said.

August looked at him. 'Is she?'

Sam took a bite and worked his brain along with his jaws,

thinking of all the time that was lost to everybody, but especially to Lily. The life of a young child is compressed existence, and a month is like a year. He tried to call up one day from his own childhood and remembered a time when he was eight, after cane-grinding season, when his uncle Claude took him on his first rabbit hunt. He still knew every detail, from loading the little shotgun he was allowed to use, to his uncle's hunting jokes in French, to the first shot and kill, to the opening with a pocketknife of the bright red world inside the animal as he was taught to clean it for the table and, that night, the rabbit stew itself. One day was intact and as long as a whole book in his recollection. If it was like that for Lily, then she'd been gone for years.

He caught a streetcar home with the last seven cents in his pocket, and when he walked in at ten o'clock his wife sat him down in the kitchen and began to warm some meatless potato stew, moving quietly so as not to wake the baby. He summarized the events of the past few days, and she touched his forehead and kissed him there.

'You found her,' she said, her breath a current in his hair. 'It's finally over.'

'Yes, I think so.'

'We can go back to like we were before, Sam.'

She was as thin as a pretty ghost. He wasn't at all sure that the months of searching could be ignored and written off, that time would gradually diminish everything like a sad town passed through on a speeding train, the glimpse of it fading into insignificance. 'That would be nice,' he said.

She brought him his plate and put her arms around him where he sat. 'I can't believe it.'

The next day he got up with Christopher, changed him, and held him in his lap for a long time. They ate breakfast together, his son sitting on his legs and grabbing at everything. At eight o'clock he said to the baby, 'Time to go start making some money so I can feed that hungry mouth.' He put on his good suit and took a quarter from his wife's purse and rode the car down to Canal Street. Inside Krine's main entrance, he stopped dead and looked around at the ceilings and plasterwork, smelled the dye in the new clothes and the light, polished smell of the glossy counters, inhaling it all like medicine. He waved at Gladys over in the men's department and took the elevator up to the main office.

A new receptionist was in Krine's anteroom. She greeted Sam with a neutral expression and asked him to take a seat while she went in to announce him. He sat there patiently, ready for the main floor.

The receptionist motioned him into the inner office and closed the door.

The owner was behind his desk, leaning back in his chair, one hand fisted on a stack of papers. 'Hello, Mr Simoneaux.'

'Mr Krine.' Sam waited to be asked to sit down. After a long moment, it was obvious that he wouldn't be asked to.

'It's been a while. I'm surprised to see you, in fact.'

'I just came by to say I found the little girl and returned her to her mother.'

Krine looked at him but said nothing. They both seemed to be listening to the regulator clock on the wall next to the window. 'I'm glad for her,' he finally said.

Sam grinned. 'I was wondering if I could get my old job back.' He thought it odd that he had to explain what he wanted. They had an agreement.

Krine didn't blink, and that frightened him.

'You've taken your own sweet time solving this problem. I thought you might take a month, at most. When you didn't come back, I hired a good man to take your place. As a matter of fact I hired two, and they've worked out very well for us.'

Sam swallowed several times, feeling a chill in the center of his chest. 'I thought we had a deal,' he said faintly.

'You know, I found out recently that that child's father was killed as a result of trying to rescue her. Is that right?'

He looked at the clock, wondering how many minutes he had left in the office. A drop of sweat ran down from behind an ear. 'More or less.'

'I'm sorry to hear that. And I'm sorry to say we don't need you as a floorwalker.'

He swallowed again and looked at the carpet, trying to make sense of the design. 'Do you have any positions at all?'

'The big stores in town are cutting back a little. I'm sorry.'

'Nothing?' He held out a hand, palm up.

Krine picked up a folder of paperwork and stood. 'Nothing,' he said, like a shot, and the meeting was over. 'We have your number. If we ever need a floorwalker, we'll call you.'

He took the elevator down and walked around the first floor as if he were shopping, touching the bright ties, the glossy shoes. He was tempted to straighten a rack of shoe-polish tins but pulled his hand back at the last moment. Across the store, one of the new floorwalkers was chatting with a well-dressed woman who'd come out of the café. Sam wanted a cup of the wonderful coffee the café brewed, but it was free only for employees. He turned around once in an aisle, taking a last look, then headed for the main doors. On the street he felt vaguely like an exile, glanced back once at the store's Italianate façade, and began walking home. Three blocks off Canal Street, he remembered the *Ambassador* was leaving port in two days, and he changed direction down to the ferry landing. He wouldn't play piano in a gangster's bar or carry a gun for a bank or the city, so second mate, if he could get it, would suit him fine.

His wife's face fell, and she sat down hard on the sagging mahogany settee in the front room. 'You'll be gone months at a time. I need you here.'

'You need the rent paid. The grocery bill.'

'I can get a little from Mom.'

'Hey, sometimes the boat lays over and I can take a train home for a couple days. Lots of the schedule's down South.'

'And you'll eat up your salary on train tickets and meals. Lucky, why can't you just play music in town?'

He looked at the bright spot against the wall where his piano had been, a fine, booming instrument he'd bought with his mustering-out pay. 'I can't get a good piano spot. This is New Orleans, darling. Everybody plays better than I do.'

She turned away, then leaned back against him. 'What'll they pay?'

'More than the last trip.'

'Put your arms around me.'

He kissed her nape, the backs of her pale ears.

'Lucky, when I walk up the street I see these nice houses with porches and big backyards. Sometimes I ask myself how *anybody* can afford to own a house, you know? To keep it up? Everybody I know rents.'

He took in a slow breath. 'There's a lot of businessmen in town, I guess. Store owners. Superintendents.' Out on the sidewalk someone passed by bouncing a basketball, the pneumatic pings rising for a time and then diminishing up the street. 'I thought I could work my way up at Krine's,' he said absently.

'This kidnapping dragged us down, baby.'

'I know.'

'I thought it would be over, but it isn't.'

'I know that, too.'

She took in a sudden breath. 'When do you leave?'

'Probably day after tomorrow.'

'Do you still have your nice Hamilton watch? The one Uncle Claude gave you for a wedding present?'

'Sure.'

She turned to face him. He thought she might want a kiss, but when she gave him a sad, complicated smile instead, he knew what she would say, and he looked away. 'You have to sell it.'

The *Ambassador* wasn't ready to steam for a week. The day before he was to leave, Sam received a call from a New Orleans assistant district attorney summoning him downtown to be deposed for an upcoming trial of the Whites in Kentucky. In an office of the federal building he met a slim young lawyer who asked him to write out a statement. He labored over four pages for an hour, signed off on them, and waited for the lawyer to step back into the room. Trying to imagine what would happen to the Whites was beyond him, but he had a dim notion that such people never saw the inside of a jail. He hoped, however, they could be fined enough to keep them away from anyone else's children.

The glass in a mahogany door rattled, and the lawyer came in and reached for the deposition as he walked by.

Sam looked up at him. 'Has the boy been in yet?'

'We took his statement yesterday. How's the little girl doing?'

'I haven't seen her again. I go to work tomorrow, and I guess she'll be on board.' Sam stood and shook his pants legs loose. 'They trying those people in Kentucky?'

The lawyer, who wore a thin mustache, turned it up on one side. 'Well, I don't know. The jurisdiction's rather confused.'

'I figured they'd get out of it.'

'Oh, I wouldn't say that. They're still in a county jail in Mississippi. The sheriff there's got his own juice, as they say, and the Whites threatened him in several ways, then offered to bribe him, so there are two or three new local charges against them. Mrs White's in the regional female prison wearing denim clothes along with the whores and lady pickpockets. Not doing too well, I hear. Mr White's still in the Woodgulch pokey.'

Sam thought about this while the lawyer examined his handwriting. 'I guess it might bother them more than it would some other folks.'

'Let's just say they're not used to such accommodations. I got a telegram from Graysoner, Kentucky, that said the local paper has the story all over the front page, and the reporter didn't gild the lily, if you know what I mean.'

'I'd have guessed the local paper would've taken their side.'

'Me too. But the reporter has a young brother on the police force who gave him some interesting details.'

Sam grinned. 'Sometimes a criminal gets his justice just because of bad luck?'

The lawyer opened the door into the marble hallway. Down the broad stairs Sam heard people talking and quick footsteps, and someone dropped what sounded like an armload of file folders. Throughout the building people were trying to propel the lumbering steamroller of justice forward in a straight line, but it seemed to him a complex business, both noble and imprecise.

The lawyer clapped a hand on Sam's shoulder. 'As for bad luck, I think the Whites have rolled snake eyes.'

The *Ambassador* ran three trips on a Saturday in New Orleans, breaking in the new band, the repaired machinery, and a revolutionary speaker system mounted on the roof and dance floor. On Sunday, Sam went to Mass at the cathedral with his wife, and at noon the boat departed, banners flying, bunting set, and twin clouds of coal smoke rising skyward. It would run a meet-the-boat trip, carrying excursionists upriver about forty miles and then exchanging the whole crowd with that from the *Buckeye Deluxe,* a big sidewheel excursion boat tramping south. The *Ambassador* would then paddle upriver to Donaldsonville and drop off the sidewheeler's tired load.

Sam caught a glimpse of Elsie through the crowd boiling around the decks, but the captain caught his arm as he was making his way to her.

'Lucky, we've got a new generator in the engine room, and Bit says he can't watch it all the time, so you're elected to learn how to operate the thing and just check its meters every couple hours. It runs all the new bulbs on the rails, plus the loudspeaker thing.'

He made a face. 'A generator?'

'Go on. It's not like learning piano, for gosh sake.'

He went down to the engine room and sat amid the hissing machines and worried through the manual, testing the circuits and learning the Bakelite control board and its tangle of fuses, rotary controls, and knife-blade switches. It was impossible to learn the manual because all he could think of was Lily and her mother. He gave up and walked forward to the main deck. After the boats tied up side by side and exchanged passengers, the purser discovered that the *Deluxe* had overbooked, and excursionists were stacked on the *Ambassador*'s forecastle trying to get up to the good music. The deck speakers were meant for colorful commentary on things the boat passed by, but the captain found Sam and directed him to figure how to connect the stage microphones to the on-deck speakers so he could forestall a riot. The Donaldsonville crowd had been floating south all morning listening to a dull hotel orchestra while sipping radiator-made shine and were primed to try the hot tempos of this New Orleans band. An hour upriver Sam figured out the crossovers, and people began to dance up on the hurricane deck and in the lower lounge. He walked up to the Texas roof and looked down on hundreds of dancers, feeling the thin lumber of the old boat rumble under him like a wooden bridge bearing a cattle drive. When he turned to look aft, Elsie was standing next to him, her little waitress crown sunken down into her sweaty hair.

'I've been looking for you,' she said. 'The crowd's going to bunch into the café in a minute, so they sent me out on a break. It's been a crazy house since noon. I was almost killed over a ham sandwich.'

She had aged two or three years in the few days since he'd seen her, her face flushed and shiny with both labor and grease from the kitchen ranges. 'How's Lily doing?'

She gave him a look. 'Not so damned well. She asks me for baby dolls every hour on the hour.' She turned and watched the darkening river as if she might jump into it. 'I don't think she understands where and what she's come back to.' She pulled out a pack of cigarettes and lit one with Ted's military lighter. 'The other night we were eating in the back of the café and she asked me for roast duck.' Her eyes grew wide, incredulous. 'What kind of little girl did you bring back to me? She thinks she's a rich kid.'

'Give her some time to fall back into your routine. She'll come around.'

'I don't know. I tried to spend some time with her by teaching her a new song, "Ma, He's Makin' Eyes at Me"? She said it was nasty.' Her voice rose. 'She said her mother was teaching her a *nasty* song.'

Sam thought of the White's many-roomed house, its manicured hill, guessed at what those people had taught her. 'She'll get used to things.' As he said this he knew he didn't believe it.

'She's just a baby. She's been gone from me for *ten* months. That's a big part of a baby's life.'

They talked until Mrs Benton called down to them from the pilothouse. 'I'm fixing to blow for a descending tow, so unless you enjoy getting splashed with hot condensate I reckon you ought to move.'

They ran three trips at Natchez against a competing boat come down from Davenport and did well. Jazz was still rare along the river, so the sports, the young people, the heartstrong dancers – whether swells or hillbillies, sawmill bucks or plantation beauties – came down the bluffs at late dusk to board the light-lavished steamer and glide out into the dark, taking on the breeze and moving their feet, or rather, having their feet moved by this strange, powerful sound come up from New Orleans against the currents.

Sam watched Lily as much as he could, talked to her as much as she'd allow. She seemed a closed vessel, not showing who she was, perhaps not even knowing, not anymore. At rehearsal, when she sang a novelty number her mother had taught her, her voice lacked energy and rhythm. She remembered the words, but seemed to have forgotten how to form or phrase them. The intelligence of her voice had been robbed away. What had stolen it, Sam couldn't guess, at least not at first. Then one night, lying in his bunk above a snoring Charlie Duggs, thinking about how children change, he figured it out. Her father had been the teacher in the family, the one with the big musical spark that could go all night, set after set without burning out, who could guide the fingers and vocal cords of the children he himself had made with his wife. Elsie taught the words, the dances, but Ted was the bearer of the notes, the lilt, the sass, and Ted was forever gone. Sam understood that Lily would still sing, but she might never again perform.

33

The river north of Vicksburg was running high and the *Ambassador* strained against the current to make its shore dates. The crowds were civilized, even appreciative, but at one malignant landing called Hurricane Slough, the boat filled with lumbermen and their whores and also the entire congregation of a Baptist church. The night trip was a brawl from landing to landing and ended with a shoreside religious war by torchlight, a hollering slugfest out on the dark bank. The crowd dissipated as slowly as a stinking smoke, and the crew was so exhausted and the boat so filthy that the captain sent the advance man on horseback to the nearest telegraph office to notify the town above that the morning excursion would be canceled. All night the boat leaned against the bank, as if the very planks and machines had lost all strength. Some time before dawn, the crew began to stir and Mr Brandywine backed her out and turned her toward Greenville, the river running ponderous as molten lead against the hull. The old pilot spotted a sandbar and figured how to steer around it, and later decided which side of an island to choose for passage as he walked spokes on the wheel. When the full disk of sun lay over the bunched pines of the eastern hills, he reached up and pulled on the whistle cord, letting the ring slip through his hand, and the big whistle grumbled half a word.

In less than a minute, Sam opened the narrow door to the pilothouse with Lily on an arm. He sat her on the lazy bench, and she looked around at the windows, then through them.

'Saul's bringing up your coffee,' Sam said.

The pilot stole a glance at the child. 'Hello, little miss.'

'Good morning, Mr Brandywine.' She fluffed her dress around her dangling legs.

The pilot nudged the *Ambassador* out of a thread of current and peeled away from the head of the island. He pulled an engine-room bell and turned his head for the western shore, watching the trees roll past. 'You being nice and quiet like you should.'

'I know.' She nodded.

Saul, a retired Pullman porter too old for railroad service, tapped at the door and Sam waved him in. He carried a bright, triple-plated tray and sat it on the cold pilothouse stove. 'I brought you a biscuit with your coffee, sah.'

'Thank you. I'll eat it when I go off in an hour.'

Saul turned the cup handle out on the tray, and when he swung around to leave, he noticed Lily for the first time. 'Little ma'am, would you like me to go and get you one of those cookies they're bakin' fresh down in the kitchen?'

She looked at him squarely. 'I'm not supposed to talk to niggers.'

Sam looked at the old porter and his face was unmoving, hardened by a lifetime of blows. Saul kept his smile and said, 'Yes, little ma'am.'

Mr Brandywine slid a hand from the wheel. 'Sam, come over and just stand here and hold her steady. Don't do anything but hold it in one spot.'

He hesitated, looking out at the water sliding by. 'I'm no wheelman.'

'Just for a minute.'

They changed places, and the pilot walked over to the lazy bench and gave Lily a serious look. 'Little miss, would you hurt someone's feelings on purpose?'

Lily shook her head.

'Well, lots of people use the word "nigger", and I know you've heard it thrown around by those folks who stole you, but let me tell you, it hurts people's feelings. Would you want Saul here to call you something like "nasty grits"?'

She began to get the idea she'd done something wrong and straightened her back. 'That's ugly. I'm not nasty grits.'

Mr Brandywine put his many-creased face close to hers and trapped her with his glossy little eyes. 'It hurts your feelings to be called that, does it?'

She nodded.

'So it's ugly to call Saul here a "nigger". That pretty young mouth of yours should have nicer words come out of it. You can refer to him as a Negro or a colored man.'

She looked at Saul, whose expression was still unreadable, and he was waiting, as he had all his life. 'I'm not supposed to talk to a Negro,' she said.

Saul laughed, and no one in the pilothouse could tell exactly what the laugh meant. He turned for the door and was gone.

Sam called out, 'Mr Brandywine.'

The pilot was watching the porter through the aft glass. 'What?'

'There's a towboat rounding the upper end of this island.'

The pilot still didn't turn around. 'Do you not see a big white house with green shutters and a gallery sitting on the bluff over the next bend?'

Sam scanned the east side in a panic. 'I think so.'

'Well, put the flagstaff on the front door.'

He turned the wheel and began to sweat as the boat swung a few degrees, then began to drive at the hallway of the farmhouse three miles away. Behind him, he heard Brandywine say, 'You feel the weight of my hand on your shoulder, girl?'

'Yes,' she answered.

'When you insult someone it puts a weight on you. Oh, you don't feel it until you get older, like me, but that's when you get to thinking and thinking about all the hurt you caused people in your life with your smart little mouth and your wise little cracks. Now, do you feel this hand on your other shoulder?'

'Yes.'

'Each pain you cause people, little miss, is a weight, and the older you get, the more they burden you like stones until you're bent over and near buried by them all.'

The shore was coming up, and the towboat had fully materialized on the port side pushing ten loads of heaped block coal. 'Mr Brandywine?'

But he was staring intently into Lily's sharp blue eyes. 'Do you not see the big gray rock some lovesick fool has painted a heart on off to your right about five hundred yards?'

Sam swung his head in several quick scans of the riverbank. 'I see it.'

'One hundred yards this side of it, split the difference between it and that descending tow.'

'But—'

'It's all water in this spot, son, and this here is a boat,' he snapped. The girl's eyes watched his own steadily, and Brandywine knew what he told her would stick. She was too smart, young as she was, for something not to stick. 'Somebody has taught you it's all right to hurt people's feelings, to try and make them less than you are. And I'm here with my bent-down shoulders to tell you for a fact that it's not.'

He stepped back to the wheel, slapping Sam's hand off a spoke. 'You and that child can leave now. It's going to get busy here directly while I try not to knock all that coal back to the mine.' He pulled a long, bluesy note from the whistle, and Lily covered her ears.

A week later above Cairo, Sam shared a table with Elsie after the last trip of the day. Her color wasn't good, and the corners of her mouth branched with the start of wrinkles. She ate her food with a habitual motion that showed she enjoyed none of it. More than once she began a conversation by blaming him for all her troubles, saying things like, 'You brought back my child, but it wasn't the same child.' At this meal she told him, 'Those people made her different. She's not sweet. She's less mine.'

Even Sam realized he was the worst person to talk to like this, because accusations stuck to him like beggar lice. 'I'm sorry about everything,' he said this time.

She wiped her mouth with a napkin and threw it in her lap. 'And August isn't the same. He's still using his talent, at least, but he doesn't talk to me anymore. He used to tell me jokes, one a day, and say how much he liked to hear me laugh, and Ted used to say the same thing.'

'He's doing well with the band. He's off the boiler gang.'

'He's learning, all right, but it's as if he's gone from kid to old man overnight.'

Nothing was good for her, everything had changed for the worse, and he could tell that no matter what happened for the rest of her life, she would blame her misfortune on the fact that a department-store floorwalker had allowed himself to be bested by a pair of backwoods thugs. He knew that event followed event, and that it was his bad luck to be first in a string of bad fortune. But once or twice some little spark of resentment flared up at her badgering, and he was tempted to ask what she and Ted were doing the moment the child was spirited away from them. How long had they been distracted while looking at men's coats or women's dresses while Lily was swept into a topcoat or lured away with a handful of candy? And hadn't he begged Ted not to go after Skadlock? He tightened his finger in the handle of his cup as though he wanted to break it off.

Elsie drained her coffee. 'You look like you have something to say, Lucky.'

He started to open his mouth, his shoulders trembling with the burden of her accusations. 'I've got to move on,' he said. 'I've got to replace about fifty lightbulbs.' He pushed through a door out onto the deck and stood there watching dark water sluice by. What good would it have done to have said anything? At worst it would've taken away the balm of blaming him for everything, making her look to herself, and most people never think to blame themselves until they're old and have time for thousands of second thoughts.

* * *

At Cape Girardeau the moonlight trip was attended by a civilized tribe of midwesterners who had leased the boat. The dancing was orderly and friendly, and the young people danced as if they'd been taught the steps in school. Sam and Charlie faced no emergencies, and after they had walked around the boat twice, took a break on the boiler deck forward rail and listened to the orchestra. Onstage, Elsie was singing in the spotlight, her alto caressing 'When My Baby Smiles at Me.' He watched her through the window, and in her makeup and shiny dress, she looked like a million dollars and sang like a mint.

Charlie had just come back from his father's funeral and had spent a week settling the small estate. 'I tell you, Lucky, the old man didn't have two nickels to rub together, and his shed was full of the damnedest stuff. It took me two days to haul it out into the yard for the sale. Stove legs, empty shotgun shells, parts to railroad lanterns, a broken plow, and I don't know what all. I made about ten dollars and had to pay that to get the rest of the junk hauled away.'

Sam leaned back against the rail and let the music pour over him. 'What'd he do for a living?'

'Watchman in a foundry. They paid him so little he could draw a week's pay in coins.' Charlie shook his head. 'I got there about five hours before he died. Someone had picked him up in the street, and he was at the clinic two days before anybody in the family knew where the hell he was.'

'It's good you got to see him before he passed.'

'I don't know. He was out of his head and cussed me for not sendin' more money. But I knew it was the sickness talkin'.' A breeze came up, and Charlie snugged his cap and slipped his big hands into his pockets. 'At least I had a father. You ever wonder what your old man would've been like?'

Sam looked upriver, into the wind. 'No.' In fact, he had thought about his father right after he realized that his cousins weren't his brothers. He'd asked his uncle what he'd been like, but Claude had only shrugged and said it wasn't time to talk about that.

For years, this was the answer he'd gotten: '*C'est pas les temps pour ça*' – an unfathomable statement that might have meant he was a bad man and his son shouldn't know this, or he was a wonderful man whose son shouldn't be made aware of such a loss.

Charlie moved a step closer along the rail. 'You mean you just didn't give a damn, or what?'

'I didn't know what to be curious about.'

'You didn't even have a picture of him or your mama?'

'There weren't too many photo studios in Troumal.'

Charlie leaned in. Two young couples were walking past them toward a companionway, the boys lighting up the night with their seersucker suits. 'I still can't believe you're not curious about who killed them.'

'I'm curious.'

'I mean serious curious. Track 'em down or somethin'. Sic the law on them at least. Damn, you got their name off one of the Skadlocks, didn't you?'

Sam stepped away from the rail, suddenly angry. 'What, you got nobody to fight tonight so you want to fight with me?'

'Calm down, Lucky.'

'I tell you what. When I get finished paying my bills and sending money for my wife and baby, I'll buy an outfit and load it on a train and track those bastards all over Arkansas for a month. You want me to hire some Pinkertons while I'm at it? Would that make you happy?'

'Look, it's all right. Forget it.'

'I've never been long on vengeance, friend. It's not exactly in my budget.'

Charlie began to walk off. 'Time to check for cigarettes.'

Sam yelled after him. 'What am I supposed to do with these people if I find 'em? Write out a bill for memories that never happened? Shoot 'em in the eye? Listen, you ever slap a dog for pissing on your leg? You think the dog understands why you hit him? What's the use, is what I'm saying.' But Charlie had rounded the deck into darkness, and he found himself enraged and near tears. He made his rounds quickly, dodging passengers and telling himself he was merely tired. He stopped at the rail and watched the moon-glazed river for a long time, then he went up to the café for coffee.

Elsie, working even between sets, slammed a cup in front of him as soon as he sat down. 'You're on the floor.'

'Give me a break. I just need five minutes.'

'After the trip tonight, August needs you to go over an arrangement for that newest DeSylva piece he's been practicing.'

He took a hot swallow. 'I don't know arrangements like Ted did.'

'Well, I thought you might want to do some of his work.' She said this in as cruel a voice as possible. He wondered if she remembered she was talking to a man who'd never even had a father.

'And tomorrow, before you play for the two o'clock crowd, can you watch Lily?'

He shook his head no, but said, 'Sure.'

'Even *you* ought not to be able to lose her on a boat.' She snapped around and walked through the crowd to go down for the next song, her fine dress swaying like water.

He went back to his cabin and dug out Charlie's new bottle of Canadian whiskey and sat with the door open, looking out into the passing dark. He'd rescued the child, but so far as Elsie was concerned, he'd brought only part of her back. 'Bits and pieces of all of us fall away,' he said aloud, staring out into the dark, waiting for a light, onshore or waterborne, it didn't matter. But no light passed his door.

The next day he was at the piano setting up for the two o'clock trip. A few Presbyterians were crossing the gangplank dressed in their snappy summer clothes. Elsie appeared at the treble side of the piano and thrust Lily's hand toward him. 'Here. I'll be back in an hour.'

He lifted her onto the bench and continued practicing ''N'

Everything.' She was looking at her sooty doll as if it were diseased.

'That your favorite dolly?'

She put out her bottom lip. 'I had some nice ones with real china faces.'

'Why, you can have just as much fun with a cheap doll,' he said, instantly sorry that he'd said anything at all. 'What's her name?'

'I don't know.' She slid next to him on the bench and watched his hands play through the Broadway tune popular a few years before. The rhythm was tricky, a sort of semi-ragtime experiment. Lily began to hum.

'You know this one?'

She quietly sang the last verse along with his playing, forgetting the second-to-last line.

'You're not interested? You'd sound good with a band behind you, I bet.'

'Maybe,' she began, 'when my fingers get long, I can play the piano.'

'But you can sing right now.' He finished the piece, took up a pencil, and made a few marks on the music, thinking how sooner or later everybody has to sing for their supper. He looked down at Lily's unbrushed hair and the drooping rickrack bow. 'You want me to play something?'

She shook her head.

'Anything you want to ask me?'

She put a thumb over one of the doll's eyes. 'Why are the rooms on this boat so small?'

'It's a boat, honey, and boats have small rooms. You won't be on one forever.'

She put a thumb over the doll's other eye. 'That's good,' she said, her voice shaking.

After one glance at her face, he began playing 'Kitty Kat Rag' and jostling her on the piano bench. 'Come on and clap.' She let her doll slip to the floor but didn't move, only watched his fingers, and at the turn she put up her right hand and began to insert grace notes an octave above where he was playing, in time and matching the melody. In the repeat she put in more notes, guessing right where he was going. Something was happening, but he wasn't sure what. She was staying with him now, bouncing on the bench.

34

The *Ambassador* broke a paddlewheel shaft in St Louis and laid up a week. Sam caught the Illinois Central to New Orleans and spent three days at home, playing with Christopher and taking Linda out one night just to ride the streetcar belt and eat beignets and coffee at the Morning Call. They sat on stools among leviathan sugar bowls and whorls of confectioner's sugar spilled across the marble counter and talked a long time, but his mind was not always on their conversation.

'Lucky, what is it?' She put her cup down with a clack, unnoticed in the café, which was always racketing with stoneware.

He held his hand over his steaming mug. 'I've been thinking about Uncle Claude. I don't know why.'

She put a hand lightly on his arm. 'Oh, you know why.'

'I thought he was my daddy for the first five or six years. But it's something else.'

'What?'

'The attack.' He wouldn't say 'the killing.' It was too final a pronouncement.

She took her hand back. 'I was wondering when this would come up. I mean, I've always admired the way you put that behind you. Other men would've gone crazy about it. I understand that.'

'I don't know why, but I feel like it's time to find out a little about it.'

'It's because you've got your own family now.'

'I don't know.'

She put her arm through his. 'Lucky, you can catch the Texas and New Orleans train west in the morning.'

'I don't want to leave.'

'It's okay. You haven't seen old Claude in a good long while.' She laughed. 'I remember him at our wedding, wearing that gray-striped suit that made him look like a dominique chicken. Is his English getting any better?'

'Oh, he can speak it when he pays attention.'

'Honey.'

'What?'

'It's okay if you speak French, you know. It doesn't mean anything.'

He pushed his cup away and stood up, leaving a nickel on the counter for the boy. 'The schoolteacher used to beat me with a stick of lath when I spoke French. Even one word. I got the idea real quick when I saw him whip the Abadie kids. He hit them like their French was a fire he was trying to beat out. And they didn't know enough English to realize why he was mad or what he was yelling at them. I thought, who needs it? "I think" works as well as "*je pense*."' He took her arm and they walked out into the humid heat, the smell of fish drifting from the market downriver. 'What time does the train leave?'

'They load it on the ferry at eight.'

'All right.'

'And call the store in Troumal to send a boy to tell Claude you're coming.'

Here he laughed. 'I remember one time a man delivered a telegram and Uncle tipped him with a sweet potato.'

The next morning the train was pulled off the lurching ferry by a switch engine, handed over to a greasy road locomotive, and proceeded west through poor, water-soaked farms into a reptile-laced swamp where virgin cypresses held up a cloud-dimmed sky. The timber was immense and close to the track. He watched out the window and imagined that from one of the new aeroplanes the railroad would look like a flaw in a vast green carpet. After an hour, one mildewed and rain-blistered town went by, and then they were in sugarcane fields, rainwater pooling silver in the long rows. Then thirty miles of timber, then sugarcane again, red-wing blackbirds flocking away from the train's clatter, flashing their crimson badges. At noon he dug in a paper bag and ate a cold piece of chicken his wife had packed, washing it down with a cone of water from the coach's fountain. There was no diner on the little consist, and the man next to him watched him closely as he ate, as if he were famished himself. The train switched off the main line and rolled to a stop in Petit Coeur and several people got off, including his seatmate. The feeling stirred in him that the train was going back in time to a place that didn't exist anymore, that maybe never had existed at all, though he knew he'd come from there. The engine whistled off, and now the few villages provided intermittent relief from the fields and swamps that the train threaded through at twenty miles an hour for much of the afternoon. At a flagstop of ten buildings known as Prairie Amer, he waited on the wooden platform until the one-car train departed for Troumal on the branch line, its little nineteenth-century locomotive lisping steam northward through drowned cane fields.

From the depot in Troumal he was planning to walk to the store and wait for a ride, but the agent put a finger in his elbow and motioned with his head. '*Ton cheval est là-bas.*' Down the street, tied off to a railroad hydrant, was an oily-looking horse with a note pinned to the saddle, 'Simoneaux' scrawled on the paper. He looked the horse over and shook his head.

The road was so sloppy he switched to the edge of a sugarcane field, riding past little farmhouses washed gray by the weather, the Boudreauxs, the Patins, the white home of Mrs Perriloux, his piano teacher. When he rode into his uncle's yard, he was pleased to see the house looking good, with new chairs and rockers on the gallery, the yard inside the pickets clean and free of weeds and junk. His aunt came out as he tied the horse to the gate and gave him a long hug. She was a tall woman with a straight back and dark hair cut medium-length, and though her face was wrinkled, the skin was clear and the even color of cream. She started to rattle off questions in French, and he held up his hand.

'Aunt Marie, I don't remember a lot of the old talk. Can you go in English?'

She put a finger up and touched her lips. 'Ah, yes. You a bigshot city boy now. Me, I forgot that. Come on in and I'll fix you a hot cup of coffee.'

Inside, nothing much had changed. Seated at the kitchen table he looked around to the whitewashed board walls and the pictures of the Blessed Virgin and Saint Martin. The stove was the same one for which he'd chopped tons of kindling. 'Where's the boys?'

'Nestor moved away to work on them oil field in Texas. Orillian married and has a place out near Petit Coeur. Arsène and Tee Claude stayed around to help with the farm.'

'Orillian found a girl to marry him?'

She poured a long rill of coffee into an ironstone mug. 'Hard to believe.' They looked at each other and burst out laughing. Orillian was the smallest of all of them and famous parish-wide for his big ears.

'How's Uncle Claude?'

'Oh, him, he's fine as can be.'

They sat in the kitchen and traded news until it was time to begin supper, and without being told he stepped onto the back porch, bent to the right, and his hand found the hatchet handle as easy as finding his own forehead with the sign of the cross. He held the tool up and smiled at it. The kindling plinked against the house until there was enough to get the stove started. He noticed a kitchen chair resting against the back wall and looked long at it.

Aunt Marie used to tell him she could set her watch by Uncle Claude. Sam no longer had a watch, so he kept an eye on the kitchen clock on the shelf above the table, and when it said six o'clock he heard the jingle of mule harness. Through the window, he saw his uncle walk stiff-legged around the corner of the barn holding the singletree and reins, steering two big dark mules into the front bay. Claude had a thick shock of graying hair and muscled, sun-bronzed arms that rippled as he turned the animals into the barn. Sam walked out from the back porch to greet him, helped unbuckle and put up the tackle. Then a cast-iron handshake, a slap on the shoulders, and a sweaty hug and kiss on the cheek. *'Comment ça va?'*

'Ça va en anglais maintenant.'

The old man popped his fist on his forehead. 'Oh, yeah, me, I forgot that. Let's go on to the house.' He turned Sam by the shoulder and gave him a push in the back. 'Go on, mule.'

They had coffee, and when his cousins came in they all ate supper, then drank more coffee. Aunt Marie lit the lamps and sat and talked with the men while they rolled cigarettes and drank blackberry wine dipped from a crock in the kitchen pantry. Arsène and Tee Claude were saving to buy the cane field next door and asked Sam for advice on how to deal with bankers. He understood they thought he was rich and wise about city things. After all, he didn't wear overalls, had an education, lived in the big town, and worked in a suit. He thought of how they imagined him and of how wrong they were.

Arsène fell asleep in his chair, and by nine o'clock nearly everyone had gone to bed. Sam and his uncle stayed at the kitchen table on either side of a glass kerosene lamp, two jelly jars of dark wine between them. Every minute the tall windows flickered grayly, and out to the northwest a thunderstorm wandered about like bad luck looking.

He glanced at a window and then to his uncle, the smiling mustache, the wild eyebrows. 'I have to ask you something.'

His uncle pulled in his chin. 'I hope you don't need no money.'

'This isn't a joke.'

'Eh bien.'

He took a sip of the wine, thick as syrup. 'It's about those killers.'

Claude sat back slowly. 'They's a lot of things you better off not knowin'.'

He put a hand palm-up on the table. 'Maybe I need to know more instead of less.'

'What, you gonna look for them people?'

'I might. I feel bad sometimes for not doing anything. I know the law can't help. It's been, what, twenty-seven years?'

His uncle took a breath so deep a spindle in his chair popped. 'If you lookin' to get back at these people, you can't do that. You can kill 'em dead with a axe and they won't even understand why you doin' it.'

'What about justice?'

'Justice works if it puts a dollar back in you pocket.'

'Punishment?'

His uncle turned toward the window as a tumble of thunder came out of the next parish. 'What I always told you?'

He looked down. 'What people do wrong is its own punishment.'

In the weak light his uncle's face was brown and furrowed like a winter-killed field. 'Listen to me. I rather be your dead papa for five minutes than one of them killers for a whole life.'

Sam looked at the lamp flame, which leapt for no reason and made a puff of smoke. He tried to imagine such people but couldn't. 'Maybe I could tell them something. If I could ever find even one of them, maybe there's something I should say.'

'Something needs sayin'? You gonna find 'em to forgive 'em?'

'I don't know. I don't know what I'll say until I find them.'

'Then they'll do you in.' With a forefinger his uncle drew a line across his throat.

'Don't worry, Nonc. A little girl I met in France gave me my nickname. Lucky, she called me. Chanceux.'

'*Chanceux* so far,' he said.

'Come on. Tell me.'

Claude sniffed, then drank down his wine and pushed the little glass away. He shook his head. 'They came in ridin' double so the horses wouldn't make plenty noise. I figured this out from the hoofprints in the yard. I went over *à pied* – how you say, on foot? – to help him put in seed cane. The sun was just up, but me, I could see the door knocked down flat.' He spread his fingers in the air. 'Holes in all the wallboard. One porch post was shot in two, yeah. I never seen nothin' like that before, and I got scared. I walked around the whole house to make sure nobody wasn't still there. Then I went in.' He raised a hand from the table and let it come down slowly.

'You found them.' Sam's voice was a whisper.

'It's funny what I thought. He was my brother and he had a hole in his head and it was floatin' in a puddle of blood, and the first thing what come to me was I'd never hear him play a fiddle again.' He looked up. 'You knew that? You papa could play the fiddle?'

'No.' A new door opened in Sam's head, and through it came notes and rhythm flowing onto a cypress porch.

'Ay yi yi, I never told you that. That cuts me like a knife. He played waltzes his own papa taught him, waltzes and old fast-dance pieces could make a chicken two-step. It wasn't what he played but how he did it that I remember, slick like lightning, you know? Sometimes smooth like moonlight.'

Sam nodded. 'Like moonlight.'

'I looked down on him and thought about all the music wouldn't never be heard. And that wasn't all, he could shingle a roof tight as a boat's bottom. His fields were plowed straight like lines on a tablet. I thought about that, too. All that was killed. Ah, Sammy, when a man kills somebody, the most important thing he takes away is all the things that person can do in a lifetime. *Tu comprends ça?*'

He nodded, understanding too well.

'And then I saw your mamma, she was shot in the chest, and I started cryin' so much and shakin' I didn't see your brother and sister at first.' He shook his head. 'All I can say is a big bullet kills a little child fast, fast. I can tell you at least nobody hurt for long.'

He put his head in his hands. 'How many did it?'

Claude shook his head. 'The house looked like a strainer. Maybe nine or ten.'

'I never heard a number.'

'Nine or ten. That afternoon the one lawman we had, that little stinking Thibodaux crook, he rode to the parish line and gave up. He said they out his territory. Me myself, I rode into the parish to the north and told the sheriff, and he sent a deputy with me down the one dirt highway they got to the edge of that parish. We found one '*tit neg* said he saw a bunch ridin' like a army north, so I went into that parish and found the red-face sheriff that said he didn't chase nobody for no dumb coonass Catholic couldn't talk good American.'

'Did you ever hear who they were, or where they were from?'

Claude got up and went to a dark corner of the kitchen. Sam could hear a cabinet door squeak open and the tap of a dipper. He came back with two glasses of wine and sat down again, the joints in his chair grinding like dry bones. 'At first, no. Six month later, the priest come over with the saddle from the man you papa knocked off his horse. He said he found some papers in it. They didn't say where the man was from. But from one of them we saw the man's name was Jimmy somebody. I can't remember that last name. I never heard that name before in my life *parmi les américains autour d'ici*.'

'Do you have the papers?'

His uncle blinked and looked up. 'I think so.'

He rose, took the lamp, and went into the front room. In the dark kitchen Sam heard him open a locker and begin to shuffle through papers. He imagined him squinting, running his eyes into the musty cabinet, trying to remember, maybe trying not to. When his uncle came back he held a hardback supply catalog with a few outsized pages stuck in the middle.

Sam took the book and opened it. Inside were two handwritten contracts for small timber leases, and the agent was the hard-drinking horse torturer, Jimmy Cloat. 'Well, well.'

His uncle's eyebrows went up. 'You know this name?'

'It's a little world for sons of bitches. I believe that. They get found.'

'You know you ought to go back to New Orleans and forget about it.'

'I know that.'

'But you won't, you.'

'Probably not.' Sam held the papers up in the yellow glow.

His uncle sat back just out of the lamplight, diminished to an amiable smudge. 'Aw, Sam.'

He stood up, holding the papers. *'Bon soir, mon oncle.'*

Breakfast was at five-thirty, and when Sam sat down Arsène came in with a gap-toothed smile and threw a patched pair of Headlight overalls at him. 'Hey, boy, I hear you stayin' here all day. We gonna get some work outa you, hanh?'

Sam plucked the overalls off his shoulder and looked at them. 'Well, the train don't go back till tomorrow, so I guess you got me.'

Aunt Marie put on the table a plate of rolled flapjacks stacked like cordwood and they grabbed the syrup pitcher and went at it, slathering on butter and pouring coffee. He looked around the table. But for the fact that two of his cousins had gone off, it was as if he'd never left. He imagined what a kitchen table would have been like in that other life, the one that stopped twenty-seven years before in a sideways rain of lead. What father would have sat at the head of the table, what mother, sister, brother, what empty chair promising a future child? And when he thought of all these meals that had not happened, he saw a whole world of life broken, gone. He dropped his fork, and his uncle looked up at his face.

'You all right, you?'

'I'm okay,' he said, looking at no one.

'You don't have to work with us.'

'I'm all right.' But he knew he looked as though he'd been conversing with ghosts of the unborn. He also felt he had to put something back together, and he had no idea how.

They started by hitching the mules and running the rattling cultivators through the young cane. After the dew burned off, they sent Sam to the barn to shovel the manure pile into the spreader and haul that out with the mare, Tante Sophie. He covered an acre his uncle intended for late-season tomatoes and then dropped the spreader off at the barn, washed it out with buckets he hand-pumped at the well, and hitched Tante Sophie up to a small plow to turn up another part of the field. By noon he was aching and sunburned, the sun straight over his head and as worrisome as the headlight of an oncoming train. His aunt brought out cornbread and buttermilk and pistolettes stuffed with ham along with a cool pitcher of homemade root beer with slices of lemon floating in it. They sat under the green, heart-shaped leaves of a tallow tree, eating and looking out over their work.

Arsène nudged Tee Claude. 'I bet Sam's gonna run all the way to that damn department store when he gets back.'

Tee Claude closed one eye. 'How'd you wind up on that dancin' boat, anyway? I thought you wanted to stay in the city.'

'The department store didn't want me back.'

Tee Claude had a round, rascal's face, and when he pursed his lips it grew even rounder. 'I read in one of you letters that you'd get you job back if you fount that li'l girl.'

Sam swallowed a wonderful rush of cornbread and buttermilk. 'It's all right. The boat's paying all right.'

Arsène shook his head. 'Damned if I'd live in a big city where they go back on their deals. I'd of threw that evil *fils de putain* out his office window.'

Sam bit his pistolette and chewed on the comment. 'He thought I took too long to find the girl and bring her back.'

'Well, hell, you got her back, didn't you?'

'I did that. But she changed while she was taken.'

Uncle Claude stuck out his thick legs and crossed his boots. 'That age, babies change day by day. Me, I'm not surprised one kid got took and another got brought back.'

'The rich people that stole her taught her things.'

Arsène laughed. 'What a pile of cowshit. I wish some rich folks would steal me, yeah. Teach me how to sleep past six o'clock.'

Tee Claude drained his buttermilk and belched. 'Who the hell'd steal you?'

'All right, shut your traps,' the old man said. 'Time to get after them potato. Sammy, you go bust up some stovewood.'

'How much?'

'Well, the stove ain't never gonna stop burnin'.'

Sam fell asleep in his chair at supper and woke when everyone began laughing at him, and he thought there was nothing better than a tableful of blood kin laughing at his expense. Nothing better than the chicken gumbo over fat pearls of rice and a tongue-popping potato salad on the side and a mug of hot coffee with fresh cream and three spoons of sugar in it. Nothing better and at the same time nothing sadder.

Everyone on the screened porch was telling stories. Arsène about a train wreck he'd been in. Tee Claude about a fistfight he'd started over a Duvillier girl. Sam about the girl in France he'd shot with a cannon.

'You shot a cannon and hit somebody?' Tee Claude made a terrible face. 'What an idiot!'

Sam straightened his back in his rocker. 'It was an accident!'

'*Mais,* who gave *you* a cannon to shoot with?'

'We just found it.'

Tee Claude shook his head. 'Hell, Sam, remember when you couldn't hit that rat in the outhouse with a rifle.'

Everybody laughed, and Sam stood up. 'It was running around and around. You ever try to aim a rifle inside an outhouse?'

Arsène told about a live rabbit in an icebox, and the tales went on toward the deep dark of eight-thirty. Aunt Marie talked about her sister's operation, how her appendix was the size of a bell pepper and how mad she was when the doctor told her he'd thrown it away. She'd wanted it in a jar, a trophy to show the ladies at the Altar Society meeting. Uncle Claude told about a great-uncle who'd drowned, a man no one had heard of before, and everybody on the porch wanted to know what he was like and what he did with his short life. The old man tried his best at reincarnation and the night ended in stories about other drownings and near-drownings, floods, roof leaks, baptisms, an accordion played in the rain.

The house was empty when Sam got up the next morning. They'd let him sleep out of understanding. All his bones hurt with yesterday's work, and he winced as he raised a cup of coffee to his mouth. He was packed and standing on the porch when his aunt and cousins came out of the fields to say goodbye.

His uncle rode up from the barn on horseback, and the cousins walked out into the sun and left for the fields.

'Just leave him tied at the station,' Uncle Claude said, getting off. 'We'll get him when we go in for feed this evening.'

'All right.' Sam took a long look at the house.

His uncle waited for his gaze to come around. 'You goin' to look for those people?'

'I think so.'

'And if you find where they at?'

'I don't know.'

'Well. What you do will say who you are.'

He looked at the dust rising in the road. 'I guess so.'

His uncle's eyes were full of thought. Finally, he said, 'The house, it's still there, all growed up.'

'House?'

'You know. Where it happened. It was cypress all of it, so it's still there. Six mile away.'

'It's been there all along and you never told me?'

His uncle dismissed his voice with a wave of his hand. 'I found somethin' else in the cabinet you can have. It's in a sack on the saddle.'

'What is it?'

'*Violon*. A fiddle. It belonged to you daddy.'

He looked toward the horse. 'Another thing you never told me. I knew there was a fiddle in the cabinet, but I never thought anything about it.' He suddenly felt as if he'd lived a thousand years on this farm, and he turned around, staring.

‘It was too sad to tell you what it was.’ His uncle looked away and put his hands in his pockets. ‘He played that thing all the time we grew up. What I think of when I look at it is the music it’s not making. *Tu sais ça?*’

The sack hung off the pommel like a sad thought. *‘Oui. Je sais.’*

‘La seule chose plus triste qu’une chanson triste est aucune chanson du tout.’

Sam put an arm on his uncle’s shoulder, the muscles oakey and warm. *‘C’est vrai, ça.’*

The old man turned his face. ‘True too much.’

35

In New Orleans he relaxed for a few days, played with Christopher, repaired a broken pipe under the bathroom, and went on long walks with the baby and Linda. She asked him to quit the boat several times, but he told her he was afraid to give up a job when he had no other prospects. He didn't tell her that his playing was much better because he was working with a good group of musicians.

When he got off the train in St Louis, he found the boat tied up below the Eads Bridge and half the crew down with influenza. The captain, his face compressed with worry, pulled him aside as soon as he stepped off the stage. 'Sam, you stay in your cabin and don't mix in. We're trying to keep the sickest folks to the back of the boat.'

'All right. How's Charlie?'

'He had a case in 1918 and says he can't catch it again. But the cook staff and the café help are knocked down bad.' The captain squeezed his shoulder. 'A cabin boy died yesterday, and the day before that, Maude Schull.'

'Big Maude in charge of the linen?' He pictured her going through the cabins, jerking sheets off their flimsy bunks.

'She'd been with us five years.'

'How's Elsie doing in all this?'

'The captain lowered his voice. 'She's had the fever three days and is out of her head.'

Sam took a step back and looked aft down the rail. 'Is there anything I can do for her?'

'You'd best try to keep well. We've canceled four days' worth of trips, and when we start up again we'll need every hand.'

He watched the captain pull himself up the stairs. Sam remembered the epidemic two or three years before. He'd gotten a skull-cracking case of it himself, but made it through. Six employees at Krine's weren't as lucky.

Later that afternoon, he met with the day band and they went over new arrangements, playing them out on the forecastle deck in safe, open air, the music running up the riverbank into town. Two black clarinetists, Will Williams and Louis LaBorde, their forearms resting on a deck rail above, listened and watched. Felton Bicks, the cornetist, called up. 'Hey, get your instruments and come on down. Teach these sight-readin' dandies a few licks.' In a few minutes they appeared and everybody started up 'Clarinet Marmalade,' and not far in, Sam noticed how the music got set free by the clarinet improvisations. August sat to his right in a deck chair, and when the clarinetists dropped out, he slid right in and embroidered a new edge onto the melody, the rest of the band setting a stage for his wandering sax. Sam was playing on the downstairs upright, which they'd pushed out into the sunshine, and he could feel the band get good and tight as they doubled the song, playing it right out of the end and into the beginning, turning the tune inside out and running it over the water. He looked at August, and the boy was pure music, eyes closed and sax waving like a flag at a parade.

He fell into his bunk at ten o'clock, and Charlie came in and sat in the chair, looking old and tired, his shoulders curled forward. 'Lucky, they just brought a cook up the stage plank. He didn't make it.'

'Who was it?'

'The little Swenson guy.'

'Why didn't they bring him to the hospital?'

Charlie looked at the palms of his hands. 'Nobody thought it was that bad, I guess.' He pulled off his cap and hung it on his knee. 'They're taking out three by ambulance in the morning, though. Unless they improve.'

'How's Elsie doing?'

'She's one of the three. Her and a fireman and the purser.'

'I'd better go down and see her.'

'You had the flu yet?'

'Yeah.' He pulled his mate's cap off a nail and settled it square on his head.

'It's a bad dose she's got.'

'I just want to see her a minute.'

He walked toward the rear of the Texas, where most of the women had their cabins. Lily was staying with another waitress farther forward while her mother was ill. He knocked, and Gladys, a ruddy pastry cook from Minnesota, opened the door for him.

'How's she doing?'

'You just set with her a minute while I get a snack. You'll get the picture.'

The room was warm and smelled of sickness. Elsie lay on the bottom bunk, and he took the small chair between it and the sink. Even in the light of the dim bulb he could see that her complexion was dark. She breathed hard, her mouth open, and when he reached to her forehead, the fever scorched his palm. She opened her eyes and coughed, rivers moving in her chest. 'Lucky,' she said breathlessly. 'Can you help watch the kids till I get better?'

It broke his heart to see her like this, and he remembered her in the spotlight onstage, all beauty and talent and music. 'That won't be a problem, girl.'

Her head rolled away from him. 'Hell of a mess.'

'You'll be all right.'

'I guess this is one thing I can't blame on you.'

He looked at the enameled deck. 'You seen August?'

'He just left. I don't want him in here too long.'

'He's getting better with his horn every day.'

She seemed desperate for breath. A crescent of blood glowed in her right nostril. 'If I can't work this season.' She stopped and swallowed. 'The only one who'll take Lily is Ted's brother.'

'You better rest.'

'No. Ted's brother is a saloonkeeper. Bad, bad temper, Lucky. It'll be terrible for the kids.'

He waited for her to go on, but she was completely exhausted and her eyes had drifted closed. A big tow went by the little window, the boat's mast light winking like a shooting star, and the *Ambassador* started to rock slightly. After a few minutes he stood up, unsure of what to do, and in the dim room her voice came, all the music out of it.

'His name's Bruton.'

He bent down over her face, appalled by what the sickness had done. 'Who?'

'Don't let him have them, Lucky,' she gasped.

'Okay,' he whispered.

Her eyelids parted like dark wounds. 'Don't let him have them.'

'Go to sleep.' He touched her forehead again, where the skin was as warm as a lamp shade. Glancing around the room, he searched for anything that might distract her from the suffering.

Suddenly, she arched her back and cried out, as from a dream, 'It's all your fault.'

He waited at the rail outside her door until Gladys returned, and then he watched the river, still broken with the passing of the last boat, shattered like his feelings. He wondered if there was a physics to one's mistakes, a chain of reactions that ran away toward infinity like waves or a sounding whistle chasing along a watercourse for miles and miles. And what could he do but make right his mistakes when he could, or unable to do that, catch some other fellow's mistake and fix it? Across the river one of the last packet boats serving St Louis rang its deck bell, the heavy notes skating across the water and up the sloped and cobbled bank into the city. He watched it leave, and then Gladys came out carrying a pail.

'What time will the ambulance come for her?'

'They said daybreak.'

'Will all three of them fit into it?'

She was walking away to the stern, but stopped and turned to him. 'Two. The fireman's done crossed over.'

* * *

The next morning started off warm and humid. The mates and kitchen staff still able to work disinfected the café, mopping everything down with bleach. The ambulance came and left while Sam was swabbing under the tables. Later, he went down to the bandstand and began playing the piano. August walked in with his hands in his pockets. He was letting his hair grow and it was oiled back out of his way and tucked over his pale ears.

Lily dawdled behind him, her face still four years old, oblivious, carrying a coloring book folded over a single-row box of crayons. She opened it on a table and pulled the chair out with both hands, then kneeled on its seat to begin coloring. 'I don't have a brown,' she complained.

'Use black,' Sam told her.

August leaned against the piano. 'Lucky,' he whispered, 'what do you think about Mom?'

'I think she should've gone to the hospital a couple days ago.'

'I know. I'm scared.'

The statement froze his fingers, and he put his hands in his lap. 'You saying your prayers?'

'I've been praying for two days straight.'

Sam closed his eyes a moment. He wasn't August's father, and the Wellers weren't his responsibility. He would help Elsie as far as he could, but ultimately that wouldn't amount to much. 'You want me to go up the hill with you to see her?'

He shook his head. 'I'm scared I'll catch it and give it to Lily. The cabin boy that died wasn't but twelve years old, and strong as a country ox.'

'Zach?'

'Yes.'

'That's kind of scary, all right. Scary as hell.'

'The captain says we won't go anywhere for ten days, and that's if nobody else comes down hard with it.'

'Good practice time, sounds like.'

August sat down on the bench beside him, facing away from the keyboard. 'I don't want Lily to wind up with Uncle Bruton.'

He looked over at his sister. 'I'll kidnap her myself if it comes to that.'

'Your mom's a tough lady. She'll pull through.'

'God, I hope so.' He slumped forward and closed his eyes.

Sam tried to remember if he had ever been that worried. When he thought of the sickness that took his first child, the baby's trembling eyelids, his blue lips, he knew that he had.

'You go on and take a walk. Get your mind on something else.'

August stood up. 'Can you watch her?'

'Well, I guess so.'

He walked forward toward the main stairs and Lily saw him go, then turned to Sam, a crayon bearing down on a page. 'I'm hungry.'

The piano key cover snapped down like a fact. 'Let's get you a sandwich in the café.'

'It smells bad.' She pinched her nose.

'That smell is medicine to get rid of the sickness.'

'It always smells bad.'

He took her by the hand, which was sticky and soot-smudged. 'We'll wash our hands and go get a sandwich.'

'I don't want to wash my hands.'

'Come on and let me show you how it's done.'

Before supper, they left Lily with Gladys and walked to the hospital, and at the main desk, when they asked to see Elsie, the receptionist called someone on the phone. When they saw a tall nurse walk down the hall toward them, a woman with iron-gray hair and a solemn stride, when they looked at her eyes and the way she held her hands, one over another in front, when they saw her face, a face good at telling the worst, they knew Elsie was dead.

August collapsed in a chair and covered his face with his hands. Sam spoke with the nurse for a few moments, then stood staring down the long hall after her retreating steps. He remembered visiting Elsie sick in bed, and that was hard enough. He didn't want to see her now. When he asked August if he wanted to, the boy trembled and shook his head.

'I'm scared.'

'I'll go with you.'

'No, I don't want to.'

For himself, he chose to remember her in a close-fitting gown the color of pearl, bouncing the notes of 'Painting the Clouds with Sunshine' as the hundreds on the dance floor quick-stepped and the river breeze streamed through the windows and the shoreline moved past like the dreary real thing it was, the thing made of smokestacks and shabby houses and overworked souls, all gilded by Elsie's gliding voice, her flash of blond hair, the spark of hard work showing in her song, in her eyes. He wanted to dwell in the remembering, but he was obliged instead to turn to August and pull him out of the chair. 'I'm sorry, Gussie. Cry all you want.' And the boy did, against Sam's cheap second-mate coat. After a while he walked him down the echoing hallway, trying hard to think of something to say, and in the entry, he pulled him aside and told him, 'Never forget that you had her for fifteen years. A lot of kids never had anything like those fifteen years.'

Captain Stewart paid the expenses for the body to be shipped to Cincinnati. Sam went up with August and Lily, who had cried a little without understanding why. After the burial Mass, there was a family meeting, some shouting on August's part, bitter accusations and dismissals from Ted's brothers, quiet resignation from Elsie's aged parents, and the result was that when Lucky got off the train days later, broke and hungry in St Louis's grand station, August stepped off behind him, Lily asleep in his arms.

In mid-June the boat was far north of Hannibal playing an isolated town, a place of machine shops and foundries stretching up the mountainside. The afternoon crowds were mostly families of running and screaming children, and Sam had to keep an eye on Lily to make sure she wasn't knocked down a stairway. He played piano for the two o'clock and convinced her to sit beside him on the bench and turn pages, though he knew the music, and it didn't matter if she turned two pages at once. Sometimes she wandered away in the middle of a song, and he'd have to play looking over his shoulder, and one time when she'd wandered out among the dancers and gotten bumped to the floor, he had to stop playing and charge out to drag her back up onto the bandstand as she bawled and rubbed her calf.

For the night trip, the boat filled up with local men and their women. Sam worked the stage plank asking for weapons and surveying the crowd. The men were all muscle from working ten-hour shifts wrestling cylinder heads and piston rods, but only two surrendered anything, a jackknife and a dollar pistol. The ones who strutted onto the dance deck either took seats at tables or leaned against the bulkheads, all of them staring grimly at the band. When Sam came up and looked around, the hair rose on his neck. The crowd stared as if they'd never seen Negroes holding anything other than a shovel or a wrench. He guessed they hadn't heard much jazz and distrusted any music that didn't sound like the conventional tunes played on their Victrolas. The orchestra was playing a grinding rendition of 'Sud Bustin' Blues,' and no one was dancing. It wasn't clear that anyone knew how.

He walked over to the trumpeter when the piece was over. 'Hey, we got a boatload of rubes tonight,' he said, his back to the floor. 'Can you do your hotel stuff?'

The man nodded, wiped his face with a voluminous white handkerchief, and scanned the crowd. 'They don't look like no dance club, do they?'

'Nope.'

'We can't play no polka music.'

'Just dumb it down.'

'Play like the day band?' The trumpeter's smile was wide and bright.

'Give me a break.'

He walked over to the main staircase and down to start his rounds on the main deck. The boat was barely a hundred feet from shore when an argument broke out in the forward lounge and he got sandwiched between two men dressed in heavy denim shirts who were trying to tear them off each other. Closing his eyes, he pushed into the muffled flailing of their fists, but two enormous hands grabbed him from behind and tossed him against a bulkhead, the concussion a star-flashing impact that sent him sliding to the floor. He tried to get up but found a large soggy boot pressing on his chest. 'Let 'em at it,' a voice above him said, cramped by a wad of tobacco. Someone else put a brogan on his ankle, and he lay down and gave up. After a while he felt a sticky sensation on the back of his head and realized he was bleeding. A whole wicker table arced in the air above him, and somewhere glass was breaking and rattling on the deck like gravel. Someone's thumb must have found a windpipe or eyesocket because an ungodly squalling ensued and the room began to reshuffle, but he suddenly wasn't there.

He woke up on the deck outside his cabin door, a wadded bedsheet under his head. Down below he could hear hundreds of shouts and the orchestra playing a waltz. Above him were stars in one eye, nothing in the other, and in the next instant he was in his upper bunk, Charlie's hand drifting above him holding a rag soaked in alcohol. A streak of fire running around the back of his skull from ear to ear roused him.

'Damn it to hell, that hurts!'

'I'll bet it does. Glad to see you're coming around.'

He put a hand over his eyes. 'What happened?'

'Well, it's over now. You been out four hours.'

He blinked and rolled his head. 'Where's Lily?'

'She's in with a maid and the maid ain't too happy about it.'

'I can't . . . Big fight?'

'You could say that. There'll be some carpenter work to do tomorrow and a hell of a lot of mop work.'

Charlie opened the door and looked out at the paintless buildings of the town. 'You dizzy?'

'I don't think so.' He touched the bandage Charlie had put on him. 'You're not going back out?'

'Still gotta work. You can't handle this.'

'Handle what?'

'Coming back from Talbot Island a motorboat pulled alongside with running lights and all and paced us about three feet out. The guy driving it was drunk, I guess, and was cussing at some jugheads on the top deck. Well, they went in the café and picked up a slot machine and threw it over the rail at him. Went straight through the bottom of his nice boat, and he sank like a woodstove.'

Sam lay back, deciding to stay in bed. 'You meeting with the law?'

Charlie stepped through the door into the night. 'It's a mess, all right. A real mess.'

He lay there listening to the rasp of brooms overhead, the rattling of bucket bails, the crash of mop water and slops in the river. His head pulsed, and an iron taste rose up the back of his throat. He heard distant sawing and nailing in the night as the carpenters propped up the boat's power of illusion, and finally, he slept.

At daybreak he heard his cabin door open and close, and he thought Charlie had come in.

'I'm hungry.' It was Lily standing under his bunk in a wrinkled baby dress, barefoot, her face dirty.

'Sweetie, I'm sick.'

Lily looked at him a long time and said again, her voice absolute, 'I'm hungry.'

He slowly sat up and waited for the cramped room to stop drifting off to his left. He pulled on his pants and looked into the mirror at a black eye, then began to wash up and shave.

Lily lay in Charlie's bunk and watched him. 'Why doesn't somebody come up and bring us something to eat?'

'Girlie, you been living in the wrong hotel.'

'What?'

He put on a shirt and looked at her. She was filthy and smelled sour. 'Where are your clean clothes?'

'In number fourteen.'

'Where's August?'

'I tried to wake him.'

They walked down to the cabin she shared with August, and he rummaged through her few things until he found a clean set of clothes. August lay like a stone and didn't move. Sam gathered up four sooty little dresses and some underwear and brought her back to his cabin, where he gathered his dirty clothes. In the boat's laundry they waited for a wringer machine to come free, and while their clothes were washing he got them breakfast in the café. On the starboard side, workmen were replacing a section of bulkhead that looked as if someone had blown it out with a cannon.

Back in the laundry he sent their things through the wringer and hung everything to dry on the temporary lines strung on the aft deck between trips. Then he looked closely at the girl. 'When's the last time you washed yourself?'

Lily shrugged.

'Do you know how to wash yourself, or does August do it?'

She rubbed her nose. 'I can wash if you soap the cloth.'

He led her back to her cabin, where August was snoring, drew a sink of water, put her on a stool, soaped up a washcloth, and told her to take everything off and scrub herself good all over, then rinse the rag clean and wipe off the soap and put on her clean clothes. He would wait for her out on deck.

'I can't put on my socks when my feets are wet.'

'Just come out dressed and I'll put your socks on.'

He sagged against the rail, something in his head spiking against his skullbones, a pain that should have been fatal.

In half an hour she came out and the little dress was on backwards. One of the cooks was coming down the Texas rail. 'Oh, for gosh sake,' she said, pulling the dress off and turning it around on her. She cast Sam a malevolent look and walked on, saying over her shoulder, 'You got to watch that baby, now.'

They went onto the dance floor, and he sat at the piano's keyboard and closed his eyes, trying to ignore the pain at the back of his head. He felt her climb onto the bench, and he kept his eyes closed.

'You sleeping, Mr Lucky?'

He began sorting through the books of music on the rack and found a simple waltz. 'Do you want to sing?'

He knew she wouldn't. He had tried to coach her on a few songs that August said she knew, but when she sang, she dragged the notes and ignored the timing. Sometimes she just whined. Neither one of them knew what was wrong with her. 'Look at that mark. It's an F. Can you find F on the piano?'

She pressed down middle F, the single note buzzing out over the hardwood.

'When the mark is in the blank line above, it's an A, and then a C.' He went on, and she touched the notes. He looked into her cornflower eyes. 'Is a sharp up or down?'

'Up.'

'How much did your father teach you?'

'Those notes. F-A-C-E and E-G-B-D-F. He's going to teach me to count.'

He was sick to his stomach and dizzy, and the bandage on the back of his head felt hot, but when Lily said this, he spiraled down into a new dimension of pain – of darkness, even. 'Who is?' he whispered, putting an arm around her.

She looked at her shoes. 'Nobody.'

He felt in her posture some notion that had not occurred to her before, that people disappear in a manner she might never understand. She began to cry gently, but he knew she didn't really comprehend why she was sad. Someone had told her that her father had gone to heaven, then someone told her that her mother had gone to the same place, and none of it made the least sense to her because she was in the eternal present tense of childhood where the motion of life keeps your mind busy, and the future and the past don't even exist. He felt sick for her, but terrible for himself as well, for the thin shoulder he cupped in his right hand might have been his own sister's or brother's, and then he was crushed by a deeper understanding of what he had lost back before he knew what loss was. He didn't know such a feeling could come so late, and to keep from crying in front of her, he grabbed a music book and started playing the first piece that opened up, a waltz called 'Falling Waters,' and he began explaining the three-four rhythm. Lily's head raised up and scanned the page. It was a simple piece with single bass notes, and she crossed behind him and stood on his left, poking out G and C more or less in time, watching his fingers complete the chords. He began to have the strange feeling that they were playing into the future, a place where there was no baggage to carry.

They'd spent an hour at the piano when August came through the starboard door covered with coal dust. 'I had to help load. I'll take Lily now.'

Sam looked him up and down. 'It's all right. You get cleaned up, then we'll go and pull the clothes off the line and iron them.'

'Hot time of day to iron next to a stove. How'd you get banged up?'

'I don't even know.'

August looked at his bandage closely. 'We've got some aspirin in our room.'

'I'll get them when I bring down the clothes.'

The boat plowed north all the way to St Paul, where the New Orleans music packed the dance floor every night. During the day, patrons desperate to escape the shore-bound heat loaded on board and sat under the cloth awnings, staring at their houses drifting by as travelers from some foreign land might, relishing the illusion that their town was exotic, special, or at least worth a look.

The crowds were mannered but large, the weather rainy and windy. The pilots fought the shallow channel of the upper river, and one time Mr Brandywine was flanking a bend when he saddle-bagged the steamer on a sandbar. A ferryboat had to be hired to take fifteen hundred people back to the landing, and the *Ambassador* was stranded until a rise came down to float her off three days later. Sam was thankful for the idle time. The child began to soak up her piano lessons as well as her short fingers allowed, and he was teaching her limits. Do not stand at the head of stairways. Stay away from the smokestacks. Never go down to the main deck, where the guard rails were sometimes open to the water. At night he read to her, seated in an armless deck chair next to her bed, until she grew tired of the same ten baby books, so he began to make up stories. She stopped him in the middle of one and said she didn't like it.

He'd just finished playing with the night band because the pianist had jumped to a hotel orchestra, and his head felt as wooden as the wall behind it. 'What kind of story do you want?'

'One about a bathtub.' She climbed out of the bunk onto his lap.

He looked at her. 'A bathtub?'

'A house with a sidewalk in front.'

He frowned. 'Okay. There was this little boy named Fritz who lived in a house with a huge bathtub.'

'Could he play the piano?'

'Uh, sure, he was a crackerjack pianist. Now Fritz fell in a mud puddle in the backyard . . .'

'Was there grass in the yard?'

'Grass? Yeah. Lots of nice grass. Well, Fritz began to cry and . . .'

'Did his mother come out and tell him it was okay he got muddy?' She put a hand in his shirt pocket and hung on.

'Of course she did, baby. It was an accident.'

'Did she take him inside a house? The house with the big bathtub?'

He sensed the soaring hope behind the question and understood at once what he had to do.

36

On a blustery July morning a west wind drove the *Ambassador* into a landing barge. There was no denying that it would have to limp down to Davenport for hull repair. Sam had been calling Linda and giving reports of how he was managing the children. He had discussed certain things with August. When told that the boat would be out of business for ten days, he loaded up August and Lily and took the train south, changing in Memphis and riding through the cinder-strewn heat and humidity down to New Orleans. The three of them showed up at his house sooty from two days on the rails, and his wife met them at the front door with a frown, the baby in her arms.

She thrust Christopher at Sam and examined August and Lily. 'Are y'all Catholic?'

'Yes, ma'am.' August put down his suitcase. 'But would it make a difference?'

She waved them into the house. 'It sure makes it easier if we all go to the same place on Sundays.' She fixed everybody glasses of iced tea, then sat Lily next to her on the sofa and asked all of them questions for an hour, paying particular attention to her. Sam could tell she was trying to get a feel for how things might be.

That night, after the children were asleep, Linda crawled in next to him, and he could feel her whole body decompress toward rest.

'Well, what you think?' He hoped he knew, but with Linda, he could never say for sure.

'I never saw a four-year-old so glad to get into a bathtub.'

'I know we can't afford another child.'

She laughed curtly. 'Baby, we can hardly afford ourselves.'

'August will stay on the boat with me. He's a real worker.'

'You know as well as me he can only work till September. He's got to finish school.'

'But I'll be back right after that at the end of the season. He can get pickup work in his spare time.'

'We'll talk about this later. Just let me try to get used to them.' She put an arm around his neck. 'Come here and let's not talk about workin' at something.'

He saw her watch August during the week, how he practiced on the back porch and wrote in the margins of sheet music while tapping his foot to some rhythm winding inside his imagination. She took him along to the market and reported that he'd asked for things Lily liked to eat. Little potatoes, he said. She liked little red potatoes. At the house, August pulled grass along the walk, went after the weeds next to the street with a sling blade. He complained about the heat, the mosquitoes, but Linda didn't hold that against him because she did the same.

The girl watched Linda as though she might evanesce at any moment, trailing behind her, showing no affection, her bright eyes searching and expectant.

On the day before he and August were to catch the train, Linda sidled up to him in the front room, catching his hand as he set the screen-door latch for the night and pushing him out onto the front porch.

'What?'

'Nothing. I just wanted to make sure you understood that things were all right. You know, as far as Lily's concerned. August isn't a problem. He can handle himself already.'

'I know we didn't talk much.'

'Yeah, you just assumed things, as usual. Well, don't worry, I think we can raise her. But she's not normal.'

He looked over her head into the house. 'What's that mean?'

They could hear August talking to his sister. She squealed, and August went past the kitchen door with Lily riding his back.

'She's kind of disconnected. I don't know how to explain it.

She won't climb into my lap or give me a hug. Maybe it's because she's so smart. You can see it in her eyes. She drinks everything in. Did you see her in church on Sunday? I mean, she fell asleep during the sermon, but everything else she watched with those shiny little eyes. I taught her the Hail Mary twice, and now she knows it every word.'

He nodded and looked into the kitchen toward the sound of knees thumping the floor. 'I'm trying not to teach her too much music. I'm scared she'll get bored or just forget it. If I had to guess, I'd say she'll be a lot better piano player than me.'

Linda put an arm around his waist. She seemed worried. 'It's like she's waiting for something to happen.'

'Honey, she's used to a lot of somethings happening to her.'

She shook her head. 'Maybe that's it. Maybe not.'

'I'll bring in some money. I'll make it work.'

'For her, you'll have to.' She pulled open the screen and halfway into the room stopped and turned to him. 'I know why you brought those kids into our home. Just don't forget what they'll mean for me.'

'Pretty lady, I won't.'

'I want a house someday.'

'We'll get one.'

'We don't have a penny in savings.'

'We'll get one, you'll see.'

The rest of the season the boat ran town to town, a different landing each night. The dance floor was worn to a dull brown abrasion, the outside paint an occlusion of soot despite repeated scrubbings, the paddlewheel a barewood rack of planks washed to splinters. The old boat was waterlogged, rain-wracked, and out of true, its hogchains and turnbuckles bleeding rust and the hull warped out of its proper curve. The whole crew was as weary as a thin-walled boiler, waiting for payoff and bonus and release.

The weather turned cool early and the *Ambassador* began to tramp south, chasing the receding summer. In mid-September the crowds thinned out, except for the Friday and Saturday runs, and eventually, in October at Memphis, a cold front blasted in off the plains and all but killed the excursion business. Captain Stewart decided to try a few more towns below Memphis, and on a day of a big west wind, Mr Brandywine was at the wheel fighting current as they started south. Mrs Benton and Sam sat on the lazy bench watching whitecaps rise up in the channel. The boat was to land at a dock near the mouth of the Wolf River but wasn't traveling where it was steered, commencing a dizzying wander. The pilothouse glazing rattled in the wind, and arching currents kicked up a dirty froth midriver.

Mr Brandywine raised a hand for the whistle ring and blew a landing signal. 'I'm going straight in with her back to the blow.' It was unusual for him to announce a maneuver, and Sam traded glances with Nellie Benton, wondering if the old man was hinting for advice. He watched the east bank come up in the bright midday. The pilot rang a stop bell and let the wind shove him along. Sam looked down at the water, figuring motion. Nellie Benton said nothing but seemed to be watching for wind direction in the trees. When Mr Brandywine rang a backing bell, the pilothouse trembled as the paddlewheel grabbed water, and Sam knew he was trying to pull the boat parallel to the dock and let the breeze push him in. But then the wind came up hard, whistling through the rooftop gingerbread and popping the jackstaff flags. They were a hundred yards offshore with the stern swinging in hard. Mr Brandywine rang a double gong, and after a moment the escape pipes barked up gouts of exhausting steam as the engines fought to draw the boat back from the wharf. Sam stood up. Steamboats were always underpowered things, and the wind treated them like box kites. Feeling one going out from under your feet, you knew that something terrible was going to happen in three or four minutes and that there was nothing anyone could do except drift along on what seemed like a county-sized piece of wood and wait for the bump that might break it open like a packing box, sending everyone, sleeping or awake, into the muddy current. Mr Brandywine put the wheel over hard, but the wind was beating both the engines and the rudders, so he blew a warning whistle of four shorts, watched the dark dock pilings grow bigger in his port windows and said, over his shoulder, 'Here's the end of *this* season.' He rang the stop-engine bell right before the stern crashed into a cluster of pilings, but the signal was too late. A series of jolts shook the *Ambassador* and a spray of shattered lumber and long bolts flew up over the stern as the paddlewheel beat itself apart against the dock. The boat rocked severely shoreward, then leveled as the deck-hands threw out lines. Later, Sam found out that the piano had rumbled over its roller chocks and chased a busboy a hundred feet down the dance floor.

By nightfall, the purser had paid off nearly everyone and asked the mates to stay an extra two days to tie up loose ends. Sam helped the pilots carry their luggage up to a taxi. He'd made several friendships on board, but he admired Nellie Benton and Rafe Brandywine the most, and felt that he was sending off legends.

The old man, wearing a bluewater uniform and bow tie, opened the door to the idling car and motioned for Mrs Benton to get in. 'Safest pilot goes first,' he said.

She gave him a startled look. 'I don't know about that, but it's a nice thing to say.'

'Next year, if there is a next year, you hit the captain up for full wages, you hear?'

She slid into the backseat. 'Come on and get in. You'll miss your train back to Pennsylvania.'

He turned to Sam and told him, 'You know, I admire the way you took in those Weller kids. I just wanted you to know that.'

'I kind of felt responsible.'

'Hell, we're all responsible for something, but most of us don't do a damn thing about it.' He got in, and Sam pushed the door shut.

As the hack pulled away, Nellie Benton called out, 'Stay in easy water, son.'

* * *

Riding quiet and broken against the dock, the *Ambassador* soon lost its magic, and the smell of dust and dampness rose from its decks. The engineers dropped the fires under the boilers, and with all machinery wound down to a stop, Sam found things too quiet, and he began to think. For weeks the noise and music kept him from imagining what lay a hundred or so miles inland, somewhere in Arkansas. People he had a history with, so to speak, who owed him voices, touches, the generation of bloodline. In the near dark he leaned on the starboard rail, his mind boring westward.

The captain came up a staircase and stopped for a moment, as if surprised to see him outside. 'The purser gave me your pay.' He stepped close and handed over a brown legal-size envelope. 'You've stuck until the end of things this season, and you've had a rough road, Lucky, so there's a fifty-dollar bonus.'

He turned and looked at the captain closely. 'You'll need a new uniform next year.'

The captain regarded the braid around his cuffs. He bent over slowly and put his arms on the rail. 'It's silly, isn't it? A uniform used to mean something twenty-five years ago, when I was on the Anchor Line hauling freight and overnight passengers, people who were really going somewhere. It's all silliness now. Just music and dancing.'

'I don't know. Some people need it like Pittsburgh needs coal.'

The captain shook his head. 'I guess fun has its place. Are you going home now? See the wife and all?'

He looked west over the water. The light had diminished, and the air itself seemed as grainy as fresh-broken iron. 'Got a little business to transact first.'

'Duggs told me a few things about you.'

'I bet.'

The captain straightened up and clapped him on the shoulder. 'Remember this. I never took a boat up a stream without a map.' Then he walked aft, nudging spittoons against the rail with his left foot.

* * *

The following evening he and Charlie Duggs were the only ones on the dark boat. Sam lit a kerosene lantern and walked down to the bandstand and sat at the piano in a yellow envelope of light, playing with an edge of anger in his fingers, aware how much he'd improved in the past few months. Perhaps of necessity: no one made a living with ordinary playing. In front of so many crowds of sweating dancers, he'd learned to pay more attention to his timing. He opened the music for a new ballad and began embellishing a bit, adding notes, replacing others. Then he heard the sound of footsteps in the dark, and said, 'Hey, Charlie.'

'I was up in the pilothouse watchin' the sun go down.'

'That right?' He changed the song, playing from memory, slowed the tempo, and placed a foot on the soft pedal. 'You heading out tomorrow?'

'Yeah. You want to ride the same train?'

'I'll be down in a couple days.'

Charlie sat in a folding chair in the banjo player's position. 'You decided to make a little Arkansas excursion?'

'I don't think I'll know for sure till I start out. The last thing I need to do is get myself hurt.'

'I'll go with you.'

'I know that.'

Charlie tilted his head. 'But it's your gig, right?'

'Solo act. Everybody's a solo act when it comes right down to it.' He began tipping slow and playful notes into 'St Louis Blues,' and Charlie sat back and fished out a flask, taking a long swallow.

While he played, Sam wondered if anyone was out there on the riverbank listening and what the boat looked like from shore, the enormous old steamer a motionless white smudge against the charcoal river, one yellow square of light in its center and the sad lilt of music tinkling out into the darkness like a luring call. The thought came to him that no one was listening, and this made his music seem smaller, hardly able to escape the piano's soundboard, even trapped under the balls of his fingers, his alone; but in spite of this he began to polish his notes, playing the song's Latin bridge into velvet, and Charlie put away his bottle.

The next afternoon they were playing gin in the café when they heard a big towboat simmering down on them. There was a jolt and a holler as the *Mountain Wizard* sidled up under a pall of coal smoke, deckhands jumping aboard with their ropes and lashing tight. They went out to the rail and looked over to the low pilothouse where a graybeard wheelman slid a section of window open.

'You boys packed and ready?'

'Yep,' Sam yelled.

'Well, head on to town, then. I'm fixin' to pull her off the bank.'

They got their suitcases and walked a plank off the second deck onto the dock. They crossed a rail spur to a road, where they hitched into town on a lumber truck. At the Y&MV station, Charlie bought a ticket and Sam sent a telegram. He thought a long time before he composed it, because it contained a lie. He rewrote the message several times, trying to lessen the falsehood.

> MORRIS HIGHTOWER AGENT GREENVILLE MISSISSIPPI AM IN MEMPHIS STATION TYING UP LOOSE ENDS FOR CHILD IN TROUBLE. CAN YOU TELL LOCATION OF OUTLAW FAMILY IN SE ARK NAME OF CLOAT. APPRECIATE HELP. SAM SIMONEAUX.

He told the clerk he would wait for a response.

'I know this old boy,' the man told him. 'He might not be on shift.'

'I'll wait.' Sam knew that every nail, sweet pea, mantel clock, hot-water bottle, and woodstove came through the hands of a town's railroad agent, and all news and secrets as well. If Hightower couldn't tell him anything, he probably could put him in touch with someone who could.

He sat with Charlie until his train steamed in, and he boarded him like a relative, waving as the engine chuffed off southward toward Mississippi, its long-bell whistle hurling blue notes at the sky.

He dozed a while, and shortly after five, the clerk walked over and handed him a telegram. 'Here you go, feller.'

He tore the envelope and held the message in the light of the western windows.

> TELEGRAPHED MY MAN IN ARKANSAS. GO TO TOWN OF RATIO. ASK CONSTABLE SONER YOUR QUESTIONS. BRING BIG WEAPON. MH

37

A local freight clattered into Greenville, Mississippi, and the conductor came in with the bills of lading. Morris Hightower began to invoice everything on the train while sacks of feed, crated Victrolas, bedsteads, harness and kegs were unloaded onto the freight dock. A local fellow, toothless and skinny, an assistant bartender out of work since the Volstead Act was passed, was coming up the street headed in the direction of the hardware store. He veered into the station and stood at the barred window, calling out to Morris Hightower to give him change for a twenty. 'Them hardware clerks don't like breaking a big bill for a quarter's worth of box nails.'

'I'm low on change myself,' the agent said, running a handkerchief over his ponderous neck.

The skinny man blinked and seemed to think about this. 'Look, I ain't askin' for no loan. Just break this bill into two fives, nine ones, and some quarters and dimes.'

The agent moved one bill of lading over to a tall stack. 'Lot of people buyin' tickets this morning. I need what change I got.'

The man at the window cocked his head. 'Damn your hide. Hightower, you ain't never lifted a finger in your whole damn life to hep somebody out.'

'Them that deserves help sometimes gets it.'

He began waving the twenty in the window as though it were on fire. 'Come over here you rock-hearted old bastard and give me my change.'

Hightower turned only halfway around. The bulb hanging from the ceiling imparted a white-hot luminescence to his bald head. After a moment of concentrating on the wall above his typewriter, he said, 'If I have to come to that window, I'll hit you so hard you'll piss nickels. Then you'll have all the change you want.' When he heard footsteps trailing off toward the door, he turned back to his work. After a while he thought about the girl that had been found. His brother in New Orleans had mentioned that he'd seen her playing on Sam's porch, singing like a bird.

Sam left the pawnshop wearing a new soft brown cap, a set of high leather boots, and a big Colt automatic pistol in a shoulder holster under his coat. He left Memphis at sundown aboard the *Kate Adams,* bound downriver for Helena. In the tiny stateroom he washed up, then went out to join five old men sitting near the open windows in the forward part of the cabin. They were discussing which stocks to buy on the New York exchange. One of them was a silver-haired farmer who declared he'd as soon bury his money in the privy as trust it to a New York broker. This engendered a half hour of carping that Sam patiently waited out. When the conversation changed to river traffic, Sam got in and told them what he did, which they all considered exotic and some sign of the new age to come.

'I hear some of them young gals shimmy to that jazz music till their drawers fall off,' the farmer said.

'I wouldn't know. I'm too busy playing.'

They laughed at that, and one of them asked if he were a Levert from south Louisiana and he said no, that he lived in New Orleans, and then everybody told what they thought of New Orleans, and within an hour he had them explaining to him where to rent an automobile in Helena. He asked how the road was down to Ratio, but none of them could remember if there was any kind of a road.

The *Kate Adams* stopped all night at plantations and dirt landings, scratching for pennies in freight. Right after sunrise it ran out its stage plank and dropped him and a large, well-made wooden crate on the wharfboat's freight platform. He caught a ride into Helena and found the man who rented cars, giving him the names of the gentlemen who'd recommended him on the *Kate Adams,* and the man handed him the key of a two-year-old black Ford roadster and didn't ask for a signature.

He got directions to Ratio, and two miles south of town the road dwindled into bumper-high grass running along the levee. He gave the car some gas and spun his way up to the top of the embankment and followed a wagon track, steering around lakes of rainwater and swales of mud, making about five miles an hour. After a time, he passed a large cotton plantation and could see dozens of workers in the fields, many mules hitched up to cultivators and spray wagons, but not a single internal-combustion machine. The trail ran down the levee at this point, and he stood on the brakes and let the Ford slide down it to flat land. The car sputtered along to a company store, a tall and broad wooden building, its shutters hanging off like oversized ears. Past this, the trail went into the woods and he drove at a crawl, the wheels tumbling over roots and stumps. This was virgin forest, and the trail wound back in time, away from civilization toward some druid-like occupancy back in the hardwood-haunted dimness.

For two hours the little car shook like a dog shedding water, and then he rolled up to the edge of a flat, fallow field that had been plowed the year before but left in unplanted rows. He got the wheels to match two furrows and proceeded until he was funneled by a fence line into the backyard of a large, paintless house where a white man sat on the back porch cradling a crock jug in his lap. He placidly watched Sam stop in the yard, scattering chickens, as though this happened every five minutes. His arm came up and briskly motioned around the side of the house, and Sam set the car forward and saw a lane under wild magnolia branches, and soon he was at a gate in front, which he opened and closed, now facing a pasture full of rickety brown cattle. This he drove across for two miles, dodging manure cakes and listing, bony animals, coming to another gate that led to a levee ramp. On top, he expected to see the Mississippi, but it had meandered off many years before and there was only willow-haunted flatland that seemed to go east for miles. He guessed that this had been a landing a hundred years before, for remnants of a cypress dock remained, pilings marching out to nowhere, to history. He tried to picture the grand steamers that stopped here fifty years before with their mural-covered paddle boxes and stained-glass clearstories, millionaire planters gesturing from the upper decks toward the worlds they owned, a time that seemed as inconsequential as smoke in light of the nothing that remained. It was only money, he thought, and that never lasts.

A trail plunged east into the willow brake, but it wasn't mentioned in the uninspiring directions he'd been given in Helena, so he again turned south on the levee, passing a cotton gin with a shake roof and a rust-perforated smokestack coming up through the middle of it. Across a field he saw a respectable-looking redbrick house, a painted wooden porch across its front. He cut the Ford's wheels and stood on the brakes, the tires locking and plowing sod down the steep slope. He drove along a cow path to a paintless barn and then through a gate into a fenced area of sawdust and dried manure, spooking three mules and five horses that ran from the machine and bunched against the mossy pickets. Leaving the Ford to steam among the animals, he climbed over the corral fence and advanced on the house.

The front door opened as he stepped up. Framed in the doorway was a barefoot man wearing a white shirt and vest, pearl-colored pants, and black cloth suspenders. Pinned to the right strap was a shield badge worn to brass. His hair was iron gray, carefully cut, and he was clean-shaven as well. There was something slightly off about his posture. 'Sir,' he began, 'is there some way I can help you?'

His civility was disarming. Sam regarded him carefully, as though there was something he didn't understand but should. 'Are you Constable Soner?'

'Indeed I am.'

'My name's Sam Simoneaux. A man I know, a telegrapher for the railroad, told me you might be able to help me find a family back in these parts.'

'Is it Sam Kivens?'

'No, sir.'

'Oh, of course. It's old Bob McFadden.'

'I'm sorry, no.'

'What railroad?'

'Y&MV.'

Soner narrowed his eyes. 'Doug Friar? Mac Divitts? Hazel Tugovich? Barry Ofel?'

'His name's Morris Hightower.'

Soner seemed surprised. 'I don't know him, son. But I imagine that he knows one of the others I named and obtained my location from them.' He looked Sam over carefully for hints of who he was, and then turned stiffly, like a man with back trouble. 'Come on in and have a seat.'

As soon as he closed the door, the front room went dark as a tunnel, and when his eyes adjusted he could see that all the windows were boarded across except for the top foot or so, where the upper sash was pulled down for air. Soner gestured to an armchair in front of an oak desk and then walked rigidly around it and sat in a wheeled office chair that needed oiling badly. In the gloom Sam saw that the wall behind the lawman was hung with guns, more of them materializing in an umber collage as his pupils relaxed. The rear wall was covered with Winchester lever actions, brass-framed carbines and rifles turning green under dust, Model 1873s, impossibly large Model 1876 big-game guns, sleeker '86s, modern-looking '95s, and semiautomatics in bear-killing .401 caliber. The walls were ten feet high, and on the one to his left were dusty military rifles, while to his right a hundred pistols hung on nails, hog legs from the Mexican War, break-action Smiths come in off the western prairie, single-action Colts by the dozen, their finish burned off according to how much misery they'd dispensed. He was afraid to turn around.

'This is some collection, all right. Where'd you get 'em all?'

Soner's expression didn't change. 'There's many of them to be had in this world.'

'You're well protected, that's for sure.'

'They're all loaded.' Here he smiled. 'Back here in the woods, I need options.'

'Yes, sir. I won't take much of your time.' He made an effort to see if in Soner's eyes there were any traces of madness.

'Take all the time you wish. Can I get you a glass of water? It's pure, though warm.'

'That'd be nice.'

When Soner returned from the back room, walking stiffly with the glass held out, he stopped behind him and held the tall glass to the left. When Sam reached out with his left hand, Soner's right hand ghosted from behind and plucked the .45 from its shoulder holster. He held the big pistol high in the air with two fingers as he returned to his seat. 'Just a precaution. I don't know your character.'

Sam gulped the water. 'Well . . . all right, then.'

'I've been the law back in here ever since I was a boy, more or less. You'd think it was just writing permits and solving little neighborly fights. Serving papers. Things like that.'

'I hadn't thought about it much.'

'Even back in here there are what you might call earth-shaking matters.'

Sam looked at the top of the window to his right. The light was fading, and he wondered if he could stay around long enough to sleep in the barn. He might even get up in the morning and drive back to Helena. 'You know everybody around here, then.'

'I know their animals, too.'

'I'm looking for a family named Cloat.'

The constable's expression froze. In the dim room his eyes, deep set and dark, glimmered like two stars reflected in a narrow well. 'I have the feeling you've got a story to tell me.'

'That's right.' He took several swallows of water, which had no taste at all, and said what there was to say. He ended by explaining that each year he thought more about the missing pieces of his life, and that talking to the Cloats, maybe just seeing them, might help him fill in the blank areas. When he finished his story, the space in the window was lavender sky.

'You think that by looking at them you'll figure them out?'

'I don't know.'

'If you look at a mountain, can you tell what's inside all that rock?'

'Sir?'

'I'm sorry.' Soner made a dismissive motion with his hand. 'You going back there to kill some of them?'

'I hope not.'

'Why else would anyone look up a Cloat?'

'To find out things.'

Soner nodded. 'Yes, of course. You're on a quest for knowledge only. That makes you lucky.'

Sam blinked. 'How's that?'

'The Cloats go through life incurious about anything at all, whether history or music or the well-being of their own blood.'

'Maybe they're the lucky ones.'

Soner shook his head. 'No. They're like animals, interested only in what's in front of them at the moment. But there's one thing that makes them different from animals.'

'And what's that?'

'Revenge.' The constable was quiet for a long time. Then he reached out and lit a Rayo lamp with a match. 'Come on,' he said, hoisting the lamp. 'Let's fix supper.'

They went into a long rear kitchen and lit more lamps. Sam got the kerosene stove hot and found a skillet while Soner brought in eggs and a smoked ham and snap beans from his garden. There was a pitcher of buttermilk under a cheesecloth and some hard bread. The little stove cooked slow, but within an hour they sat down to eat, and Soner said a blessing. He asked Sam to tell him about his work on the *Ambassador* and listened to the long story about why he hired out on the boat in the first place.

After the dishes were put away, the constable poured them some old sour mash in glasses of the good water and they went out and sat on the porch in rush-bottom rockers. The dark was so total the mosquitoes couldn't find them.

'Mr Simoneaux, you can spend the night in the upstairs bedroom. It should be cool enough for sleep in about an hour. But do not for any reason come down before daylight. There's a chamber pot under the bed. Do you understand?'

Sam nodded. 'What's your bedside firearm?'

He heard Soner take a long draw from his glass and then a knocking sound as he set it on the floor. 'An eight-gauge Greener double-barrel. I loaded the shells myself.'

'Good Lord. What's in them, buckshot?'

Soner chuckled. 'My father was a watchmaker in Memphis. He died when I was young, and I was left for years with boxes of used watch parts, little steel gears, balance wheels, winding stems, case-hardened screws. I loaded a whole box of eight-gauge shells with the stuff, jammed it in tight.'

'Damn. You ever fire one off?'

'No. I call it my time machine. You know, when somebody dies their soul travels one of two ways – back where they came from or forward toward what they deserve, and whoever comes against my Greener will make the journey.'

'Is it something everybody around here knows about?'

'Oh, yes. Even the clan of Cloats you want to find.'

'I'd like to drive out and meet some of them.'

A little laugh came out of the darkness as Soner reached down for his drink. 'I think "meet" is too nice a word, son.'

'I figured they'd be a bad bunch.'

'The family has fallen off considerably in the past twenty years.

When your family experienced their unfortunate meeting they were in their heyday. Usually, a meeting with a Cloat entailed a straight razor across the throat or a .45 slug in the back of one's cranium. If you were a man. Women dealt with other initial penetrations. The Cloats aren't your ordinary bad-seed murderers. Even on a cold day they stink like whoresex. They violate their animals. If they kill someone in their camp, they'll feed his carcass to their hogs. But nowadays, well, I hear less and less about them as the years go on. But still there's not a lawman in a hundred miles who would go in to find them. They came into this part of the world in the 1830s, run out of Georgia, I believe, along about the time Island Sixty-five began to form in the big river. They worked up and down the Natchez Trace cutting throats before crossing the river over to this side. Some settled back in the inland swamps for a time, but by the war they'd all moved out on the island.'

'Have you had any run-ins with them?'

'Yes.' The word came after a long pause, freighted with meaning.

Sam took a long drink. 'Not as bad as my family's, I hope.'

There was another pause. 'In 1901, Aubrey Bledsoe bought a quart of whiskey off the Cloats on Saturday morning and was dead by four o'clock. The Bledsoe men, good people who used to live south of here, rode up and asked me if I could locate the still. I was a good tracker in those days, and if I could find it, I could do the busting up. I saddled a horse for Island Sixty-five, which is connected on this side of the river, and located it in two days along with three fly-ridden Cloats around it, killed by their own whiskey. They'd galvanized that cooker with a hundred pounds of lead solder, and added xylene to the batch to jack it up. They must've gone stark raving mad before they died because they were naked and had painted designs on their backs and stomachs and all over. With mercurochrome, for I found the empty bottles.'

'Designs?'

'Like caveman pictures, but nasty. I don't want to tell you about it. I had a fire ax in my saddle holster and gave the still a good chopping, then turned it over and put a hundred blows into the bottom of it. The next day I told the Bledsoes the story, and good people that they were, they were satisfied that somehow justice had been done.'

'Was that the end of it?' He imagined the sorrow of the Cloats at losing three of their own.

Soner squirmed in his rocker, and Sam guessed he was crossing his legs. 'The next morning I woke up and every hog, chicken, and cow I owned had its throat cut. My wife was bawling, and my son, who was six then, just stood in the yard and stared. They left me one horse, so I saddled up and rode over to the Bledsoes. All their animals were down, even the beeves in the big field, one man dead in the yard and the women howling like a hurricane. Mrs Bledsoe, the grandmother, asked me who I left with my missus, and like a flash I understood how stupid I was, how much I could still underestimate inborn cruelty.' Here Soner stopped, and they listened to the deep throbbing of a steamboat whistle ten miles away.

'Were they safe?' Sam prayed they had been.

'Son, I'll not inflict more of this story on you than you need to know. But you require a certain amount of preparation for your meeting tomorrow. Let's just say that two Cloats, Batch and Slug, were standing in my backyard wearing muddy dusters when I rode up, flies in their beards around their toothless smiles. They made my wife and boy watch as they tied me to a pecan tree, arms and legs, me sitting on the ground hugging that trunk. They owned a big stinking dog, a rottweiler with a diseased face, and they turned him loose on me.' Soner stopped here and cleared his throat. 'That devil tore at my neck and ate the flesh off my back until the bones came to the surface, and right before I died they pulled him off me and rode away. I imagine they figured it was better vengeance to leave me alive than to put me out of my suffering. It was my boy who cut me free and helped me crawl into the house. My wife had lost her mind. Absolutely. This is the short version, let me tell you. The very shortest.'

But even this abbreviated telling seemed to last a full hour, and after hearing it Sam felt sure he would leave for Helena in the morning.

But Soner had more to tell. 'A year later, when I could get around, she left me. She couldn't hardly step into the yard without every nerve in her body winding up like a clock spring. The boy stayed two years more, then left to join her. He writes me every month, and he's married now with kids of his own and lives west of Chicago.'

'You wouldn't go with her?'

'I would've in a heartbeat, but she said she couldn't have me. Not wouldn't. *Couldn't*. She said every time she looked at me she saw those men and that dog.'

'You didn't go after them? Or tell the county sheriff?'

'Ha. I've got a lot of guns, but I'll admit I'm afraid. Not a match for them. All these years, I figured to leave bad enough alone. I didn't have the evil imagination to do to them what they'd have done to me.' He took another swallow from his glass. 'If I'd called the sheriff, he wouldn't have gone against them. If they'd heard I'd brought other law in, I'd have paid for it again. Call me chickenhearted, but I still enjoy watching the sun come up every morning. I still draw my pay, help the locals. The only thing that hurts is that I'm incomplete. My family's gone, but still out there.'

Sam saw a firefly combust in the yard. Only one. 'I think I would've done something. They're only men.' In the dark, he thought he could feel the anger Soner must have felt.

The constable drained his glass and began to move in the rocker. 'Come here, son, I want you to know something.'

'What?'

'The work of men.'

Sam stepped over to where he guessed by a shadowy motion that Soner was taking off his shirt.

When he finished, he rolled his shoulders forward and put down his head. 'Run your hands over my back.'

'I don't think—'

'Don't be scared. You'll learn something.'

'I can't see a thing.'

'You don't need to.'

Sam reached out with both hands the way he would search for something in a dark house at night. Placing them on Soner's right shoulder, he let his palms ride carefully over to his backbone. 'Aw, God almighty,' Sam gasped. He moved his hands over to the far shoulder, whispering something in French. Down toward the middle back, his fingers found a skinned-over wreckage of bone, and lower, wide pulsing hollows not to be imagined. He drew back his hands but hovered there a moment, frozen by his inability to change the horror he'd touched.

Soner's voice came dry and small. 'That should be a good lesson to you. But I've lived long enough to know it won't be. Not good enough to keep you away from them. Nobody understands what a snake is until he's been bitten.' Soner stood up and pulled open the screen door. 'I'll see you right after dawn.'

'Yes, sir.'

That night Sam rubbed his fingertips against the sheets again and again, as if to cleanse off memory itself. He woke at false dawn and lay on his back, watching the room develop around him in its gray plainness. Dew hung in the window screen like cloudy rhinestones, and he knew it would be a sunny day.

At breakfast, he noticed that Soner turned his whole body when reaching for something at his side. 'Thanks for all your hospitality.'

'I don't get many civil visitors. I hope to see you again sometime.' He stopped buttering his bread and looked up. 'I hope anyone sees you again.'

He was still thinking about riding on and forgetting. 'How many of them are back in there?'

Soner looked off to his left and squinted. 'At one time there were twenty Cloats, plus their Indian women. They liked Indian women. There were children from time to time, but most didn't last.'

'Didn't last?'

'Sometimes the women would run off with them. Or, when they got to be nine or ten, sometimes the kids would take off by themselves. Girl child or no, the Cloats would rut on them all.'

Sam stopped eating. 'What's wrong with those people?'

Soner's eyes were clear and bright. 'Why, nothing. They're exactly like you and I. They've just fallen a few more rungs down the moral ladder than most. It's because they live in their chosen isolation so that nothing good can touch them. And they insist on seeing themselves as normal, abetting each other's notions. The worst thing that ever happened to them is each other.'

'The men who did that to you, are they back in there?'

'Batch and Slug? They're somewhere else. They acquired some hashish, I hear, and smoked it and smoked it until they decided to play tandem double Russian roulette with their pistols. Instead of one bullet, they installed five in each revolver and both crossed over on the first try.'

'How many men are left?'

'The big one named Grill dropped dead of who knows what. He was pretty old for a Cloat, maybe forty-eight. Box and Babe are still alive, so far as I know. Percy died a couple of years ago.'

'Percy?'

'They say he was covered head to toe with syphilitic chancres and took five howling months to die. His woman came up from the island later and told me about it before she left for Memphis. She seemed very sick herself. That was five years ago.' He looked at the ceiling. 'Maybe six.'

'I see.'

'You're going?'

'Yes.'

'Throw away that shoulder holster. Wear the pistol in the hollow of your back between your drawers and your trousers.'

Sam swallowed the last of his buttermilk. 'Can you tell me how to get in there?'

Soner chewed his toast and thought. 'Well, you'll have to take my horse.'

38

By seven o'clock he was on the constable's mare riding back to where he had seen the relics of a cypress dock. He took the trail leading east onto the island, and within an hour, he was lost. The terrain was lumps of river sand sprouting trash forest. He rode in and out of old scours filled with dead water and up hogbacks topped by patches of poison oak running up the willows. After four hours of wandering, he smelled wood smoke. Turning back, he rode south and crossed a ghost of a trail he'd missed before and rode down it for a mile before dismounting and tying the horse off on a long lead. After a little while on foot he smelled privy, and not much farther along spied a clearing in which six houses lay scattered as though landed there by a flood. They were swaybacked, each made out of secondhand lumber, some weatherboard, some shiplap, some plain plank, some beaded, just boards fished out of the river and nailed up as they came by, mossy and waterlogged. In front of the nearest house, a three-room box propped with saplings against collapse, a balding man wearing a crazed expression sat in a straight-back kitchen chair on a patch of bare dirt. Sam considered him for a while and decided to walk up from the front and did so, stepping around thistles and animal droppings. He expected a pack of snarling dogs, but none appeared.

The man was mumbling, sitting where a front porch had been, the old frowning roof held up over him by one two-by-four. Sam stopped in plain sight. The man looked over at him and his mouth fell open a bit. 'It don't mean,' he said.

Sam looked around at the other houses, then turned back. 'I came here to ask a few questions. Are you named Cloat?'

The man's hands were in his lap, swollen and furry. The crotch of his overalls had split open and spilled him out onto the caned seat. His graying beard was braided and ran down onto his left thigh like a greasy snake. One overalls strap was missing and he wore no shirt, his skin botched and sun cratered, his eyes running like sores. The ground around the chair was littered with a mat of small bones as though he'd sat there for years eating chicken and squirrel. 'Six mile,' the man growled.

Sam could smell him over the rot of his garbage, a fecal putrescence that caused him to step back.

A woman who seemed half-Indian, half-Negro lurched out of the doorway and stared at him in amazement. 'Who the fuck you?'

He scanned her hands for a weapon. 'I'm looking for anybody named Cloat.'

She nodded the words into her head one at a time as if translating them into Cherokee or whatever language she was born under. 'He Cloat. No speak right. What you talk?'

He gestured behind him. 'This bunch rode down into Louisiana in 1895 and shot up a family.'

'What that?'

'What's what?'

'Eighteen ninety-five. That wagon?'

He tried to imagine how she thought, and after a while he said, 'It was twenty-seven winters ago. Killed my family.'

She pointed to the ground. 'Make winter mark.'

He bent down and with a stick made twenty-seven scratches in a bare stretch of dirt. 'This long ago.' He looked up.

The woman added ten marks with a dark forefinger and clawed a line under them. 'He this many. No kill no one yet ten winter.'

'But he *is* a Cloat?'

'Babe. Babe Cloat. You go see Box.' A hand rose out of the folds of her dust-caked skirt and she pointed to a mildew-blackened dwelling across two hundred feet of weeds.

'How many men live back in here?'

'Ask Box.'

'I'm asking you.'

Her eyes were on him, annoyed, uncomprehending. She held up three fingers.

'That's all?'

'Babe, Box, Box daddy.'

He surveyed the houses, the weather-crippled sheds out back. 'What happened to everybody?'

The woman mashed a nostril with a thumb and blew out a slug of snot. 'What?'

He waved an arm. 'Where are all the Cloats?'

She nodded. 'Die, rot. Some rot, then die.'

He watched her go up to Babe Cloat and hand him a potato, which he drew to his face and gnawed as would a squirrel.

A headache rose up in the back of his skull as he walked across the compound. He was hot, angry, and wanted out of the sun but stopped when he saw a long rifle barrel slide over a front windowsill. 'Are you Box Cloat?' he called.

A wheezy voice came from the window. 'Before I kill you, tell me what the hell you think you doin' back in here.'

The rusty octagon barrel swung slightly in the window. He hoped the shot, if and when it came, would only wound him. 'If you're Box Cloat come out and talk to me, damn it. I might not do a thing to you.'

He heard the hammer drop on the rifle, *snap,* and a raspy string of cursing and knew at once the man had pulled the trigger on an empty chamber and was fumbling with the action to throw a live round under the firing pin, so he pulled his .45 and put two blasts through the front wall above the window. He ran at the door, throwing himself against it, and it flew apart like a chickenyard gate as he fell into the room five feet from a tall man with enormous eyebrows trying to lever a jammed rifle. Sam aimed and hollered for him to drop the gun, and it hit the floor.

His heart was squeezing blood like a fist, and he stood up quickly, holding the pistol out at the other man's head. 'Are you a Cloat?'

The man was frozen, staring walleyed in Sam's direction and

trying hard to focus. 'You a Lobdell, ain't you. You not lookin' for me, you want Clamp and he died three year ago.'

'Are you Box Cloat?'

'Yeah. You a Bledsoe?'

'No.'

Box tilted his head to the left. 'Then you a Clemmons or Terranova? Maybe Walting, or a Mills? Say, you ain't no Levers, are you? . . . A Smollet?' He continued down a staccato list of twenty names, his hands rising higher above his brushy head before Sam stopped him.

'Shut up. You got a lot of people mad with you, don't you?'

Box gasped. 'You not a Kathell, is you? God lands, not no Kathell,' he whined, looking away. 'Listen, them little girls was a accident. We thought they was somebody else's.'

Sam raised the pistol thinking of how he could kill him and people would care more for the corpse of a mole rotting in its burrow. His eyes narrowed for a moment, along with his conscience. Living in the present is so easy. You just do a thing and not think about what could happen the next day, or how you might view your own actions in ten years. At last, he said, 'Sit on the floor. How old are you?'

Box squatted in the floury dust of his room. 'Forty-some-odd.'

'What do you know of Jimmy Cloat?'

'Uncle Jimmy? He been dead and gone a long time, feller.'

'Who killed him?'

Box closed one eye. 'One of them Frenchies down south.'

'Did you pay 'em back for it?'

Box went through another spasm of focusing, trying to see who was holding the big pistol at his head. 'I don't know nothing about it.'

Sam knelt down, moved the long black beard out of his way and placed the pistol's muzzle under the man's chin, leaning close through the smell of him. 'Can you see me?'

'Some.'

'My name's Sam Simoneaux. Don't you even blink. You people

came down to Louisiana and murdered my whole family, didn't you?' In his mouth he could taste the words like a metallic poison.

Box's milky eyes widened. 'I ain't did nothin'. I was just a kid.'

'Look, I didn't come down here to kill anybody. Understand that. I just want the truth.'

'You sure enough sound like them Frenchies.'

'Who did it?'

'What part Louisiana?'

'Down south. Sugarcane country.'

He squirmed against the pistol. 'Yeah. All they let me do was to hold the horses. Said they wouldn't trust my eyes with no gun.'

'Right. So who did it?'

'I ain't telling you shit.'

'Then I guess I'll have to tie you up and go talk to your daddy.'

'He's sick as a dog. Rotten sick. He ain't got no breath to tell you nothin'.'

'Where's your rope?'

'Bring me along, you got me covered. I can talk to him yit.'

Sam glanced around the room. The floor sagged, and the splayed wallboards showed the daylight beyond. There was only a shuck mattress killed flat and greasy and a poplar-wood washstand leaning away from a wall, a handful of corroded rifle shells spread over its alligatored top. 'All right. If you get me the answers I want, I'll leave you alone. But if I think you're lying to me I'll paint the wall with your brains. You understand?'

Box nodded and struggled to his feet. 'You ain't the first what said such.'

'Who else lives back here?'

'Just who you seen.'

'You have a woman?'

'The last up and died on me.'

He thought a moment. 'Do you miss her?'

Box's face screwed up at him. 'What?'

'Come on.' He put the Colt against his back. 'Let's go see Daddy.'

Outside, he was watchful for an ambush from the other five

houses, though three were homes for vines only. Ropes of poison oak ran into windows, carpeted porches, barberpoled up stovepipes, leaders scouring the blank sky for someplace better to grow. One house was lined with termite tracks, its front wall spotted with bullet holes, not a pane of glass intact anywhere.

Box stepped up onto a leaning porch made of barge boards. There was a pen next to the house and an enormous hog poked its dripping snout through the rails, its huge eye on them. The stink was intolerable. A cow with one horn was in a second pen, leaning against a post and holding a raw hind leg out of the mud. The woman came over, sneered at the pistol, and went inside. The front room was a jumble of unwashed clothes, furniture strewn about as though whoever brought it didn't know what it was or where to put it. In a single bed against an open side window lay a skeleton drawn over by rashy skin. Box made a coughing noise and the skeleton opened its yellow eyes.

The woman sniffed and glanced at Box. 'Holler when go so's I clean shit off him.' She walked out into the yard, leaving the door wide.

Box stood next to the bed looking down cautiously, as if the figure below him might leap up and tear out his throat. 'Daddy?'

The eyes rolled past him and looked at Sam. 'Who's that?' The voice was parched.

'Stranger.'

'Why'nt you kilt him?'

'My rifle stovepiped another shell on me.' He looked back at Sam's pistol. 'This here's Daddy Molton.'

'My guts burn.'

'You want water?'

'I'm afeared.'

'He says he ain't gonna kill nobody.'

'What's he want, then?'

'He come up askin' about Uncle Jimmy.'

Molton tried to turn his head, but after two small jerks gave up. 'Jimmy was kilt.'

'He knows that,' Box said impatiently.

'So what's he want?'

Box looked at Sam and squinted.

'I want to know what you did about it.' Sam tried to control his voice, to filter all the disgust out of it.

'Did?' This time the head managed to turn. 'Jimmy was the smartest one in the whole family. Could do numbers in his head. Could read and write like a schoolmaster. He was a travelin' businessman. When somebody kilt him, we got word. We went ridin'.'

'My uncle told me you shot through the house two hundred times,' Sam hollered.

The head rose off the pillow, its spidered eyes glowing. 'I won't gonna risk gettin' another of us dead.'

Sam placed his pistol behind Box's ear. 'You killed my daddy, mamma, brother, and sister.'

The elder Cloat took a gulp of air and said calmly, 'I was there.'

'You old bastard. Your brother was a stupid drunk jerking the head off a good horse. My father gave him a little jolt with a switch and he fell off and hit his head on a step. My daddy never meant to kill him.'

'But he died anyways.'

'And you killed a whole family for it?'

Molton tried to speak, but began coughing. Sam hoped he might have said something that bore a hint of regret. When the words did finally roll out on a string of red phlegm, he said, 'Appears I missed one.'

Box closed his eyes. 'Daddy.'

Sam's grip tightened on the Colt. The veins in his neck felt full of lead. 'How many of you were there?'

'We was nine.'

'Where are they?'

'What?'

'Where *are* they?' he yelled.

'Lemme die in peace.'

'Batch, Slug, Grill, and Percy – were they there?'

'They was along but done gone on.' He drew up his legs and began to whine. 'It hurts. Hurts like hellfire. Leave me be, damn you.'

'Who else? That's only six.'

'Box, call me that woman.'

'Who *else*?'

'All right, damn it. Sim, my other brother; Loganthal, who used to run with us; and that woman's daddy, Payette.'

'I want to talk to them.'

'That'd be kindly hard. They dead,' the old man groaned. 'Dead,' he said again, as though the word were a delicacy to be enjoyed a long time.

'You're lying.'

'Sim was kilt by the Rayville posse, strung up from the railroad trestle. Payette got on opium and died two year before he stopped breathin'.'

'What happened to the one called Loganthal?'

Molton squeezed his eyes shut. 'I couldn't say.'

Sam looked at Box, who shifted his gaze away and said, 'I don't rightly recall myself, but he's dead as dirt, that's for sure. Ease up on that grip, won't you?'

Sam pushed Box onto the bed and a rancid stink rose from the blanket. 'Tell me how he died.'

'I don't know how to call it,' Box said.

'Was it a disease?'

'Won't no disease. He started not talkin' and about a year after that we'd hear him jabberin' in the night. All night. Then he commenced hollering out of nightmares and Daddy like to went over and shut him up a bunch of times good. His woman lit out.'

A voice rose from the bed. 'Then he shook for two year.'

'He what?'

'Like they was a rattlesnake in his bed. Like he seen the end and didn't like it none. Now leave me be.'

'There wasn't anybody else?'

'Nine of us,' Molton whispered. 'By God, can't you hear?'

'There wasn't a Skadlock there?'

'Skadlock,' the man said slowly. 'I knew that batch. Little stealin' folks. Not cut out for the big show. Stupid. Spent more on makin' their liquor than they could get for it, most times. Ah, blazes, here come another.' He gritted his few yellow teeth, his lips drawn back, the enamel grinding, *ric-ric*.

In the yard the woman threw something into the pen, and the hog grunted like fleshbound thunder.

'I want to know one more thing,' Sam said.

'Aw.'

'Did you see them dead?'

Molton gasped a breath. 'Yeah.'

'What'd they look like?' He put the gun down at his side, and Box remained still.

'Look like? They was dead.'

'I want a picture. If you give me a picture, I'll leave you alone.'

'Box'll tell you. I'm give out.'

'I stayed with the horses, Daddy.'

'Tell me.'

One eye opened. 'Then you'll clear the hell out?'

'Tell me.'

The voice now was low, fired with a deep, anxious rasp. 'They died all at once. Nobody was movin' when we got in.'

'Go on.'

'The woman was on her stomach and the girl was under her left arm.'

'What color was their hair?'

'Damn it to hell, I can't recollect that. Don't you know?'

He got down on his knees and put the pistol on the edge of the blanket. 'You've got to understand. That's why I'm here. I never saw my mamma's hair.'

Molton looked him in the eye. 'It was brown,' he said. 'Clean. And so was the little girl's.'

'Where was the boy?'

'Agin the back door.'

'How was he dressed?'

The old man wet his lips. 'I remember that. He had him on a new bandanna. A slug passed through it and broke his neck.' He looked up and focused. 'He went quick, too, that one. Hardly any blood.'

'Broadcloth?'

'Striped broadcloth. We saw the loom out back.'

'My father?'

'He was the one we come to get.'

'Were you drinking?'

'Well, hell, yes. And I don't guess we thought he was in there with nobody.'

'Where was he?'

He writhed. 'I checked his damn eyeballs to make sure that one was dead. I remember he was startin' to bald. Ain't that picture enough for you?'

'Where was my father?'

'Dead agin the stove. We pulled him under a light, seen he was finished, then we rode off.' His eyes blinked and watered with the pain of telling.

Sam stood up and looked around at the filth in the room, at the walleyed son. He lowered the hammer on the pistol, knowing there was nothing he need do. The hog under the window, angry and wheezing, bumped against the house as if it wanted in for more slops.

'Where was you?' Molton asked, staring up now into Sam's face.

He looked down at him and smiled.

'We saw a son-of-a-bitchin' dog and heard a cat somewheres, but we didn't see no baby. Where was you?'

He slipped the pistol into the hollow of his back. 'I was somewhere biding my time. I didn't know it, but I was already on my way to meet you.'

'Won't worth the trip, was it?'

Sam's eyes went from one man to the other. 'I wouldn't take a million dollars for it.'

Suddenly, the black hog scrabbled up against the house and put its hooves on the windowsill, its monstrous head filling the frame over the old man's body. Sam backed away as Box gave it a punch in the snout, and it fell back with a splash.

The old man began to shiver. 'Great day, don't let him get me.'

Box wiped his hand on the blanket. 'Shit, Daddy, he's just a-huntin' slops.'

'Is that feller left yit?'

'Naw.'

Molton's head turned toward the center of the room. 'You think I'm goin' to hell, don't you?'

'I don't know where you're goin'. You already put yourself and others through a ton of hell.'

'I say I ain't goin' no place.'

Sam turned for the door. 'Well, you'll find out.'

The old man's voice came out as a growl. 'There ain't nothing to find out.'

Sam stopped at the door and looked back into the room. 'That's the one thing nobody can avoid. One way or the other, when you die, there's always something to find out.'

39

He stood before the husk of Babe Cloat, still sitting in the yard like an effigy of his clan. 'So long,' he called.

'Twelve of 'em,' Babe Cloat said, his eyes vacant. 'And a boat.'

At the edge of the compound he turned and looked back. The Indian woman shuffled toward Molton's shack, dragging a blanket through the dust. Within a year or two the houses would be eaten by weeds and insects. An inevitable flood would reclaim the drift lumber and wash clean the land of any sign. What would last, as some believed, would be the long mystical tally of terrible acts done by loveless hearts. He watched a long time, confirmed in his belief that punishing the Cloats would be a waste of good revenge, if that quality could ever be called good. He found the horse and mounted, riding west without a backward glance.

He figured he could make it back to Soner's place by dark, and on the way he did visitation, examining the details he'd found out about his family until like seeds they began to sprout memories he never had, or would've had, and he was glad of that. 'Anything more than nothing,' he said to the constable's mare, 'is something.'

He was putting the horse up when Soner came out with a lantern.

'Are you hurt?'

'Nope.'

The constable stared at him. 'Then you didn't find them.'

'Oh, I found them, all right.'

He raised the lantern high so Sam could replace the saddle on its board. 'Then you must have killed them all, because I don't see a bullet hole in you anywhere.'

'There's not but one whole man back in there, and he's about blind. Will be soon. You can start unloading your gun collection.'

Soner studied Sam's face as if suspecting a lie. 'You didn't find the ones who killed your family?'

'Two of them were there.'

'You're a fool if they're still alive.'

'Well, then.'

Soner put down the lantern. 'Come in and tell me about it. I'd appreciate it if you could spend another night.'

'I guess I'd appreciate it myself.' They began walking across the lot. Sam felt a lightness in his arms, as though finally he'd put down a weight he'd been carrying for years. Suddenly he stopped and turned toward Soner. 'Say, did I catch sight of a piano in the front room, left of the stairs?'

'Yes. It was my wife's. It hasn't been played in years.'

'Fix me a sip of something, and I'll let you hear some real music.'

He opened the door and motioned Sam in ahead of him. 'Why, that'll be fine. You'll want a bite of food, too.'

Soner lit the table lamp and the men sat and talked over bread and ham and the contents of an old jug of wine.

When they were finished, he asked, 'What brand of piano is it?'

'I forget, but it's a good one. My wife . . .' his voice trailed off.

Sam stood up and stretched. 'Let's take a look, then.'

And later that night, a boy out on horseback could have seen all the constable's windows yellow with light high up, where they weren't boarded. He could've taken in the tinkling of an out-of-tune piano as if it were his first sip of fine bourbon. A little girl wandering home late from berry picking could have heard the music and wished she had a piano and the time to learn it. A husband and wife could have been passing through on a journey, lingering there to listen and grateful for the pianist's fine technique. A murderer crouching in the wind-rattled weeds could have been distracted from his plans, envious of the good time.

Within an hour, the men were singing, their voices wavering

and sailing across the empty land. It was something to hear, this sound of profound release. But out in that darkness, nobody heard, and this vacancy would go on forever, a painful void Sam would feel later that night as he came out onto the porch, emptiness falling like a schoolboy's rock into the well of his heart.

The next morning he left the holstered pistol on the bed upstairs, had breakfast with Soner, then drove back to Helena. After turning in the muddy Ford, he walked down to the wharfboat. No upbound steamer was expected that day, and from his splintered desk inside the freight house door the agent asked him where he was going.

'Memphis.'

'And after that?'

'New Orleans.'

'Well, hell, the *Kate Adams* is makin' a New Orleans run. Why don't you take her all the way down?'

He looked out toward the river and noticed a big wooden crate outside on the dock. 'All in all, the train ride'll be quicker.'

'The *America* might stop northbound tonight, if it don't sink from old age first.'

Sam cocked his head. 'Wasn't that crate here when I got off the other day?'

'Yes, by damn. The lady ordered it didn't come get it when she should, and it rained before she finally did show up with a dray. Said she didn't want no piano been left out in a thunderstorm.'

'A piano. What'll happen to it?'

'The shipper's insurance already paid off. The agent sent me a wire to sell it for sixty bucks, but hell, I don't have no way to sell it, and I ain't about to drag it inside my warehouse. They'll probably send me a note in a month to ship it off somewheres.'

Sam pointed behind the agent. 'Let me see your little crowbar there.' He walked over and read the shipping label. The piano was a high-grade Knabe. He pried up one of the top planks and saw a full upright sheathed in heavy waxed paper, and the little rip he made in the covering showed a golden oak veneer. He banged the board back in place and ran his hand carefully over the rough-cut poplar case.

That afternoon found him standing on the forecastle of the *Kate Adams* as the sidewheeler huffed southbound. Behind him was the new Knabe, and he fought the urge to uncrate it and play right there in the open afternoon. He stayed out until they passed Island Sixty-five, the domain of the infirm and mind-darkened Cloats. He stared at the river-thrown sand and twisted willow brakes, trying to imagine how those people came to be. He thought about it until sundown and he could come to grips with snakebite, random illness, war, lightning strikes, and the death of loved ones, but the Cloats remained for him a mystery. Then he remembered what Constable Soner had said two nights before: the worst thing that ever happened to them was each other.

40

By early November he had gotten a steady, contracted job playing downtown in the orchestra of the Hotel Sterling. The Sterling was an impressive venue, and its ballroom showed off the plasterwork of a Viennese opera house across its high ceilings. By the end of the month he managed to get August hired to play three nights a week for the supper-and-dance crowd until eleven o'clock, and each day after school they spent an hour going over new music, learning the grand sound of a sixteen-piece group playing tight fox-trot and one-step rhythms for the city's smart dancers. During the first month, August had written quick and playful alto-sax duets into a dozen existing arrangements that earned the respect of the other musicians. Sam noticed a change in his own playing during the first two months at the Sterling, and decided it was working with August that made his fingers limber, his timing more on the mark.

He encouraged Lily to sing, but whatever spark she'd had for that was gone. She willingly played simple tunes on the oak Knabe every day, and he half expected to come home and find her working patiently through a more complicated fox-trot. What he did hear as he was coming up the walk one afternoon was a simple Chopin waltz. The piano bench had come loaded with a beginner's set of classical music, and Lily treated the pages as her private treasure. The simplest Bach pieces soon began coming together under her fingers. When August pointed out the classical structure of piano rags, she started to practice a few basic ones, and 'Dill Pickles' mixed with the first Bach Two-Part Invention in her morning sessions.

One day in mid-February of 1923 he handed Linda an envelope full of five-dollar bills for the month's household expenses, and she took it and pressed it against her stomach.

'You might have to start including an extra fiver.'

'How's that?'

'I'm pregnant.'

He pulled her close. 'You can have whatever I've got.'

'I know.'

'Don't worry about anything. We're doing swell.'

Lily walked in leading wobbly Christopher by the hand and looked up at them. 'Why're you hugging?'

He put a hand on top of her braided hair. 'You're going to get a new sister or brother, kiddo.'

She gave them each in turn a distant look, then dropped Christopher's hand and walked out of the room without a word.

'So, it's like that,' Linda said. 'It's going to take years.'

He stepped back and looked into the other room, where Lily sat holding a doll on the piano bench. It was an old doll dressed in seersucker. 'She's ours now.'

'She might understand it, but she doesn't feel it. You of all people should know.'

'What?'

'Can you speak German to her? Are you a cheerleader for smart and funny music who can make her love singing so much she couldn't imagine doing anything else?'

Late summer of 1923 saw the birth of Lisette, fair-skinned with a healthy shock of fine black hair. Because he was home now, he could hold the child every morning and watch her blossom day by day through the subtle changes: the strengthening of her eyes, the discovery of her own fingers. He had missed much of this with Christopher, and giving her her afternoon bottle was a daily marker that made him feel even more of a father. He bought a camera and recorded the first smiles, the first time she chose a toy and grabbed it up, and as he reviewed the photographs taken over the spread of months, he was always surprised at where she'd started and how much she'd changed.

Christopher was a year and a half when Lisette was brought

home, and though he looked up to August and tolerated Lily's bossing, he seemed to sense the blood bond with his sister, and when she was in Sam's lap, he wanted up on the other knee. When he was two, Sam found him on the bedroom floor, holding one of Lisette's baby books upside down, pretending to read to her. He motioned for Linda to come out of the kitchen and see.

'They're just playing,' Linda said. Then she watched his eyes. 'It's what it's like between brothers and sisters. It's what you missed, honey, and now you can see it. All you want.'

It was a blossoming year for August as well, who earned high marks in a school that was full of musicians, rawboned German kids playing accordions and Italians with their clarinets and drums, and when he was playing in the Sterling orchestra, the other musicians watched him during his solos, his animation and precision building fire under their own notes. He kept getting taller and began smoking cigarettes, but when Sam saw him slip a silver flask into his jacket one evening, he demanded that he hand it over. Though the boy was sullen about it for a few days, there was no rift between them that couldn't be bridged by the music.

Lily, though, by her fifth birthday had become an island unto herself. Through her sixth and seventh Sam taught her, treated her as his own, and paid for lessons when it became clear that she was an artist rising beyond what he knew. Sometimes when she was practicing, he would sit beside her and take over the left hand. Another child might have looked up and smiled, scooted closer or moved away to make room, but Lily treated him as if he were an anonymous brown sparrow that had landed on her bench, and she kept her eyes on the music, stretching her growing fingers out to the sharps next to his hand, but never touching him.

His own children were slobbering babies crawling over him like puppies, and he took his time with them, but they needed no convincing that they were part of his life. Lily went wherever the family went, downtown for doughnuts, to church, out to the lake for a picnic and a swim. She played with the younger children and cared for them, but at any idle moment she would seem to be elsewhere in her thoughts, separate, more like a visiting child than a member of the family. Watching her, Sam would feel a subtle lack of connection. He was making decent money, August was contributing half his salary to the family, and things, he realized, were good for him. Really good. But sometimes when he looked into Lily's blue eyes, he knew he'd never really found her.

One night, when she was six, he was reading her a bedtime story and noticed she wasn't paying attention. 'What you thinking about?'

'My parents.'

'What about them?'

'I'm praying for them.' She turned her sharp eyes on him. 'Do you pray for your family?'

He looked away, embarrassed. 'You want to finish this story?'

'I heard it already.' She turned toward the wall, but he knew her eyes were still open.

Over time, Sam settled into the rhythms of work and home, his salary covering food, rent, and all the other expenses of a family of six, but there was seldom much left over to place in savings. His life was running in a straight line with no surprises, and he was glad, as he'd had enough of them. Then, in October 1926, Linda handed him a letter postmarked from Lyon, France, addressed in an unassuming scrawl.

He looked up from his newspaper. 'What's this?'

His wife shrugged. 'It was in with the rest of the mail. Who do you know in France?'

He tore the letter open and inside were five pages written in sound English, and by the end of the first sentence he knew who it was from and sat straight up in his kitchen chair, holding the pages in both hands. It was signed Amélie Melançon. She was now eighteen and studying to become a teacher. She hadn't been able to write him before because she'd been displaced for a long time and hadn't lived at any permanent address until now. She'd stayed in her abandoned village for three months, then moved through a series of orphanage schools that American relief organizations had set up.

'Who's it from?' Linda turned from where she was cutting up onions for the noon meal.

'That little girl I injured in France.'

'My God. What's she say?'

'She wanted to thank me.'

'For what? Blowing her finger off?' She banged a spoon on the edge of her skillet.

'I don't know. Maybe it was something I told her? Who knows? Anyway, she seems to be surviving all right.'

Her sentences were densely packed with both information and feeling, painstakingly composed. He read the letter through three times. Near the end she wrote:

> When I think of that final blast, I marvel that it was followed by a messenger who tried to comfort me. I think often that is the way it ought to be. If each artillery shell had an escort, each bullet, each aerial bomb was followed by a soldier who would arrive and look around and ask 'Is everyone all right? How can I help?' then war would not last so long or be so bad. When I look at my right hand today, I could feel sorry to be maimed, but instead I have nine reasons for gratitude. Monsieur Chanceux, if you had not blown apart my house, I might have starved or lost heart. I've learned to take the good with the bad and want to thank you again, not for the explosion, but for your wonderful visit.

That night the boat whistles down on the riverfront moaned through the fog, keeping him awake, so he got out of bed and planned the letter he'd write back. He would tell her how often he'd worried about her over the years, and about how his life had veered so far away from where he thought it would go. He sat there at the kitchen table until one o'clock, then returned to bed and dreamed he was in France again, walking down a frozen road in a feathery snowfall. He came to a plastered house with a thatch roof and left the lane to knock at its door. Amélie answered, still eleven years old, and held out her hand. He took it slowly, his forefinger joining the place where her little finger had been, settling there as if it completed her – then he woke up, startled at her touch still trembling on his skin. He turned on the bedside light.

'What is it?' Linda said.

He stared at his right hand and rubbed it with his left. 'I was having a dream.'

She yawned and turned toward him. 'What about?'

He opened his mouth, but he couldn't turn such a dream into words. Finally he said, 'About coming full circle.'

41

At eight years old, Lily was an indifferent helper around the house, though she watched Christopher and Lisette carefully and worked with Linda in the kitchen without being asked. She would seldom speak with Sam, and when she did answer a question, he felt a subtle edge of resentment bordering everything she told him. She treated him like a landlord more than a father, demanding, for example, that the piano be tuned once every three months, that he hire a tutor for technique she felt she had to know, that he buy new music for her monthly. This pattern of distance might have continued permanently but for two things that happened.

The first was that Linda demanded that they buy a house, a larger place. In January 1927 after a long search, she found a rambling cypress bungalow two blocks away, four bedrooms, big yards and porches, for two thousand dollars. She had to have it. Among her reasons, Lily had just turned nine and wanted her privacy. Even though they had no savings to speak of and owned nothing that would secure them a loan, Linda wanted that house more than the next gulp of air. She told Sam she could get a few hundred from her folks as a loan and that he should try to borrow something from his uncle.

The second thing that happened was that Lily was cleaning out mildew from the closets, a chore she undertook once every two months, going over all leather shoes and belts with a cloth soaked in a weak bleach solution, when she happened to open a sack containing a fiddle and a bow.

That afternoon Sam came in about four o'clock from playing a morning wedding at the Sterling ballroom. Lily sat next to him on the sofa and showed him the fiddle. 'What can you tell me about this?'

He watched her carefully, checking her eyes for deceit. 'It belonged to my daddy. You tune it G-D-A-E.'

'I know. I tuned it against the piano. Where does your father live?'

'What?'

'Your father. I know Linda's but never met yours.'

He made a face. Somehow she didn't know and he became aware of the few links he'd built between them. He put a hand on her blond curls. 'He's not alive anymore.'

She flicked the E string with a little finger, then brushed away his hand, but not roughly. 'Did he teach you about music?'

'I didn't know him. He died when I was a baby.'

She looked at him, her eyes wide. 'You didn't know him *at all*?'

'I think I told you about this years ago.'

'Maybe I wasn't paying attention.' The way she said this, with a whiff of sarcasm, let him know she couldn't possibly remember what people had told her years before. 'What did you tell me?'

He was tired and felt a headache coming on. 'That at least you had your parents for a few years, and I never had any at all.'

She gave him a hard look. 'I know what I'm missing, then,' she said. 'You don't.'

That made him angry, and he went into the kitchen to chip a cup of ice and drink a glass of sweet tea and lemon. He'd always considered Lily a fellow orphan and thought they could imagine each other's pain, but it wasn't that way. Someone else's pain is just that. A fiddle note came from the front room, then others. She was playing scales, and in five minutes was testing minors and feeling her way through 'Oh! Susanna.' A single double-string drone convinced him it was time to take her to meet Uncle Claude, to show her where he'd come from. He stood in the doorway, sipping his tea, watching. 'Bend your wrist,' he told her.

The train stopped on the branch line at Prairie Amer, where they got off and stood out of the chilly wind in the little waiting room, waiting for the bus. The tracks to Troumal had been taken up the year before, but there was a road of sorts and a bus of sorts that rattled down to the village twice a week.

Lily looked through a station window at the fields of sugar-cane, the crossroads store, the handful of cypress buildings. 'Is the town we're going to bigger than this?'

'Smaller. You're way out in the country, city girl. Are you afraid?'

'No.' She watched a cow dreamwalking across a fenced lot. 'I like it. It's different. Quiet.' Her hair was cut short and Linda had sewn her a stylish drop-waist dress.

The little gray bus crawled down a poorly graveled road and stopped for them. The ride was slow and noisy, the bus creaking down into ruts and stuttering over cattle guards in a way that made the girl laugh.

His aunt Marie was waiting near the station in a Ford pickup, its wooden bed holding spools of fence wire. *'Mon Dieu,'* she called out. *'Une jolie blonde.'*

'You bought yourself a truck?'

'Oh, yes. So this is Lily?'

The girl opened the door and climbed onto the seat, Sam following after. 'Yes, ma'am.'

'You ready for supper, you?'

She looked from one to the other. 'I'm more than ready.'

By the time they got to the house, everyone had come in from the fields and washed up. Uncle Claude pushed open the screen door to greet them. 'Eh, Sam, why didn't you bring the whole bunch?'

He exchanged a handshake and shoulder slaps. 'We'll do that this summer.'

'When you called me on the phone I told you bring everbody you want.'

'Well, I had my reasons for coming alone with the girl.'

'Yeah, *je sais*. So she won't get lost in the shuffle, hanh?'

'Something like that. I wanted to show her around.'

His uncle cocked an eyebrow at Lily. 'Ain't much to see, but look all you want.'

Aunt Marie began herding them inside. 'Come on, come on. Wash you hands and both of you can help me set the table.'

Supper was rabbit stew on rice, drop biscuits, mustard greens, smothered okra, and fried apple pies. Arsène and Tee Claude were at table along with a hand named Beaupré, and they made a game of teaching Lily the funny French words for 'bullfrog,' 'wet hen,' and 'coot.' Afterward, Claude and Sam took glasses of blackberry wine out to the front porch to sit for a minute in the cool weather, the wind having died off.

'So, Linda found her a house she likes?'

'She's set on it for sure.' He looked around the farm, everything showing hard work and wear. The thought of asking for money pained him.

His uncle told him about his own house, where the lumber had come from, how long it took him to build it with a handsaw and hammer. He listed all the storms it had survived. For Claude, the matter at hand was always surrounded by narrative, placed in a frame of family history. After half an hour, Claude was quiet for a full minute, then asked, 'So, *combien?*'

He told him how much he could get by with, and his uncle made a face. 'Whatever I give you, I'm takin' away from the boys and Marie. And the farm. That fence wire in the truck? We borrowed money ourselves for more land next to us.'

'I understand. But it would be a loan. We'd pay you notes.'

Claude waved the back of his hand at him. 'Hey, don't get all excited. I knew this day was comin', yeah. I knew you'd need money for *enfants* or the hospital or a business, someday. When I heard you voice on that telephone, I knew. It's time, I told myself.'

'Time for what, Nonc?'

Claude leaned over and clamped a hand down hard on Sam's arm and shook it. 'To give you your farm.' With his other hand he pulled a folded document from his overalls bib and handed it over. Sam could see in the light falling through the door that it was a deed.

'What's this?'

'Can't you read?'

'This is my daddy's farm?' He stood up, amazed. 'I didn't think he ever owned anything.'

'*Mais* yeah. I had it put in you name a long time ago. The tax ain't nothin' at all, and I been payin' it along the way.'

He held the document out to his uncle. 'Why didn't you tell me?' He remembered sitting on this very porch as a teenager, unable to imagine how anyone could progress to the point of owning anything except clothes and a name.

'Sammy, I never thought you was no farmer. Didn't think you'd want to spend you life on *that* place.'

He looked at the paper, still holding it in both hands. 'How big is it?'

'Fifty acres.'

He looked toward the north into the deep dusk, where bats were harvesting insects in the glow above the trees. 'How much do you think I can get for it?'

'It needs clearin' again. Quick sale, maybe eighteen hundred.'

He sat down. 'Linda will dance on the ceiling when I tell her.' He looked out into the dusk again, in the direction of the property. 'Last time I was here you mentioned a house. Is it still there?'

'Like I said, a cypress house. It'll never go nowhere.'

'Can you tell me how to get to it?'

Claude made a face. 'It's all growed up.'

'I want to see it.'

'Well . . .'

'And I want the girl to see it with me.'

His uncle shook his head. 'No you don't.'

'I have my reasons.'

'Ain't no good reason to show a kid that place.' He looked at Sam suspiciously. 'What you gonna tell her?'

'What she needs to know about me.'

His uncle stared at him a long time, then gave an exaggerated shrug. 'I never told you nothing till you was old enough. A child deserves a childhood.'

Sam folded up the deed and slid it into his shirt pocket. 'She'll understand, this one.'

The next morning was very cool when he saddled an old grease-black gelding and set out after breakfast riding double, Lily behind. They rode cross-country through thousands of acres of cut-over cane field, an ocean of blond stubble. Following Claude's directions, he found the big cross-ditch and traced it to a plank bridge, and over that they were in the woods. He was glad it was winter, that some of the brush had died back so they could see.

The girl hung on to his belt and sat back in the saddle, staying balanced and keeping her feet away from the horse as she'd been told. She was quiet during the ride, but once they went among the bare trees, she said, 'This doesn't look like a farm.'

'Thirty-some years ago it was.'

She flinched at a branch that slid past his shoulder. 'It just looks like nobody's ever lived here.'

'Believe me, they did.' Fifteen minutes into the oaks and gum trees, he stopped and sat the horse. 'I never came all the way out here, even to hunt. I don't know where anything is.'

She looked around him. 'Maybe we should get down and walk.'

They led the horse through a broad, shallow ditch, and on the other side the animal's hoof clinked and Lily kicked the leaves off a chipped tin washbasin. She looked up at him and he nodded. He knew she was smarter but was surprised that she also had better instincts than he did. They moved on, watching the ground, and soon found an ox yoke, then looked up and saw something two hundred feet away that was the same color as the dun and frostbit woods but arranged in different form, and their brains told them it was the house though their eyes couldn't yet see it. They walked up and stood in front, and even the horse raised its head and looked, its breath steaming. Frost-scalded vines ran up the sides and wisteria the size of a child's arm had grown through the open front door, then curved around and grew back out onto the porch as though not liking what it found inside, the dearth of light, the drought. The house was four rooms and from the front porch a steep set of steps rose into an attic. The roof was high-pitched and some of the cypress shingles had taken flight in storms, but as a whole, the structure sat square and sound on its eroded brick piers.

'This is where you lived?' Her voice was respectful, as if in church.

The tree trunks hid the sun, and he shivered. 'Until I was six months old.'

'Six months.' She said this slowly, as if tasting the words.

He watched her eyes take in the bullet holes, dime-sized punctures that stippled the front wall, splintered the window frames, door frames. 'Those are from bullets.'

She kept looking. 'I know what they are. Your mother and father, they were killed here. When you were six months old.'

'And my sister and brother.'

She caught her breath. 'Did they catch who did this?'

So even she thought first of revenge, of justice. 'No. They lived out their lives.'

She turned to him. 'That's not fair.'

He shrugged. 'I don't know. What kind of life do you think they had?'

'What?'

'People who would do this, what kind of life do you think they had?'

'I don't know.'

'Well, you've got a long time to think about it. I'm going in.'

'It's scary.' Suddenly her voice was small.

'You can stay out here, then.' He tied the horse to a chinaball sapling and went up the pulpy steps to the porch. He looked inside, tested the floor, and slid a foot into the dim light, the sweet peppery smell of the cypress lumber making his head spin like a compass needle. The wood of the big room bore the brown-silver tint of the outside, but was less weathered. Nothing remained except a big potbellied stove, its pipe a streak of rust on the floor. Walking past without looking at it, he felt a shudder rise through his shoulders, and he quickly stepped into the kitchen, which held only low, warped cabinets and a broken spindle-back chair lying facedown. The window here was intact and outside of it was the *tablet* where his mother had washed dishes, as did every Frenchwoman in the region in the days before indoor plumbing. The rear bedroom was an empty box and some of the ceiling boards had come down, showing the joists. He passed through a door into the front bedroom, bare but for the dirt caused by newborn daubers breaking free of their mud. Maybe he was born in this room, saw his first dawn in the window, his first lamp flame, and he stood long and thought about what had happened here.

He heard the girl come into the house and he went to her. She turned and saw the bullet holes glowing like electric lights with the winter glare flowing through. She glanced down at the floor, and he was glad that it was dusty.

'This is where it happened?'

'Yes.'

'You don't remember anything about them at all?'

He turned his head. 'Not one second.'

Then she said something that was unusual for her. 'I'm really sorry. It's awful, isn't it?'

The statement opened a door that had been locked between them, and he walked to where she was standing next to the stove. 'I'd say so.'

'Is this rusty thing all that's left?'

'Yes.'

Her face brightened. 'We could take it back to New Orleans and put it in the backyard. Think how it would look with ivy growing out of the top and hanging down.'

When she reached to open the fire door, he bent over suddenly and pressed both hands against it. 'I don't think that would be a good idea,' he said, his voice trembling. He kept his hands on the metal as if testing it for warmth. She stepped away, her clear eyes watching him carefully, and after a moment she walked toward the back of the house. His hands still welded in place, he listened to her move through the place and realized that her guess was as good as his as to what life and death had happened inside these plain walls. When she had passed through all the rooms, he heard her push open the back door. Only when he heard her cry 'Look!' was he able to move away from the stove.

She was on the back landing pointing up under its overhang. 'Look at that. Could you get it down?'

He reached up with both hands and lifted a medium-sized washboard from a galvanized nail. His mouth fell open for a moment.

'You could take that home as a souvenir,' she said. He began walking slowly back inside, turning the washboard in his hands.

He paused by the stove again, aware that what he had in his hand his mother had held a thousand times, that his clothes had been scrubbed clean over its metal ridges, and he didn't know whether he should smash it against the stove in a weeping rage or take it home and hang it on his kitchen wall to see for the rest of his life and sometimes hold in his lap, as though it contained the phantom touch of his lost family. Hearing Lily come in behind him, he set it down and leaned it against the stove. 'Maybe not.'

'Well, can I take it?'

He put a hand on her shoulder and turned her toward the door. 'What would you do with that?'

'I just want it.' She darted back around him and tucked the washboard under her arm.

'What for? That thing'll just keep me looking back.' He glanced past her toward the kitchen, not understanding.

Her blue eyes were reddening and brimful. 'I think we should keep it. It doesn't have to make you think only about the bad things.'

He reached out to her. 'Just leave it. I don't remember any good things.'

She clamped her arm against the washboard and stepped back. 'You came here to find something. Here it is. It's to imagine what happened before those.' She pointed to the bullet holes.

He turned his head up and stared at the shafts of sunlight blazing through the wall. In a small voice, he said to the dust-haunted room, 'I found something from before the shooting.'

She walked up and stood close. '*We* found it,' she corrected, and for a heartbeat she leaned into him.

Outside, they saw that the horse had sidled up to the porch and was scratching his head against a post. Sam swung Lily into the saddle, untied the reins, and got up behind her. 'Your turn to drive.' She handed him the washboard, and he stood it up on the saddle between them. 'Now your seat's got a back.'

The horse began to whinny and sidestep away from the house, and she yelled, 'I don't know how to work the reins!'

He rested his chin on the top of her head. 'Lily, if anybody can figure it out, you can.'

Tim Gautreaux

The Next Step in the Dance

Paul Thibodeaux is married to the best-looking girl in town. The problem is that Tiger Island, Louisiana is small, sleepy, and miles from anywhere – and Colette Thibodeaux wants out. She sets off for California, abandoning her husband and the backwater world of gossip, auto repair shops and run-down dancehalls they grew up in. But for Paul, the rich Louisiana landscape is barren without the woman he loves; he follows her out west, and back again.

'He writes like Raymond Chandler on a Deep South safari' *Evening Standard*

'Impressive . . . thoroughly gripping' *Big Issue*

'[It] may tell an old, old story – that it is only when you are in danger of losing someone that you begin truly to appreciate them – but it has rarely been told so well . . . the depiction of his native landscape, with its Spanish moss and snapping turtles, its "white heat and green humidity" is superb.' *Sunday Telegraph*

'A mighty first novel told with cinematic grip . . . Gautreaux himself takes the next step in the moody, sweet dance of southern literature.' *GQ*

'[It] holds you snug and won't let go' *Entertainment Weekly*

SCEPTRE

Tim Gautreaux

The Clearing

Byron Aldridge, heir to a timber empire, returns from the First World War a changed man and finds refuge as a company policeman in a rough, backwoods Louisiana sawmill. Soon his younger brother Randolph tracks him down amid the swamps, assuming charge of the mill in the hope of rescuing his former idol. But as the brothers try to understand each other and their wives contend with their own hopes and fears, it is Randolph who starts a feud with the Sicilians who control the whisky and girls, and the future grows fearsome for them all.

'One of the best novels I've read in years' Annie Proulx, Books of the Year, *Daily Telegraph*

'Astonishingly powerful . . . brilliantly written and the characters in their mire are superbly realised' Toby Clements, *Daily Telegraph*

'This is a novel so firmly located and vividly realised that you can almost smell the Louisiana swampwater as you read . . . A gripping, action-packed tale' Jem Poster, *Guardian*

'The relationship between the two brothers is sensitively and brilliantly drawn; the strength of the women in the book, which is at odds with the harsh physicality of a land governed by violence, is deftly depicted . . . *The Clearing* carries an emotional charge far beyond its pages and does what all great fiction does: gives insights allowing us to understand human nature and a distant time and place. I cannot recommend it highly enough.' Peter Straus, *Literary Review*

'Gautreaux captures the fetid atmosphere of a frontier society poised to join the modern world with great skill, each sentence polished to perfection.' Steve Jelbert, *Independent on Sunday*

'Confident, absorbing, monumental' Alan Warner, Books of the Year, *Daily Telegraph*

Tim Gautreaux

Waiting for the Evening News
Stories of the Deep South

In stories filled with heart and humour, the acclaimed American novelist Tim Gautreaux explores the stresses and strains of everyday life as his characters struggle to make amends for their mistakes and maintain their hope for different, better days to come.

A petty thief is bested by a widow and her card-playing friends; a farmer must cope with raising his baby granddaughter; a train engineer inadvertently causes a major disaster and finds himself caught up in a media frenzy; and a camera repairman discovers a woman's family history in a roll of undeveloped film. Ordinary people are confronted with extraordinary situations, with results that are sometimes comic, sometimes tragic, but always life-changing.

'If you were wondering where all the great southern American writers were these days, he's in Louisiana and his name is Tim Gautreaux' Annie Proulx, *Daily Telegraph*, Books of the Year

'This man is a wonderful writer . . . I love to read his stories. He never exaggerates, never manipulates the reader's affections, but nonetheless he always captures the heart.' James Lee Burke

'In the tradition of Faulkner or Joyce (or for that matter Philip Roth or Nadine Gordimer), Gautreaux mines a deep cavity – his own place and people and their concerns – that he may never exhaust. The world of literature is all the richer for it.' *Australian*

SCEPTRE